April Snow

Also By Lynn Steward

A Very Good Life

April Snow

A Dana McGarry Novel

Lynn Steward

For Richard

You know how it is with an April day.
When the sun is out and the wind is still,
You're one month on in the middle of May.
But if you so much as dare to speak,
A cloud come over the sunlit arch,
And wind comes off a frozen peak,
And you're two months back in the middle of March.
    –Robert Frost, *Two Tramps in Mud Time*, 1926

Chapter One

Dana McGarry, on vacation for the first time as a single woman, arrived at the Lansdowne Club at 9 Fitzmaurice Place, just steps from Berkeley Square, in London's fashionable Mayfair on the morning of April 8, 1975. Her lawyer had filed papers for a legal separation from her husband Brett in January, and after four months of being under the watchful eyes of well-meaning family and friends, Dana was savoring every moment of her solo trip across the pond. She and Brett had always stayed at the nearby Chesterfield Hotel, but her beloved Colony Club in New York City enjoyed reciprocity with the Lansdowne Club, where she'd previously attended lunches and lectures while her husband met with clients for his Wall Street law firm. Undeterred by the steady English rain and dark clouds hanging over the slick gray streets, she stepped from one of London's fabled black taxis with renewed spirit, excited to think that the distinguished house in Berkeley Square would be her home for the next five days. After Dana checked in, the hall porter asked her if she would like tea brought to her room and then discreetly disappeared with her luggage, a small, welcoming gesture that stood in contrast to an impersonal hotel. Rather than immediately taking the lift to her room on the fifth floor, Dana stepped into the entrance hall and surveyed the club's interior, intending to explore Scottish architect

Robert Adam's stately masterpiece commissioned in 1761 for King George III's prime minister, the Earl of Bute. Previously, she had limited herself to the dining room, never taking time to appreciate the club's historic beauty. Although rich with finely-crafted embellishments and Neoclassical splendor, the house was clearly showing signs of fatigue, and its understated elegance made the environment that much more comfortable. Dana knew she'd made the right choice. The club was an oasis of tradition and tranquility affording her the peace and privacy she needed.

When Dana arrived in her junior suite, she noticed a bouquet of flowers sitting on a table in the sitting area. Thinking they were compliments of the club, Dana opened the attached note and laughed out loud. The flowers had been sent by her childhood friend, Johnny Cirone. The message read, "Take Phoebe shopping and buy up the town. Whatever you do, enjoy yourself. Love, Johnny."

Dr. Phoebe Cirone, who was in London attending a cardiology convention, was Johnny's sister. Their father, John Cirone, known affectionately to Dana and her brother Matthew as Uncle John, was the head of the House of Cirone, a manufacturer of ladies eveningwear. Having a passion for medicine from an early age, Phoebe had never expressed interest in clothes or haute couture, leaving Johnny to reluctantly carry on family tradition by working for his father. Dana's parents, Phil and Virginia Martignetti, had been friends with the Cirones since before her birth.

Dana, pleased to see a porcelain tea service had already arrived, took her cup to the window and sipped the Darjeeling as she observed the new plantings in the courtyard garden. The peace she'd felt a few minutes ago was gone, however. Something about Johnny's note, as thoughtful as it was, unnerved her. Johnny and her mother called daily to see how she was doing. Dana sensed their concern, although she felt it was unwarranted. What did they think—that she was going to kill herself because the divorce would soon be final? They obviously didn't recognize her personal strength and resolve. Dana worked at New York City's B. Altman, and the previous December she'd formed the department store's first Teen Advisory Board. She had also succeeded in getting Ira Neimark, the store's executive vice president, to sign off on installing a teen makeup counter on the main selling floor over the objections of Helen Kavanagh, junior buyer, who thought youth-oriented strategies like those at London's Biba, were a waste of time and money. Despite these personal triumphs, she'd taken aggressive steps to further advance her career, leaving her comfortable job in the marketing department for the position of junior accessories buyer. She had requested time off for this visit to London immediately after settling into the new assignment, and that alone was proof that she knew how to take care of herself.

Dana had been equally aggressive in terminating her marriage to Brett. Papers for a legal separation had been filed in January by Dana's lawyer when she discovered that Brett was having an affair with fellow litigator Janice Conlon, a saucy and impertinent young woman from California. Negotiations for a final settlement were proceeding smoothly, with no protests originating from either Brett or his lawyer lest the firm be apprised of his misconduct with the audacious Conlon. In the four months since their separation, Dana had realized that Brett's dalliance with the abrasive Conlon had merely been a catalyst for the end of their relationship since there had been something far deeper and more troubling in their marriage: Brett's growing neglect of Dana as he vigorously pursued partnership with the firm. His work always served as a convenient excuse to pick and choose his time with Dana and in the long run, that grim reality had proven intolerable. Within days of learning of Brett's infidelity, Dana contacted an attorney and moved from her Murray Hill apartment to a carriage house a few blocks away in Sniffen Court.

Given the decisive actions in her personal and professional life, Dana therefore felt smothered at times by the daily concerns of others. As for her traveling abroad alone, she felt more than competent to take care of herself. When Brett had been with her in London, they were rarely together. He usually spent days working, and evenings meeting with clients, joining Dana for late dinners, if at all. He was up and out by 7:00 A.M. She'd always hoped that the next trip would be better, but this was never the case. Traveling alone? It was all she knew.

Yes, it had all happened just four months ago, illustrating how the course of a life can change so radically and quickly. But was she ecstatically happy now that a new phase of her life and career had begun, with Brett being almost surgically excised from the picture? No, she wasn't jubilant about anything at present, but she was content, at peace with the decisions she had made to take care of herself and her future. In the words of her father, she had discovered that she had "a very good life" despite longstanding marital woes and formidable professional challenges. Many of her friends had urged her to re-enter the dating scene since she was almost thirty and the clock was ticking, but Dana didn't miss married life in the least and had no interest whatsoever in dating, especially guys described as the perfect match: upwardly mobile professionals, or "Brett clones," the apt description provided by Andrew Ricci, Dana's good friend and display director at the store. Besides, marriage was not the only path to a fulfilled life. In Dana's estimation, happiness also resulted from pursuing a creative dream, enjoying good friendships and the myriad interests that gave her immense pleasure, such as travel, literature, films, and lectures on a wide variety of topics. Being suddenly single was not a condition to be cured but rather an opportunity to be savored.

A line from Dickens came to mind as she thought of events that had altered her life: "It was the best of times, it was the worst of times." Dana had survived the tumultuous weeks of the previous December, when she realized her marriage was over, but surely this was now the best of times, was it not? She smiled as she contemplated her walk tomorrow morning to Piccadilly for breakfast at Fortnum & Mason, followed by a long and leisurely visit to Hatchards, London's oldest bookshop. The thought of Dickens reminded her of the delight she took in finding rare editions of the classics, or even first editions of lesser-known authors. Today, however, she was going to enjoy Richoux's delicious risotto when she lunched with Phoebe, who was staying within walking distance at the Grosvenor House on Park Lane. Filled with a new surge of energy, the blue-eyed Dana freshened up, brushed her short blond hair, and grabbed a shawl and a pair of unlined leather gloves. The clouds were beginning to part, and the steady English drizzle had let up, but it was still a nippy fifty-four degrees—a perfect spring day in London.

Rays of sunshine were reflected by leaded windows in the rows of eighteenth century townhomes Dana passed as she strolled leisurely through Berkeley Square. It was only eleven thirty and she had an hour before meeting Phoebe at her hotel, enough time for a short detour across Hill Street and Hays Mews to the Farm Street Church, also known as the Jesuit Church of the Immaculate Conception. Years earlier, she'd been sitting on a bench in Mount Street Gardens when she looked up and beheld one of the church's open gothic portals that seemed so inviting, beckoning her to enter and pray. Then as now, it had been a glorious April day, the kind celebrated by Chaucer in the opening lines of the *Canterbury Tales*, when spring rains provide rich "liquor" for flowers suffering winter's drought.

Dana arrived at the church and chose to enter from Mount Street Gardens rather than Farm Street, as she'd done on her original visit. In the transept to the right of Our Lady of Farm Street statue was the Sacred Heart Chapel, and this is where Dana chose to pray in deference to the Sisters of the Sacred Heart, who'd taught her for twelve years in her youth. She knelt in the third pew, said a decade of the rosary, and then sat, looking up to admire, as she always did, the glorious painting of the Sacred Heart flanked by four saints above an inlaid marble altar with three brass reliefs. But instead of finding peace in this pious setting, the silence suddenly became deafening, and the alabaster walls of the chapel began to feel close, confining. A wave of emotion engulfed her, and she cried uncontrollably, questioning her impulsive decision to end her eight-year marriage—and without considering her vows taken before God, family, and friends. What a hypocrite she felt herself to be—a selfish hypocrite who had turned her back on the faith that was such an integral part of her life.

Glancing at her watch, Dana saw that it was almost noon. She needed to pull herself together and be on her way to meet Phoebe. She took a deep breath, wiped away her tears, and walked outside to a bench in Mount Street Gardens, where she would spend a few moments composing herself.

In the sacristy, a priest was marking the readings for the twelve-thirty mass in the gilt-edged lectionary when he heard anguished sobs emanating from the Sacred Heart Chapel. Curious, he stepped into the sanctuary in time to see a young woman exiting the side door leading to the gardens. He followed her and observed her sitting on a bench fifteen yards away. He folded his arms, closed his eyes, and said a brief prayer.

• • •

Looking in her compact mirror, Dana wiped away the mascara beneath her eyes and reapplied a bit of powder to her cheeks. She didn't want Phoebe to see that she'd been crying. What could she possibly say in answer to any questions her friend might have? That she was upset over the abrupt manner in which she'd dissolved an eight-year marriage to an inattentive man who'd cheated on her? No, the emotions that had spilled forth in the chapel had taken Dana by surprise, and they needed to be processed in private moments of reflection.

Dana had been resting her eyes when she looked up and saw a priest approaching the bench. The Jesuit, a tall man in his early fifties, walked with a confident gait, and the smile on his face was evident when he was still several feet away.

"Good morning," he said. "Lovely day." He could tell the young woman was upset and, in point of fact, she wasn't the only one he'd encountered on the grounds who needed consolation or, at the very least, a friendly smile.

"Yes, Father, it is," Dana replied. "A splendid day."

"Are you on holiday, or are we blessed to have you as a new parishioner?" he asked.

Dana examined the priest's face more carefully. He wore rimless glasses, and pale blue eyes regarded her kindly beneath close-cut salt and pepper hair. He was dressed in a black clerical suit and looked to be strong and vigorous despite his gentle manner.

"On holiday, Father," Dana replied. "I come here whenever I'm in London and wanted to stop in and … visit. I was taught by the Sacred Heart sisters back in New York."

"A New Yorker!" Father Macaulay said. "And a member of the family, so to speak. May I sit?" he asked, motioning to the bench.

A member of the family, Dana thought, again fighting back tears. *Not anymore.*

"I'm sorry, Father," Dana mumbled, rising to leave. "I'm meeting someone and I'm late."

Father Macaulay nodded. "I hope you'll visit again. I'm here in the church or the gardens every morning from nine until I say mass. If you can't find me, just tell the sacristan that you're looking for Father Charles Macaulay."

"Thank you, Father. Have a good day."

Biting her lip to fight back fresh tears, Dana and Macaulay shook hands. The priest watched Dana walk out of the gardens, sensing that she was in distress. He was a good judge of people, and he thought that Dana would surely return to the church before she boarded a plane for New York City. Somewhere in her soul, he thought, there was unfinished business.

Wearing sunglasses, Dana walked for five minutes along Mount Street until she reached the Grosvenor House. Phoebe was waiting in the lounge, and after they exchanged warm greetings, they left the hotel for Richoux, which was two blocks away on South Audley Street.

The two women were shown to a small table in the dimly-lit restaurant owing to the dark wood paneling in the main dining room. When Dana removed her sunglasses, Phoebe immediately saw that Dana was upset. Her eyes were puffy and her smile was forced. Phoebe cocked her head and raised her eyebrows, as if to say, *Do you feel like talking about it?*

"I'm fine," Dana said, brushing aside the concern. "Nothing worth discussing. Now tell me about you, how's the convention?"

The two women chatted over lunch, Phoebe speaking of the lectures she'd attended on anticoagulation therapy, angioplasty, and catheterization for the diagnosis of coronary artery disease.

In turn, Dana described her new duties at B. Altman. They laughed at Johnny Cirone's daily calls and continued concern for Dana since her separation, although Dana was reminded yet again of the excessive attention she was receiving.

"We have to get him married off," Phoebe said, "or at least find him a serious girlfriend. He's becoming a mother hen." She paused, knowing that Dana was holding back something painful, but decided not to press the matter. "By the way, my dad has an offer on his house, and he's in contract to purchase the estate sale on East 79th Street. It's a big renovation, so he's hoping to get approved by the co-op board quickly and start the demo. Johnny is already interviewing contractors."

John Cirone was moving to Manhattan since his Long Island home seemed far too large since the death of his wife two years earlier. He'd accepted a seat on the board of the Metropolitan Opera, and Johnny was helping his dad make the long-overdue transition to the city—and to the present, away from thoughts of his deceased wife, Lena.

"It sounds like the convention is keeping you pretty busy," Dana said. "Would you like me to pick up Uncle John's cigars at Sautter's? It's a few blocks from the Lansdowne."

"That would be a lifesaver," Phoebe said. "I have two days of seminars on using something called a stent to open up clogged arteries instead of always resorting to bypass surgery. It would be a non-invasive procedure, but most cardiologists think it's still years away." Phoebe suddenly burst out laughing. "And here I am, bringing my father cigars, which is the last thing a cardiologist should do."

The two women finished lunch, Phoebe heading to the convention for afternoon lectures, and Dana returning to the Lansdowne Club, where she finished unpacking.

Dana sipped afternoon tea while paging through a book of poems she'd found lying on the end table by the sofa, her thoughts returning to her display of emotion that morning. Brett had indeed been quickly and surgically excised from her life, perhaps too quickly, and yet she had received no judgments about the decision to do so from her parents. She was aware, of course, that Virginia had always been a bit leery of Brett, even at the very beginning of their courtship. As for her father, he was quite unflappable and had reminded Dana that things always work out in the end, which was a part of his lifelong, homespun philosophy that she found so comforting. And yet Dana couldn't shake the realization that Brett, despite all of his shortcomings, was a man she'd loved for over eight years. Should she have given him another chance? After all, the marriage hadn't been *all* bad. The visit to the chapel, she concluded, had reminded her of Catholic dogma regarding marriage: it was indissoluble. Mount Street Gardens, the chapel, the brass panels—they'd brought to mind her many years with the Sisters of the Sacred Heart, causing her to second guess her decision.

Leafing through the slightly-worn pages—she thought that older books had such character—she saw Wordsworth's "Ode on Intimations of Immortality." It was one of her favorite poems. She especially liked the lines towards the end.

Though nothing can bring back the hour
Of splendour in the grass, of glory in the flower;
We will grieve not, rather find
Strength in what remains behind;
In the primal sympathy
Which having been must ever be;
In the soothing thoughts that spring
Out of human suffering;
In the faith that looks through death,
In years that bring the philosophic mind.

The sentiment was essentially that of her father, who had a "philosophic mind" when it came to handling disappointment. There had been good times in the marriage, but some things were beyond repair, and Dana had indeed retained strength in what remained behind, which was a full life that included friendships and opportunity. Dana realized how important this trip was—far more than a break from her daily routine or an enjoyable shopping spree. On her own, she could privately mourn her marriage and process her emotions, opening her mind and heart for whatever lay ahead. She was at peace again, ready for the rest of her stay in London. Still, she wondered if Father Macaulay would share her perspective. The priest had emanated kindness and understanding in the brief minutes she'd been in his presence, and now, feeling stronger, she decided to visit him again before she left London. He'd demonstrated genuine concern, and she wanted to hear his soothing voice one more time.

Chapter Two

*A*fter a good night's sleep, Dana arrived at Fortnum & Mason, located at 181 Piccadilly, at eight o'clock in the morning. An hourly tribute to the founders begun in 1951, the four-foot models of William Fortnum and Hugh Mason emerged from the turquoise and gold clock and bowed to each other with punctual civility as the carillon bells sounded eight times. Dana was seated in the Buttery, an intimate dining room on the mezzanine level. She ordered coffee and a croissant and began reading the *Times* when her thoughts drifted to the shifting tide of events at B. Altman since January. While she had experienced great success with the teen makeup section and the Teen Advisory Board, new challenges had presented themselves almost immediately, and she'd found herself at odds—not for the first time—with Helen Kavanagh, the former junior buyer.

Struggles were unavoidable in everyone's career, but Dana felt like progress was achieved at a pace of two steps forward and one step back. In January, Helen's junior department had been broken up, and she became the divisional manager, overseeing women's sportswear and dresses as well as juniors. In turn, Dana had stepped up to the position of junior accessories buyer. For Helen, however, her new job, while a promotion, no longer had power or status thanks to the arrival of Dawn Mello two years earlier. Mello filled the newly-created position of vice president and fashion director and had been hand-picked for the task by Ira Neimark, who was hired to make B. Altman more competitive in mainstream retailing, thus updating its stodgy image. Dawn was solely responsible for charting the store's fashion direction, approving new lines and making buying decisions that were influenced by her extensive European travels to scout for new trends. With twenty-five years of buying experience, Helen resented reporting to Dawn and was now angry that she had no control of her staff's merchandise choices, leaving her with boring budgets and operational issues.

In the months following Helen's promotion, Dana enjoyed a good working relationship with Dawn, who wholeheartedly approved of Dana's suggestion to build a small free-standing accessories "store" in the junior department. Dawn had challenged the buyers to think of creative ways to compete with boutique-mania thriving all over the city, from Madison to Third Avenue, and she especially liked Dana's idea to market the proposed accessory section, called "Nantucket," with merchandise popular on Nantucket Island: handmade lightship bags decorated with scrimshaw pieces, colorful ribbon belts, and canvas duffle bags from Marblehead, Massachusetts. Dawn not only gave Dana the green light but approved an expensive build-out to replicate cedar shingle houses on the island, custom-designed by Mark Senger, president of Senger Display Company, B. Altman's vendor for holiday windows and major store renovations. Helen went directly to Dawn, asking her to halt the project or defer the cost to the store, but she was overruled. Dawn thought the Nantucket concept had potential for growth and believed that Helen should be responsible for the expense because her department would ultimately benefit from the new brand. Dana had found herself in the middle of a power play between two formidable women, and she was an easy target for Helen's misery. Her exciting new job had once again become nothing more than a game of politics.

Dana lingered over breakfast until the store officially opened so she could buy a few favorite items for her room at the Lansdowne, ginger and lemon tea and ginger chocolates, before dashing next door into Hatchards Bookshop. She had almost an hour before the lecture on portrait miniatures, and enough time to browse the tables and shelves, picking out several titles, and a lovely edition on eighteenth and nineteenth century portrait miniatures that would be the perfect complement for the upcoming lecture.

She purchased the books cradled in her arms and took a short taxi ride to the historic Hertford House on Manchester Square, where the Wallace Collection was located. The small museum had been established in 1897 from the private collection acquired by Sir Richard Wallace and the third and fourth Marquesses of Hertford. Wallace's widow had bequeathed the entire collection to Great Britain on the condition that admission would always remain free to the general public. The collection included European paintings, portrait miniatures, sculpture, eighteenth century French furniture, Sevres and Meissen porcelain, and Oriental and European arms and armor. Despite its many renovations over the years, the Wallace Collection still had the graciousness of a private town mansion of the period.

Dana immediately went to the Sixteenth Century Gallery on the main floor where twenty chairs had been arranged. Just as the lecture was about to begin, Dana seated herself next to a slim young woman who, although conservatively dressed in a tweed skirt and sweater, wore large antique Art Nouveau silver jewelry. The woman had thick, wavy hair parted softly in the middle and pulled behind her head in a bun. Her large brown eyes were attentive and aimed at the front of the gallery except for a brief moment when she turned slightly towards Dana and smiled.

The lecture began, and Dana focused her attention on the speaker, a balding English gentleman in his sixties named Basil Trivett. He wore a dark gray suit and a burgundy foulard bow tie, with half spectacles perched on the end of his nose. He spoke slowly and distinctly, as he explained that miniature portraits first appeared in illuminated manuscripts painstakingly produced by hand in the High Middle Ages. By the early sixteenth century, portrait miniatures were used by royalty at French and English courts and were painted in watercolor on stretched vellum parchment or enamel. The first glimpse Henry VIII received of his fourth wife, Anne of Cleves, was courtesy of court painter and miniaturist Hans Holbein. King Henry carried images of some of his wives in lockets before they lost his favor—or their lives.

In 1768, artists in London established the Royal Academy of Arts, with miniatures displayed at its annual exhibition. When photography was introduced in 1839, however, miniature portraits were eclipsed by the accurate likenesses produced by early cameras. A revival occurred in 1896 when the Royal Society of Miniature Painters was founded. Trivett concluded by explaining that miniatures were still highly prized by art patrons and were quite collectible. A question and answer session ensued, during which the woman next to Dana asked several questions that clearly demonstrated her superior knowledge of miniatures

When the lecture concluded, Dana turned to the demure woman and said, "Your questions were as interesting as the lecture, particularly your inquiry on the British colonial period, which I love." She paused. "Pardon me—my name is Dana McGarry. Would you care to join me for lunch in the courtyard? "

"I'm Abby Kempf," the woman said, extending a small, frail hand. Her head was slightly lowered even though she looked Dana in the eyes as she spoke. "Yes, I'd be happy to join you. It's a beautiful day."

During the first few minutes of their lunch, Abby spoke quietly, expounding on Trivett's facts about miniatures to include stories about their history in France and Germany. Dana was overwhelmed by Abby's continued display of artistic knowledge, but at times she was distracted by the intensity she brought to the subject. Dana was more than a bit curious about her passion for the miniatures.

"Are you a collector?" Dana asked.

"No, but I do have three enamel miniatures, one by Henry Bone. They were wedding gifts from my mother-in-law." Abby explained that she'd majored in art history at Sarah Lawrence, spending her senior year in Florence and remaining there an additional two years after graduation. She had then interned for a year at Sotheby's in London.

"I don't enjoy a nine-to-five routine," Abby said with a shy smile, "so I share my knowledge and passion by giving art lectures in England and the U.S. I book my travel schedule around the lectures."

"Then you must know Rosamond Bernier," Dana said enthusiastically. "I attend all her lectures at the Met. We were introduced last year, and she invited me to her after-party at Café des Artistes. A beautiful lady and so gifted."

"She and my parents have mutual friends in Peapack, New Jersey, and we've spoken at summer parties. When she heard I was putting together slide presentations, she was very generous and gave me invaluable advice. She's exceptional."

"Are you from Peapack?" Dana asked.

"No," Abby replied. "From nearby Bernardsville."

"I grew up on Long Island," Dana said, "although I've been living in Manhattan since I graduated from college."

"I have a flat in London, but I consider Manhattan my home," Abby said. "I'll be traveling most of the summer before returning to New York in the fall."

Dana and Abby exchanged phone numbers, and Abby once again grew more reserved as she stood to leave.

"I hope we'll visit in New York," Dana said. "It's been a lovely lunch."

Abby merely nodded, smiled, and left.

Dana had thoroughly enjoyed both the lecture and the lunch, although she sensed a very mysterious air surrounding Abby Kempf. It was also strange that, aside from a brief reference to her mother-in-law, there was no mention of her husband or marriage. Well, strange or not, Dana was grateful to be in the company of someone who didn't ask personal questions. She looked forward to seeing her again.

While Dana had listened to Basil Trivett's words intently, her thoughts had occasionally drifted to her new Nantucket boutique and how she would merchandise it. After all, Helen had to approve her budget since the department would carry junior accessories. In spite of Helen's brusque manner, business would go on. Dana had no doubt that the concept would be successful and, as soon as it was, that Helen would come around.

Chapter Three

*B*rett McGarry strode down the corridors of Davis, Konen and Wright, which was located at 80 Broad Street in the heart of New York City's financial district. He was currently trying a case in San Francisco and made it back to the East Coast once or twice a month to check on other cases and put out any fires that had flared up in his absence. His chief client at present was the owner of a building in Manhattan, a building that had caused considerable health problems to employees due to the presence of asbestos in the walls and ceilings. The owner was suing the construction company, but in December the judge ordered a change in jurisdiction since the builder's pertinent files had been found, upon discovery, to be located at his main office in San Francisco. Brett's lover and fellow litigator, Janice Conlon, had remained on the West Coast to handle various trial motions.

Brett stepped into his office, smiled, and took a deep breath as he sat in his familiar chair, his hands rubbing its brown leather arms as if to remind himself of their feel. His office had been his second home even before Dana had discovered his affair and filed for divorce. Brett settled back in the chair and looked at his well-appointed office. Nothing had been changed or moved in the past four months, and even the pictures of Dana remained untouched. He wondered what Janice would have thought if she'd returned to New York to see the photographs of Brett's soon-to-be-ex-wife still prominently displayed in his office. He was certain she would be displeased since she had encouraged him—and rightly so—to move on with his life, to live and breathe a little. According to Janice, his life had become stuffy and predictable, an assessment he had begrudgingly agreed with in the long run. Still, leaving the pictures had been strategic inasmuch as doing so conveyed to his colleagues and the managing partner of the firm that he was indeed grief-stricken over the separation, thus deflecting any suspicions of his affair with Janice.

Brett sighed deeply as he ran his fingers through thick brown hair parted on the side. His clandestine relationship with Janice had been exciting but also draining due to the necessity of monitoring his every word and action when around his colleagues. To alleviate the tension, he'd doubled his exercise regimen, adding daily runs with Janice. He had square shoulders, a strong jaw, and worked out at the New York Athletic Club when he wasn't traveling.

Brett stood and paced around his office, looking at family pictures depicting the stages of his eight-year marriage. Had the affair been worth it? He'd been ambitious to make partner, and it had cost him dearly. It was a tragedy, of course, but Dana had failed to understand the demands of his job, his need to advance. If one was just marking time at a prestigious Wall Street law firm, it was considered by the partners to be a waste of talent. The biggest and best firms looked for hungry sharks, men and women who were aggressive and pursued their careers with tenacity. No, Dana had never fully understood how important it was for him to go the extra mile in order to maintain their New York lifestyle.

Or so he had convinced himself. In his heart, he knew she had been the quintessence of patience, giving him abundant understanding over the years, always forgiving his inattentiveness in order to preserve the marriage. It was who she was, and her religious faith had only reinforced her determination to make the relationship work. Dana had even bought his lame excuses when his eye began to linger more and more on the seductive Conlon. Deep down, he knew he couldn't blame Dana.

But it had all worked out for the best, hadn't it? He had avoided all but the most cursory questions from his colleagues, and the delicious and sexy Janice was an amazingly irreverent and iconoclastic woman, not to mention a voracious lover. In fact, she was even more extroverted in her native California, where she'd spent her college and law school years absorbing the freewheeling lifestyle of the coast.

"To the business at hand," Brett said aloud as he returned to his chair. He'd been summoned back to New York by managing partner Richard Patterson because Jack Hartlen, CEO of Hartlen Response, hadn't joined a consortium of oil companies proposed by Davis, Konen and Wright to act as first responders to the increasing number of oil spills in the world's oceans. Hartlen Response possessed cutting edge technology that was considered to be the gold standard in repairing ecological disasters before they could affect wildlife or thousands of miles of coastline along the eastern seaboard. Jack and his father Ralph, CEO of Hartlen Oil in Houston, had originally shied away from signing the consortium proposal put forward by the firm because it was waiting for patents on its equipment to clear. Brett had pointed out that it could take years for the patents to be issued, during which time other oil companies might develop their own response technology. It was a persuasive argument, but it hadn't won over the powerful and wealthy Hartlens of Texas, who had recently opened an office in New York. Brett had succeeded in putting the younger Hartlen on the defensive, however, when he'd discovered that Jack was having an affair with Dana's gay friend, Andrew Ricci. Jack's wife Patti was a grant manager for the Altman Foundation, and Brett knew that Patti and her in-laws would have been shocked and devastated to learn of Jack's infidelity and sexual orientation. Jack had therefore been quite chastened and pliable when Brett had seen him and Andrew engaged in a lovers' quarrel at the Sugar Plum Ball the previous December. Shaken, Jack had promised to join the consortium, but he had apparently balked in the intervening months. Richard Patterson was getting anxious, and Brett, who had been made partner on the strength of bringing Hartlen Response into the fold, was nervous as well. His reputation was on the line, and Brett feared that Jack was making him look foolish, not the way a new partner wanted to be perceived.

Jack would obviously need a little coaxing by way of reminders of what Brett knew about his private life. Brett had his secretary put in a call to Jack to set up a lunch meeting at the Polo Lounge. Brett suspected that Jack wasn't taking his blackmail scheme seriously ever since he'd been sent to the West Coast. It was time to take the pulse of the young CEO of Hartlen Response.

Brett entered the Polo Lounge, located in the Westbury Hotel on Madison Avenue. Brett was running late, but Jack hadn't yet arrived. It wasn't a good omen. Brett chose a seat at the rear of the lounge and waited nervously. After ten minutes of constantly checking his watch, he looked up to see Jack, tall and slender, approaching the table. Jack had thinning brown hair, and his laidback manner was antithetical to Brett's desire to always keep business on a professional footing.

"Sorry to be late," Jack said with a confident smile as he seated himself. "Our office has been open less than four months, and we're still not up to speed on staffing. I tell you—it's a busy life here in New York."

"Busy in more ways than one," Brett said dryly.

"Now that didn't take very long," Jack said, his eyes fixed on Brett. "So let's get right to it, shall we? Here's what I'm seeing: you've been gone four months, I haven't signed the consortium papers, and yet you haven't divulged my wicked little secret to anyone or placed a single call to me to urge me to sign. Looks to me like something is holding you back. To be honest, I'm not that worried anymore." Ever the gentleman, Jack's manner was straightforward yet calm even though he detested the opportunistic lawyer sitting across from him.

"Your *little* secret?" Brett said. "Hardly little, Jack. What counts is that I'm back today, and it only takes one word from me to destroy your marriage and possibly even your reputation. What's it going to be?"

Jack rubbed his chin thoughtfully before clasping his hands on the table. "After a lot of careful consideration," he said, "I've concluded that you would never go through with outing me. Not now, not ever."

Brett, clearly irritated, knitted his eyebrows and frowned. "What makes you so sure?" He took a sip of scotch as he waited for a reply.

"Because you'd hurt Dana. Badly. She loves Andrew dearly, as do I, and she's also getting quite close to my wife now that Patti is with the Altman Foundation. You may be getting divorced, but you're not going to hurt that very adorable wife of yours even when she becomes your ex. After all, you spent eight years with her, and I'm willing to bet that without her considerable patience, you wouldn't be where you are today."

Brett took another sip of scotch, certain that Jack knew nothing of Janice and therefore couldn't turn the tables on him when it came to blackmail. "It seems I've already disappointed

Dana," he pointed out. "What do I have to lose? The damage is already done, and I'll do what I have to. As for Andrew and Patti, they're nothing more than collateral damage to me. You've put my reputation with the firm on the line, and nothing is going to jeopardize that. I sacrificed my marriage to make partner, so don't presume I'll stop there to further my career."

Jack smiled and stood to leave. "But I don't think you will. I know how to read people, and I'm also a gambler." He winked. "It's what we do down in Texas. My great-grandfather was a wildcatter, and we know something about risk. No, you're not going to pull the trigger on this, Brett ole boy."

Jack turned and left before Brett could respond.

Brett was nonplussed. Was Jack correct in his assumption? Would he—Brett—not go forward with his blackmail plan for the sake of sparing Dana since her dear friend Andrew might be caught in the cross-fire? He'd been busy in San Francisco, enjoying his new-found freedom, but why indeed had he not called Jack? Was it because, as he'd realized in his office, he knew Dana didn't deserve any more grief?

Or was there another factor to consider? Brett could certainly find numerous ways to disclose Jack's affair without leaving a trail that pointed to himself or the firm lest the Hartlens find new reasons to sever ties with Davis, Konen and Wright. But despite the method of disclosure, Andrew would learn from Jack in short order that he, Brett, was the one who'd stumbled across their affair, and it would only be a matter of hours before Dana found out. When she did, what would her reaction be? He'd learned a few months ago that Dana was now willing to be pushed only so far. Would she go after Brett? His career? Would she, in turn, expose his affair with Janice? There was no way to predict what she would do, but one thing was certain: Dana was no longer hesitant to operate in her best interest and that of her friends.

Have I seriously miscalculated, Brett wondered. *Is this about to blow up in my face?*

Four months ago, the blackmail had seemed logical, had seemed the obvious way to secure his partnership. But now Jack had hesitated, and ugly possibilities were creeping into the picture.

He finished his scotch and returned to his office, trying to think of additional leverage to use against the obstinate Mr. Hartlen.

Brett was back at his desk for only fifteen minutes before Janice called from San Francisco. They exchanged a few amorous greetings before Janice informed him that Ralph Hartlen had been trying to reach him all morning.

"Did he say what he wanted?" Brett asked.

"No," Janice said, "but he said it was urgent and that you should get back to him as soon as possible. He'll be at his Houston office all day."

"I'll call him now."

"Call me when you're finished," Janice requested. "You know how I love intrigue."

"Janice," Brett said, "you're the very definition of intrigue."

"That's why you love me. Like I said, let me know what's up."

Within minutes, Brett had Ralph Hartlen on the line.

"Brett McGarry here, Ralph. What can I do for you?"

"Quite a lot actually," Ralph said. "Let me explain."

Brett said nothing for the next ten minutes as Ralph spoke at length about a serious concern at Hartlen Oil. Brett could tell that he was extremely upset.

"I'll have to speak with Richard," Brett said when Ralph had finished talking, "but I'll do whatever I can. Let me get back to you."

Brett put the receiver back on its cradle, leaned back, and smiled broadly. Fortune had smiled on him once again. Hartlen Oil was immersed in a scandal, and Ralph wanted Brett's help. The request would send Jack reeling.

Life was so sweet sometimes.

Chapter Four

It was overcast when Dana left The Wallace Collection, with a few drops beginning to hit the pavement as black umbrellas popped open up and down the length of the block. She decided to return to the Lansdowne Club to quickly retrieve her raincoat before heading to Regent Street. She stopped at the front desk before going to her room and was given a phone message from Andrew Ricci that had come in while she was at the lecture. It read, "Please call any time, day or night. Try home, try work, but call. It's urgent."

Brows furrowed, Dana went to her room and dialed Andrew's work number. It was early morning in the states, and she figured that Andrew had been at the store for at least an hour. She was concerned. Was someone ill? Had Andrew received bad news? Had Brett returned from San Francisco in order to cause further trouble? Was there a problem with the divorce settlement? She assumed her parents were okay since no one from her family had called, but perhaps something terrible had happened to Johnny or Uncle John. Dana's mind raced as she waited nervously for the overseas call to be put through, static crackling on the line.

Five minutes passed before she heard Andrew's distant voice. "Dana? Is that you?"

"Yes, Andrew. I got your message a few minutes ago. Is anything wrong?"

There was a pause that seemed to last forever. Was there a problem with the connection or was Andrew too overwhelmed to speak?

"Are you there, Andrew?"

"I'm here. Listen, I'm really sorry to call you about this on your vacation, but I thought you should know as soon as possible."

"Andrew, what is it? Please get to the point."

"Dawn resigned."

"You're kidding. What happened?"

"You can't guess?"

"Well ... yes, of course, she's joining Ira at Bergdorf's."

"Yep. She's already gone. Left yesterday. We should have expected it. They've been close for years."

"What a loss for the store. No one has Dawn's vision. Do you know if they will try to replace her?"

"I have no idea. Not a peep coming from senior management, but lots of hushed conversations around the store."

"Remember, Andrew, that the position of fashion director was Ira's idea, and not everyone understood what Dawn did or the difference she was making. She had a lot of power."

"Good point. There's a good chance they won't replace her."

"Well, I'm just lucky that Dawn helped me get Nantucket into production before she left."

"Dana, that's why I'm calling. Dawn's news could have waited. Helen is killing the Nantucket boutique."

There was silence on the line.

"Dana, did you hear me? Are you okay?"

"Damn it, I'm not okay! I'm livid! She couldn't wait until I got back to the store? She's a spiteful woman! Andrew, are you absolutely sure about this?"

"The news wasn't even an hour old before Helen called me into her office and ordered me to tell Mark to halt production." Andrew paused, second-guessing his decision to tell Dana the news while she was away.

"But … I mean … that doesn't make any sense at all. You said Dawn left yesterday and that no replacement has been announced. Helen can't make that kind of sweeping decision without consulting someone!"

"She can and she did," Andrew said. "Until further notice or a new fashion director is named, the divisionals once again have full control of their buyers, just like they did before Dawn came on the scene. No one can override Helen's decision, Dana. I'm sorry. I just thought you shouldn't hear this your first day back."

Dana was stunned and angry. The boutique would have gone far beyond an idea such as the placement of a small teen makeup counter against a side wall, a counter that Dana had to fight for last December. The boutique would have been her biggest accomplishment to date, not to mention a boon to B. Altman. Ira had been brought in to give a facelift to the store and energize its stuffy atmosphere, but with his move to Bergdorf Goodman, the winds of change had suddenly died down and the old guard, represented most notably by Helen, might well impede innovations necessary to keep the store competitive. Boutiques were appearing in many stores in New York City, and once again Helen was balking at a popular current trend.

Dana sighed deeply. "You're right. I need to take some time to accept this. Helen didn't even give me the courtesy of a phone call to tell me herself. The build-out was already under way. What about the money that's been wasted with Senger Display? I know Helen is concerned about cost, but it's about much more than that. It's about control, and ever since she's been divisional manager, she thinks she's nothing more than a paper tiger. She saw an opportunity in Dawn's announcement and pounced on it. Andrew, I'm mad as hell."

"I don't blame you, kiddo, but I don't see anything to do except bite the bullet and live to fight another day."

"Oh, there's going to be a fight all right," Dana said, her voice rising in pitch.

Andrew paused. "Why not finish your vacation and come back fresh. Give things time to play out. Maybe Bob Campbell will weigh in on this."

"I doubt it. Bob gives Helen a wide berth in just about everything. Maybe he, too, doesn't believe in the Nantucket boutique. I don't know what to think or who to trust anymore."

"Try not to think about it while you're away. Things will work out."

Dana didn't place much stock in Andrew's cliché, but he meant well and was always willing to do anything to help his friend. "Okay, Andrew. You're right. I'll use this time away to try to process everything. It's going to take a while."

"I'm sure it will, Dana. Take care, and we'll talk when you get back."

"Bye now." Dana hung up and paced anxiously around her suite, hardly able to believe what she'd just heard. *Helen can't do this*, Dana thought over and over again. *She's overstepped her boundaries this time. I won't let her get away with it.*

But Dana knew that Andrew was correct. With Dawn no longer present to overrule Helen, and with no replacement named, Helen had both the right and the leverage to stop the build-out cold. What Dana's response would be was another matter. In the minutes following the call to Andrew, Dana considered walking into Helen's office and tendering her resignation. If B. Altman didn't value her creativity, she could certainly find another store or company that would. Maybe she had gone as far as she could at B. Altman.

Maybe it was time for a change. She'd filed for separation from Brett because she'd grown weary of the drama. Maybe it was time to divorce B. Altman as well. The bureaucracy was stifling.

Dana sat on one of the many wooden benches that lined the main walkway cutting through Berkeley Square near the Lansdowne Club. A light mist in the air had ceased, although the day was still gloomy, a stark contrast to the sunny spring atmosphere she'd enjoyed the previous morning. The mood seemed fitting to Dana since the bleak, chilly day mirrored the emotions in her mind and soul.

Why didn't Helen understand the marketing potential of the Nantucket concept? It was endless and could reach far beyond juniors into housewares, children's, and, of course, menswear. The boutique was a small investment with a huge up-side. Yes, Helen had pride and was someone who liked to have firm control of situations, which wasn't always a bad thing. Every company needed leadership, and Helen was a talented, savvy businesswoman, but leadership without vision was doomed for failure. Furthermore, outside of work, she had always been a friend to Dana. But nothing static could survive indefinitely, not marriages and certainly not businesses when the competition was always looking to build the better mousetrap. Even portrait miniatures had been an innovation hundreds of years earlier, a unique art form that had gained the attention of kings and emperors. As Dana looked at the green trees of the square, heavy with raindrops, she realized that all of life depended on cycles and change, and change at B. Altman was being stifled by Helen Kavanagh.

Dana's thoughts turned to the indomitable Nina Bramen, B. Altman's antiques buyer and a staunch, outspoken feminist who inspired Dana to pursue her vision for the teen makeup counter when her idea had been dismissed at every turn. Nina had convinced Dana that a determined woman could accomplish anything if, above all, she didn't lose the spirit to fight for what she believed. It's what Estée Lauder did, as well as all successful women who carved a new career path.

Remembering Helen's wrath when Dawn approved the Nantucket boutique, Dana recalled a comment Helen made that had stung like a bee: your "little idea." What, Dana wondered, did Helen really mean by the remark? Was the idea small because the items were accessories and low ticket items? But Helen's refusal to even discuss the topic made Dana think *she* was the one who was small and not willing to explore the possibilities. Now that Dawn was gone, however, Dana realized that she had to find a way to renew the relationship if she wanted Helen to eventually support the Nantucket boutique or any other creative idea. Dana decided not to show Helen how angry and hurt she was about the way she had abruptly killed her pet project, but rather she would request a meeting to get Helen's fashion direction before buying her spring accessory line. At the right time, Dana would change the subject and ask Helen for her vision of boutiques at B. Altman. Even without Dawn Mello, top merchandising executives at the store would soon want to ride the wave of this new business model, and Helen would have to get on board. Dana would take her comments back to the drawing board and tweak the Nantucket boutique accordingly. If politics was the name of the game, Dana was determined to learn how to play. Giving up was not an option.

Dana stood proudly and walked quickly towards Regent Street.

• • •

Regent Street was located in London's West End, and when it came to shopping, it was as well known and iconic as Fifth or Madison Avenues. Its layout was designed by architect John Nash, and the street itself was named after George IV when he was Prince Regent. The street exhibited the Beaux-Arts school of urban design, assembling several small buildings in great numbers to produce an overall effect of architectural harmony. As Dana made her way past the dozens of shops on the fabled street, the day didn't seem dreary any longer despite lingering gray clouds. It was the 150th anniversary of Regent Street since its completion in 1825, and colorful banners and flags hung from the triple-globed street lamps in the center of the thoroughfare. Posters in the windows of many shops advertised a procession on Regent Street on April 23rd and a costume ball at Café Royal. After a visit to Liberty & Co. to see its newly-opened wallpaper department, she headed straight for Jaeger at 204 Regent Street.

Jaeger, both a brand and retailer of menswear and womenswear, was founded in 1884 by Lewis Tomalin, who had published a translation of the book by naturalist Dr. Gustav Jaeger on the merits of wearing clothing made from high-quality natural fibers such as wool, silk, cashmere, and alpaca. In fact, it was Jaeger that introduced camel hair clothing to Great Britain in 1908. In 1956, the legendary dressmaker Jean Muir, a self-taught designer who honed her sketching and business skills during a six-year stint at Liberty & Co., joined Jaeger as one of its youngest designers, exclusively using Jaeger's knitwear and jersey fabrics. Aimed at a younger and less conservative customer, Muir created the name "Young Jaeger," which defined the generation. During this time Audrey Hepburn and Marilyn Monroe modeled Jaeger clothing. By 1970, Jaeger represented the epitome of the quintessential British look and the first Jaeger boutique opened on Madison Avenue.

Dana entered the store, noting as she did that the clouds were parting to reveal slivers of blue sky and weak rays of sun. Hopefully, this was an omen that the murky issues regarding Helen's intransigence would also dissolve. She was greeted warmly by Mrs. Llewyn, store manager, and her two assistants, Sarah and Maude, to whom she always sent notes before her visits. Dana met them during her first trip to London almost eight years ago when she became a devoted customer, purchasing her first camel hair blazer.

"How wonderful to see you again!" Mrs. Llewyn exclaimed, giving Dana a polite kiss on each cheek. "We've been expecting you."

"Are you here on business or pleasure?" asked Maude.

Dana laughed. "It was planned as pure pleasure, but I can't get my mind off work. I suppose if I spent all my time in museums, I could forget, but once I walk into a store, my mind always travels back to B. Altman."

"Have you been visiting our Madison Avenue boutique?" asked Maude.

"Of course!" Dana replied. "I don't have to tell you that they're doing very well. They are always busy, even at off hours during the week. I think they need a store *this* size!"

Jaeger's six-story building was, surprisingly, an emporium of plate glass and chrome modernism, a minimalist setting that featured the classic, tailored clothing as the main attraction. Each floor was divided into small, open departments categorized by style and fabric, and all separates, sweaters, and outerwear were color-coordinated for easy mixing and matching.

"We have a surprise for you," Mrs. Llewyn said. "Samples arrived yesterday for our autumn fashion show. It's a beautiful collection!"

Dana glanced at Sarah and Maude, who were beaming. "We couldn't wait to tell you, Dana," said Sarah. "You will love everything! Let's take a look! We set up a room on the second floor."

"I'll stop by shortly to see your selections," the store manager said.

Dana followed Sarah to the Camel Room, where the autumn collection was arranged on racks. It didn't take half an hour for Dana to make her selections: a gray and camel argyle lambswool sweater; full-cut gray flannel trousers; a side button lovat green kilt; and a raspberry cashmere sweater-set.

While Dana thought how much she loved the little black wool dinner suit that she no longer had use for, Sarah said, "Brett would want you to have that suit. It was made for you." Dana was startled by the sudden jolt back to reality. She decided not to tell Sarah about the pending divorce. The news could wait for the next trip. The mention of Brett, however, was a sharp reminder of her heartache during the past few months and, in a split second, she decided she deserved the suit and said, "I'll take it."

While Sarah was writing up the order that would be sent to Dana in August, Dana overheard two American tourists discussing the Jaeger brand and how all the pieces coordinated perfectly with each other.

"This is such an efficient way to shop," said a well-dressed woman who had a slight Boston accent. "All the matching pieces are within steps of each other."

"I agree," said her friend. "I spent a month carrying a sweater from store to store trying to find a pair of trousers in the same shade, and I finally gave up."

This was precisely the point of the trending store-within-a-store concept, Dana thought. The average American woman was busy raising a family or launching a career and didn't have the time or the patience to coordinate a separates wardrobe. If Helen thought Nantucket was a small idea, she just might go for a full-scale tailored British boutique using Jaeger's philosophy of matching separates and accessories in one location. The fine fabrics and knitwear, combined with classic British style, would be compatible with B. Altman's conservative image and customer. Unlike Jaeger's contemporary interior, however, Dana envisioned a boutique more like Brooks Brothers, with dark wood paneling, brass lighting fixtures, and chairs upholstered in wool plaid and tweed fabrics. Management would surely consider the idea because in December of 1972 they invited Fortnum & Mason to open a token branch of its London gourmet shop on the eighth floor, and it had been a huge success.

Dana thought she had done enough damage with the little black suit and was ready to leave as soon as she paid the bill for her fall order. She visited Mrs. Llewyn and Maude before she left and thanked them for their warm hospitality. "I hope to see you in New York before too long," Dana told the three women. "I'd love to show you B. Altman. I might even have a few surprises for you."

Dana returned to the Lansdowne Club, her mind swimming with ideas and images for the British boutique. After ordering afternoon tea, she sat at the writing table and began planning a fall buy and Christmas promotion. If Helen jumped on board, they could open before Thanksgiving. After several minutes, she began sketching what the boutique would look like. She couldn't do the drawing justice, of course—not like Mark and his brilliant ability to conceptualize—but she was excited enough to commit her dream to paper.

The fact that Helen might be positively apoplectic over the suggestion to resume and modify the build-out didn't even enter Dana's thinking.

Chapter Five

Feeling renewed by her visit to Jaeger the previous day, Dana returned to the Church of the Immaculate Conception so she could attend the twelve-thirty mass. She also wished to say goodbye to Father Macaulay and thank him for the concern he expressed two days earlier. The day was sunny and warm, and Dana felt buoyed by her plans to lobby for the boutique. She therefore arrived early to sit on the bench in Mount Street Gardens and enjoy the spring weather. She was surprised to see Father Macaulay busily trimming some hedges several yards away. He wore khakis and a blue work shirt and, after five minutes, he paused to wipe his brow with a handkerchief and noticed Dana observing him from the bench.

Leaning his hedge clippers against a wheelbarrow, he walked towards Dana and removed his wide-brimmed straw hat.

"Good morning, Dana," he said. "What a pleasant surprise!"

"Surely you have gardeners to trim the hedges," she commented, laughing.

"Of course, but I love to do a bit of gardening when our resident groundskeeper takes a day off. It keeps me grounded."

"I must confess that I arrived early for mass so that I could tell you that I'm returning home tomorrow, which is a few days earlier than I planned because I've been told that things are really busy at work. I also wanted to thank you for your kindness the other day."

"A confession and expression of thanksgiving all in two sentences," he said with a warm smile. "You are indeed a member of the flock—and in good standing."

Dana cocked her head. "Well, I don't know about the good standing part. I'm trying to figure that out."

"Well, maybe you should stay in London a little longer. It doesn't sound like you'll have much time for reflection once you get home."

"So true, Father. But my job is starting to distract me even though I'm here."

"Will a few more days make a difference?" Macaulay asked. "What do you do, if I may ask?"

Dana described her position at B. Altman and how much she loved the store. "I'm going home early because my boss—her name is Helen—is always fighting my ideas, always fighting change. I could do so much if only I had a free hand to use my creativity. It's terribly frustrating at times. Truthfully, the situation has made me downright angry in the last few days. I'm angry at Helen, angry at Bre—" Dana said, annoyed at letting her husband's name start to slip out.

"Excuse, me, Dana," Macaulay said, "Did you say Brett?"

"Yes, Father," Dana answered, her head still lowered. "My husband. Or my soon-to-be-ex-husband, to be precise. I'm waiting for our divorce to become final." She glanced up to see that Macaulay's expression hadn't changed. His caring eyes were fixed on her face as he listened attentively. "My husband and I separated in January after I caught him cheating on me with a lawyer at his firm. They've been together for a few months in San Francisco while working on a case."

"So there's no possibility of mending the fences?" Macaulay commented.

Dana shook her head. "He's an ambitious man, and he's been inattentive for many years now. I was in tears the other day because I felt that maybe my decision had been a little too rash. To be truthful, however, I really want my life back and don't believe that he's capable of change." Looking directly at Father Macaulay, Dana added, "I don't know. Maybe we should have gone to counseling."

"So you're a bit conflicted at times. Welcome to the human race, Dana. If you had walked away without the slightest look back at the love you had for your husband, I would say that you belong to the large number of people who don't examine their actions through the eyes of faith and reflection, who never look inside."

"That's precisely what happened when I was in the Sacred Heart Chapel," she continued. "I was looking deeper at my decision even though I'm convinced it's the right one."

"The church does not consider separation to be a sin," Macaulay explained. "Sometimes relationships are quite difficult and don't work out despite the considerable effort we put into them."

"Thank you, Father. I'm sure I'll be fine. I'll be keeping busy with my job and my friends. I'm volunteering at the Metropolitan Museum's Costume Institute, I'm joining a reading group, and I'll be boating with family on the weekends. I'll be very grounded."

Laughing, Father Macaulay responded, "I think the word is exhausted! Keeping busy is not necessarily the same thing as staying grounded. In fact, sometimes it's a way to avoid making decisions or really living the life we want. Your life is going through a lot of changes right now, but you can't keep your emotions bottled up. Sooner or later, they'll come pouring out, like they did in the chapel. Anger and doubt are normal human emotions. They only become dangerous when you hold onto them for too long. You shouldn't be angry at yourself for having feelings." He paused. "When I'm mad, I go to a gym and pound a punching bag for an hour. It's all in *how* you handle your emotions, Dana. But here's my concern. You're grounding yourself by attending to duties at the store in order to work through your impending divorce. As you've explained it, however, work carries its own unique frustrations. How do you ground yourself from those?"

"So you're saying that I need to find something that helps me cope with everything. Do you mean prayer?"

Macaulay laughed. "Well, that certainly helps, and it's what I'm expected to say, of course. But I'm also talking about continuing to find your own center of gravity, if I may phrase it like that. Trimming hedges, beating a punching bag, and singing Cole Porter tunes at the pub every Wednesday—they help me remember who I am and what I'm called to do with my life. We're all on a journey and you need to always return to who you are deep down inside. You have to take care of Dana first. Does that make sense?"

Dana nodded. "It makes a *lot* of sense, Father. But how does one begin?"

"That's something only you can discover, but maybe you can start by not cutting your vacation short to get back to work. What does Dana *really* want to do? While you decide, I need to clean up and vest for mass."

As Father Macaulay rose from the bench, Dana asked, "Father, do you really sing Cole Porter tunes in a *pub*? "

"Every Wednesday night, at the Four Farthings."

"What fun! I love Cole Porter. Brett…um…well, we always celebrated my birthday at the Café Carlyle with Bobby Short. He only sings Cole Porter, Gershwin, Noel Coward … "

"I'm a big Bobby Short fan, too! I saw him when he performed here many years back. Safe trip home, Dana."

The priest walked towards the side entrance to the church but stopped and turned around, removing a slip of paper and a yellow, stubby pencil from his shirt pocket. "Here's my mailing address," he said after scribbling on the paper and handing it to Dana. "Transatlantic calls are rather expensive, but I'd welcome hearing from you any time you feel like you wish to share something. Or just to know how you're doing."

"Thank you, Father. I'd like that very much."

Macaulay went inside to prepare for mass, and Dana entered the church and sat in a pew before the main altar. She still had many unresolved issues, but she suddenly felt she could handle them without bitterness or anger. In fact, she felt so good that she was no longer in a rush to get back to work or Helen. Her conversation with the Jesuit had reminded her that she needed to maintain an internal balance, that she had to stay grounded. Taking back those two vacation days was a gift she was giving herself and a step in the right direction. She knew that things would get hectic again when she returned to New York, and she would welcome the opportunity to correspond with this kind and wise man who had given her such inner peace during the brief moments they had spoken.

New trials awaited her, but she was content to go to mass and just be Dana McGarry right now. For the moment, she was very grounded.

Chapter Six

*T*wo days had passed since Brett had spoken with Ralph Hartlen by phone. Ralph had explained that the FBI was investigating donations to Hartlen Oil, donations intended to facilitate environmental responsibility. Donors had been promised that their money would be used to help safeguard marine and wildlife along coastal areas, as well as to promote clean water in rivers, streams, and oceans. The goal was to ensure water that was free of oil and industrial pollutants, with the assurance that Hartlen would work with reputable environmental groups to help achieve these purposes. The environment had become a hot-button issue since the 1960s, and pollution of the air, land, and oceans was being investigated by congressional subcommittees. Ralph believed that working towards a clean environment would be a wise PR move since oil companies were being singled out by many organizations as acting irresponsibly and negligently given recent oil spills. Oil refineries were also being named as major polluters compromising air quality. The federal government, however, was not satisfied with the way donations were being handled by Hartlen, and the FBI had gotten the IRS involved as well. Brett had dispatched one of the firm's private investigators, a specialist in forensic bookkeeping, who had taken the red eye to Houston to make a preliminary assessment of the situation and had just returned to New York City that afternoon. Davis, Konen and Wright did not send lawyers out of town on a new case without having specialists first make an assessment on the merits of a given case.

"What did you find out, Wade?" Brett asked while sitting at his desk.

Wade Forrester was a slender man whose features were thin and harsh-looking, but despite his no-nonsense appearance, he was a consummate professional who wore tailored dou-ble-breasted suits and spoke with the precision of a university professor. He sat opposite Brett and looked at the lawyer with steely gray eyes.

"Hartlen Oil has taken in approximately eighteen million dollars in contributions for their environmental campaign. Donors are primarily corporate, although individuals—like the well-meaning John Q. Public who wants to shell out a few dollars to save the world—comprise about twenty percent of the donor base."

"That's an awful lot of change going into the coffers of Har-tlen Oil," Brett commented. "So why is the FBI investigating the donations? Is our good friend Ralph Hartlen not being fis-cally responsible?" Brett tendered the remark with considerable sarcasm.

"It's hard to say at this point," Forrester answered without any change in his facial expression. "Hartlen Oil has letters of intent on file from several high-powered environmental orga-nizations who wish to partner with Hartlen to clean up air and water and also preserve wildlife along coastal regions. We're talking big boys like the Environmental Defense Fund, the Sierra Club, the Ocean Conservancy, and the Coastal Ocean Institute, to name just a few."

Brett raised his eyebrows, hands clasped as he sat sideways, listening to Forrester' report. "Sounds legitimate enough."

"This is where the waters get murky," Forrester said. "No pun intended."

Brett suppressed a laugh. Forrester was the last person to employ humor when discussing business.

"The donations are accounted for down to the penny. In fact, I've rarely seen such thorough and accurate books. The problem is that the organizations it's partnering with haven't seen a dime of the eighteen million yet."

"Is that why Hartlen is in trouble?" Brett asked. "Did an environmental group start complaining that the cash wasn't flowing?"

Forrester shook his head. "Quite the opposite. No one has said a word. The letters of intent to partner with the oil company are rather vague and open-ended. No deadlines or dates have been stipulated for the donated money to move from Hartlen to the various environmental groups. The agreements Hartlen has with these outfits say that money will be held in a fund that Hartlen Oil calls its Responsible Use of Natural Resources Account. The money is to be disseminated to its partners after various environmental studies have been conducted and concrete action plans have been formulated."

Brett shrugged. "Bureaucratic, but it still sounds rather routine."

"This is where it gets even more interesting. There's only ten million dollars in this Responsible Use account."

"And the other eight million dollars?"

"It's been deposited in a discretionary account at Hartlen Response."

"Meaning Jack's company can do whatever the hell it wants with the money."

"Not according to Ralph. He pointed out that the letters of intent specify Hartlen Response to be its subsidiary in all matters pertaining to environmental responsibility. It's in fine print, to be sure, but it's there."

Brett swiveled, a puzzled look on his face as he leaned forward, elbows on his desk. "I'm still not following. Hartlen Response is all about clean-up and safeguarding the environment. If I'm Ralph Hartlen, I'd hand the football to junior and let him dole out the funds anyway. It's the most logical thing to do."

"True, but I looked very carefully at the name of the account to which Hartlen Oil is transferring these donations. Hartlen Response simply calls it Hartlen Discretionary. Pretty vague."

"And the feds are interested in all of this because ... "

"Hartlen Discretionary only has a million dollars in it. Seven million are unaccounted for."

"What does Ralph say about this?"

"Says he wasn't aware of the discrepancy until a few days ago. He claimed that Jack told him that the money is being invested in order to give the environmental groups interest only in order to safeguard the principal."

Brett smiled. "If there's nothing in the partnership agreements giving Hartlen Response that kind of flexibility, then ... "

"Then Jack Hartlen is violating federal laws protecting charitable and philanthropic donations. Hence, the FBI and IRS are sniffing around. Ralph has referred their inquiries to Hartlen Response, which apparently isn't giving the feds satisfactory answers."

"What's your take, Wade?"

"I think Ralph and Hartlen Oil are on the up and up. Ralph trusts his son. Thinks it's all a big misunderstanding."

Brett thought for several seconds and looked at the investigator. "Great work as always, Wade. I'll be in touch. I may need you to do some legwork here in New York at Hartlen Response."

Forrester nodded and left Brett's office.

Brett felt confident he had Jack in his sights once again. He was willing to bet that there were no investments being made from Hartlen's discretionary fund. His gut instinct was that, whatever Jack was calling the account, it was an auxiliary monetary fund. A lot of companies had them. They were also known as slush funds, and companies used them for a lot of off-the-book activities.

Corporations could do a lot of creative bookkeeping with their internal funds, and it was often difficult to trace where money was flowing. But when you started to be creative with charitable donations, that was a different matter, and it raised eyebrows very quickly. If the federal government had gotten involved, Brett felt certain that someone had blown the whistle on Jack, someone who knew where the money was really going. Money was going from donor to Hartlen Oil to Hartlen Response to unspecified investment funds. The feds didn't like such paper trails, especially when the money was not generated by regular corporate activity to begin with.

Brett broke into a laugh. He owned Jack Hartlen, pure and simple. Details would follow, but he could already see Jack signing the consortium agreement within the week to make Davis, Konen and Wright happy. He would have bet his partnership on it.

Chapter Seven

Dana awoke on Friday morning in the familiar surroundings of her 1863 carriage house in Sniffen Court, a
landmarked cobblestoned mews on East 36th Street in Murray
Hill. Lifting Wills, her Cavalier King Charles Spaniel snuggled
at the bottom of her bed, she walked out to the book-lined
landing overlooking the living room and twenty feet of leaded
glass windows. She may have left the sights and sounds of London but her charming home was as aesthetically pleasing to her
as the historic Lansdowne Club or an English cottage.

As Dana dressed, she was surprisingly calm and optimistic
as she faced her first day back at work, a day that should have
been filled with anger and frustration. There was no doubt in
her mind that the kindly Father Macaulay was the reason for
her tranquil mindset. He had not expressed condemnation
or judgment about her situation, only listened with a patient
ear. He'd given her sound advice that most people paid for
dearly while lying on leather couches in richly- appointed offices with diplomas hanging on the walls. Aware that the daily
pressures of her New York lifestyle would soon descend upon
her at lightning speed, she was determined to maintain the
balance that she discovered in London. Even the phone calls
from Johnny and her mother, which she'd received within an
hour after arriving at the carriage house the previous evening,

had momentarily pulled her away from her peace of mind, but she'd listened to them patiently and told them how much she'd enjoyed herself. They were ostensibly calling to see if she had arrived home safely, but she knew that both were, in reality, still checking up on her.

Dana arrived at B. Altman at 8:00 A.M., ready to see what had piled up on her desk in her absence. As expected, she had to return a dozen phone calls and get up-to-date on the previous week's sales reports from the branch stores. And there were the usual memos from department heads—they seemed endless—that she received on a daily basis.

By midmorning, Dana knew there was no putting off seeing Helen any longer. She had already decided that she was not going to charge into Helen's office and contest her decision, as she had implied in her overseas call to Andrew. She would stay focused and consult Helen about the direction she wanted her to take with the spring accessories buy and the display of Nantucket-labeled accessories in a corner of the department. Whatever Helen said would be accepted without challenge. Dana had her sights set on much larger matters since revisiting Jaeger, not that Nantucket would be neglected. She would segue into what she'd seen on her trip, broaching the idea of a free-standing boutique from a different point of view. Helen was more than familiar with Jaeger's long history, success, and stellar reputation, not to mention its relatively new Madison Avenue store. Helen would have a frame of reference this time for what Dana was suggesting so that her idea would not be discussed in a vacuum.

Dana found Helen in the conference room on the fifth floor, where the executive suites were located amid wood-paneled corridors. The middle-aged woman was a portrait of concentration, her blond hair pulled behind her head as always and secured with a black velvet ribbon.

"Yes?" Helen said, looking up from a stack of papers on the conference room table. There was no "Hello" or "Welcome back," which wasn't that unusual. Helen was perfectly capable of pleasant conversation, but at work she was all business. Over cocktails in the evening, she would surely have asked Dana to describe her time in London.

"I made my spring line selections, and I thought you'd want to see them before I place the orders," Dana responded, not mentioning that Dawn had already approved the merchandise before she left for Bergdorf's.

"Schedule an appointment with Clare for next week," Helen answered, not looking up from her files. "Clare Bradley is my new assistant. I want to have an all-buyer meeting before I look at spring buys."

Her strategy thrown a curve, Dana paused, swallowed, and proceeded to the subject of the cancelled boutique. "Andrew called me in London to inform me that the Nantucket build-out has been scrapped."

"I had no doubt that he would," Helen said without looking up.

"Actually," Dana continued as she slipped into a chair a few feet from Helen, "I agree with your decision and your original idea to simply use Nantucket hangtags and to merchandise the items in a corner of the department. I think there's a much better way to utilize the space, one that can tie in a *few* of your departments."

Dana succeeded in getting Helen's attention. Helen leaned back, removed her glasses, and turned her head towards Dana, eyebrows knit. "Really now. And to what do we owe this epiphany?"

"While I was shopping at Jaeger's, I realized that smart merchandising is as important to success as the beautiful fabrics and designs."

"And?" Helen impatiently asked, not acknowledging that what Dana said was true.

"And I think we should explore a free-standing boutique of coordinated separates and matching outerwear with a British country look. I know our customers will appreciate not having to travel from department to department to find matching pieces."

Helen put her glasses back on and looked again at the papers on the conference table as she spoke. "I'm against a boutique regardless of whatever concept it espouses. And I'm certainly not interested in constructing a Jaeger knock-off." Helen frowned as she uttered the last few words. "Dana, you shouldn't be so impressionable, influenced by the latest trend on the street. This year it's in-store boutiques. Next year it'll be something else."

Dana would normally have gotten upset at the mild insult, but she wanted to maintain an even temperament. Letting Helen know that she was aggravated would send the wrong signal.

"Helen, we've already spent time and money since Mark has cleared the space and begun the first stage of the build-out. And more money will have to be spent to redesign the area. Why can't we simply look at it as a test? We can be up and running by Thanksgiving. I think it's a perfect concept to market for holiday selling since the matching items will lead to multiple purchases. Dawn told me that she heard Bloomies is opening five new boutiques for the holidays."

Dana immediately knew that injecting Dawn's name into the conversation was a mistake.

Helen removed her glasses again and looked Dana directly in the eye. She spoke with a hard edge in her voice, as if correcting a child who has not assimilated what she's been told. "Let's be clear about this, Dana. Dawn isn't here anymore, and while I admired her very much, you're well aware that I never approved of the Nantucket boutique. I'm in charge of the matter now, whether you like it or not, and my decision stands. Yes, we started the build-out, but that doesn't mean I'm going to throw good money after bad. It will be less expensive to have Mark convert the space to something more conventional—something, I may add, that will actually turn a profit for the store. I know you had your heart set on this trendy idea, but I strongly believe that it would be a poor business decision."

Voice level, Dana tacked in another direction. "Helen, think how this shop would appeal to Grace Mirabella! It's exactly the look she wears and loves, and tailored separates are on the editorial pages of *Vogue* every month. As the editor-in-chief of *Vogue*, Grace just might do a spread on the merchandise *and* the boutique!"

"Dana, you're a dreamer. Women have been coordinating their separates for years, and our sportswear business has never been better."

"Helen, it's not just putting pieces together. Jaeger's success is in their dyed-to-match woolens and yarns. Knitwear matches perfectly with wool trousers and skirts. Monochromatic separates are more formal and sophisticated for work and evening. It's a great marketing story, and no store in town is selling it that way!"

"Well, Dana, there's your proof," Helen said with a sarcastic smile. "No one is selling it because there is no value or story in a coordinated separates boutique with a tony British style."

Dana's mouth was dry from nervousness, but she retained her composure and continued.

"Helen, I'll do all the legwork. I think it's a perfect fit for B. Altman. Remember, we already have Fortnum & Mason on the eighth floor."

"Dana, I'm not ready to consider the boutique concept. The answer is no."

Helen opened the spreadsheet in front of her, and Dana got up to leave.

"Thank you, Helen," Dana said. "I'll see you at the buyers meeting."

Dana returned to her office and sat glumly at her desk. She had prepared herself for resistance from Helen, but Helen's tone of voice, her stubbornness, her body language—it all added up to more than a "no." It was akin to a personal assault. Why couldn't Helen at least engage in a productive discussion on the pros and cons of an issue rather than summarily dismissing an idea outright? How could she ignore that Grace Mirabella would like the merchandise and the boutique? It was, after all, her signature style. There were so many factors to consider. Bob, Ira, and Dawn—they all knew that change was inevitable, but Helen was simply too comfortable with the tried and true. She was highly effective in her job, but she didn't possess the vision that a store's management needed to compete in the marketplace in the long term. Dana believed that unless Helen became more attuned to the changing winds of fashion and women, she might be harming herself as well as the store. It wouldn't happen overnight, but for now there was no alternative route for Dana. Helen was the boss.

The day dragged on, and Dana went through the motions, exhibiting little enthusiasm.

"I can tell you spoke with Helen today," Andrew said while Dana was gathering her things and preparing to leave for the day.

"Yes, but I'd rather not talk about it now if you don't mind."

"Of course not," Andrew said. "Go home and get some rest. We'll talk when you're ready."

Dana kissed Andrew on the cheek and left. She recalled Father Macaulay talking about how he used a punching bag to get out his pent-up frustrations. Dana, who'd started jogging again after filing for separation, decided to have a run along her favorite path in Central Park. It might clear her head and help dissolve the funk she found herself in after her first day back at work.

Dana halted at the end of a gently-curving path, bent over, hands braced against her knees. She'd run three miles and was breathing fast and shallow. Slowly, her breathing returned to normal as she walked across the grass, noting people enjoying the spring weather of an April evening. Dogs chased Frisbees, and young couples sat on blankets, talking and looking at a sky that still had streaks of orange and yellow blending into the deeper blue overhead.

Dana took a breath and realized that she did indeed feel better. She was no longer angry, but neither did she possess the unbridled enthusiasm that she'd brought back from London. The run notwithstanding, she felt frustrated. She knew that Helen was dead wrong about the boutique, but for now, there was nothing Dana could do. With Dawn having left, Helen was holding the reins, and her response had been unequivocal: there would be no boutique of any kind within the walls of B. Altman.

Dana's thirtieth birthday was the next day, but she didn't feel like celebrating. She planned on spending most of the day reading one of the books she'd purchased at Hatchards, have an early birthday dinner with Andrew, and go to bed early. There was a family celebration at her parents' home on Sunday. The less fanfare about turning thirty, the better. She didn't think she could muster a smile even if forced to by her family and friends.

For the time being, the only way to stay grounded was to read and stay secluded. She thought Father Macaulay would approve of her distance from the madding crowds.

Chapter Eight

*D*ana spent her birthday as planned, doing a few errands before enjoying a quiet afternoon reading Henry James' *The Outcry*. The novel was a lighthearted story about a British lord's decision to sell a painting by Sir Joshua Reynolds to an American billionaire. The plot hinged on the patriotic outcry in the British press with the lord's decision to ultimately keep British treasure in Britain. Dana appreciated the book despite its obscure references—it wasn't for the average American reader—because she was so emotionally invested in English art as well as the manners and proprieties that accompanied the British mindset. Reading the book was like being in England again or listening to Basil Trivett's lecture on portrait miniatures. Spending the afternoon within the pages of a book that took her back to England for a few hours was just what she needed. Father Macaulay had told her in so many words that she needed to find a way to relieve the pressures of work, and she hadn't thought of Helen all day long.

The phone rang at four o'clock. It was Andrew, reminding her that he would pick her up for their dinner date at the French restaurant La Grillade. Throughout the day, Dana had considered calling him to cancel, but she knew he would never let her be alone on her birthday, especially this one, her thirtieth and the first one in eight years without Brett.

Dana sighed and decided it was still worth a try. "Andrew, you're a sweetheart as always, but may I have a rain check? I'm still a little jet-lagged and would love to call it an early night. Trust me when I say that I don't have the birthday blues."

Andrew didn't hesitate for a second. "Sorry, kiddo, but you've had your heart set on La Grillade since Nina told us about it. It took me a month to get the reservation. You can cloister yourself another time. I'm picking out a suit as I speak. I suggest you do the same. I'll be over at seven thirty. Be ready."

"But I'm really kind of tired, and—"

Andrew had hung up.

Well, I did indulge myself all day by reading, Dana thought, consoling herself. And I do love being with Andrew. He's expecting an update on my meeting with Helen, and I might as well tell my tale of woe over a good bottle of French wine.

Andrew arrived ten minutes early, and to Dana's surprise, he insisted that she change from the black suit. "Dana, you're not having dinner with an English gentleman. Hey, it's me—Andrew. Come on! Find something a little less serious."

"What are you talking about, Andrew? It's my new dinner suit. A birthday gift to myself—an extravagant one, I might add. I bought it at Jaeger's. Perfect for La Grillade."

Andrew smiled and shook his head. "Nope. Something more festive is in order for your birthday. Now go upstairs and change. That's an order."

"Sometimes you're worse than a mother hen, Andrew Ricci. Even my mother, who is capable of being quite unyielding, wouldn't ask me to change. Personally, I—"

Andrew held up the palms of both hands to signal that further protest from his colleague and friend was useless.

"I surrender!" Dana said. "I'll be back in a few minutes. Would you mind taking Wills for a walk? We were on our way out when you arrived."

Ten minutes later, Dana was wearing a blue and white Diane von Furstenberg wrap dress.

"That's more like it!" Andrew said when he returned. "But wait a minute. Let me look at those shoes."

"Now what?" Dana asked.

"They're the sexiest slingbacks I've ever seen. Are they Chanel? Where did you get them?"

"Lady Continental."

"They're no proper lady's shoe. You're lookin' good, kiddo. Thirty suits you."

"Will you please stop! Let's get going before I change my mind."

After a brief taxi ride to La Grillade, Dana and Andrew entered the restaurant. Dana's hope that the evening would be quiet and mercifully short wasn't fully formed in her mind when she realized why Andrew had requested a change in wardrobe. She was walking into her surprise party.

"Surprise!" everyone shouted on cue.

"I'll kill you, Andrew," Dana mumbled out of the side of her mouth as she smiled at the applauding guests who were gathered in a private corner of the dining room. "Thank you!" Dana said warmly. "It's a cliché, but I really had no idea."

La Grillade, located on Eighth Avenue at 51st Street, was a pretty French restaurant decorated with dark wood, lace curtains, contemporary art, and enormous bouquets of flowers. Dana made the rounds, greeting Phoebe, Nina, Jack and Patti, and Max Helm and his wife. Meredith Varga, a friend of Dana's from Cabrini College, arrived with Johnny.

"I got your last letter," Dana told Meredith, touching her on the arm, "but we'll have to catch up later."

"Absolutely," Meredith said. "I'm going to stay with the United Way but am considering a transfer to the New York office. I'll tell you all about it when you have time, but there's a good chance we might be neighbors soon."

"That's wonderful!" Dana exclaimed. "I can't wait to hear the details."

Ever the gentleman, Johnny had offered to pick up Meredith at her hotel, and although he didn't regard her as a date per se, he dutifully guided her into conversation with the other guests to make her feel more relaxed. Meredith had a crush on Johnny when he attended Villanova, Cabrini being its sister school, but Johnny had been dating someone else.

"So, did I do good?" Andrew mischievously asked. "Isn't this how you should be celebrating your—"

"Stop reminding me! Diana Vreeland told me not to count the candles! But yes, I'm happy to be with my dearest friends, and you're the dearest of them all," Dana said as she kissed Andrew and gave him a hug. "Thank you."

Andrew bowed as he extended his hand towards the dinner party.

Dana was seated at a round table with Andrew and the eight guests he had invited.

Drinks were served and appetizers were ordered as the guests engaged in three different conversations. Andrew carefully avoided glancing at Jack, although he made sure to speak with Patti to avoid arousing suspicion. In turn, Jack joined in discussions with those not directly speaking with Andrew. He held forth about his recent relocation to New York while Patti and Meredith discussed their charitable work. Phoebe and Johnny talked of their father's pending move to Manhattan, as well as Phoebe's seminar in London.

"Everyone seems quite content for the moment," Nina said, "so that leaves the three of us who toil for the glory of

B. Altman. We haven't been together for a powwow since we drove to Bucks County last December to buy Dana's Christmas tree."

"Yes, but tell us all about India, Nina," Andrew said, alluding to the antique buyer's month on the subcontinent to buy merchandise for the store's Indian extravaganza.

"If I start in on India, I'll talk for the next three hours," Nina said laughing. "At some point it will become inevitable, but before I can't control myself, I hear Dana has done a little globetrotting of her own. Tell me all about London."

"Well, actually I had something of an epiphany while I was there, but Helen doesn't share my artistic vision. I probably shouldn't bore you with all the drama."

"An epiphany?" Nina said. "Artistic vision? I'm intrigued! Tell me immediately!" Nina was an outspoken, gregarious woman who brushed away the mundane as others shooed away flies.

"If you insist," Dana said. "It's no secret that Helen put the kibosh on the Nantucket boutique the minute Dawn was out the door, so I suggested that instead of scrapping the entire concept, we modify the build-out to a British country boutique that would highlight color coordinated separates and knitwear."

"Brilliant!" Nina declared. "A boutique inside the store? It's a wonderful idea!"

"Not according to Helen," Dana said. "To her, I'm nothing but a dreamer who needs to keep both feet planted on the ground."

"My feet haven't been on the ground for twenty years," Nina proclaimed. "Thank God for dreamers!" Her voice was slightly raised from its previous conversational level.

Max, Phoebe, and Johnny had tuned in to Nina's remarks.

"Don't get me wrong," Nina said. "I like Helen, but sometimes she can be downright—"

"Stubborn," Andrew said.

"I was going to say rude," Nina countered.

"She rejected the idea without discussion," Dana confessed, "but I don't see that I have any choice. With Dawn and Ira off to Bergdorf's, I'm alone on this one. Helen said no one would buy into a tony British style, which is not at all what I meant. There's nothing tony about Jaeger. It's an understated, tasteful brand, and the look is timeless. That's the boutique I see for B. Altman."

"Absolutely!" Nina blurted out. "What's wrong with her? *I* can see your vision, and I think it's a wonderful idea!"

Dana, Andrew, and Nina now had the ear of everyone at the table.

"Dana, I agree," Johnny said. "It's a great idea! Or should I say another great idea that Helen shot down. Even *our* eveningwear is going in that direction. We looked at sketches last week for wool jersey shirtwaist gowns with belts. You're right on."

Dana sipped from her glass of Burgundy. "I know, I know! I even told Helen how Grace Mirabella would probably endorse us and that Bloomies will be opening five boutiques before the end of the year." Dana shrugged, resigned to her superior's decision. "Coordinating separates as Jaeger does would be hugely successful, but what can I say? Helen's the gatekeeper."

"The answer is simple," Johnny said. "Find another gatekeeper."

"Huh?" Dana said.

"I think you should join us at the House of Cirone. You can develop new business."

All eyes on Dana, the table suddenly became quiet.

"I know you want to rescue me, Johnny," Dana said, "but I have to work through this on my own."

"Why? You get nothing but tsuris from Helen. She's an obstructionist at every turn, and I don't like the way she treats you. Dad would love you to join us." Johnny took a sip of scotch before adding, "And so would I."

"I don't know. I can't imagine leaving B. Altman."

"At least think about it. Hell, Ira and Dawn went to Bergdorf's because they saw an opportunity. I think it's high time *you* had some clout."

Dana looked at Andrew, who said, "I can't help you on this one. Would be a conflict of interest, plus I'm not impartial. I'd hate to see you go."

Dana looked at Phoebe next, whose smile and nod indicated that she agreed wholeheartedly with her brother."

"I guess I'll have to weigh my options," Dana said.

Meredith raised her glass and offered a toast. "To old friendships and new opportunities!"

The guests again broke into separate conversations, but Dana was suddenly lost in thought. She knew Johnny's offer was genuine and that Uncle John would indeed sign off on giving her a great deal of creative latitude. The House of Cirone was a manufacturer, not a store, but she might have enormous input into design, choice of fabrics, and even marketing to the buyers at major retailers throughout the country. Working with Johnny and his father might be the break she was looking for. Who knew how far her influence might one day extend? Perhaps an idea by Dana McGarry might even be embraced by the likes of Grace Mirabella or her contemporaries. This was heady wine, and Dana found it difficult to do anything more than smile and nod as Andrew and Nina talked about the Indian bazaar and other events at B. Altman.

The entrée course was served and conversation grew more animated as wine glasses were refilled. La Grillade's specialties included poached striped bass, London broil, roast leg of lamb aux flageolets, and paupiettes of sole. Dana spoke and laughed with all of her friends, glad to be in their company. Her thoughts, however, never strayed far from Johnny's intriguing offer.

It was over dessert—coffee, opera cake, and platters of macaroons—that Andrew turned to Dana. "You're thinking seriously about Johnny's suggestion, aren't you?" he said.

"You know me too well," Dana said almost dreamily. "And yes, I think I should at least consider it and talk to Johnny and Uncle John. I think I've gone as far as I can go at B. Altman. The freedom the House of Cirone would offer me is compelling."

Andrew smiled wistfully. "I'll support whatever you decide. And let's face it. You're being penalized for your youth, and that wouldn't be the case with the Cirones."

"I thought you were going to remain neutral."

"Too much Burgundy, but I'm behind whatever you decide."

"Thank you, Andrew, but I must take you to task over something."

Andrew raised his eyebrows, puzzled.

"You've talked Patti's arm off all evening, hardly speaking with Jack at all."

"Guilty as charged. I'll try to make amends, but right now I want to show you the second floor of the restaurant. It has a private dining room that you may want to keep in mind when you start wining and dining buyers."

"Be right back," Dana informed the table as she and Andrew stood. "I'm going to take a quick tour."

"Take your time," Max said. "Believe me—we're not going anywhere."

The table erupted in laughter that Dana attributed to the cocktails and wine served in the course of the evening.

Andrew led Dana to the rear of the main dining room and up a flight of stairs on the left.

"It's the weekend, Andrew. I don't want to barge in on anyone's private party."

"Not to worry. The manager told me that the room is empty this evening."

Andrew opened the door and led Dana into a room that was almost completely dark. For the second time that night, Dana heard the shout of "Surprise!" as a glittery disco ball came to life and spun overhead in the middle of what was a very large room. As a disc jockey cranked up the music, lights began to strobe as Dana was welcomed by a new set of birthday revelers: buyers from the store, members of the marketing department, two grant managers from the Altman Foundation, classmates from Cabrini, and volunteers from the Costume Institute at the Metropolitan Museum of Art.

In happy disbelief, Dana tapped her fist on Andrew's shoulder. "You got me again, Mr. Ricci."

"I told you we weren't going anywhere!" Max said.

Dana pivoted to see the dinner guests from downstairs coming through the doorway behind her.

Mark Senger emerged from the shadows and hugged Dana before kissing her on the cheek. "Room for one more?" he asked with his trademark sense of humor. "Personally, I'd hate to put on my resume that I couldn't get into a disco party."

Dana smiled and returned the kiss on the cheek. "Mark, thank you for coming. So nice to see you."

"The bar is on the right, everyone!" Andrew called out. "Let's party!"

Dana, of course, thanked the second wave of guests one by one, and when she'd finished the amenities, she approached

Andrew at the bar and took a glass of champagne. "This is definitely over the top, Andrew. I can see why you wanted me to change!" She looked at the room, people sliding across the center of the dance floor.

"Well, you won't be surprised to learn that it was Johnny's idea to rent the disco. Nobody likes to party like Johnny."

"I'm lucky to have such good friends, Andrew. I am grateful for so much."

"Then show Johnny you're having a good time and let's start dancing!"

Dana cocked her head quickly from side to side and held out both arms. "I have no choice!" She was feeling better than she had since returning to New York. "I can do this!"

Andrew and Dana took the dance floor as Johnny mingled with women who'd gone to Cabrini. Phoebe, who had refrained from drinking at dinner, said a quick goodbye as the music grew louder since she began a seventy-two hour call rotation the following morning at New York Hospital. Patti and Jack danced next to Dana and Andrew but, after several moves, Jack managed to spin his wife to the far side of the floor, putting distance between himself and Andrew.

After ten minutes, Mark approached with a wide grin. "I don't know if the term applies to disco, but I'll have to cut in here, Andrew. I can't let you have all the fun."

"She's all yours," Andrew said above the music.

Mark put his left hand on his hip while raising his right arm in the air, spinning in a circle as he did so.

"You're good!" Dana cried.

"It's not that difficult," Mark replied.

Dana laughed, and the pair danced to the Bee Gees' "Jive Talkin'" and "Night Fever."

"How about a drink?" Mark asked as a new song blared from the speakers.

"Good idea," Dana said.

At the bar, Mark, who had light brown hair, blue eyes, and an athletic build, looked at the guests and sighed. "At least no one is wearing a green polyester leisure suit."

Dana laughed, "No, not this crowd. Parochial schools and jobs at B. Altman. Not a chance. But they've got the moves."

"Yep. I'd say they're having a good time," Mark said, raising his glass and turning to Dana with a big smile. "Best wishes for an exciting new decade, birthday girl."

Returning the smile, Dana said, "I'm ready. It's time for a new chapter."

Mark, aware that she was referring to her pending divorce, quickly changed the subject.

"I hear you were in London last week. See any plays?"

"I did! I stayed at the Lansdowne Club. They had extra tickets to the opening of *The Importance of Being Earnest* at the Theatre Royal. It was wonderful! Dame Flora Robson came out of retirement to play Miss Prism. It was one of those special evenings."

"Did you go with Phoebe?" Mark asked. "Andrew said she was there for a cardiology convention."

"No, I went alone, but I'm glad Phoebe could join me to see *Equus* at the Old Vic. Now that it's won a Tony, it'll be impossible to get tickets."

"What did you think of *Equus*?" Mark asked.

"I'm still reflecting on it," Dana answered somberly. "That's why I'm glad Phoebe was with me. We had a late supper and talked about the characters for an hour and a half. She's so smart and her thoughts about Dr. Dysart led us to explore feelings about our personal goals for a fulfilled life. Have you seen it?"

"Yes. Anthony Hopkins was outstanding as Dysart. I couldn't go right home either. You need to discuss it."

"That's how I feel about foreign films, so many layers to peel away. Do you like foreign films? Do have a favorite foreign director?"

"Gosh, do I have to name just one? Hmmmm. Everyone likes Fellini, of course. I loved the Italian vignettes from *Amarcord*, but I think my favorite is … " He paused, as if thinking of film titles, although in reality he had decided not to name *Juliet of the Spirits*, a mystical film about a woman's decision to leave her unfaithful husband. "Well, it's a tie between *Sweet Charity*—what great choreography by Bob Fosse—and *La Dolce Vita*."

Dana rolled her eyes good-naturedly. I think *La Dolce* is overrated, but there's no denying that Fellini is a genius."

"And you?" Mark asked. "Which directors do you like?"

"Truffaut, hands down," Dana said. "*Day for Night* was brilliant in its simplicity. A movie about making a movie. *Jules et Jim* is perhaps my favorite, but what range Truffaut has. He even did Bradbury's *Fahrenheit 451*."

"Bradbury is a national treasure. Much more than a science fiction writer, in my estimation. *Something Wicked This Way Comes* has been heralded as a literary epic rather than mere sci-fi. His prose style is highly inventive."

"When it comes to literary fiction," Dana said, "I'm a fan of ——

"That will be quite enough," Andrew said as he grabbed Dana by the arm. "We're here to dance."

Dana stuck out her lower lip and exhaled, causing her bangs to fly upwards. "No rest for the weary," she said.

"Happy birthday!" Mark said, raising his glass.

Over the course of the next hour, Dana danced with many of the guests, but her gaze kept returning to Mark as he spoke with Max as well as people from the store. She noticed that he commanded their attention with his mannerisms and facial expressions or had them laughing out loud and wiping tears from their eyes. He occasionally looked in Dana's direction and winked, thumbs up, as if to say "nice dance move!"

During a much-needed break from the dancing, Dana noticed Mark approaching her again.

"I have to be on my way," he said, taking her hand in his. "But once again, happy birthday. I'll let you know if I find out that anything unusual is playing at the Paris or the Plaza. They have some great foreign and independent films. I hear Lina Wertmüller has one coming out called *Seven Beauties*."

He kissed Dana on the cheek and left.

Dana was momentarily confused since Mark's comment seemed deliberately ambiguous. Did he intend to ask her on a date or was he simply going to apprise her of a good movie that was coming to town since they both had an interest in foreign directors?

"What are you thinking about?" Andrew asked. "You're lost in thought again. Still contemplating Johnny's offer?"

"Huh? Oh, not really. Just getting a bit tired."

"Well, the crowd may be thinning, but as the guest of honor, you have to marshal on."

"And I will, but I think I've seen the last of the dance floor."

The DJ continued to work the turntable on his slightly raised platform, and more dancers headed for the middle of the room.

It hadn't been a quiet evening but it had been thoroughly enjoyable, not to mention thought-provoking. Dana turned to the bartender and asked for a ginger ale as Meredith sought her out to talk about her work with the United Way and her possible move to New York.

It had been great connecting with old friends.

• • •

Dana arrived home at two in the morning, quite exhausted. She quickly removed her make-up, put on cotton pajamas, and climbed into bed. She stared into the darkness for a few moments, thinking about her short conversation about the theater and literature with Mark.

Her thoughts then turned to working for the House of Cirone. Maybe she should remain loyal to the store, or "keep Britain's treasure in Britain," as Henry James might have phrased it. Leaving B. Altman would represent a major change in her life, and she would be sorry to leave, assuming it came to that. But was there any point in staying where she wasn't fully appreciated? She debated the change of employers for a few minutes, but her eyelids grew heavy and she fell asleep, having made no decision.

Chapter Nine

*D*ana awoke at ten in the morning, and far from being tired from the previous evening's festivities, she was completely energized. She'd needed to be among friends and connect with people she loved and who, in turn, cared deeply for her. A life worth living, she realized, had to be shared with others. Quiet time was one thing, but being a recluse wasn't who she was, something that Andrew and Johnny knew instinctively and hence Andrew's insistence that she accompany him to La Grillade.

She thought of Brett, but this time she was not spontaneously moved to tears or unchecked emotion. She and Brett had reached a point in their marriage where they did not share the wondrous moments of life, large and small. Most of all, they had no longer shared themselves with each other with the kind of joy and trust she'd experienced with her friends at the party. They had married young, and there had been no maturation of love as they grew older. Brett had only one way to keep grounded, as Father Macaulay would have put it: his relentless career pursuits with the firm. It was a shame, for he was an intelligent man who at one time had enjoyed the simple pleasures of life with Dana.

After making coffee and a toasted bagel, Dana, still in her bathrobe, sat at the antique English secretary in her living room overlooking the ivy-covered courtyard. She wanted to tell Father Macaulay about life in New York since she'd returned from London.

Dear Father Macaulay,

I hope this letter finds you well. I wish I could leisurely stroll along Hays Mews to meet you in person for a conversation in Mount Street Gardens, but I suppose that this is the next best thing. I sometimes think that the art of letter writing, so prevalent in your country's literature, is becoming a lost art. It forces one to think deliberately as opposed to quick conversations on the telephone.

One of my good friends from the store waylaid me last night and took me to dinner, which turned out to be a surprise birthday party—I'm officially thirty now!—with a disco party afterwards. Of all things! My friend Andrew forced me out of my comfort zone, which, I suppose, was the point of the whole evening. I had a wonderful time, even though I felt a bit foolish at first since I know as much about disco as I do about the Galapagos Islands. But it was a great deal of fun.

An old friend of mine, Johnny, offered me a job at his father's company, which makes ladies eveningwear. I'm going to seriously consider the job and talk with them when I get a chance. One of my present bosses is a bit old-school and disapproves of my latest idea to have an in-store boutique, but I won't bother you with the details. I'll just say that I'm always struggling to have my creative visions implemented, and it's getting more than a little frustrating. Working for my friend's company—it's called the House of Cirone—might be a breath of fresh air. I could have creative freedom without the distractions of office politics.

And yet I do love my present employer which, if you recall, is B. Altman. I don't wish to be disloyal since I love the staff and management dearly despite the restrictions they impose on me. It's not unlike the moment of grief I experienced in church when I thought of my eight-year marriage to Brett. The idea that it was all over suddenly hit me, and I suspect the same thing might happen if I left B. Altman. The store gave me a chance to learn and grow when I was fresh out of college, and it has taught me so much. I'm sure that leaving might be terribly sad, but we must keep growing, mustn't we? As you can see, I'm a bit conflicted.

You'll be happy to know that I'm jogging and making some quiet time for myself to read or just sit and think. Here in my carriage house the other day, I realized how wonderful it is to savor my time away from work. I've always enjoyed my career, its frustrations notwithstanding, but I'm beginning to hear an inner-voice, and it's important to stay in touch with that person, just as you told me in the garden. I can't let work alone drive me, although I'm eager for a successful career. I hope I'm not sounding contradictory. I'm still trying to understand. Is the relationship between work and our inner lives perhaps symbiotic?

I felt the same about the surprise party last night, which I really didn't want until I got there. But I loved it all—the conversation, the friends, and the dancing. Without cutting loose once in a while, maybe the quiet time wouldn't seem so precious. Is it all a question of balance? Whatever the case, I'm going to do my best to maintain the tranquility I discovered in London and stay in touch with my inner voice.

Please write and tell me how you are doing and feel to free to comment on my musings. I look forward to hearing from you.

Best wishes,
Dana

Dana had intentionally left out details about her enjoyable conversation with Mark Senger, a conversation she'd replayed in her mind many times earlier that morning. Mark worked closely with Andrew at B. Altman and was often in his office when Dana stopped in to discuss business or just to chat. He was always interested in her job and was so personable. In January, Mark consulted almost daily with Dana on the design and implementation of the teen cosmetic counter, but aside from a pleasant and professional relationship, she never sensed that he'd taken a personal interest in her. Of course, she had been distracted at the time because she was dissolving her marriage and probably wouldn't have noticed even if he had.

Still, she felt their short time together at the party was of a personal nature. He'd avoided the subject of Helen's killing the Nantucket boutique, which was possibly a further indication that he was more than a little sensitive to her feelings. They'd connected over their mutual interest in foreign films, but it was the easy rapport they'd had, together with his playful comments, that kept dancing in her head. She was seeing him for the first time, not as president of the Senger Display Company, an important vendor for B. Altman, but as a forty-two-year-old man who was bright, witty, engaging, and absolutely adorable. Just thinking about him brought a smile to her face.

Glancing at her watch, Dana realized she needed to quickly shower and dress if she were going to attend the twelve-thirty mass and then take the train to her parents' home on Long Island. She decided to put aside thoughts of Mark Senger and regard him as a business associate who'd been invited to her party, nothing more. Johnny and Uncle John would be joining the Martignettis for dinner, and her thoughts should be focused on a possible career with the House of Cirone.

Chapter Ten

Dana sat among family and friends in the den of her parents' home located on Macy Channel in the Long Island community of Hewlett Harbor. Her parents, Phil and Virginia Martignetti, sat on the couch, although Virginia popped in and out of the kitchen frequently, checking on dinner. John and Johnny Cirone relaxed in nearby chairs, sipping from their glasses of Vietti. They faced the double doors set in knotty wood paneling, offering views of Macy Channel in the late afternoon light.

Dana had regaled the small dinner party with tales of her trip to London, describing her trip to the theater, the Wallace Collection and, of course, her shopping expedition to Jaeger, the latter naturally being of interest to the owner of the House of Cirone.

"Phoebe called this morning and raved about the dinner at La Grillade," John said. "I hear it's only been open a few months."

"Yes," Dana said, "and it's already so popular that it took Andrew a month to get a reservation. Did Phoebe tell you about the disco party? Courtesy of your son?"

"She did!" John said laughing. "She also said it was her cue to leave."

"Well, Phoebe missed a good time," Johnny said. "What about you, Dana? Did we usher in the next year of your life on a high note?"

"It was more fun than I've had in a long time," Dana said, "although I never thought I'd celebrate my thirtieth birthday under a disco ball."

"I've got quite a few years on you," John said, "but I'm feeling younger than ever now that I'm moving back to Manhattan. Age is truly a state of mind. Here's to many more, Dana."

Glasses were raised as Dana said, "Thank you, Uncle John. If I can stay as active as you, I'll know I'm on the right track."

Uncle John settled back in his chair, his features becoming more reflective. "You brought up Jaeger a moment ago, Dana, and Johnny told me how things stand at B. Altman and his decision to offer you a position with the House of Cirone. I want you to know that his offer has my full blessing. Have you given it any thought?"

Dana had expected the subject to come up since she knew the Cirones had been invited, although she hadn't made a decision yet.

"I'm not trying to rush you," Uncle John stated, "but I want you to know how honored we'd be to have you with us."

Dana wasn't quite sure what to say, but she couldn't be rude and dismiss the subject altogether. Uncle John was like family, and he and Johnny no doubt had the best of intentions. She had the feeling that the subject of her possible job change had come up before her arrival, especially since Johnny and Virginia stared at her, eagerly awaiting her response. Dana again felt annoyed that they didn't seem to trust her ability to handle the circumstances of her own life.

"I guess it's no secret that Helen and I have some fundamental disagreements over my idea for an in-store boutique. Truthfully, I'd be reluctant to leave B. Altman, but I remain open to a change at this point. Uncle John, what role would I have at the House of Cirone?"

Phil was listening to the conversation, making no comment. A tall man with salt and pepper hair, he was composed as usual. Virginia, however, sat forward, holding her wine glass with both hands, a study in concentration as she looked at her daughter. She was a slender woman with blond hair and blue eyes that now seemed to beg for an affirmative answer from her daughter.

"I would make you fashion director," John said. "Frankly, I think you're hiding your light under a bushel basket."

The response dispelled Dana's temporary annoyance at having to discuss the matter at her birthday dinner. As fashion director, she might be able to exercise her full range of talent and use her creativity in ways that B. Altman would never even consider, let alone implement.

"I'd expect you to spot new designs and fabric trends and to work closely with Frances, our in-house designer and her two assistants, all of whom I believe you've met," John continued. "You'd naturally need to attend the European shows to keep your pulse on trends and help us keep a competitive edge. And I can promise you that whatever ideas you bring to me will always be met with serious consideration, and that goes for Johnny and Frances as well. I'm looking for new ideas, not reasons to shoot them down. I can't promise that you'd get everything you want, but we work as a close-knit team. No office politics at the House of Cirone. We're family! So then, what do you think?"

Dana didn't know how to respond. The position sounded great, of course, but she couldn't give an immediate answer. Leaving B. Altman would be a big step. Her inclination was to accept the offer, but there was that old adage about burning bridges. And what would it be like to work alongside Johnny?

She'd known him for so long. Would she be smothered by his current role as self-appointed guardian angel? It was also a given in her family that Johnny's heart wasn't in the business and he stayed on to please his father. How would that affect her position? Furthermore, did she want to work in a family business as opposed to a corporate environment despite the restrictions of the latter? The questions in her mind were endless.

"Sounds like a fantastic opportunity!" Virginia said, unable to contain herself any longer. "I know you and Johnny would make the perfect team."

Dana let the remark pass since she knew her mother had always assumed she would marry Johnny before Brett entered the picture. Virginia was not above subtle matchmaking.

"It goes without saying," John said, "that I'll beat whatever B. Altman is paying you now, with bonuses for whatever innovations you bring to the table."

"Your generosity precedes you, Uncle John" Dana laughed. "I know your offer will be very attractive. I … I think—"

"I think it's time to adjourn this board meeting," Phil said affably, rising from the couch, "and go into dinner."

"I agree," John said with a broad smile. "I've given you a lot to consider, Dana. I just want you to know that you're welcome at the House of Cirone. Take all the time you need. There's no time limit on the offer."

John left after dinner, and Dana and Johnny walked to the edge of the pier extending over Macy Channel, the water reflecting the golden sun of late afternoon.

"What do you think, Dana?" Johnny asked. "Wouldn't you love being our fashion director? Not to mention how much we could use you. Frances is a wonderful designer, but she's getting up there, and I think she would appreciate your fresh eye. Hey, you can attend the Milan shows with Nonna. I think she still has a reserved seat at most of them. She'd be ecstatic to hear you joined the business."

"Your grandmother should be the fashion director!" Dana laughed.

"She was, unofficially, but she was always at war with Dad."

"To tell you the truth, I'm seriously considering your offer. I don't see any way around Helen. Today it's the in-store boutique. Six months from now it will be something else, and I'll go through the cycle all over again."

"Cycle?"

"Getting enthusiastic about an idea, working out the details, and then having someone tell me that it's not the way B. Altman does business."

"Playing the devil's advocate," Johnny said, "maybe Helen won't be in charge forever. Dawn was behind you one hundred and ten percent. As much as I'd love to see you at the House of Cirone, I want you to be happy."

"I suppose that's true," Dana said, "but I can't count on Dawn's replacement being as open-minded as she was." Dana shrugged. "If that's the case, I'll have missed a great opportunity."

Dana picked up a pebble and threw it into the channel. Ripples spread out from the splash in perfect circles.

"A single act can cause so many repercussions," Dana said, staring at the water. "Brett was unfaithful, Helen doesn't like my ideas—we have to live with the consequences of other people's actions. The question is how long do the ripples last."

"That's why I think you'd be happy working with us." Johnny said. "The only ripples to spread out would be positive because you'd be making them."

Dana smiled. "You're very persuasive, Johnny. I promise that I'll give you and your dad an answer soon. The incentives you're giving me are quite attractive."

"Fair enough. In return, I promise not to nag you about it or put any pressure on you. It will be my way of showing you that things are more laid-back with us."

"Deal."

Dana and Johnny shook hands and returned to the house, where Virginia was serving a second cup of coffee.

Dana arrived at her carriage house at eight o'clock that evening. After taking Wills out for his evening walk, she sat down to read, but her mind was distracted.

"What's the matter with me?" she said aloud. "I feel tired and can't focus."

Dana stood in front of the large windows in the living room and peered outside as a spring shower caused the flagstones in the alley outside her front door to turn a dark shiny gray. She folded her arms and watched the slanting rain for several minutes, lost in thought. The rain finally let up, but Dana noticed a single drop fall into a small puddle. Tiny ripples spread out from the impact.

Dana turned around and sat on her sofa, feeling a new peace of mind. She didn't have to keep enduring the grief inflicted by others—the negative ripples. No one could force her to be unhappy—not Brett, Helen, or anyone else. She'd been proactive in dealing with Brett, and it was time to do the same with her career. At the House of Cirone, she could become a fashion director and be a trendsetter. How could she take care of herself, especially the part deep inside that Father Macaulay had told her to nurture, if she let others continually thwart her ambition? As always, taking care of Dana McGarry meant making decisions, even hard ones like resigning from B. Altman.

Her mind was made up. She still had a few projects to close out at the store, such as the Nantucket line, and she wasn't the type of person to just walk away and leave someone else to finish her work. She took pride in what she did and, when she left, she would have the satisfaction that she'd taken everything she'd begun as far as she could. When she was satisfied that all loose ends were tied up, she'd give her two weeks' notice.

Until then, there would be no announcement. She would keep her decision to herself lest there be a lot of discussion or advice from Andrew, Johnny, Helen, Bob, or anyone else. She didn't want to listen to protracted goodbyes or discuss plans with Uncle John while she was wrapping up her career with B. Altman. It would be distracting and perhaps even maudlin. That was part of taking care of herself as well. She would make the announcement when she was ready and not before.

Content with her decision, she went upstairs and read until it was time for bed. When she fell asleep, all doubts had been erased from her mind.

Chapter Eleven

Dana had gone jogging after work and was standing next to the table by the front door of her home, sorting through the mail, when the phone rang.

"Hi, Dana. It's Mark Senger. How's the party girl?"

"Still recovering," Dana laughed. "Too much attention for one birthday! It wasn't so much the dancing as all the talking and catching up with old friends. It was great. And thank you for coming."

"By the way, how did you like La Grillade's dinner?" Mark asked. "I can't buy my way in. Reservations are six weeks out."

"Dinner was excellent and the staff wasn't intrusive. You should give it a try. I think you'd like it."

"I'm on the waiting list. I have four weeks to go, but I'm calling about a more immediate request. Do you go out on school nights?"

"As long as I'm back in the dorm by ten," Dana responded.

"I know how to sneak you in at eleven," Mark said, "but for a first date, I promise we'll make the curfew."

There was that rapport again, Dana thought. She wasn't imagining it.

"A date, Mr. Senger?" Dana asked playfully.

"A proper date, Ms. McGarry. Dinner, *and* a movie. How's tomorrow night? And we forgot to discuss Vittorio De Sica at your party."

"Ah!" Dana said. "*The Garden of the Finzi-Continis.*"

"I was thinking more along the lines of *Two Women, Marriage Italian Style, Yesterday, Today, and To—*"

"All right, I get it!" Dana interrupted, laughing. "We'll battle it out over dinner."

"Did you see Mazursky's *Harry and Tonto* last year? The Paris is bringing it back for a return engagement since Art Carney won the Oscar."

"No," Dana said. "That one slipped by."

"Good. I didn't see it either. That's where we'll go. I'll pick you up at six. We'll have a quick bite and make the eight-thirty show."

"Okay," Dana said. "I live at Sniffen Court. The gate code is 009, and the house number is eight."

"Great," he said. "I'll see you then."

Dana hung up and stood frozen in disbelief. They'd picked up the conversation from Saturday night as if nothing had transpired between then and now. Since her birthday, she had made futile attempts to dismiss thoughts of Mark. He'd already accomplished for her what no one else had been able to do for a very long time: he made her feel happy. That positive feeling was empowering, especially at work. Maybe it was because he was a fresh face, someone new to talk to that was outside of her inner circle, or perhaps it was their shared interest in film and literature. Dana wasn't going to over-analyze it, however. As her father would say, things always worked out in the end.

Dana glanced at Wills, who was looking up at her, patiently waiting for dinner. She picked him up and gave him a big hug and a kiss. "Just between you and me, Wills," Dana said as she carried him to the kitchen, "Mommy has a crush on a very sexy man."

● ● ●

Dana and Mark sat opposite each other at a small table at the rear of Café Pierre in the Pierre Hotel at Fifth and 61st. In the background, pianist Dickson Hughes played tunes from Broadway shows.

"Okay, back to De Sica," Dana said. "I know no man can resist a film with Sophia Loren, but you *had* to be moved by *The Garden of the Finzi-Continis*. Mark, I saw it three times." Dana's gaze was intense.

"But it's so disturbing," Mark said. "Why would you torment yourself."

"I loved the cinematography, the costumes, and the lighting. Most of all, it's a moving and emotional story. I was fascinated by the Jewish-Italian family as they went about their lives behind their garden wall, believing they were immune from the spread of Fascism. After I saw it the first time, I immediately visited my grandfather and said, "Papa, I think we're Jewish.""

Mark laughed. "Why do you want to be Jewish?"

"For one thing, the Finzi-Continis are blond blue-eyed Italians like, well, like me, my mother, my aunt, and my grandfather, who has the most beautiful blue eyes. And listen to this—my mother's maiden name is Sommer."

"Wait a minute," Mark said, sitting back and rolling his eyes, pretending to be reflective. "Let me understand this. You're an Italian girl with an Irish name, look like a WASP, and you appeal to a Jew."

"Mark, I'm a little Jewish," Dana said seriously.

"And how is one a *little* Jewish?" Mark teased.

"When my mother visited Bari, a city in Italy where my grandfather grew up, she did a little digging and learned that the Pesoli Vineyard was originally owned by the Sommer family. They were Jewish. Sure, I had a Catholic upbringing and education, but my ancestry clearly has both Jewish and Italian roots, just like the family in the film."

"Dana, every politician in town would be lined up to marry you if they could hear this," Mark said in between laughs. "You have almost every voter base covered!"

"You're pretty comfortable in all situations, too" Dana said. "I've watched you interact with different groups at the store."

"True," Mark answered, "but to quote Groucho, I don't want to belong to any club that will accept me as a member. When I was sixteen, I was turned down by a polo team, and I never got over it. It was the only club I wanted."

"You were an equestrian?" Dana asked. "In the heart of Manhattan?"

"I was, and still am. I was first put on the back of a horse at summer camp in Maine. It was a Tennessee Walker, which is a beautiful animal. It has a mild gate and an even disposition, which makes it perfect when riding for pleasure even though it's quite popular on the show circuit."

"You've been riding from childhood? I'm guessing your family owned a horse."

Mark creased his forehead for a split second, head tilted. "Horses were a bit too extravagant for my father. He had a rough time during the Depression, and no matter how much money he had, it was never enough. He didn't like paying for my riding lessons, plus my father wanted my head in the books. He dreamed of my becoming a doctor."

"Was he disappointed that Dr. Senger never materialized?"

"Of course! What Jewish parent doesn't want to talk about my son, the doctor?"

Dana felt as if Mark were covering a more deep-seated conflict within his family, but she listened as he spoke further of his love for riding.

"We lived at Central Park West and 90th, just two blocks from Claremont Riding Academy. My mother let me take lessons over my father's objections, and I still love riding to this day. Sometimes I just amble down trails in Central Park. It really keeps me ... centered. I'm able to get away from things, and there's something comforting about the measured, steady gait of a horse that relaxes me. When the horse stays in rhythm, so do I. My daughter Amanda inherited my love of riding, so much so that she's a show jumper. She's excellent, if you don't mind my bragging."

In the background, Hughes was playing Cole Porter's "I've Got You Under My Skin," and for a few minutes Dana just looked at Mark, not hearing a word he was saying, her mind wandering with the lyrics. She *was* trying hard not to give in, but she knew her heart: she was clearly crazy about him.

"I understand," Dana responded. "I feel the same way when I run. There's a rhythm to jogging, a comfortable repetition that keeps my thoughts from flying all over the place."

"Scientists say that running causes the brain to produce something called endorphins. It makes a person feel tranquil and balanced."

"Is there anything you *don't* know, Dr. Senger?"

"Quite a lot, actually."

"Such as?"

"Whether or not you'd like to dance while we wait for our entrees."

Dana smiled and extended her hand.

"I think that answers my question nicely," Mark said, standing and taking Dana's hand in his.

Hughes was now playing a slower tune, "Where or When," and she followed Mark's every step for the next three minutes as they slow-danced. He held her right hand softly, and as the song progressed, he brought it closer to his body. Dana didn't have to concentrate on Mark's steps, for she instinctively anticipated his every move. She felt relaxed and secure in his gentle embrace and wasn't conscious of the room or anyone else in it. Endorphins? Apparently, dancing with the right partner could produce them just as well as jogging. Except on a crowded floor at a wedding, she and Brett hadn't been dancing in years, and as she let herself be guided by Mark's effortless flow across the floor, she realized that she hadn't had such a pleasant evening out in—well, she couldn't remember when, nor did she want to. She was enjoying the music and the moment too much.

Hughes stopped for a break, but Mark and Dana continued dancing for another fifteen seconds before looking at each other and laughing.

"When did the music stop?" Dana asked, blushing.

"I didn't think it had," Mark said as he stepped back and looked Dana in the eyes.

The waiter interrupted their reverie as he brought their entrees to the nearby table, but Mark's words echoed in Dana's mind. *I didn't think it had.* Could he have said anything more endearing at that moment?

Dana thought it unlikely, and she felt mesmerized by her date as he asked her about her parents and brother over dinner.

"Matthew is at the University of Hawaii studying marine biology," Dana said. "When he's not surfing, that is."

"Did you know that certain species of whales can talk to each other even when they're thousands of miles apart?" Mark asked. "Especially humpbacks."

"I've heard that they sing, but I don't know much about it," Dana confessed.

"I find it utterly fascinating that two whales can communicate over such long distances."

"What do you suppose they're saying?" Dana asked.

Mark looked thoughtful. "Scientists aren't sure. Some say the sounds are mating songs. Others believe the whales are helping guide each other during their migrations."

"What do *you* think they're saying to one another?"

Mark put his fork down and leaned closer to Dana.

"Maybe they're just saying hi to make sure they don't feel lonely." Mark paused and then smiled ever so slightly. "Or maybe they're just telling each other how much they enjoy dancing when they get together."

Dana thought her heart would melt right then and there.

Three hours later, Dana and Mark strolled down the sidewalk after leaving the Paris Theater. In the movie, Harry Coombes was an elderly widower forced from his condemned building on the Upper West Side. Rather than become a suburbanite at his son's home, he begins quoting from *King Lear* about his life and children and eventually buys a used car and sets out on an odyssey across the country with his cat Tonto. The people he meets on the way to Los Angeles are diverse: an evangelical hitchhiker, a childhood sweetheart suffering from dementia, a hot redhead named Ginger, his divorced daughter, and a Las Vegas hooker. After being seduced by the prostitute and then being arrested in Vegas for drinking too much, he spends the night in jail with a Native American man before moving on to Los Angeles to find a new apartment.

"I loved it," Mark said. "How about a nightcap? The only thing better than seeing a wonderful film is discussing it. We can go to the Palm Court."

"Okay, but what about Mother Mary. It's past my curfew," Dana said, taking Mark's arm as they walked around the corner to The Plaza Hotel.

"You mean you don't know about the kitchen door trick?" Mark said. "I'll have to show you how to get around Mother Mary."

Sitting next to each other in a booth, Mark couldn't contain his enthusiasm for *Harry and Tonto*. "Each of Harry's encounters was more disheartening than the one before. He's seventy-two and keeps experiencing one disappointment after another on his journey."

Dana cocked her head thoughtfully. "For me, the most poignant moment in the film was Harry dashing frantically after the stray cat, thinking it was Tonto. Even though you knew Tonto was dead, didn't you feel a rush of excitement, hoping that the new cat would heal Harry's heartache?"

"Yes, I did," Mark said. "I wanted another Tonto to make things okay for Harry."

"Then he picks up the cat, rubs its little head, and lets it go. And you know that Harry will return to the bench and the woman who had invited him to move in and share expenses." Dana said, closing her eyes. "Mark, that scene will remain with me more than any other in the film. In less than a minute, it said so much."

"You can't go back."

"No, you can't, and as much as he wanted to replace Tonto, Harry was wise to know that. In that moment he had a choice. Discover another path with a roommate or try to duplicate his past life with Tonto's look-alike. From the happy expression on Harry's face, he was ready for a new adventure."

"Are you concerned about that?" Mark asked. "Concerned you might try to duplicate what you had?"

"Not really. Although I do think it's easy to fall into that trap—the comfortable world you knew. In my case, I'm surrounded by well-meaning friends and family trying to put me back together. They think that the right guy will wash away the pain of the past year so I can pick up where I left off as though nothing happened."

"And what do *you* think," Mark asked.

"I think what I had was what I needed at one time, but it's not right for me now."

"And what *is* right for you now?" Mark asked.

"Frankly, I don't know. I only know that I don't want to go back." Dana said, smiling coyly at Mark. "I'm rather enjoying being *pas engagé.*"

"Really, Madame," Mark said, leaning closer to Dana. "Might you make an exception and engage in a delicious French dinner with me Friday night at La Fleur?"

Dana's smile and the twinkle in her eye said it all. "J'adorerais."

Mark reached out and squeezed Dana's hand. "I'll be by at eight."

The pair took a taxi back to Sniffen Court. At the front door, Dana took out her key and began to speak. "I had a lovely time to—"

Mark put his index finger against Dana's lips and quietly said, "Shh" before kissing her lightly on the lips.

"See you Friday," he said with a big smile.

Dana entered her apartment as Mark walked away beneath the gaslight at the end of the flagstones.

After a quick walk with Wills, Dana went to the kitchen, got a glass of water, and climbed the stairs. She hadn't planned on dating again for some time, but the night with Mark had been magical, as though it was meant to be. Glancing at the alarm on the nightstand, she saw that it was one o'clock, so she got in bed and turned out the light. As she slowly drifted into the twilight of sleep, she saw herself on a calm, moonlit ocean. In the distance, a whale was singing a song to her.

She wondered if Mark was thinking about her—wondered if he'd enjoyed their dance as much as she. And maybe—just maybe—he was at his apartment on the Upper West Side, listening for a song in the distance, just as she was.

Chapter Twelve

*P*atti Hartlen spent most of Tuesday morning on the sixth floor of B. Altman with the special events coordinator, making sure everything was ready for the private viewing and cocktail reception that afternoon to celebrate the opening of Lord Snowdon's retrospective exhibition of photographs for the benefit of the Association Residence for the Aged. Antony Armstrong-Jones, 1st Earl of Snowdon, was married to Princess Margaret, sister of Queen Elizabeth II. A famous portraitist and photographer, his work included fashion photography, images of urban life, and pictures of celebrities such as Laurence Olivier and J. R. R. Tolkien. Much of his work appeared in *Vanity Fair* and *Vogue*. Patti had been informed that he would be giving interviews at the reception, as well as signing copies of his new book, *Assignments*.

Since the doors opened, the store had been filled with shoppers hoping to get a glimpse of Lord Snowdon when he arrived, and there was a considerable buzz circulating among the store's staff as well. But Patti was distracted, finding it difficult to focus on the visit of such a luminary. She was thinking about her husband's recent change in mood and temperament, something she initially blamed on their relocation to New York and the stress from working feverishly to open Hartlen Response's new office. But that was four months ago, and the company was up and running. Patti was highly intuitive—nothing escaped her notice—and she'd helped identify burglars at the Sherry-Netherland Hotel the previous December because she'd seen them and remembered their car's license plate when she'd gone down to the lobby at six in the morning. As much as she tried, her instincts told her Jack's irritability stemmed from something more serious. Always an easy-going, quiet, and congenial man, Jack now had a short fuse, was anxious and distracted much of the time, and when Patti expressed her concerns, he became defensive. The situation was puzzling, and her astute mind knew that if she didn't find the missing pieces, her marriage might not survive.

Patti's thoughts were interrupted by the Altman Foundation's executive director, who wanted to discuss a topic he planned to bring up that afternoon with the director of communications for the Association Residence for the Aged. Although the day was more hectic than most, she was thankful for her position as grants manager, a title she'd held with the Houston Endowment. Her work at the foundation had become her entire life, but without it she would have been alone in New York City. Fortunately, her colleagues were warm, friendly people, and Dana, who'd recommended her for the position, came by at least once a day to say hello or ask what she was working on.

And yet Patti was feeling depressed and isolated despite being surrounded by so many caring coworkers. Whether or not Jack was at home, she felt lonely most evenings, staring at the television or reading a book after dinner, the antithesis of the active social life she enjoyed with her husband in Houston. If she attempted to engage him in conversation, his canned response was that he was tired and had to get to bed since the following day's schedule was going to be brutal.

As for intimacy, she could count on one hand the number of times they'd made love in the past two months. When she gave him a hug or held his hand, he would smile weakly and give her a quick kiss on the lips, but his mind seemed elsewhere. Moving to New York had been difficult enough, but didn't he realize that she needed him all the more after being uprooted from their stable lives and extensive circle of friends in Texas? Jack had always been a hard worker, but he'd always made time for Patti and enjoyed leisurely evenings at home or sitting in neighbors' backyards for a barbecue. It was as if he'd become synchronized with the faster pace of New York. Or was he depressed because he, too, missed their home and lifestyle in Houston while trying to successfully run the East Coast office?

Patti closed the file on her desk, her head bent forward, resting in her hands. "Maybe it's all in my imagination," she sighed. "Maybe I'm the one who hasn't adjusted to the move, and I'm expecting too much attention from Jack."

Patti raised her head and recalled how Jack had bought her an Elsa Peretti necklace from Tiffany's the previous week, adding, "Sorry I've been distracted lately." While the gesture was kind and loving, the message was hollow, and she sensed he was merely going through the motions. Still, he'd made an effort to show his affection. Perhaps he would slow down and she would find her concerns had been exaggerated.

Perhaps. It was just that her intuitions seldom proved to be incorrect, and her hunch was that something was very wrong with Jack or their relationship.

Patti was exhausted after the reception but stopped in her office to check for phone messages. There were two that would keep until the morning. She was ready to go home and relax. One of the foundation's secretaries, however, brought her a third pink message slip. It was from Jack. "Have to work late again. Don't wait up. Love, Jack."

Patti sighed. Jack knew how important the Snowdon exhibit was, as well as the Association Residence for the Aged. They had plans for a quiet dinner at one of their favorite restaurants that evening to discuss the highlights of the day and her introduction to Lord Snowdon.

But it wasn't going to happen. She had given him the benefit of the doubt over and over, but she'd been disappointed yet again. There was nothing to do but go home, take a hot bath, and call it a day.

She picked up her briefcase and walked to the elevators on the fifth floor. She was more than just frustrated, however. She was holding back tears.

"How was the reception?" Dana asked, approaching from the left. "I was hoping to stop by and have a glass of champagne, but I couldn't get in the room. The line at the door was five deep. Did you—"

Dana paused, noting Patti's drawn features.

"Is everything okay?" Dana asked.

Patti bit her lip and shook her head.

Dana took Patti by the arm and led her down the corridor to her own office. "Here," Dana said, motioning to a chair by her desk. "Sit down while I get you some water. You look pale."

A minute later, Dana handed Patti a cup of water from the cooler down the hall. Patti took a sip but couldn't suppress her tears any longer.

Dana placed her hand on Patti's forearm. "Did something happen at the reception? Would you like to talk?"

Patti swallowed hard, inhaled, and tried to speak. "I'm so tired of Jack changing plans at the last minute. We're never on the same page anymore. Never!"

Dana nodded. "I've had some experience with that."

Patti, usually the perfect image of confidence, looked at Dana tentatively. "I was wondering—would you mind if we could talk one day when you have the time. If it isn't any trouble, that is."

"Trouble?" Dana said. "Of course not. And you're not going home to eat by yourself tonight. We'll go to my house, and I'll fix dinner. We'll have more privacy there than talking in a restaurant, and we can open a bottle of wine and relax."

"Are you sure? I don't want to be any trouble."

Dana sensed Patti was not somebody who felt comfortable asking for help, especially with a personal matter, but she was clearly distressed about her marriage.

"It's no trouble at all," Dana said. "I'll make sinfully rich Fettuccini Alfredo and put you to work grating the Parmesan. That will release some stress, and I have the perfect white wine to go with it."

"Thanks," Patti said in a hoarse whisper. "I'm so embarrassed. You must think I'm crazy."

"No, what I think is that you need some company and a few hours away from your routine."

Patti's lips formed a weak smile as the two women left and headed for Sniffen Court.

After putting water on the stove to simmer slowly, Dana opened a bottle of Fiano di Avellino and sat with Patti in the living room.

"I know you've gone through tough times recently," Patti began, "and I was wondering ... well ... did you notice trouble coming on in your marriage? Is there something I should be looking for? I mean, Jack and I always had a solid marriage, and now, out of the blue, he's hardly ever there, physically or emotionally." Patti sniffled and wiped away tears with a Kleenex.

Dana was keenly aware that she was no expert when it came to dispensing personal advice, especially about marriage, but she'd never seen Patti looking so distressed.

"Brett and I married awfully young," Dana began. "I think that had a lot to do with our problems. I believe my mother felt that way when Brett and I first started going out, and she was certainly disturbed by our engagement, believing Brett to be immature. We shared some interests, but in retrospect, I wonder if he and I were really suited for each other. Youth can gloss over so many important issues. How long have you and Jack been married?"

"Just four years. I didn't think twenty-three was too young to get engaged, and my parents really loved Jack. Until we moved to New York, I thought we had the perfect marriage."

Dana, who sat next to Patti on the couch, sipped her wine and moved it in a gentle circular motion, watching the wine's legs briefly creep up the side of the glass. "I guess age is relative when it comes to marriage. It depends on the individual, but it sounds like you knew what you wanted. I'm not so sure I did, though. The most important thing to know is that there's no such thing as a *perfect* marriage."

Patti's eyebrows furrowed. "I guess I know that intellectually, but since we've never had any major conflicts, I haven't really thought about it. Do you think I might be overreacting to Jack's behavior or his change of mood?"

Dana moved her head from side to side slightly, weighing the question. "It's hard to say. In Brett's case, he worked long hours for many years. Sometimes the late nights at the office were warranted, but ... " Dana paused in order to choose her words carefully. "Even people who work hard can take time to do the small things that let you know they're aware of your needs. In the long run, I believe spouses can make time if they really want to. Even the busiest. That's not to say people don't get caught up in their jobs and become neglectful or self-absorbed. I don't think it's possible for couples to share everything with each other, but that's why a level of trust is so important. There could be something troubling him at the office, and he doesn't want to worry you."

Patti was steadier now, more composed. "He was always eager to tell me about his work," she said. "In fact, in a family company like ours, especially in the oil business, it's very common for wives to be kept in the loop about most matters. As for the little things, Jack gives me presents occasionally and even says that he's aware that he's not around much, but it doesn't seem that his heart is in it."

"In what?" Dana asked.

"In his words. Or—" Patti took a sip of wine and looked away from Dana. "Or in the marriage."

Dana nodded her understanding. "I know the feeling all too well, unfortunately. Have you sat down and had a serious talk with Jack? Told him how much his absence is affecting you? Have you asked him to make more time for you in his schedule while demonstrating understanding for the stress he himself might be under?"

Patti shook her head. "Not really. I've started to broach the subject a couple of times, but I think he senses what I'm going to say and he cuts me off, suggesting we go to a movie or an exhibit at the Met. Anywhere there's a crowd so we aren't alone. Then we come home and he's either too tired to talk or gets on the phone."

"I would insist that he make time for the two of you to have a serious discussion," Dana said. "Don't let him off the hook." While Dana was hesitant to give any specific advice for fear of being intrusive, Patti had thus far asked straightforward questions, and Dana was merely suggesting that the couple talk.

It was what any therapist would have recommended as a first step.

"You're right," Patti said. "I'm going to do it when he gets home tonight." Patti paused yet again. "But tell me honestly, Dana. Are the things I'm describing … are they, you know, warning signs?"

"Yes, but what kind of warning signs is another question. I think you're asking whether or not Jack's neglect might signal that he's having an affair, right?"

Patti sighed and spoke reluctantly. "I have to admit that the possibility has crossed my mind."

"That's one question I can't answer," Dana said. "Maybe he just needs a wake-up call. Until you two talk, try not to jump to any conclusions."

"Okay. And thanks, Dana. I really didn't know who to bring this to. I couldn't discuss these personal problems in brief, long-distance telephone conversations with my friends in Houston. Besides, I wouldn't want them to know that I was concerned about Jack or that there might be trouble in my marriage."

"I understand completely," Dana said. "You can talk to me anytime. Please—never hesitate to get in touch."

The two women ate dinner, and Patti described how Lord Snowdon had been swamped by women fighting to get near him.

"We have to get through two more days of this," Patti said, "and I heard that security is working on a new plan to control the crowds. The lines were too disorderly tonight, winding all over the sixth floor."

"I walked through the exhibit when it was first installed, and I plan to see it again before it comes down," Dana said. "I'd like more time to study the portraitures, although Andrew is getting me a copy of *Assignments* when he buys his."

"I'll get it autographed for you," Patti said. "We're having a meeting with Lord Snowdon in the morning. I hope I can concentrate. He's so handsome!"

"That he is," Dana said, "and much too charming. He's so ... "

The two women glanced at each other over the small dining table and burst out laughing.

"To Lord Snowdon," Dana said, raising her glass.

"To Lord Snowdon."

Patti helped with the dishes and left after giving Dana a hug. She wasn't sure what was going on with Jack, but unburdening her soul and spending the evening with a friend had made her feel much better. At least she knew how to proceed.

Patti arrived at her apartment at ten o'clock that night. She paced about nervously for an hour, rehearsing what she was going to say to Jack. She was certain that he would try to put her off, assuring her that they could talk in the morning because he was dead tired, but she wasn't going to take no for an answer. The talk suggested by Dana couldn't wait any longer.

The clock on the mantel chimed eleven ... and twelve. Jack hadn't come home, nor had he called. Patti decided to relax in bed and read *Assignments*. It had been a long day, and between the champagne reception and her talk with Dana, she was exhausted.

At one-thirty, she fell asleep with the light on, the book having slipped to her lap. At some time during the night, she turned over in her sleep and noticed that the light was off and that Jack was lying beside her. For a moment she tried to sit-up, but she had been sleeping too soundly to initiate a conversation. She closed her eyes and fell back into a dreamless slumber.

Before opening her eyes in the morning, she remembered the task at hand. Turning to her left, she propped herself on her elbow and saw that Jack was gone. He had already gotten up, dressed, and left for the office.

Chapter Thirteen

*B*rett had not called Janice daily, as he'd promised, since arriving in New York City. He'd been consumed with looking into Hartlen Response's slush fund and making sure that Jack would sign the consortium agreement. He had also been unable to resist the temptation to see what Dana was up to, so he had asked Wade Forrester to do a small job on the side—strictly off the books—with Brett paying out-of-pocket for the information. Brett, therefore, learned in short order of the surprise party thrown by Johnny and Andrew and that Dana was thriving at work. He'd also discovered that Dana had gone out with Mark Senger, and it hadn't been just an innocent evening with a friend.

After receiving Forrester's report, Brett gazed from his office window to New York's financial district with a distant look in his eye. Like most husbands, he would have been happier to learn that his soon-to-be ex-wife was foundering without him, regretting her lightning-quick decision to seek a divorce, not that he would have sought a reconciliation. He was still caught up in the excitement and bohemian lifestyle that Janice offered him. Besides, what Forrester had told him was mere validation. Brett had instinctively known that Dana, a strong and deter-mined woman, would move on with her life. She was not one to wallow in self-pity. That she would date so soon, however, was most definitely a surprise. A small part of him, buried beneath his winning smile and confident demeanor, was jealous and hurt even though he knew it was hypocritical to be upset.

His curiosity having been satisfied, Brett settled into his desk chair and dialed Janice's number.

"Are you so busy that you can't pick up the phone and keep in touch more often?" Janice asked, sounding mildly irritated.

Brett flinched, knowing that he'd let too much time pass since his last call two days earlier. "Sorry," he said. "The Hartlen slush fund has taken a few weird turns. The money is being diverted to Hartlen Response, but a lot of it is missing, so I'm staying on top of it."

"Good. Keep the pressure on lest Richard become really impatient. People at the firm tell me that he's not happy that Jack has delayed committing to the consortium so many months after you officially declared the Hartlen signing a done deal. In terms of your partnership, remember that you're the new kid on the block."

"I've spoken with Richard and told him in so many words that Jack was able to drag his feet since I've been on the West Coast handling the asbestos case. He told me he understood, although I agree that results are what matter in the long run."

There was a pause on the other end of the line before Janice spoke again.

"So what have you been up to in New York?" she asked. "Playing squash? Keeping fit?"

Brett laughed. "I have to. You're physically demanding. Not that I'm complaining, of course."

"I should hope not. And what is Mrs. McGarry up to?"

Brett cleared his throat. "Haven't a clue. I suppose she's still working at B. Altman. I haven't heard anything from her attorney, so I assume everything is still on track for the divorce to become finalized."

"Is she dating anyone?" Janice asked. "Anything special going on in her life?"

"I wouldn't have any way of knowing since I've had no contact with her. Anyway, it's you I think of, not Dana."

"A wise answer," Janice said. "So when are you returning to San Francisco?"

"That's one of the reasons why I'm calling. This slush fund business is going to keep me in New York a few extra days, maybe longer. Going through the books of Hartlen Response to track down where the charitable contributions are ending up isn't going to be easy."

"I understand," Janice said. "Keep in touch. I miss you."

"I miss you, too. I'll call again tonight."

"I'll be waiting."

Brett hung up the phone, feeling that the call had accomplished its purpose. He had reestablished contact, plus Janice was well aware that forensic analysis of a company's books was difficult. As for her questions about Dana, they were natural. Janice was territorial in the extreme, and all mistresses asked a few probing questions to make sure their prey remained loyal, right?

Of course. Brett had things in hand as usual.

Janice grinned and shook her head. Men were so transparent—and easy to trick. She'd worked with Brett long enough to know a good deal about his personal life with Dana, and she'd had easy access to his office in New York before their temporary assignment began on the coast. She knew when Dana's birthday was, and if Brett had been one hundred percent honest, he would have mentioned that there had been a special event in her life.

Janice grabbed the yellow pages, looking up airline phone numbers. She would hop back to New York for a day or two— the paralegals could handle matters in San Francisco—to see exactly what Brett was up to. Dealing with the slush fund was indeed something that could take time, but Brett's calls had been sporadic since returning to New York, and he sounded slightly evasive.

Several possibilities occurred to Janice. Brett was perhaps in contact with Dana, or at least reaching out to her. He was a novice at living a new, less structured life. She'd seduced him, and it was much too easy. The poor baby was probably still nursing some degree of guilt for his unfaithfulness to Dana, whom Janice had privately nicknamed Little Miss Priss.

But the opposite might be true as well. Freed from the constraints of his stuffy upper-class marriage, perhaps he was *too* accustomed to her California lifestyle and was using his time in New York to practice his newfound freedom with someone else entirely.

Brett McGarry was her conquest, someone she was grooming according to her own tastes, a project that was both fun and, in the long run, could be financially lucrative. She would look in on Brett and make sure that her investment was protected.

Chapter Fourteen

Dana and Mark sat in La Fleur, located in a townhouse on East 58th Street. It was a small yet elegant restaurant that, to Dana, had the perfect ambience for a second date.

Dana was on the verge of asking Mark if he'd seen the latest Lina Wertmüller film, but he leaned forward before she could speak a single word. His eyes sparkled as he covered Dana's hand with his.

"I think it's time we get you on a horse," Mark suggested in a whisper.

Dana was taken aback, unsure what had prompted the remark. "A horse?"

"Why not?" asked Mark. "We could get you started at Claremont any time you want. I think you'd really enjoy it. You told me how you like the rhythm of jogging, so I was thinking you could learn a different kind of rhythm. Once you get the hang of it in the ring, we could go riding together in the park."

Dana was flattered. Mark was clearly implying that he wanted to explore the possibility of a deeper relationship. His suggestion had come out of the blue, but he appeared quite serious.

"But I haven't been on a horse in years," she countered, "and even then, it was only for a few minutes when I visited a friend's home in the country when I was a teenager. Other than that, pony rides as a kid are my only experience."

Mark clasped his hands as if Dana had already proven his point. "Ah, you've taken the first step then! We'll go from there. With the right training and the perfect horse, you could take up where you left off."

"Huh? More pony rides?"

Looking delighted, Mark laughed, enjoying his unorthodox invitation. "No, no, no. You'd be taught English riding style, starting with the horse's tack—the saddle, halter, the bit, and the like. Then they'd select a horse for its gentleness and let you lead it around the paddock. Just to get acquainted. After that, you'd learn how to sit in the saddle properly since the body's alignment is everything when riding a horse. Then a topnotch instructor would lead you around until you felt comfortable. No cantor or loping yet, at least not until you learn to give your mount the right commands. Nice and easy at first. When people think of the sport, they envision riders madly dashing across a meadow, but Claremont knows what they're doing. Plus you'd get to wear an absolutely stunning riding outfit and impress the hell out of everyone." Mark folded his arms and looked at Dana. "No question about it. You'd be a Ralph Lauren model. Imagine wearing stretchy white breeches, a fitted navy hacking jacket, a ... "

"A *four-button* navy hacking jacket," Dana said playfully, folding her arms and mimicking Mark.

"As many buttons as you wish. A pink ascot shirt, tall English dress boots in rich brown leather—"

"Stop! I'm feeling weak!" Dana laughed as she mockingly dropped her head. "Wait. Gloves. A girl needs gloves. Yes, luscious leather pigskin gloves ."

"*You're* luscious," Mark said as he kissed her before he sat back in his chair.

"And you're very persuasive, Mark. I'm tempted. I just don't know how I can start a new sport now. There have been so many changes in my life at work and at home. I ... I don't think it's the right time."

"It's the *perfect* time," Mark said. "You should mark your thirtieth birthday with a new challenge. Push the envelope. It's the only way we learn and grow. When I turned forty, I climbed Mount Kilimanjaro to overcome my acrophobia."

"Kilimanjaro? Mark, you're amazing," Dana said, loving his energy and enthusiasm. "You really think I can do it?"

"The question is whether or not *you* think you can."

Dana knew that Mark was right. A milestone birthday should be celebrated with something more exciting than a divorce.

"Okay then," Dana said confidently, her chin raised. "I'll do it."

Dana could see that Mark was pleased. She had no idea where their relationship was headed, but suddenly riding was a daunting goal she wanted to accomplish. Unlike her over-ly-protective family and friends, who wanted to provide her with a sense of security, Mark was encouraging her to step out of her comfort zone and test new waters. He seemed sure that she could ride, at least well enough to enjoy the trails with him in Central Park, and she was determined to prove him right.

Dana and Mark talked during their meal as if they'd been going out for years. Mark could segue from one subject to an-other with ease, and by the time they'd finished their entrees, Dana wasn't even aware that they were on a formal date. As she'd told Patti, she had married young and she'd therefore never experienced this kind of easy rapport with a mature, cul-tured man with such diverse interests. Mark also stood in stark contrast to Brett inasmuch as Mark was eager to share his pas-sions with Dana. He was just as busy as Brett, but he was a man with a voracious appetite for life, savoring every moment. And unlike Jack Hartlen or Brett, Mark was making time for Dana despite his work and fast-paced life. As for Dana, she herself was savoring everything Mark had to say.

There were times, however, when staring into his eyes made it hard to concentrate.

With Mark standing by her side, Dana opened the door of the carriage house and spotted Wills at his usual spot, eagerly awaiting his final walk of the evening. The door still open, Dana instinctively reached for the leash hanging from a coat rack on the entrance wall. Turning, she noticed that Mark was already on one knee, patting Wills on the head. Barely looking up, he took the lead from Dana's hand and snapped it securely onto the dog's collar.

"Come on," he said to Dana. "Let's go for a walk. It's a beautiful spring night."

"Wills will like that," Dana said. "We're usually back within minutes in the evening."

The two headed out into the April evening, Mark holding the leash.

"Amanda has a yellow Lab at the house in Connecticut," he said. "Rex. She brings him to my apartment whenever she visits. We love taking him to the park when the weather's nice. Of course, if it were up to Amanda, we'd have three Labs."

"Is she in high school?" Dana asked.

"I *wish* she were still in high school. No, Amanda's in the College of Veterinary Medicine at Cornell."

"You must be very proud," Dana said. "Do you have any other children?"

"Just Amanda. She's spoiled rotten, especially by her grandfather, but there aren't many kids in Greenwich who *aren't* spoiled." Mark raised his eyebrows, looking almost philosophical. "She's a keeper, though. Doesn't let all the attention go to her head. At least not too much."

"And you say she's a show jumper? That's pretty impressive."

"Since the age of thirteen. She was such a great student—advanced placement and honors courses—that we didn't have much reason to deny her the privilege of taking up riding. She hit the books hard so she could groom her horse Pepsi."

"Cute name," Dana said. "Like Caroline Kennedy's pony, Macaroni."

"Pepsi is a chestnut Dutch Warmblood, which is a show hunter in the hunter jumper division. I bought Pepsi from my friend Judd Baumann, who owns a horse farm in Muttontown, on Long Island. I'd like to show it to you sometime. Beautiful place, with hundreds of acres set aside for preserves and horse trails. That's where Amanda started show-jumping lessons."

The night air was chilly, and Dana unconsciously hooked her arm through Mark's, drawing herself closer to his body.

Mark walked steadily on, allowing Wills to investigate the sidewalk, trees, and side streets.

"Murray Hill is a nice pocket-neighborhood right in the heart of midtown," he remarked as he looked up at the tall, stately brownstones they passed. "I bet you never take the subway. You can walk everywhere."

"Yes, but when I go to Lincoln Center, I—" Dana stopped in mid-sentence to brush away a bug hovering near her face. When she quickly averted her head to the side, pushing against Mark's shoulder, he unexpectedly kissed the top of her head.

"The bugs can't resist because you smell so good," he said casually.

Dana looked up to find Mark gazing down at her. He lowered his head and kissed her again, this time gently on the lips.

Dana said nothing, for there was no need for conversation after an evening when everything had been easygoing and relaxed. Their words and glances had fit together seamlessly since the moment they'd been seated at La Fleur. Dana merely looked deeply in Mark's eyes and smiled, holding his arm a little closer as he guided her and Wills down the street with a steady hand. He tilted his head to the side, leaning against hers.

"Think it's cold enough for a fire?" he asked.

"I never need an excuse," she answered.

At the carriage house, Mark unhooked the leash from Wills' collar, dropped his jacket on the sofa, and walked to the living room bar, where he poured a glass of red wine for Dana and a scotch for himself. Squatting by the fireplace, he told Dana that he'd bring her a basket of kindling the next time he went riding in the country. Meanwhile, he tussled with Wills as he lit the fire, at last standing and stepping back to make sure the flames had caught sufficiently.

Dana picked up his coat from the sofa to hang it in the closet, but couldn't resist resting her face against the fabric. In that one brief moment, her heart pounded and her face blushed, but she recovered before hanging up the coat and taking her glass of wine from the bar. She inhaled, still intoxicated by Mark's scent on the coat.

Sipping his scotch, Mark turned in a circle and studied the room, noting the soft lighting and the reflection of the fire in the tall leaded glass windows. The small house seemed to be a model of tranquility, complete with a bouquet of flowers on the coffee table.

"Well, well, well," he said, motioning to the flower arrangement. "Who's my competition?"

"I bought them for *moi*," Dana said.

Mark laughed. "That's not what you're supposed to say, Dana. You're supposed to make a guy jealous."

"Well, professor, you can add a course in dating when we finish our lessons on the trail."

"It would be my pleasure, Ms. McGarry," Mark said as he moved closer to Dana. "But only if you can give me a few tips on stage design."

"What could I possibly teach the president of a display company?" Dana asked.

"How you staged this beautiful English setting," Mark said as he observed every detail of Dana's home. "Did you work with a designer?"

"Thank you. I'm flattered, but, no. I decorated it myself, although it was easy because there was a perfect spot for everything I brought from the apartment. My mother and I had everything in place in a few hours. Even *I* fell easily into place," Dana said with a laugh. "I love being here."

"I can see why," Mark said. "How did you find this gem?"

"Max Helm's friend was living here but had to take a sudden assignment in Paris. Max practically handed me the keys overnight. I think you remember the rush I was in to move out of my old apartment. If you recall, you were the one who recommended my divorce attorney, Alan Rudnick. I can't thank you enough, by the way," Dana said, facing Mark and putting the palm of her right hand against his chest.

"Alan's a good man and a good lawyer," Mark commented. "I should know. I think I've paid off his house and bought him an automobile or two."

"He's the best," Dana said. "I'm so thankful that Alan enabled my battle to be short and sweet."

"I was happy to help," Mark said. "But let's leave the past behind and toast the present. It's been a wonderful week."

"To the present," Dana said.

Mark continued walking around the living room, shaking his head and smiling as he observed the coffee table books and the art.

"What's so funny," Dana asked.

"Excuse me. After twenty years, I'm still haunted by my mother's request to report to her on every detail of the art and books I saw in the homes of women I dated."

"Why did she do it?" Dana asked.

"Mother was screening potential daughters-in-law. She insisted that I marry the right girl from the appropriate socio-economic background. She got what she wanted all right, but it didn't make for a very happy marriage."

Dana nodded, remaining silent. She wasn't the kind of person to pry into someone else's affairs, nor was she inclined to ask any follow-up questions about Mark's ex-wife. Given Mark's tender, amorous displays throughout the evening, it wasn't the time to discuss other relationships, let alone his marriage. The night belonged to them, and she wasn't going to spoil the magic.

"And this picture," Mark said, picking up a silver frame. "I presume this is your mother? Has anyone ever told you she looks like Blythe Danner?"

"All the time."

"Handsome couple," Mark said, referring to the photo of Dana's parents.

"A happy couple," Dana said as she looked at the photograph in Mark's hand. "They make it seem so easy."

"What do you mean?"

"Being married," Dana said. "Their personalities are so different, but they're always on the same page."

"It may *seem* easy," Mark said, "but they obviously work at it in their own way. It's never fifty-fifty. Someone always gives more. "

"That would surely be my father. He's probably giving ninety percent!"

"Spoken like a true daddy's girl. I suppose he can do no wrong."

"Never," Dana said. "I'm sure Amanda feels the same about you."

Mark laughed. "True. To her mother's chagrin."

"My son's my son till he takes him a wife," Dana said, quoting from *Sons and Lovers* by D.H. Lawrence, to which Mark quickly added, "But my daughter's my daughter the whole of her life."

"I love that quote," Dana said. "I always include it in my note to friends when they have a baby girl."

"Let's continue the tour," Mark said, his arm around Dana.

She led him upstairs and pointed out the master bedroom and the adjoining sitting room that offered a view of the landscaped deck outside. It was at the bookcases, however, where Mark paused, running his fingers along the tall, leather spins of the many volumes in Dana's personal library. His eyes darted up and down, right and left as his lips softly mouthed his favorite titles.

"More biographies than I would have expected," Mark said, "but I see you've got the classics covered as well." He gave Dana a glancing kiss on the forehead. "That doesn't surprise me in the least."

Dana rested her hand on Mark's shoulder, saying, "When it comes to having everything covered, you'll be even more impressed by what's in the kitchen."

"I don't think I can be more impressed than I already am," Mark said. "Everything is just as it should be, but go ahead—surprise me."

"Follow me and prepare to be amazed by something worthy of the Senger Display Company."

A few moments later, Mark saw why Dana was so eager to bring him downstairs.

"A stone fireplace in a New York kitchen!" Mark said. "This room belongs in a cottage in the English Cotswolds. Do you use it?"

"I assume you're asking if I cook," Dana said. "Of course I do."

"And what is on the McGarry menu on any given day?" Mark asked, leaning against the upholstered banquette.

"Every month I try at least two recipes from *Gourmet* magazine," Dana said. "But the focus is on seafood, pasta, soups, crepes, frittatas, and pancakes. I want you to know, Mark, that I happen to make really good blueberry pancakes."

"Tell me about the frittatas," Mark said.

"You mean you've never had a frittata?"

"Not *your* frittatas. What are your favorite fillings?"

"It depends. Sometimes mushrooms, spinach, and tomatoes. Maybe smoked salmon, dill, and goat cheese. Or—"

"Okay, I think I like the salmon, dill, and goat cheese."

"Don't you want to try my pancakes?" Dana asked, pretending to pout.

"Dana, I'm not a breakfast-for-dinner kinda guy."

"Then you've come to the right place. It's only pancakes for breakfast in this house."

Mark dimmed the lights in the kitchen, leading Dana back upstairs.

He paused at the bookcase, his finger pressing the START button of the cassette deck on the middle shelf.

"Stan Getz and Astrud Gilberto," Mark said. " 'Quiet Nights of Quiet Stars.' Now who in the world could listen to this music and not want to dance?"

"Not me," Dana said. "How did you know what would play?"

"I saw the tape when we passed by a few minutes ago."

"Is there anything you don't miss?" Dana asked.

"I miss *you* when you're not around."

Dana put both arms around Mark's neck and they slowly glided into the master bedroom. Mark's next kiss was not playful, but rather warm, tender, and long. A few minutes later, the lights in the master bedroom dimmed while the music, low and slow, filled the upstairs of Dana's house.

Chapter Fifteen

Mark and Dana sat down to breakfast the next morning in the brick-enclosed, bluestone patio off the kitchen. As promised, Dana made pancakes and set them on a bistro table near the flower bed that lined the base of the brick wall. Both wearing robes, they lingered over a second cup of coffee, happy to begin the day together.

"I've been meaning to ask you," Dana said, "whether you got a chance to see Snowdon's exhibit?"

"I walked through it with Andrew before the store opened yesterday morning. I'm glad I didn't miss it. What a talented guy—and a nice chap, too. I met him last year when he came to New York to start planning the space with Andrew and Bob."

"I didn't know you worked on the installation," Dana said.

"I didn't. I was invited to the meeting as a consultant. Snowdon designed the environment himself, and it was built to his specifications. Do you realize how much department stores have changed in the last four or five years? Bloomies gets all the attention for their over-the-top extravaganzas, but B. Altman has hosted an impressive list of notables, and many more are on the calendar for next year. Great PR that also brings traffic to the store. Did you hear that ten thousand people showed up each day to see Snowdon?"

"That's shocking! I don't think we'd get traffic like that even if we gave away the merchandise for free. As for events at the store, I have some news I've been meaning to tell you, but my mind has been on other things lately—in case you haven't noticed."

Mark was bringing his coffee cup to his mouth but froze, his arm suspended in midair.

"Tell me? Tell me what?"

"I'm leaving B. Altman."

Mark remained speechless for a moment before flashing a wide grin. "I knew it was only a matter of time before you got a better offer, and I think it's long overdue! Where are you going? Bloomies?" He paused, as if a light had gone off in his mind. "Of course! Ira and Dawn are bringing you to Bergdorf! That's it, right?"

"Not Bergdorf, but you're on the right track. I'm going to be fashion director at the House of Cirone. Last week Johnny and Uncle John asked me to join them."

The grin disappeared from Mark's face, and he suddenly looked troubled.

"What's the matter?" Dana asked. "I'll have considerable creative input, European travel, and I'll get a healthy salary increase."

"Are you sure about this?" Mark asked, settling back in his chair.

"I didn't make the decision lightly. I've just had my third go 'round with Helen in less than nine months, and I'm drained and frustrated. I thought I had won her favor with both the Teen Advisory Board and the teen cosmetic counter which, as you know, she's expanding. But here we are—a new idea, another battle. This isn't a job, Mark. It's an endurance test. She not only killed the Nantucket boutique, but also my suggestion to modify the concept of selling coordinated separates and matching outerwear with a British country look. Just like Jaeger! She has been more obstinate than usual lately, and while the world awaits a mood change in Ms. Kavanagh, my career is on hold."

"I'm sure it's a wonderful position, but … "

"But?"

"I've had some experience with family businesses, and while you may not have office politics, there may be parental control issues."

"I don't understand. What are you getting at?"

Mark sighed and chose his words carefully. "I got to know Uncle John when we were redesigning the ladies eveningwear department at the store. He's a lovely, gracious man, softer around the edges than my father, but he can be just as controlling. Didn't you tell me that Johnny couldn't choose his own profession? Plus a person's demeanor can change quite a bit in the workplace when money and reputation are on the line."

Dana shook her head. "I can't envision Uncle John not honoring his promise to give me a great deal of latitude."

"Dana, Uncle John is family. He loves you like a daughter. I get it. But I don't believe you'll have the freedom you anticipate as fashion director. Family ties notwithstanding, it's a new position, and every little brainstorm you have will need his blessing. Trust me—I know what I'm saying. I live it every day with my father." Mark paused and covered Dana's hand. "I'm sure the position with Uncle John will keep for a few months. I just want you to think about it."

"I really want this job, Mark. I'd planned to be on board in time to implement my ideas for the spring collection. I have to admit that you've caught me off guard a bit."

Mark shifted his chair closer to Dana's. "I understand." He kissed Dana on the cheek and put his arm around her shoulder.

"But I have an idea that I think you could sell to Helen. A really big one."

"Which is?"

"A private label for B. Altman."

Dana raised her eyebrows. "Um … interesting, but where is this coming from?"

Mark removed his arm from Dana's shoulder and clasped his hands on the edge of the bistro table. "Senger Display is designing and implementing a build-out at Brooks Brothers, which is launching a women's department with clothing designed and made at menswear factories. They're not going to buy off the racks on Seventh Avenue."

Dana looked confused. "Then who are their suppliers?"

Mark smiled, seeing that he'd succeeded in getting Dana's attention.

"That's the beauty of it," he explained. "The women's buyers at Brooks Brothers buy the piece goods and give them, together with their ideas and clothing samples, to men's manufacturers so they can be inspired to design women's patterns."

Dana sipped her coffee as she digested what Mark was saying. "It's intriguing all right," she admitted, "but I'm not sure Helen would sign off on it. In fact, she might shoot it down just because it came from me, given her abrupt dismissal of my suggestions lately. If I say white, she says black."

"I'm not saying it would be easy," Mark said, "but it's a way to salvage the boutique. Instead of a Nantucket setting, we'll build out a clubby English room. You could sell the line from your brainchild."

"But who would I work with?" Dana asked.

"Let me think about that for a bit," Mark replied. "For now, lay the groundwork and see if Helen will at least discuss the idea. A private label would give B. Altman a great deal of prestige. Surely she'll see the wisdom of such a proposal."

Dana stared at the brick wall a few feet away for several seconds before speaking. "All right, I'll approach Helen, but I'm not promising anything. I may still decide that working at the House of Cirone is in my best interest. But ... "

"Yes?"

Dana laughed. "I have to admit it's a fantastic idea!"

"Good!" Mark said, nodding his approval. "Put Cirone's evening gowns aside for now, and start thinking about classic separates. I think you'll find the sample patterns for your first line are hanging in your closet! In the meantime, I want to run this by a friend of mine who might be in a position to help. I may have more input in a few days." He pushed back his chair and stood. "Right now I need to go upstairs and get dressed so I can get back to my apartment. Amanda is coming by around noon, so Dad here needs to get ready."

Dana and Mark were both dressed as they descended the stairs and stood by the front door thirty minutes later.

"By the way," Mark said, "that's a handsome secretary. It appears that you're using it as it was intended."

"And you can obviously tell that, my dear Holmes, because the desk is unfolded, with blank stationery and my fountain pen in plain view."

"It's elementary," Mark said, putting his arm around Dana's waist. "I'm a big fan of Conan Doyle, by the way. And, I may add, there's an unopened letter from London waiting to be read. I noticed it during our tour last night. An English admirer?"

"A Jesuit priest, if you must know. He became my unofficial spiritual advisor when I visited his church."

Mark leaned over and kissed Dana on the forehead and then the lips. "I'll call later when Amanda gets settled in and is pleasantly distracted." He nodded towards the letter. "Be sure to tell the good father all about me."

"There's confidentiality between a member of the flock and her spiritual advisor. What I decide to tell him about you shall remain sealed."

"How deliciously mysterious," Mark said, opening the door.

He kissed Dana one last time and disappeared across the flagstones.

Dana cleaned up the breakfast dishes and sat on the sofa, staring through the large windows overlooking Sniffen Court. She felt light, happy, optimistic. Mark brought a new joy to her life and waking up in his arms was a beautiful way to start the day. It had been quite a while since she'd smiled for the sake of smiling. She'd worked beside Mark on so many occasions when he was building a display at the store but had never entertained romantic thoughts about him. And yet here he was, deeply attracted to her, awakening her heart and spirit with a joy she could never have imagined. She was happy beyond belief.

There was, of course, a new hesitation about joining the House of Cirone. She thought it unlikely that Helen would agree to the business model being used at Brooks Brothers, and yet Mark's instincts were sound. Helping to develop a private label for the store, if she were allowed to do so, would be exhilarating and challenging in a way that wouldn't be possible if she worked for Johnny and his father.

And Mark had struck a nerve when he'd mentioned Johnny, who was only at the company to please his father. Could the Cirone family dynamics be more complicated than Dana anticipated when it came to business? Dana reluctantly had to admit to herself that it was possible.

She decided to open Father Macaulay's letter and see how he'd responded. Perhaps there would be some small gem that would guide her in the choice she would have to make in the weeks ahead, if not sooner. She slipped her silver letter opener beneath the flap of the white envelope and removed the vellum stationery.

Dear Dana,

How delightful it was to hear from you! And a belated happy birthday. I hope you don't regard turning thirty as getting old as so many people your age do. Dare I say you have your whole life in front of you at the risk of seeming so very trite?

I'm equally delighted that you are jogging and getting out of your house. The birthday party sounds like it was quite enjoyable. I wish I could have been there. As for my own diversions, my pub closed and I am temporarily left without a place to give voice to my renditions of Cole Porter songs. Some of my friends have jokingly told me that this is Mayfair's good fortune, but that won't deter me when I find another pub that's right for me. It's not the quality of my voice that counts, but the opportunity to belt out a few tunes regardless of what others may think. It's for fun, of course, but I do think one must take the bull by the horns once in a while. I'd hate for my parishioners to say, "That's the priest who used to drink a pint and sing until midnight." Used to? That's not for me.

I think this also answers your question as to whether our deepest selves and our work are symbiotic. The answer is a resounding yes. It's who I am, and I don't think I'd be a good priest if I couldn't be myself in the process. My parishioners rather like my boldness and slightly unorthodox approach to having fun. I think they respect me all the more when I go to work because they realize that I'm human just like they are and not somebody who simply wears a Roman collar and mumbles prayers on Sunday.

As for your being conflicted about possibly leaving the store, I'm sure you'll make the right decision. Being conflicted is also a part of being human and forces us to make difficult decisions because we can't tread water indefinitely when it comes to saying yes or no.

I hope you'll continue to write, and I look forward to hearing what you decide about the job. Meanwhile, keep jogging!

Keep me in your prayers as I keep you in mine.

Sincerely,
Father Charles Macaulay

Dana was stunned by how sage Father Macaulay's letter was and how closely it addressed the present quandary about her employment options. His attitude about finding another place to sing and accepting the challenge of being himself resonated with her. He wasn't going to throw in the towel because of a setback. If people didn't approve of his creative outlets, he didn't care. In his own words, he was bold and took the bull by the horns.

Dana, who already had a glow about her, now felt even more lighthearted. She was going to try to convince Helen to allow her to develop a private label for B. Altman. What's the worst thing that could happen? Helen might say no, and if that eventuality came to pass, Dana could still accept Uncle John's offer. The important thing was not to let her goal slip away so easily.

Dana loved a good challenge and now knew that, under the right circumstances, staying at the store was what she wanted most. She wasn't going to tread water when it came to making a decision.

Chapter Sixteen

Brett walked confidently into the offices of Hartlen Response in the Chrysler Building, location of the company's New York office. He'd asked to see Jack but was told that the CEO was in an important meeting and couldn't be disturbed.

"Trust me," Brett told the receptionist. "He'll make time. Tell him I'm here to talk about the company's discretionary account holding donations to Hartlen Oil ... " Brett glanced at his watch for dramatic effect. " ... and that I'm in something of a rush."

"One moment, please," the receptionist said, picking up a telephone and relaying Brett's message.

Five minutes later, a secretary appeared in the waiting room and ushered Brett to the executive office of Jack Hartlen.

"Good morning, Jack," Brett said. "Sorry to barge in unannounced, but we have some things to discuss—important things that can't wait for an appointment."

"I've already told my father that I have everything under control and that we don't need your help with the FBI or IRS investigations. We have our own set of lawyers—quite competent, I might add—so if you'd be so kind as to turn around and leave, I have a busy day ahead of me."

In defiance, Brett sat down in a chair in front of Jack's desk, crossed his legs, and made himself comfortable.

"Whatever your legal advisors are doing isn't deterring the federal government from continuing to scrutinize your company very closely," Brett said. "Perhaps a recap is in order so you'll understand how firm my grasp is of your current situation. The donations to Hartlen Oil's Responsible Use of Natural Resources Account seem to be disappearing into a black hole here at Hartlen Response—what you're calling your Hartlen Discretionary Account, which is missing ... " Brett rubbed his chin and tilted his head back slightly. "Oh, about seven million dollars? Sound about right? None of the environmental organizations that you and your father are partnering with is seeing one red cent of the money originally given to Hartlen Oil."

"I'm not interested in discussing the matter," Jack shot back coldly. The affable tone and swagger Jack had exhibited at the Polo Club had vanished. "This is company business. Family business, for that matter. I want you out of my office or—"

"But here's the rub," Brett continued, undeterred. "Your partnership agreements with environmental groups, though tenuous, don't give you the flexibility to invest philanthropic donations given what the law calls intent and reasonable expectation for funds to be used towards predetermined purposes. It's legalese, but diversion of such funds is a violation of numerous federal statutes."

"Our partners have signed letters of intent while we conduct environmental studies and formulate specific action plans," Jack explained. "They're in no hurry."

"I've looked into that as well," Brett said. "Your company doesn't have even one scientific study on the drawing board let alone what you call action plans. But you're missing the point, Jack! The money isn't where it should be!" Brett uncrossed his legs and shook his head. "You're breaking the law. You're going to get your father in a lot of trouble since the donations are first given to Hartlen Oil. So what's going on? The donors and feds aren't happy, and sooner or later your environmental partners won't be either. As for your legal department, I'm willing to bet they don't have the slightest idea what you're up to because you're not telling them what you're really doing with the money. As a lawyer, I know from experience that I can only be effective when clients are honest with me."

Jack, now angry and red-faced, stood and straightened his coat. "I've tried to be civil with you in the past, but leave now or I'll call building security."

"Sit down, Jack. Your dad has done more than ask me to look into these matters. He's retained my firm to represent your two companies. I haven't shared my suspicions with him … yet." Brett smiled, the fingertips of his two hands touching as he rested his elbows on the arms of the chair. He loved cornering opponents, and Jack was clearly in his sights yet again.

"You have no right to meddle in my affairs!" Jack shouted.

"Your affairs? I made the decision to keep myself apprised of your affairs several months ago, or don't you remember. Here's what's going to happen. You're going to tell me where the seven million dollars is. It's hidden in some kind of slush fund—we both know that—but I doubt it's in any kind of discretionary account that the IRS would approve of. Then you're going to start releasing the money to your environmental partners and become a model of transparency. You're also going to contact marine biology experts at various universities and begin to do pilot studies even if it's to determine how much salt is in the damn ocean. Then you're going to release even more money. Are we clear on this?"

Jack was about to speak, but Brett held up the palm of his hand, silencing the CEO.

"I'm not doing this for you," Brett continued, "but for your father. I intend to protect his business interests, which include Hartlen Response, because they coincide with mine and the firm's. Finally, you're going to sign the consortium agreement. This goes way beyond you and Andrew now. I can cause you a lot of trouble on any number of fronts, but I'd rather not."

Jack was visibly upset and had swiveled his chair sideways so as not to face Brett. His tone of voice was now subdued, somber. "What gives you the right to interfere in my life?"

"Right? I have *no* right. I simply do it because I can and, more importantly, because it furthers my career."

Brett softened his approach and stood, leaning forward so that both of his arms were braced against the desk.

"Listen, Jack. The terms I originally laid out for you last year will protect your proprietary technology for several years. After that, Hartlen is established as an environmental leader, and you've made a bundle of cash for the company while your competitors develop their own response technology, which, as we've discussed, is going to happen long before you're granted a patent. You're a smart businessman, so let's get this done. Don't lose profits just because you dislike me personally."

Jack once again faced Brett and attempted to compose himself. "I don't know what to do. I—"

"Where's the money, Jack?"

Jack scribbled two words on a memo pad and shoved it silently across the desk. Brett picked it up and read "Cayman Islands."

"That a boy. My lead investigator has been granted access to your books, and he'll make sure that everything I've laid out goes off without a hitch."

"You can wipe the smirk off your face now, Brett. You got what you wanted. Now leave Andrew and me alone."

"And the consortium?"

"Just tell me when to show up and sign the papers," Jack said with resignation. "I'll be there."

"Thursday morning. Ten o'clock."

Brett turned to leave, but stopped. "Jack, out of curiosity, what the hell were you thinking? How could you put your company at such risk? The federal government is breathing down your neck, for God's sake!"

Jack cleared his throat. "For what it's worth, the environmental partners were eventually going to get their money, but ..."

Brett smiled knowingly as he suddenly realized how simple it all was. "But you were going to skim some of it for you and Andrew. A little nest egg as you transferred the money back into legitimate accounts. That's why the letters of intent are so vague. If done discreetly and slowly, you could have written off millions as operating expenses or created a dummy environmental corporation and deposited some of the funds there. I suppose living a double life is a bit dangerous, so you were hedging your bets. Does Andrew know about this?"

"No," Jack said, tapping his index finger nervously on the edge of his desk. "Are you going to tell him?"

Brett shook his head. "Just be in my office on Thursday morning. As long as you give my firm what it wants, I'm not interested in your personal life."

"What about my father?"

"Once the wheels are in motion and the feds are off your back—and you'll have *me* to thank for that—he'll be none the wiser. You'll be in the clear, and dear old dad in Houston will continue to think you're the salt of the earth."

Jack simply nodded.

"Just remember that I'll always be watching you," Brett said. "As long as the consortium can use the technology, Richard is happy. And when Richard's happy, so am I."

Brett left the office feeling exhilarated. He hadn't lost his touch.

• • •

Brett arrived at Davis, Konen and Wright an hour later. He wasn't expecting to see Janice Conlon sitting in his desk chair when he opened the door to his office. He stood perfectly still, his mouth open. The tall blue-eyed blond stared back at him.

"What are you doing here?" Brett asked. "I mean, San Francisco and the asbestos case and ..."

"It's nice to see you too, Brett," Janice said, folding her arms and staring at her lover. "Your warmth is overwhelming. No wonder Dana got fed up with you."

"Uh, I'm sorry. It's just that, well, I've been busy all morning, and my secretary didn't tell me you were here." Brett had no vestiges of the confidence he'd displayed at Jack Hartlen's office.

"Because she doesn't know I'm here. I waited until she was away from her desk and let myself in."

"Come on," Brett said, approaching his desk. "I've missed you. How about a more proper greeting?"

"Not just yet," Janice said coolly. "Why didn't you tell me it was Dana's birthday when we spoke on the phone the other day?"

"Birthday? Why should I?"

"Listen, Brett, I always had access to your office, so I know where you keep things." Janice produced several stacks of papers from a desk drawer. "You had a private investigator look into Dana's comings and goings. What am I to make of that? Don't tell me that you're longing to know about that boring little life of hers."

Brett sighed and raised both arms in the air like a frustrated, innocent man. "I just wanted to make sure she wasn't asking for anything else," Brett lied. "She pretty much dictated all the terms of the separation, so I thought it prudent to see what she's been up to. And to make sure she wasn't spreading any gossip about you and me."

"I see she's going out with a man by the name of Mark Senger." Janice looked up at Brett, searching his expression for the slightest hitch. "Does that bother you? Make you jealous?"

"Absolutely not. It's just a detail that my investigator turned up."

Janice remained silent as she looked through another sheaf of papers. "And why didn't you ever tell me that you've been blackmailing Jack Hartlen?"

"To protect you! I can't imagine that you'd disapprove of my methods, but I didn't want to risk getting you involved in case anything went wrong."

Janice frowned and shook her head. "I thought we were partners, Brett. Both in and out of bed. I thought you trusted me, but maybe I've been naïve."

"What are you accusing me of?"

"It appears you have agendas you're not telling me about, one of which might be getting your darling little figurine wife back."

Brett backed up several steps. "No, no, no. I'm being honest with you. I just wanted to keep Dana from seeking further financial gain from the divorce. And to protect you. Nothing more."

"I'll see you at my apartment," Janice said, rising to leave. She made no attempt to hug or kiss Brett, who simply watched her leave the office.

Brett slumped in the chair Janice had vacated, reminding himself that she was sharp and not to be underestimated.

Looking into Dana's life had been a miscalculation. As for not telling Janice about his blackmail scheme, he'd done it to protect himself, not her.

He would take her out to dinner when he got home. She now knew about his vice-like grip on Jack, so he would tell her everything about what had been happening with Hartlen Response and make her feel a part of his triumph. If he succeeded in doing so, the evening might yet end on a very pleasant note.

Chapter Seventeen

Dana heard from Mark throughout the weekend between his activities with Amanda, which included a spur-of-the-moment decision to drive to Muttontown for a lesson with her riding instructor. The timing of his daughter's visit wasn't ideal, but even if Dana had been dating Mark for months, she knew they would still want private time when Amanda was home from college. Dana looked forward to joining them for dinners, however, and perhaps for rides on the trails in Central Park. She was excited about meeting Amanda, for whom she already had a special place in her heart.

The rest of the weekend was relaxing and non-eventful: Saturday errands, a run in the park, a quiet evening of reading and phone calls, Sunday Mass, and brunch with volunteers from the Costume Institute. Through it all, she enjoyed thoughts of Mark and the changes he was bringing to her life. Dana was again reminded that the course of a life can be altered radically and quickly, only this new state of affairs was one she welcomed. Mark was Jewish, twelve years older than she, and the father of a college-age daughter. How in the world could they fit in each others' lives? Surprisingly, Dana found that she wasn't concerned. Maybe Mark didn't check all the boxes as perfectly as Brett had, but she was no longer interested in a scripted life. She would leave her future to Fate, trusting her instincts to know what she needed to be happy and fulfilled.

She suspected that her family and friends would be surprised by her unconventional choice of Mark, and her mother, most of all, would have plenty to say about it. But Dana knew that, above all, they loved her and wanted her to be happy. Her father would be the one to remind them that the latter was what truly mattered. In fact, Dana couldn't wait to introduce her parents to Mark. She knew that he and Virginia would enjoy each other's quick wit and, in spite of her mother's concern about her seriously dating a Jewish man, Virginia would soon be challenging him to a game of mah-jongg, reminding him that he better be good to her *shaineh maidel*. Dana hadn't expected her heart to be awakened so quickly after the separation, although the impending divorce wasn't necessarily the only reason for her openness to a relationship. For at least a year she'd been going through the motions of married life. Presently, her only thought was of Mark and of the next time she would see him.

Dana's optimistic mood was still in evidence as she entered her office at B. Altman on Monday morning. After pouring herself a cup of coffee, she'd immediately asked Helen's secretary if she could have a few moments with B. Altman's feisty divisional manager. She would normally have been nervous to make a major request of Helen so soon after being summarily rebuffed, but she was actually eager to pitch Mark's idea for a private label, an idea that might yet save the in-store boutique. There was no point in being afraid of presenting a solid business model that Dawn and Ira would have applauded in an instant.

Dana entered Helen's office on the fifth floor at ten o'clock. As was so often the case, Helen looked up briefly to acknowledge Dana's presence and then returned her attention to the mountain of papers on her desk.

"I'd like to talk with you about umbrellas for a moment," Dana said, sliding into the chair across from Helen. She thought the unusual statement was a better strategy than launching directly into her pitch, and it worked better than she'd hoped.

Helen removed her glasses and looked at Dana. Helen seemed relieved that the word "boutique" hadn't been uttered and appeared open to hearing about accessories. "Okay, what miracles are you going to work with umbrellas?"

"I was at the Mespo Umbrella Company the other day," Dana began, "and an advertisement for The Decoy Shop in Connecticut caught my eye. It occurred to me that we could replace those boring umbrella handles with wooden duck heads. I suppose it's a small change in the larger scheme of things, but I think they would be unique and fun and could be displayed as novelty items in other departments. They'd be good impulse gifts."

"I like it," Helen said, nodding. "What's involved in making this happen?" Her curiosity had obviously been piqued.

"Marvin at Mespo contacted The Decoy Shop and will have samples for me in a week, as well as nylon fabrics in taupe, hunter green, and brown plaid."

"Good work. Simple enough."

"It is. We could market them as B. Altman exclusives. The umbrellas would carry our logo. It's that simple."

Helen tapped her pencil on the desk for a moment and raised her eyebrows. "Cute idea. Let me know when the samples arrive."

"I will," Dana said, beaming. "Also ... " Dana paused before beginning her description of the much grander idea she and Mark had hatched.

"Is there something else?" Helen asked.

"As a matter of fact, yes. Speaking of private labels, did you know that Brooks Brothers is opening a women's department with totally exclusive merchandise? They're even coloring the fabric patterns for shirts they're designing. Imagine—even the shirts! They want a tailored Brooks Brothers look for women, and the only way to achieve that is to make the clothes themselves. It's brilliant!"

Dana paused to gauge Helen's reaction thus far.

"What's the point you're trying to make?" Helen asked warily. "I sense that this is leading somewhere."

"It dawned on me that we could do the very same thing. In fact, the British separates boutique would be the perfect place to market our private label. It's no different from the umbrellas. We design the samples, buy the fabrics and trims, and have the garments manufactured. Since Senger Display hasn't dismantled the frame for the Nantucket boutique, they could quickly and easily insert the appropriate fixtures and cabinets." Dana put her palms together and looked intently at her boss. "I know you didn't like the idea of an in-store boutique, and I respect that, but if we can sell our own private line, I think it's an idea worth reconsidering. The boutique would give the private label a backdrop and provide a good marketing tool."

Surprisingly, Helen didn't look frustrated, nor did she become irritated with Dana, who quietly studied Helen's features.

"I suppose the idea is not completely without merit," Helen sighed, "but where would we get the fabrics? Who would design, manufacture, and price the line? I'm afraid it's all a bit too involved for me. You've given me an idea without any specifics as to how we could implement it."

"But we could work out the details, Helen. I'll handle it all. I can do this! A private B. Altman line would lend enormous prestige to the store. Look at Peck & Peck. Their success was built exclusively on its private label."

"Why are you always trying to reinvent the wheel, Dana?" Helen said, growing impatient. "Even if you could answer every one of my questions, what's the point in going to so much trouble?"

"Because the store—"

"Let me finish," Helen interrupted. "B. Altman already carries all of the top designer lines. Just look at the excitement being generated by Donna Karan's new sportswear collection. Everything we need is already hanging in the showrooms on Seventh Avenue."

Dana had come this far, so she attempted to drive home her point.

"Helen, all of the major department stores carry the very same designers as we do. With an exclusive line, however, we could create our own excitement in a way that could never happen simply by offering someone else's name, no matter how well known it might be. Our own line of clothing would almost certainly create a buzz, especially if it's sold in the boutique. It's a win-win situation."

Helen's patience was now clearly wearing thin. "Dana, even if I were inclined to let you try this, which I'm not, it would take you away from your regular duties. You're an accessories buyer for the junior department, not a one-woman act. Your idea entails entirely too much work. Designers? Manufacturers? Brooks Brothers has been manufacturing exclusive men's clothing for years, so it's no wonder they're using the men's factories. But I'm not going to ask B. Altman's menswear manufacturers to make room on their cutting tables for women's clothing! Dana, I can't believe I'm having this conversation.

The whole idea is absurd. I wish you could keep your feet on the ground for more than a week."

"Could I at least gather some sample fabrics and look for manufacturers on my own time?"

"Absolutely not. We don't need our own line of clothing. And certainly not an in-store boutique, which is a concept I'm not going to keep revisiting. I don't want to hear about this ever again. If you want to proceed with the umbrellas, fine. But that's as far as it goes. Do we understand each other?"

Dana smiled. "Perfectly, Helen. Thanks for your time."

In the hallway, Dana didn't experience the emotional downward spiral that was all too common after leaving Helen's office. It was par for the course and, by now, Dana had grown toughened to Helen's abusive responses. Helen was certainly entitled to her opinion after many successful years in the industry, but her harsh tone and deaf ear were inappropriate. Still, unlike five months earlier, the dressing-down rolled off Dana's back. More than ever, she was determined to carry private label separates in The British Shop. Mark had indicated that he might know people in the industry who would be willing to help, although he hadn't provided any specifics. But Dana knew Mark well enough to understand that he wouldn't have floated the idea of a private label without having some way of realizing its implementation.

Dana, therefore, remained optimistic. She'd gone around Helen before, and she was prepared to do so again. Helen didn't have the final word on all matters in the store, and Dana was prepared to talk to others on the fifth floor when her plan was in place.

A B. Altman line of classic women's separates? It would definitely fly. Sold from a British-toned, wood-paneled in-store boutique? Even better. The idea wasn't dead yet.

• • •

Dana proceeded to her office, closed the door, and called Mark right away. She related Helen's response, which they both found humorous more than troubling.

"I didn't want to share you with anyone tonight," Mark said, "but I've invited friends to join us for dinner. Irwin's wife is in town, and they were planning to have dinner before driving back to their home in Cedarhurst. I have to run into a meeting now, but why don't you pack up Wills and come for a sleepover? Can you be ready at five thirty?"

"I'll be ready," Dana laughed.

"Good. I'll see you then. We'll have time to drop Wills and your things at my apartment before meeting the Bauers at Carrousel. Miss you."

"Miss you, too. Bye."

Helen wasn't on board with the boutique, at least not yet, but for Dana, the day—indeed, her life—was shaping up just fine. Her spirits were high, and she moved on to a meeting of buyers in the executive conference room.

Chapter Eighteen

As soon as Patti heard Jack's key in the lock of the front door of their apartment, she poured herself a glass of wine and bourbon on the rocks for Jack. Jack entered, dropped his briefcase by the door, and kissed his wife on the cheek. Patti recalled how, back in Houston, Jack had always greeted her with a warm smile every evening and kissed her on the lips. She handed him the glass of bourbon and slipped her arm around his waist.

Jack had seemed so much happier in Texas, and she continued to believe that, at least in part, his mood might be caused by the abrupt change in their surroundings. The weather was cold in New York City, and sunlight was absent for days at a time. It was a stark contrast from the long, warm days in Houston.

"How was work?" she asked as she led Jack into the living room, where they both sat on a couch facing a large window that offered sweeping East River views. The lights of distant buildings were beginning to wink on against the twilight sky.

"Long," he said, leaning his head back and closing his eyes.

That was something else that bothered Patti. Jack now spoke little, and when he did, it was often in short phrases or sometimes just a word or two.

Patti placed her right hand on Jack's left shoulder and gently massaged it. His muscles tensed immediately, and he leaned away from her after less than a minute. Patti retained her composure, but pulling away from her physically had also become a frequent habit of late.

"I'm preparing a special dinner," she announced, motioning to the candlelit table in the adjoining dining room. "Your favorite. Prime rib."

Jack sat up straight and opened his eyes. He was on the verge of saying, "Thanks, but I'd rather make it an early evening and turn in after a quick bite." Thinking better of it, he smiled weakly. "That sounds great. I'm really hungry."

Patti took a deep breath. Why was she so nervous about talking with Jack? Shouldn't she be able to say anything to him? It felt as if she'd made an appointment to speak with her own husband.

"Jack, remember when I told you this morning that I wanted to talk about something when you got home?"

"Huh? Oh—yes, but can it wait 'til after dinner?"

"No, Jack. You already look like you're falling asleep, and I don't want to wait. This has been weighing heavily on me for weeks."

Jack furrowed his brow. "Is everything okay? I mean, you're not sick, are you?"

"I'm fine," Patti said. "Actually, it's you I'm worried about. You come home late on most nights, and you're usually exhausted. We hardly talk anymore, and you just don't seem happy. What's wrong, Jack? Please tell me what's going on."

Jack was keenly aware of how observant his wife was. In point of fact, he'd known that this conversation was coming sooner or later, so he braced himself, already knowing how he was going to answer Patti's every question.

"It's the company," he replied. "Opening this office has been so draining."

Patti's nervousness had dissipated. She was suddenly annoyed, and she shook her head slowly as she spoke with candor and directness. "You've been telling me that for months now. I know the move has been difficult, but we've been living here since January, and your father recently told me that your office is humming as smoothly as a Rolls Royce. I think you had more pressure before we moved—when you were traveling every week between Houston and New York—but that never made you sullen and withdrawn. Something's different." Patti looked directly at her husband. "You're changing right before my eyes. You're hiding something, and I want to know what it is. If you can't give me a plausible reason for the change that's come over you, then frankly I think you need to see a doctor and get a checkup."

Jack sat up straight and faced Patti. His serious demeanor appeared genuine. "I'm really sorry, honey. I guess I haven't been much of a husband lately. That's why I've been thinking … " Jack paused, as if searching for a way to deliver his next words. "Thinking that maybe you should go back to Houston for a few months. Connect with your friends again. I'm sure they could use your help with the summer zoo ball."

"What? You've got to be kidding, Jack. The very idea is ludicrous!"

"Hear me out," he said. "The production of our equipment is being held up by several suppliers around the world. They're really dragging their feet. How can Hartlen Response possibly respond rapidly to an oil spill when we can't even manufacture our equipment? I don't want to be a burden on you. When production is back on track, you could return to a more enthusiastic spouse."

Patti was speechless for several seconds, stuck in disbelief. "Why didn't you tell me about the suppliers? You've always kept me informed about what's going on in the company.

We've never had any secrets from each another, just like Ralph and Sandy. And besides, I have a job, or have you forgotten that I work at the Altman Foundation? You never even bother to ask me how things are going, by the way, or how *my* day has gone. I just can't quit and say I'm going back to Houston. What am I supposed to tell them? That my husband is busy and making me take a sabbatical?"

"No, Patti. You've got it all wrong. I'm just thinking about you. I want you to be happy."

"I'll be happy when I get my husband back.," Patti said tersely as she stood. "I'm going to get dinner ready."

Jack sighed and sipped his bourbon. "I'm sorry, honey. It was a stupid suggestion. I can't wait to tear into the prime rib."

Patti, however, was not in the mood for conversation. They ate in silence, after which Patti washed the dishes, holding back tears. When she finished, she walked into the den and saw Jack asleep in front of the television.

She turned out the lights and walked down the hall to their bedroom, but she couldn't sustain her anger at Jack even though she felt like screaming. Something was definitely wrong—that much was certain—but she loved him despite the mysterious and eccentric behavior he'd displayed since moving to New York. Just as importantly, she knew that he loved her. She had no intention of going back to Houston. The fact that Jack would propose such an idea was proof that something was clouding his reasoning. It was clear that he needed help and, for now, her own needs had to be put aside. She would stand by her husband and see him through whatever was troubling him.

She only hoped that his difficulties would resolve quickly. Living in the dark was becoming harder by the day.

Chapter Nineteen

Mark knocked on the door of 8 Sniffen Court at a little after five. "One of your neighbors was opening the gate and thought I had a trustworthy face. I'm running a bit early."

"Early is good, but give me a few more minutes," Dana said, admitting Mark into the carriage house. "I just got home and I'm still getting Wills' things together."

Mark took Dana into his arms and gave her a long, passionate kiss. "Okay," he said, "but we have to keep our priorities straight. It was a long weekend, and I'm glad you're coming home with me." He petted Wills, who was demanding his attention. "And you, too, little fella. We have a date in the park early tomorrow morning." He turned back to Dana. "Can I help with his things?"

"You can clean his water bowl in the kitchen and put it into the canvas bag on the counter. His dry food is in the pantry, and his leash and toys are already packed. I'll be upstairs getting the rest of my things together. Don't worry. I travel light."

"The true sign of an adventurer," Mark said.

Fifteen minutes later, they were in a cab headed to the Upper West Side.

• • •

Dana entered Mark's apartment and was surprised by its sleek, imposing style. The expansive, loft-like space, unusual in a pre-war building, was created by removing a wall between the living and dining rooms, displaying five bare casement windows that framed breathtaking views of Central Park. The rich wood floors were uncarpeted, and the white walls were adorned with abstract Japanese art. There was a brown suede sofa, two tan leather Bauhaus chairs, and an original marble fireplace. Uncluttered teak tables displayed art books, and the bedroom wing was lined with bookcases.

"What are you thinking?" Mark asked as he observed Dana's expression. "That we're chalk and cheese, as the Brits like to say?"

"Did you bring in the Brits just to make me feel at home?" Dana asked as she put her arms around Mark.

"I'll hang the Union Jack if you stay all week."

"You won't have to do that," Dana laughed. "I rather like your cool moderne style. And your home is appealing, too. Actually, I find it very peaceful."

"Thank you, but I think you'll bring the warmth that's been missing," Mark said as he kissed her again.

"I'm glad I'm here," Dana said, smiling and giving him a hug.

"I'll get Wills some dinner," Mark said, "while you hang up your clothes. Then we better get going. Carrousel is cross-town on Third Avenue at seventy-fifth.

"Welcome, Mark!" Irwin Bauer said, standing up at his table in the center of the bistro. "My wife Susan is running late, but why don't we order a bottle of wine while we wait. I'm sure she won't be long."

"Irwin, this is Dana McGarry. Dana, Irwin Bauer."

Irwin extended his hand before sitting again. "It's my pleasure," he said. "Mark has told me so many things about you, all of them good, by the way."

"I simply tell the truth," Mark said.

Irwin was forty-two years old and had been a lifelong friend of Mark's as well as a neighbor while growing up on Central Park West. Their families had attended the same temple and they'd been classmates at Bronx High School of Science. After graduation Mark attended the Wharton School while Irwin studied at Syracuse. Both joined their fathers' self-made businesses and had remained close throughout the years.

"My wife Susan drove in today for a board meeting," Irwin said. "I usually take the train since it's much faster, but this worked out perfectly. We decided this morning not to fight the rush hour traffic and were planning to stay in town for dinner. In fact, I was going to give Mark a call to join us, but he beat me to it."

The waiter brought a bottle of chardonnay to the table and poured a sample into Irwin's glass. "Very nice," Irwin said, motioning for the waiter to pour a glass for everyone.

"Irwin's wife is a college admissions consultant," Mark explained.

"What an interesting and rewarding career," Dana said, "but it can't be an easy one. I'm sure it entails much more than just helping students navigate the complex application process."

"Indeed it does," Irwin laughed. "The moms and dads need counseling first so that they have realistic expectations. Susan claims it's an art more than an exact science—matching people and their goals with the right college or university. We live in Cedarhurst, and Susan has been able to build a thriving practice in the surrounding Five Towns, which was convenient while the children were growing up."

"I grew up on Long Island, too." Dana said. "In Hewlett Harbor, not far from you."

"Are you related to Dan McGarry? I took the train with him for years before he moved to Connecticut."

"No relation. My maiden name is Martignetti."

"Really!" Irwin said. "I would have never guessed!"

"It's a long story—and a bit complicated" Mark said. "Actually, Dana acts British but thinks Yiddish."

"Is that because of your career in the garment center?" Irwin teased.

"Everyone in New York and Long Island, for that matter, is a little Jewish," Dana said. "But my mother did find Jewish origins on her father's side when she visited his town in Italy a few years ago."

"Well, there's always been a closeness between the Italians and the Jews," Irwin said, "and it looks like it's working well for the both of you. From what I'm hearing, you two have a lot in common."

"Surprisingly, we do," Dana said, smiling at Mark. "But we're pushing the envelope and—"

"A common practice of Mark's," Irwin said.

"Mark's convinced me it's time for a new challenge, and I'm starting riding lessons at Claremont. I just want to be good enough to meander with him in the park."

"Between Claremont and Mark, you'll be show jumping with Amanda before you know it! But it seems you're balancing another challenge at B. Altman. Mark told me that your idea for a private label collection is falling on deaf ears."

"I filled Irwin in this morning on what we talked about over the weekend," Mark said. "Including the in-store boutique."

"My divisional manager isn't wildly enthusiastic about any of it," Dana said, sipping her chardonnay. "She dismissed it as being too complicated. In a way, I'm blaming myself for not being better prepared before I presented a completely new concept to her. I didn't have a manufacturer lined up, and I couldn't answer her basic questions."

Mark and Irwin once again exchanged knowing glances.

"Allow me to reintroduce myself," Irwin said with a mischievous smile. "I'm Irwin Bauer, and my company has been manufacturing menswear for forty years. I think your idea is fantastic."

Dana's jaw dropped. "Mark, you're amazing! When you think of an idea, it's already done! I can't believe this!"

"Let me tell you why Mark was able to pique my interest so quickly," Irwin continued. "Aside from the fact that we've been friends forever and I'm somewhat obliged to listen to him."

Both men laughed heartily.

"I told you I knew someone who might be willing to help, didn't I?" Mark said.

"You did," Dana said, "but I thought we might be talking weeks before you could line anything up. It's only been two days."

"I'll be candid," Irwin resumed. "I'm currently overstocked with fabric. Gray flannel, tweeds—even camel hair since orders were so short last year. With men running around casually dressed with epaulettes and unconstructed jackets, my business isn't what it should be. So when Mark called me this morning and told me about your idea, I thought why waste the fabric."

"What do think about manufacturing ladieswear?" Dana said. "Is that something you'd be interested in?"

Irwin leaned forward. "I hear you have a closet-full of Jaeger clothing, Dana. Bring in your favorites and let's see what we can do. My head tailor is a master fitter and has a good eye. We'll tweak the patterns any way you want. Who knows? B. Altman may become my best account."

Dana's face lit up with unexpected enthusiasm. "I can't tell you how flattered I am that you're willing to entertain my—I mean *our*—idea," Dana said, acknowledging Mark's encouragement. "I've got to be honest, though. Getting into B. Altman might be an uphill battle."

Irwin simply smiled. "Mark seems to have the utmost faith in you, my dear. Having faith in someone or something—that means everything to me, both in business and friendship."

Dana felt as if she were falling for Mark all over again.

"Mr. Senger here is of the opinion that most uphill battles can be won," Dana said. "And we have one more chance to get it through. I can present the entire concept to someone on the executive level who I think will be very receptive to it, especially since I'm prepared to give him the name of an established manufacturer."

"Excellent!" Irwin beamed. "This is just the thing to jump-start a stagnant business. I trust Mark's instincts. Always have. But now that I've met you, I also trust yours. I think the British spin you put on this takes it over the top. Boutiques are popping up everywhere, and this is an innovative way for a department store to compete. If you ask me, it would be the perfect platform."

"I've felt that from the beginning," Dana said, hoping she wouldn't wake up and discover she'd been dreaming. I was able to visualize every detail as soon as I stepped into Jaeger."

"I can tell that from your enthusiasm," Irwin said, "but why don't we put business aside for a moment, at least until Susan gets here since she'll want to hear all about it. I'd like to propose a toast."

Irwin ordered a bottle of champagne, which arrived at the table five minutes later. Raising his glass, he proclaimed, "To a happy and profitable business venture!"

Mark leaned over and kissed Dana on the lips. "I told you this was worth pursuing."

"And you were right," Dana admitted.

"Am I interrupting anything?" asked a female voice.

"Susan!" Irwin said, standing. "How are you, honey? Here, have a seat and join the celebration."

"Susan, good to see you," Mark said as he stood and leaned over to kiss her hello.

"You, too," Susan said as she looked at Mark and Dana, whose kiss had clearly caught her off guard. "What are we celebrating?" she asked, sitting next to Irwin.

"Susan," Irwin began, "this is Dana McGarry. Dana's a buyer at B. Altman. Let me give you the short version. She and Mark have had nothing less than a brainstorm. I'm going to manufacture an exclusive line of tailored womenswear for B. Altman. The private label merchandise will be sold in a stand-alone boutique in the store. Here, honey," Irwin said as he handed Susan a glass of champagne. "You're just in time for the toast."

Susan was speechless. Smartly dressed in a navy pantsuit, she was thirty-nine, a tall woman with short brown hair, little makeup, and a medium frame. She continued to look around the table, trying to find the right words.

"When did all this happen?" Susan asked. She glanced at Mark and Dana. "You'll have to excuse me. This is the first I'm hearing about any of this. And I'm happy to meet you, Dana. Sorry I ran so late."

"It all came up quite suddenly," Irwin explained. "Mark and I spoke this morning, which is when he told me what he and Dana wanted to do. Dana and I have been talking shop in the last half hour, and I think this is how I can pump some energy back into the business. You're aware of how our sales have been steadily down for the last three quarters."

"Yes, of course," Susan said, "but ladieswear?"

"I'm a garment manufacturer and I'm overloaded with fabrics," Irwin countered.

"I know," Susan said, "but who will design the line?"

Mark spoke up quickly. "That's the beauty of it all since—"

"I'm going to design it," Dana interrupted, unable to contain herself. "I've spent quite a bit of time in England during the past eight years, and my wardrobe was built around Jaeger sportswear. We're going to use my clothing for patterns."

"It sounds very intriguing," Susan said, sipping from her fluted champagne glass. "But didn't you say something about a boutique, Irwin?"

"I certainly did."

"It's a concept I came up with for an accessory line I was buying," Dana said, jumping in once again. "I was going to call it Nantucket. Mark already started the build-out. This idea, however, has greater marketing potential, and it's in keeping with today's popular separates look for the active career woman. We'll also carry some outerwear, as well as wool and cashmere sweaters, and all of it will have a distinctive British character."

Susan smiled. "You three have my head swimming! Jaeger, boutiques, ladieswear, private labels." She paused and looked at her husband before speaking again. "I love the enthusiasm here at the table, but isn't this all a bit too ambitious, Irwin?"

"Mark's already begun the boutique," Irwin said. "He'll finish it once B. Altman gives its approval."

Susan swallowed her champagne quickly and coughed. "Oh my goodness—please excuse me. You caught me off guard again. Irwin, you don't even have B. Altman's approval yet and the boutique isn't finished? How can you commit to something at this early stage?"

"I have the ear of our executive vice president," Dana said. "I think he'll jump at the chance. A private label is cost effective, giving the store a higher mark-up."

"Think?" Susan said.

"Dana has done some amazing things at the store," Mark interjected, "and she's overcome some formidable obstacles in the process. I have every confidence that she'll be able to sell the whole concept."

Irwin laughed. "So do I. I'm getting the impression that she's intrepid at both work and play. Mark's even thrown down the gauntlet on riding, and Dana's picked it up. She's going to start lessons at Claremont."

"That's wonderful, Dana," Susan said. "That's how Amanda started. I'm sure Mark's told you she's a show jumper. Mark, is Amanda still working with the trainer in Muttontown?"

"Yes she is," Mark replied. "Pepsi is still boarded at Judd's. In fact, she's going straight to Muttontown when exams are over. She'll be there all summer, preparing, for a competition in August. This is her first year in the adult division. "

"Well, I wish you all the best," Susan told Dana. "I assume you live in the city?"

"I do. In Murray Hill, which is just a four-block walk to B. Altman."

"Dana's a Long Island girl, Susan," Mark said. "Her parents have a home on Macy Channel."

"Oh, have you met them?" Susan asked.

"Not yet, but I'm looking forward to it. Dana's mother is a champion mah-jongg player. I may take on the challenge."

"Did you go to Temple Beth El?" Susan asked.

Dana, Mark, and Irwin laughed.

"No," Dana answered. "I'm Catholic, but my mother's dear Jewish friends taught her to play mah-jongg years ago. She loves the game and is really good."

"That's interesting," Susan dryly said. "I guess you met at B. Altman? Okay, tell me what's going on. I feel a little romance in the air, Mr. Mark."

"Well, Ms. Susan, as a matter of fact there is," Mark said. "Dana and I have known each other for about four years, and we've worked together on a few projects at the store, and here we are."

"So why did it take so long? Why now?" Susan pressed on.

Dana decided to let Mark respond to the line of questioning.

"Because now we're both available," Mark said. "As they say, timing is everything."

"Do you have children?" Susan asked, hoping to find out a little more about Dana's prior relationships.

"No, we didn't have children," Dana answered softly, starting to resent the inquisition, thinking Susan might have the impression that an affair with Mark broke up her marriage.

"There's plenty of time for that," Irwin quickly added.

"Well, Dana, it sounds like you're focused on a career right now anyway. It's not easy doing both, especially in a corporate environment. I was lucky that my business had flexible hours and was close to home."

"You must have worked hard to make it happen," Dana said. "Nothing comes easily."

"Some things do," Mark said, drawing close to Dana, knowing that Susan was making her feel uncomfortable. Changing the subject, he said, "I not only have a new love in my life, but also a new pet. Wills."

"Wills?" Susan asked.

"Yes. Dana's Cavalier King Charles Spaniel. I'm going to cause quite a stir in the park tomorrow morning when we run into Rex's buddies."

Susan, who was still good friends with Mark's ex-wife Marsha, suddenly fell silent. She didn't have all the answers, but she knew Mark well enough to know that he wouldn't be spending this much time with Dana or exerting so much effort to propel her career forward if he didn't deeply care for her. She and her dog were already spending nights in his apartment, and she wondered if he'd considered how Amanda would react. As Irwin's childhood friend, she knew Mark as well as she knew her husband, and unlike the other women he'd dated since his marriage ended, he was clearly enjoying this relationship and wasn't shy about letting them know. They were living in a romantic bubble, oblivious to real-time challenges in the life of a forty-two-year-old man. Susan was curious to see how Dana would react to such issues and if Mark would be able to quickly work his magic on her, just as he'd done by soliciting Irwin to advance her career at B. Altman.

As for the business partnership that everyone was excited about, she would discuss it with Irwin later. She'd always had confidence in Mark's business acumen, but perhaps Irwin was jumping at this a little too fast given the recent downturn at Bauer & Sons . Worst of all, everything seemed to hinge on Dana's ideas, and she barely knew the woman seated next to Mark. She couldn't have been more than twenty-eight, thirty tops. Susan knew virtually nothing about Dana's own business experience. The whole enterprise sounded like something that was being cobbled together at the last minute.

She turned over these thoughts during dinner. Irwin was a shrewd businessman, although he tended to be spontaneous and gregarious. Susan was more cautious—more analytical and reserved—especially in the presence of an unknown like Dana McGarry who, to her way of thinking, was a little too outspoken when she wanted to get her way. She had no hesitation about jumping right into the conversation when other people seemed ready to speak. Were it not for the possible business venture with her husband and her tight hold on Mark, Susan wouldn't doubt Dana's motivations and, under different circumstances, could imagine a casual friendship. But considering how close Dana was getting to her life, Susan was concerned that what you saw was not necessarily what you got, and the sweet demeanor that caught Mark's eye might be skin deep.

The evening ended with coffee and dessert.

"We'll be in touch very soon," Mark told Irwin.

Everyone stood, and Susan hugged both Mark and Dana warmly. "It was a pleasure to meet you," she said. "And please forgive my endless questions. When I first arrived, I had no idea what was going on. When Irwin starts talking, sometimes there's no stopping him if he's excited about something. I enjoyed meeting you. Good luck with your riding. "

"Thank you, Susan. I look forward to seeing you again very soon."

The two couples parted, and Mark and Dana headed back to his apartment.

Dana and Mark took Wills out for his final walk, something else that Dana loved about Mark: sharing small moments together. When they returned to the apartment, they discussed dinner with the Bauers.

"Irwin is such a delightful man," Dana said. "Brimming with enthusiasm."

"And best of all, he loves your idea."

"I can hardly believe this is happening. Do you really think everything is going to fall into place?"

"We'll know soon enough, but for now, I'm optimistic."

"But what about Susan? She was pleasant, but did you notice how she scrutinized me? I felt a bit uncomfortable."

"Susan has been a good friend for many years. But she's overly protective and forgets that even my mother can't influence my decisions any longer. You know, couples don't like it when their friends separate. If you haven't noticed, you will. And Susan, like Amanda, for that matter, wants things as they were. In addition, you're very different from Marsha, so she's trying to figure that out, too. She was caught off guard tonight in more ways than one."

"Just like you continually catch me off guard," Dana said as Mark wrapped his arms around her in the bedroom. "Starting with the disco party all the way through the movies, riding, and a way to keep the boutique."

"Any complaints?"

"Not a single one," Dana said.

They kissed, and there was no more conversation about business or dinner as Mark led Dana to bed.

Chapter Twenty

Johnny made his daily call to Dana on Monday afternoon. He was aware that Dana knew that he, like her mother, was in reality still checking up on her, and he thought that she tolerated their intrusions in her busy schedule with patience and good spirits. She'd sounded more rushed and distracted in the past week, however, although Johnny didn't sense irritation. Quite to the contrary, Dana sounded upbeat and energized, although lately she'd kept the conversations shorter than usual. Sometimes she wasn't available and failed to return his calls altogether, which was out of character for his longtime friend. On Monday afternoon, their call was interrupted when Helen stopped into Dana's office just as Johnny was about to invite Dana to a meeting at the House of Cirone. Since their discussion at her parents' home, Dana hadn't asked Johnny anything about his business, nor had she mentioned the offer to join them. Johnny was always careful to avoid bringing the subject up so as not to put pressure on her, but he was beginning to suspect that she was avoiding the issue or, worse yet, had decided not to accept the position as fashion director.

Returning home from work at nine o'clock, Johnny immediately followed up with his idea to test Dana's level of interest in joining his family's business. He decided to invite her to attend a breakfast meeting the next morning with him, Uncle

John, and the design team to review the initial sketches for the Spring '76 line. Additionally, they would study the latest reports from the European shows, a subtle reminder to Dana that her attendance twice a year would be an integral part of her job and a perk that he knew she would love. If she were seriously considering joining the company, wouldn't she want to observe the creative process from its inception? He didn't think that such an invitation would be construed as pressure.

He called but there was no answer. He tried watching television for thirty minutes, but he was too distracted, so he called Virginia. She related how she'd spoken with Dana late that afternoon. She, too, had noticed that Dana seemed to be in a hurry. In fact, Dana had said that she had to finish up and get home before five so that she could get changed, although she hadn't specified where she was going.

"You don't think anything's wrong, do you?" Virginia asked.

"No, nothing like that," Johnny replied. "I just wanted to ask her to join us at a breakfast meeting in the morning. We're starting to plan next spring's collection, and I thought the creative session would appeal to her. I guess she's out. No cause for worry."

"So she hasn't given you or John an answer yet?" Virginia said.

"Not yet. I'm still hopeful though. I just don't want to force her into making a premature decision. If I rush her, she'd probably be inclined to say no."

Virginia sighed. "You're probably right, but I think it's a dream job for her. I know you and John agree. I can't imagine what could be holding her back. I think meeting with the creative team might be the perfect nudge."

"I'll let you know if she's able to attend," Johnny said. "Dad and I would love to get her input as soon as possible."

"Thank you, Johnny. Give my best to your father."

Johnny called Phoebe next, asking if she knew Dana's whereabouts. Phoebe was in the middle of a forty-eight hour shift at the hospital and said she hadn't heard from Dana for several days.

Holding the receiver, Johnny exhaled and tapped his finger on the cradle of the plastic beige telephone. He tried Dana again at eleven, but there was still no answer.

He decided to call Andrew. Andrew was a good friend, and if Dana had made plans for dinner or a late night, Andrew would know what they were. They worked together closely, and he was her confidante in matters both personal and professional.

"Hello?" Andrew said.

"It's Johnny Cirone, Andrew. I was wondering if you knew where Dana was. I've been trying to get in touch with her all evening, but she's not at home. I tried calling her mother, but she doesn't know where she is either."

"Sounds rather important. Is it an emergency of some kind?"

"No, nothing like that. It can keep."

"Hmm, let's see. I know she had dinner plans with Mark Senger, but I'm not sure where they went."

"Thanks, Andrew. Hope I didn't disturb you."

"Not to worry. I'm a night owl. Take care."

It was a Monday night, and restaurants were usually closed by ten thirty. Surely Dana was at home and already in bed. Since he was calling to invite her to an early meeting, she wouldn't think he was checking up on her. There was still no answer, and the same held true at twelve thirty and one.

Johnny dropped the receiver onto the cradle and then froze. He opened his eyes wide, as if experiencing a revelation. "She's not going home tonight," he said to himself. "She's staying at Mark's. I can't believe it." He decided to call Dana at seven in the morning, thinking she may have returned home to get dressed.

It was time for bed, and the last words he uttered as he turned off the light were "Mark Senger? That's not what I would have guessed. Not at all."

• • •

Johnny wasn't surprised when he couldn't reach Dana at home the next morning. Later, he stepped away from the breakfast meeting and called her at the store to arrange a lunch date at one o'clock. Johnny gave no indication as to why he wanted to meet, so he was surprised when Dana herself asked the first question when they were seated at Bienvenue on 36th Street, one block from B. Altman.

"My mother and Andrew said you were looking for me late last night," Dana said. "Mom said something about a creative meeting?"

"Inviting you to the meeting was a last-minute brainstorm of mine, although Dad thought it was a great idea, too. We met this morning to look at Frances' initial drawings for next spring and to discuss the trends from the European shows. I thought it might be helpful for you to actually see the creative process at work so you can make a more intelligent decision about working with us. Like Dad said, the offer has no time limit, but we thought you'd enjoy talking with Frances and meeting our new piece goods buyer."

"Thanks, Johnny," Dana said, "but I'm afraid the next few weeks are going to be incredibly busy. I'm hoping to resurrect the in-store boutique, although nobody knows about it except Mark Senger and his friend."

Johnny furrowed his brow and cocked his head. "I thought that ship had sailed. In fact, the collapse of the Nantucket boutique was why I offered you a position in the first place since you seemed so frustrated."

"True," Dana said, "but Mark introduced me to a manufacturer who believes he can help me revamp the whole boutique concept."

"Whoa! You lost me. Manufacturer? Revamp?"

Dana explained that she hoped to open The British Shop in order to sell B. Altman's exclusive line of women's separates.

"It sounds like you've got a lot of time and energy invested in this project," Johnny said thoughtfully. "And that you may be at B. Altman's longer than anticipated."

Dana decided that she had to be forthcoming with Johnny since she knew he had her best interests at heart. "The bottom line is that I need more time to decide what career path I'm going to take. Mark agrees that my concept is great, as does his friend Irwin, the manufacturer he introduced me to last night. He owns Bauer & Sons Clothiers. Irwin is going to make some sample pieces based on my Jaeger wardrobe. Plus I'll even get to design the line, something that goes far beyond my aspirations for the Nantucket collection."

"How did all of this come about?" Johnny asked, aware that designing an entire line of clothing might well rival the position of fashion director.

"Mark has been working with Brooks Brothers, which is basically doing the same thing—using menswear manufacturers to make a clothing line for its new women's department rather than buying off the rack on Seventh Avenue. If I can get Bob Campbell on board, then Mark can finish the build-out."

"Wow. This sounds like a really huge undertaking," Johnny observed. "But what if Bob sides with Helen, which he's done before? You'll have wasted an awful lot of time and might get burned again?"

"Mark thinks that I gave up too easily, and I tend to agree with him. He thinks that, in the long run, the idea will be too good for B. Altman to resist. If we can manufacture some solid samples, I can at least make a compelling argument."

Johnny paused, concerned that Dana's interest in working for the House of Cirone was waning. "Mark owns Senger Display, right?"

"Yes, but between his work at Brooks Brothers and his friendship with Irwin, everything just fell into place. Trust me when I say that Mark knows the industry."

"Does Mark know about our offer to make you fashion director?"

"Absolutely. I've discussed both of my options with him."

"I see." Johnny fell silent and sipped a glass of water.

"Is anything wrong, Johnny?"

"I hope you don't mind my prying," Johnny said, "but it looks like Mark's becoming an important part of your life beyond B. Altman."

"He is, Johnny," Dana said. "I can't deny it. I like him very much."

Johnny smiled thinly. "I thought I'd detected a little flirtation at your birthday party. It sounds like he's a pretty special man."

Dana couldn't suppress a smile. "He's wonderful, and we have so much in common that ... well, what can I say? We've been spending a lot of time together."

Johnny didn't confess his suspicions, but the name Mark had surfaced several times in the space of a few minutes, and Mr. Senger was clearly advising Dana on her professional life— exactly what Johnny himself had tried to do at Dana's birthday dinner. Unfortunately, it sounded like Mark had gained quite a bit more influence over Dana than he or his father, and he wondered if his job offer could compete with a romantic interest, especially in its early stages. Johnny decided to keep his concerns to himself for now. Since he called Dana frequently, he would keep his pulse on what was happening in her life. He didn't want to see her get hurt by a whirlwind romance, nor did he want to see her suffer more grief at B. Altman if what he considered to be her overly-ambitious plan fell through.

To Johnny's way of thinking, things with Mark were moving way too quickly. Everything was Mark this and Mark that. He also felt that Dana had perhaps been blinded to the opportunities at the House of Cirone by Mark's aggressive plans, at least temporarily. Johnny had met Mark before, and he'd had always seemed to be a genuine and trustworthy gentleman. But was he right for Dana? Johnny had his misgivings.

"Have to get back to the store," Dana said when lunch was over. "And thanks for keeping an eye out for me. What would I do without you and Phoebe?"

Dana kissed Johnny on the cheek and left.

Standing near the front of the restaurant, Johnny watched her melt into the lunchtime rush on Madison Avenue. He was concerned that she might be losing herself in a relationship that was foreign to every aspect of her life. For the time being, he knew that neither he nor her family would have much influence on Dana.

Chapter Twenty-One

*A*ndrew stopped by Dana's office in the afternoon to show her the schematics for a new display on the main floor. She'd just returned from her lunch with Johnny, and she knew he was expecting a decision about the job offer he made at her birthday dinner. She trusted Andrew more than any of her co-workers and told him of the plans she'd made with Mark and Irwin. If all went well, there would probably be no move to the House of Cirone.

"You are one tenacious woman," Andrew declared. "When Helen finds out about it, I want to be as far away from ground zero as possible. This will represent the most serious challenge you've ever given her. If you succeed, however, you might be on the inside track to becoming fashion director."

"What would you do if you were in my shoes?" Dana asked.

"I'd push for the private line. The store has no energy since Ira and Dawn left. The drain is palpable."

"What do you think my chances are?"

"Fifty-fifty, but I say go for it. Nobody in this business ever got anywhere without taking risks."

"You sound a lot like Mark."

"Mark? I suppose you could say that he—"

A ring from the telephone on Dana's desk interrupted the discussion. Mark was on the other end of the line.

"Listen," he said, "I'm finishing up a meeting with Revlon, and I've got the afternoon free. What's the rest of your day look like? Can you play hooky?"

Dana glanced at the planner on her desk. "Sure. Nothing too earthshaking in the works. I suppose the store can manage without me for a few hours," Dana said with a laugh. "Where are we going?"

"It's a surprise. Just meet me at the Fifth Avenue entrance at two-thirty. I'll swing by in a taxi."

Andrew shook his head and smiled. "Tell Mark hello for me," he mouthed.

Ignoring Andrew, Dana told Mark that she'd be waiting and then hung up.

"How did you know who that was?" Dana asked.

"Please," Andrew said with a sly grin. "It doesn't take a detective to figure out what's been going on. I knew one of your manufacturers couldn't put that smile on your face. Monday night dinner dates, Mark's interest in your career—you're on top of the world, kiddo."

"Is it that obvious?"

"To me it is, but I know you far better than anyone else around here, so your secret is safe."

"I'm not trying to keep it a secret," Dana said as she straightened the papers on her desk and prepared to leave. "The British Shop—now that's another matter. That stays between you and me until I've got some samples in hand and am ready to go to Bob with the whole thing. Loose lips sink ships, Mr. Ricci."

"I'm the soul of discretion," Andrew said. "We never even had this conversation. Where are you two going, by the way?"

Dana laughed and shrugged her shoulders. "I don't know. He wants to surprise me."

"You've got it bad," Andrew said, "which I suppose is good."

"Very good," Dana said over her shoulder as she left the office. "Very good indeed."

• • •

Mark jumped out of the cab and gave Dana a quick kiss as she got into the taxi. He then slid in on the other side and instructed the cabbie to proceed to their next destination.

"Well, we're not going in the right direction for Claremont or Bauer & Sons Clothiers," Dana observed. "I'm in suspense."

"Having second thoughts about placing yourself in my capable hands?" Mark asked.

"Second thoughts? I never had 'any hesitations to begin with. I'm yours for the rest of the afternoon."

"That's all? I was going to suggest that we grab dinner, too."

"Whatever you say, Mr. Senger. I'm guessing that we're on one of your adventures."

"They're *our* adventures now. And yes, we are. Your curiosity will be satisfied soon enough."

Several minutes later, the cab came to a stop in front of Miller's Harness & Saddlery at 124 East 24th Street, the equine epicenter of New York. Miller's was the city's premiere tack shop for the well-heeled English-style equestrian. The two LLs in "Miller," a logo in the shape of boots, had become iconic in the riding community around the world. The company supplied fifteen hundred stores throughout the country, as well as Europe and the Far East.

Mark paid the cabbie, adding a generous tip, and turned to Dana. "Ready to go shopping?" he said proudly. "The first step to becoming an equestrian is dressing like one."

"I don't know, Mark," Dana said, looking at the saddles, bridles, and tall boots in the display window. "I'm not sure I'm ready for this. This store is for serious riders."

"Honey," Mark said. "There's only one way to approach riding, and that's seriously. Come on. I think you can be convinced."

They entered the store and were greeted by a salesman named Travis Smith.

"Good afternoon, Mr. Senger," Smith said warmly. "We've been expecting you."

Dana noted that Smith stood perfectly erect, hands clasped behind his back. He, as well as the entire shop, looked thoroughly English, with saddles, clothing, and various tack gear, such as harnesses and bits, lining the walls.

"Everything's ready, just as you requested, Mr. Senger," Smith said.

"Ready?" Dana said, flashing Mark a puzzled look.

"My assistant Ms. Harris will escort you to the dressing room, Ms. McGarry," Smith said.

"I took the liberty of asking Travis to make a few selections for you," Mark explained. "He knows exactly what I'm looking for. He's been outfitting Amanda for years. I think you'll be pleased, but you can make any changes you wish. It's just to get you started."

Dana looked stunned. "I'm surprised you don't have a horse waiting outside," she told Mark.

"Actually that would have been possible at the turn of the century," Smith said with a smile, "but thank goodness today you can still find a horse to ride at Claremont."

"That's on Saturday's agenda," Mark said, "but Dana can't ride in her Belgian loafers, so first we have some serious shopping to do."

"Let's take a look, Ms. McGarry," Ms. Harris said.

Dana followed Smith's assistant, and fifteen minutes later she emerged from the dressing room wearing white stretch breeches, a four-button navy blue hacking jacket with side vents and slanting pockets, and a pink oxford shirt.

"Delicious!" Mark said. "I think you nailed it out of the gate. Honey, you look fabulous."

"Do you think I should get the khaki breeches? I love the white, but I feel like I should be on a runway, not a bridle path."

"Get the khaki also," Mark said. "In fact, you better get two khakis. They're always out of stock."

"Here, Ms. McGarry," Smith said. "We have two khakis in your size. Would you prefer black or brown boots?"

"Black," Dana said as Smith handed her a pair in smooth cowhide.

"Please, have a seat," Smith said, motioning to a brown leather wing chair. "This will take a little practice, but you'll quickly get the knack. Here's one suggestion that always helps. Slip these socks over the breeches. They will help your foot slide down the shaft. Then insert these boot hooks in the tabs inside and slowly draw the boot up with the hooks."

"Very snug," Dana said, standing. "But they feel a little too high. They're over my knee."

"They're fine, honey," Mark said. "They're supposed to be about an inch or so taller than you'd expect. With wear, the ankle area will soften and wrinkle, and the boot will drop."

"Ms. McGarry, please step this way," Smith instructed. "I want to check the foot bed, and the best way to do that is when you're seated in a saddle."

"I love this jacket," Dana whispered to Mark as they walked to a corner of the saddlery. "Maybe I should have Irwin copy it for The British Shop."

"Will you please forget about work?" Mark said as he gave Dana a quick kiss on the cheek.

Smith grabbed a platform of two wooden steps and helped Dana climb onto an English saddle atop a mockup that resembled an upside-down U.

Smith knelt down and examined the boots as Dana slipped them into the English stirrups.

"We need a proper fit," he continued, "to prevent the saddle from pinching the leg or having the boot catch on the saddle's flap. And the heel must be adequate so that it doesn't slip through the stirrup. Heels down. There you go." Smith pressed the fingers and thumb of his right hand against all parts of the boots and wiggled the heels left to right before pushing them against the stirrups. "Good fit," he said. "How do they feel, Ms. McGarry?"

"A bit unusual, but overall, they're comfortable."

"That's to be expected," Smith said. "I recommend that you walk around in them as much as possible at home before you start your lessons. They'll be a bit uncomfortable the first few times you ride, but after a month or two you won't even notice that you're wearing them."

Mr. Smith helped Dana from the saddle as Ms. Harris appeared with a stock—a white silk scarf to be worn as an ascot around the neck and held in place with a pin. She also carried a brown tweed hacking jacket.

"Unfortunately, we don't have your size in the tweed jacket," Ms. Harris said, "but I think this one will work with a little alteration."

"That's fine," Dana said. "I don't need another jacket."

"Yes, you do," Mark said. "It's a great jacket with jeans, too."

Dana was led down a hall to the dressing area for the alterations.

As Mark wandered around the shop while waiting for Dana to return from her fitting, he noticed a green enamel dragonfly pin that he thought she would like—and need—for the stock.

"Travis, do you have a note card? I'd like to surprise Dana with this stock pin when she receives the tweed jacket. Would you mind gift wrapping it and sending it along with my note. You can enclose it with the jacket."

"Certainly, Mr. Senger. Where shall we send it?"

Dana reemerged from the fitting room as Mark signed for the purchases. They thanked Mr. Smith and Ms. Harris who, in turn, wished Dana good luck with her riding.

"Mark, thank you," Dana said as soon as they were alone outside the shop. "You have gone above and beyond. You're much too generous. This won't become a habit."

"Are you happy?" Mark asked.

"I'm very happy, and I love everything. But what if I only look like an equestrian? I don't want to disappoint you after you've made this investment. Maybe we should have waited until—"

"You'll never disappoint me," Mark said, "unless you're going back to Sniffen Court tonight."

"Aren't you being picked up at six in the morning for your flight to Dallas?"

"I am, and we can drop you and Wills off on our way to the Midtown Tunnel. Right now, let's bring these packages to my apartment and relax a bit before dinner," Mark said as he hailed a taxi.

In the cab, Dana put her arms around Mark's neck and kissed him. "No disappointments today."

"Good," Mark said as he returned the kiss.

Chapter Twenty-Two

Dana returned home with Wills early the next morning after spending the night at Mark's. She got Wills settled in, unpacked her clothes, and went through her mail. It was only six-thirty and she decided to have a cup of coffee at her secretary so she could answer Father Macaulay's last missive. She was anxious to relate developments in her life and how she was growing more optimistic by the day.

Dear Father Macaulay,

I was sorry to hear that your pub closed, but I'm sure that you will find a new one, given your indomitable spirit. One day I would very much like to hear your renditions of a few Cole Porter songs.

I am happy to report that I'm much closer to deciding whether or not to stay at the store or work at the House of Cirone. I spoke with Johnny again, this time in the presence of his father, the owner of the company and a man who we affectionately call Uncle John. Their offer is extremely generous. I would be made fashion director, giving me the opportunity to work with the head designer and even travel to Europe frequently. That, of course, would be one of the biggest perks of the job and would allow me to visit my beloved England often.

My friend Mark, however, thinks I threw in the towel too quickly when my boss rejected an idea that we came up with jointly, which is to sell a private B. Altman label from a boutique within the store. Thanks to Mark (he owns a display company and is a man I've worked beside on occasion), I am in touch with a manufacturer who would make the clothes that I myself would design. My inclination, therefore, is to do just what you're doing about finding a new pub, which is to take the bull by the horns, as you put it. Mark is somewhat of an adventurer who once climbed Mount Kilimanjaro, and he thinks that working for a family business might entail its own frustrations. That might be the case, and the more I've thought about it, I believe that working for the House of Cirone might not give me the same satisfaction in the long run. My career is very important to me, and I want to be able to look back and know that I did it on my own, which is another way of saying that maybe working for Uncle John would be like having everything handed to me on a silver platter.

Mark is trying to challenge me in so many areas of my life, and I think that taking on such an ambitious project (with his help, of course) is just what I need right now. He has even urged me to take riding lessons, and this afternoon we went on a shopping spree for proper English attire. I'm very excited about the lessons, and before too long I will hopefully be riding with him and his daughter down some of the lovely trails in Central Park. His daughter is a show jumper, so I have every confidence that I'm in good hands.

I do feel like I'm taking good care of myself for the first time in years. I feel connected to work in a new and exhilarating way, and I also feel that I have struck a better balance between my career and my life outside of work, a subject we spoke of early on. For now, I can say unequivocally that life is very good. I have not been in such high spirits for quite a long time. There were days when I might have felt guilty for being so happy, but that's not the case at present. I'm going to enjoy what life has to offer.

Rest assured that you are in my prayers daily. I'll keep you up-dated on how I do on horseback, and I look forward to your next letter.

Your friend,
Dana

Dana addressed and sealed the envelope before going up-stairs to change for work. Once in her room, she fell backwards onto the bed, arms spread wide. She was happy—incredibly so, in fact—just as she told Father Macaulay. Her work and personal life were coming into sharp focus. They were indeed balanced, and she could hardly wait to see what the months ahead would bring. She supposed that Johnny would be very disappointed when she informed him that she wouldn't be joining the House of Cirone. Between Mark's support and Ir-win's enthusiasm, she didn't see how The British Shop could fail, and she had all but abandoned the idea of working for Uncle John without having closed the door completely on the move. Helen seemed like a minor obstacle now that she would be able to actually show Bob finished samples manufactured by Irwin. She wanted to get started and, with Mark behind her, she felt certain that the preliminary steps at Bauer & Sons would be quickly set in motion.

Dana closed her eyes to savor the moment, feeling a peace and contentment that had eluded her for years.

Chapter Twenty-Three

*B*rett had been informed that opposing counsel for his case in San Francisco had been granted another continuance, allowing him to remain in New York for a few extra weeks. He would consult on some of the firm's current cases, but he would also have time on his hands. Perhaps, he thought, he and Janice could have a romantic holiday in the city that was still in his blood. California represented an interesting lifestyle, but it was going to be temporary, and Janice needed to learn how to enjoy the rhythms of New York. Janice, however, had been somewhat distant since arriving in town and had continued to ask more questions about Brett's whereabouts on any given day. She also continued to ask an inordinate number of questions about Dana's activities, questions that Brett honestly couldn't answer. He decided to relieve some of the tension from their last conversation by asking Johnny Cirone to play squash at the New York Athletic Club. He'd helped Johnny the previous year to extricate himself from a disastrous engagement to Suzanne Farnsworth, a young woman whose family had gotten him entangled in questionable business dealings with a subsidiary of its textile company. Johnny had therefore chosen not to take sides when Dana sought a divorce since Brett had been instrumental in saving him from possible indictment on a number of charges that could have ruined his reputation and career. He was more than willing to take time from his work to accept Brett's invitation.

They met at the club on Wednesday morning and, after exchanging pleasantries, played three matches, with Brett taking the last two handily.

"California life must agree with you," Johnny joked as they got dressed in the locker room. "Hell, you're in better shape now than when you first went out there."

"There's a totally different lifestyle on the West Coast" Brett explained. "For one thing, I'm out of the office most days by six, so I'm on the court at least four nights a week. I even squeeze in a little tennis and am trying my hand at golf. Say, why don't we catch up and have lunch here at the club. Unless you're needed back at work."

"Sounds good to me," Johnny replied. "I'm free until two. Our chief designer has the house going at full speed ever since she came back from Europe, and I could use a break since I've been putting in six days a week. We're planning to test a younger line with our collection next spring, which is why I wish Dana would finally agree to come on board."

Brett was slipping on his coat jacket but stopped abruptly, an arm in the air, when Johnny mentioned Dana.

"Really?" Brett said. "I hadn't heard about that. Why don't you fill me in at lunch?"

"Well, it came up rather suddenly," Johnny said, having second thoughts about mentioning Dana at all.

Brett finished slipping on his jacket and waved off Johnny's remark. "Hey, even though I don't know the details, I think joining the House of Cirone would be a great change for Dana."

Brett and Johnny went to the club's dining room and ordered. Brett's curiosity about Dana had been piqued for the second time since he'd gotten home, and as the two men ate, he realized that a golden opportunity had fallen into his lap.

There would be no need to pay a private investigator since Johnny could probably tell him chapter and verse about Dana's life. Maybe he could finally answer some of Janice's probing questions.

"Is Dana having problems at B. Altman?" Brett asked. "You mentioned that the job offer came up suddenly."

"I offered her a position—my father wants her to be fashion director—when I heard that Helen was giving her a hard time again about some idea for a boutique."

Brett nodded matter-of-factly. The more nonchalant he acted, the more likely Johnny would be to keep volunteering information. As a lawyer, he learned long ago to let people talk as long as they wanted. Listening usually yielded as many answers as asking direct questions.

"Helen can be a real tiger," Brett said. "I thought Dana was going to walk out of the store last December. What would Dana do as fashion director?"

"Eventually she would be the one who, with Dad, would chart the direction of the company, such as spotting new trends and fabrics, approving the designs, and styling the collection. I'm better in the field, servicing our accounts and managing operations. I think it would be her dream job in more ways than one since it entails European travel which, as you know, she loves."

Brett laughed. "I do recall her penchant for travel. Keep reminding her of that, Johnny, and she'll give in. It sounds to me like she would almost have partnership status."

"Funny you mention it. I can tell that Dad's been thinking along those lines from a few of his comments. Yep, in time I can see that happening."

"Sounds like a good plan to me," Brett said. His interest was now no longer a matter of sheer curiosity. He was about to hand over a lot of cash and assets to Dana in accordance with their separation agreement, and he wanted to hear more.

"But she told me at lunch yesterday that she needs more time to consider the offer," Johnny said. "What more is there to think about?"

"I agree. I would think she'd welcome the chance to have more creative freedom. I'm surprised she's not jumping at the offer despite her allegiance to the store."

"My point exactly. But Mark wants her to redouble her efforts to get the boutique up and running at B. Altman. He—" Johnny paused, unsure if he should continue.

"Don't worry about it," Brett said. "Mark Senger. They've worked together for years, and I heard they were going out. It's not a problem."

Looking relieved, Johnny continued. "Anyway, Mark has upped the ante. He wants Dana to work with a friend of his who manufactures menswear to produce a private label for B. Altman."

"And from what you're telling me, they'd obviously sell this new line in the boutique you mentioned," Brett said.

"That's their plan, but I think Dana might be setting herself up for a big letdown."

"How so?"

"Mark's idea is not only ambitious, but it's more than a bit risky. Assuming his friend can turn out a really great line, Dana has to find somebody at the store to sign off on the whole project."

"Let me guess," Brett said. "Bob Campbell?"

"Yep. Bob's been her mentor since she started."

"True. He's been in Dana's corner a number of times," Brett said thoughtfully. "But not always. I wouldn't consider it a done deal if I were she. She shouldn't lose this good job with you and John since careers at the store can be so competitive. Too much in-fighting there, if you ask me."

Johnny sighed. "That's what's so distressing. Dad told her that the offer will remain open indefinitely, so there's no incentive for her to make a quick decision. In the meantime, she can pursue this new line of ladieswear for her boutique."

"So what you're telling me is that Dana has the House of Cirone as a safety net if her project with Senger falls through," Brett said.

"I hadn't thought of it like that, but yes—I guess that's as good an assessment as any. She's sitting in the catbird seat."

"Well, it goes without saying that I hope she chooses to work with you and your dad," Brett said. "I wish her success either way, but I think she'd be much happier among people she regards as family. It sounds like a terrific opportunity, not to mention that it offers advancement, job security, and an equity position."

"Well, Dad's not discussing partnership yet. Too premature, and it would be added pressure for Dana. We just want her to get started, especially developing the new young line."

"I think she's just being cautious, Johnny," Brett said. "Don't forget that it's been a difficult six months for Dana. But knowing how much she loves you and your dad, I'm sure she'll soon be on board."

"I'll let you know what happens either way," Johnny said.

"Yeah, keep me in the loop," Brett said. "I'll be concerned until I know the situation is resolved. Dana puts so much into her work, and I know she's miserable when it's not going well."

"I'm glad you and Dana parted amicably. It's too bad more people don't take the high road."

"So true," Brett said. "So true."

• • •

Brett returned to his office after lunch with Johnny and looked out of his office window, lost in thought. He never had any plans to see Dana—until now. She was in a win-win situation as far as he could tell. She would either become fashion director at the House of Cirone, with a possible partnership down the road, or she would be a rising star at B. Altman. Either career path meant that she was almost certainly going to be earning more money than at the time they separated. Quite a bit more, in fact. She'd already moved up from special events coordinator to buyer, and now she would go even farther regardless of where she planted her flag.

And then there was Mark Senger to consider. Brett hadn't figured Dana for someone who'd start dating so quickly. Was she in a serious relationship with this man, who was wealthy and could give her anything she wanted? If so, she was advancing her life in more ways than one. And yet their settlement amounted to Brett giving away the store. Maybe he'd acted too hastily, granting Dana far too many concessions out of guilt as well as fear of having his affair exposed. Fortunately, they were still in the legal separation period, and the divorce would not be final until December. There was still a chance that he could alter the terms."

The first step was to find out a lot more about Mark Senger. He would once again enlist the aid of private investigator Wade Forrester, having him follow Mark everywhere he went and learning as much as possible about his lifestyle. He would also keep in touch with Johnny Cirone and find out which way Dana was leaning in the coming days.

He'd been truthful with Johnny. He didn't begrudge Dana having a successful life and career, but he didn't think she should realize her dreams at his expense. Literally. From what he could tell, Dana might not need his bank account to find all the happiness and fulfillment she desired.

Chapter Twenty-Four

ndrew Ricci's afternoon was proceeding like any other. The schematics for the current House & Garden Home Furnishings exhibit were undergoing daily modifications—typical in the design phase—and Andrew was in perpetual motion, going from the eighth floor, where the display would be located, to his office, to the conference room, to Bob Campbell's office—and then repeating the entire route. The pace was frenetic, yet Andrew loved his job and always thrived on the excitement at the inception of a project. His creative juices were flowing, and as was usually the case, he was lost in his thoughts. He stepped out of the elevator onto the sixth floor and started walking down the corridor before realizing that he was passing the offices of the Altman Foundation. He'd pushed the wrong elevator button. Reversing direction, he trekked back toward the elevators but stopped cold when he saw Patti Hartlen sitting at her desk and sobbing uncontrollably. He quickly slipped into her office, closed the door, and sat across from Patti.

"Hey, what's wrong?" he asked, handing her a tissue from the box at the edge of her desk.

"It's nothing," she said dismissively as she wiped tears and mascara from her face. "I'll be okay."

"Come on, Patti," Andrew said, handing her another tissue. "You're obviously pretty upset about something. Is everything all right here in the office? Anybody giving you a hard time?"

Patti shook her head. "No, nothing like that. Everybody here is great."

"Then?"

"It's more personal."

Andrew was about to get up and leave rather than intrude on a private moment, but Patti burst into fresh tears.

"Look," Andrew said, leaning forward, "whatever's wrong is none of my business, but maybe it would help if you talked it out. I promise that whatever you say won't go beyond this office."

Patti sniffled and wiped her face again. "It's Jack."

Andrew sat up straighter at the mention of his lover's name. "Is he okay? I mean, he hasn't been in an accident or anything, has he?"

"Maybe this will seem silly to you, but we had dinner reservations last night, but he didn't make it. Didn't even call. He got in at three o'clock and didn't say a word, but I knew he had been drinking. He just went straight to sleep, which is nothing new. I wanted last night to be … special."

Andrew took a deep breath. He knew exactly where Jack had been. They'd gone out to dinner and then back to Andrew's apartment. Jack had far too much to drink, and Andrew had poured black coffee into him for two hours before sending him home in a taxi. In fact, Jack had been drinking a lot more in the past two weeks, although he'd never gotten outright drunk until last night.

"Did he say anything this morning?" Andrew asked. "In the way of an explanation, that is."

"Only that he'd been entertaining clients who didn't want to call it a night and that he'd been thoroughly exhausted before the evening began. He apologized for not calling and then hurried off to work. The apologies are a part of his daily routine now."

"I guess opening a new office here in the city is probably—"

"I'm not buying that excuse any longer," Patti interrupted. "Dana suggested I make him sit down and talk, which I did a few nights ago. He admitted that he wasn't very good company any longer and claimed that the suppliers for Hartlen Response were dragging their feet. He even suggested—" Patti successfully fought back a new wave of tears. "He suggested that I go back to Houston until he got things sorted out here."

Andrew looked at the folded schematics he was holding and spoke quietly. "It sounds like he's under a lot of pressure. What did you tell him?"

"About returning to Houston for a few months? I told him that it was out of the question. Andrew, I don't know what he's going through, but there's something he's not telling me, and I intend to stand by him regardless of what's troubling him. It's just that some days are almost impossible to get through."

"Like today," Andrew said.

"Like today," she repeated. "He knew how important last night was to me. I wanted to go out and have a romantic dinner. Just the two of us. No clients and no talk about business. But he couldn't even call me. I'm sorry you had to see me like this. I feel like I'm falling apart."

"It's okay," Andrew said. "I understand."

In truth, Andrew realized that he was only beginning to understand the difficulty of Jack and Patti's situation. He saw Patti on most weekdays and occasionally had lunch with her at Charleston Garden, B. Altman's eighth-floor restaurant. As for Jack, he rarely spoke of Patti when they were together. Andrew loved Jack, but his love had blinded him to what Patti might be going through. Andrew had never coerced Jack into a relationship when they first met. Rather, they had both been immediately attracted to one another, and Andrew had helped Jack discover, month by month, who he really was and what he wanted in life. In an instant, however, Andrew knew that he would have to reevaluate his relationship with Jack. Seeing Patti so distraught was tantamount to a punch in the gut. He still wanted to be with Jack—that hadn't changed—but Patti could not be allowed to linger in her painful no man's land any longer. To do so would be cruel and insensitive. He decided to call Jack that very afternoon.

"Try to hang in there," Andrew said, standing. "I'm late for a meeting, but maybe you should sit down with Jack again and see if he'll open up to you, just as Dana said."

"Thanks, Andrew," Patti said, now looking more composed. "Jack and I will somehow make it through this together. Thanks for lending me your ear."

Andrew smiled thinly and left. He felt awful, when Dana stopped him moments later in the main hallway on the fifth floor.

"You look pale," Dana remarked. "What's wrong?"

"Feels like I'm coming down with something," Andrew said hurriedly. "I'm going home early."

"Give me a call if you need any—"

Andrew had already entered the elevator before Dana could finish her sentence.

Andrew returned to his apartment on East 55th Street. He slumped on the couch and thought for several minutes before picking up the telephone, dialing Jack's private line at Hartlen Response.

"I just had a talk with Patti," Andrew said, his voice subdued.

There was a long pause on the other end of the line. "About what?" Jack asked. "You sound terrible."

"Yeah, well, I *feel* terrible. I saw Patti sobbing in her office. Sobbing, Jack. She told me that you two had dinner reservations last night."

"I know. I forgot all about them. I guess I—"

"No, just listen for a second, all right? She said she confronted you. And she told me about your suggestion that she go back to Houston for a while. About your excuses and apologies and her intention to stand with you until you resolve whatever's going on. She knows you're hiding something, Jack, and you—no, *we*—can't do this to her any longer."

"Wait, wait, wait," Jack said. "I know she's upset, and I should have told you. But I'm handling it, okay? It's going to take some time, but I'll take care of it."

Andrew said nothing for a full minute.

"Hello?" Jack said.

"I'm here," Andrew said, his throat dry. "I love you, Jack, but that's not good enough. I want to spend my life with you, but I can't go on until you're out of the marriage."

"And I will get out of the marriage. It's going to take time. I need to break this to her gradually. Hey, it's my fault. I get it. I should have dealt with this much sooner, but I didn't. Just give me a little more time. Please, Andrew!"

In his mind's eye, Andrew could still see Patti, her spirit numb and crushed as she sobbed at her desk, a look of desperation in her eyes.

"Do what you have to do," Andrew said, his voice barely audible. "You know where to find me."

"What are you saying?" Jack asked, panic in his voice.

"I'm saying that I can't see you until things change."

"You're overreacting, Andrew! Please don't. Listen to what you're saying. Just give me—"

"Goodbye, Jack," Andrew said, hanging up the phone.

• • •

Andrew cried before pouring himself a gin and tonic. He paced back and forth in his living room, his mind replaying his conversations with Patti and Jack. Was he being too hasty? Didn't Jack deserve a chance to work things out at his own pace? Perhaps, but Jack did indeed love his wife, a wife who was undergoing incredible pain and wanted her husband back. Andrew also considered Jack's strong family ties, which were strengthened by the Hartlens' commitment to their family-owned oil companies. Jack was a conflicted man, and Andrew doubted his long-term resolve to leave Patti or break the news to his family.

He was about to pour himself another gin and tonic when he decided that he wasn't going to sit in his apartment alone all evening. The room suddenly felt depressing and claustrophobic. Down the hall, the master bedroom contained several changes of clothes for Jack. The two men had gone to museums, the theater, and places in New York that the average tourist never discovered, but most of all they'd spent countless hours at Andrew's apartment discussing the changes Jack was going through. Andrew looked at the walls with a blank stare, unable to fathom that he might never see Jack again. Sitting in the room where Jack had been less than twenty-four hours ago was oppressive.

An hour later, Andrew jumped in a cab to the East Village. He walked for a while, head lowered, hands in his pockets. He saw a gay bar up ahead and entered without hesitation. The lighting was dim, which suited Andrew just fine. Usually upbeat and optimistic, he felt empty and alone.

Six hours later, he was still inside the bar.

Chapter Twenty-Five

*A*manda Senger was five-four and had a small frame. With blue eyes and brown hair, she'd inherited her father's features. She was highly intelligent, but she was more serious and intense than her father, whose wit and humor she appreciated but didn't share. At nineteen, she was a highly-focused young woman excelling in Cornell's veterinary medicine program. She loved animals and was equally passionate about her riding. Although she lived with her mother in Greenwich, Connecticut, she spent a great deal of time with her father, who frequently joined her when she trained at Judd Baumann's horse farm in Muttontown, Long Island. Judd, a high school friend of Mark, had arranged the purchase of her Dutch Warmblood, Pepsi, and Amanda could never seem to find enough time to visit her beloved horse. She loved Pepsi from the moment she'd first seen him, and she was allowed to groom the animal, given her equestrian knowledge and abilities. When she rode the horse, the two functioned as one. She instinctively knew each move Pepsi was going to make, and she felt that Pepsi, in turn, could sense the commands that she would be giving him. In fact, her trainer, Paul Arnoff, had told Amanda years earlier that one of the most elemental traits of a great rider was to have a deep bond with a horse and always operate in tandem with it, especially when one reached the competitive levels of riding.

Amanda was currently training to compete for the first time as an adult exhibitor in the High Performance Hunter Division at the Hampton Classic, which was held each August at Bridgehampton, New York. Starting at the age of nine, when she finished first place in the Pony Hunter Division, Amanda had been participating in this annual event. Such hunter classes in the High Performance Division required horse and rider to clear a series of fences three feet nine inches high and four feet six inches wide. When more than one competitor completed the course without missing a fence, they competed against the clock, with the rider posting the fewest mistakes and the fastest time taking the prize. It was a demanding course and called for consummate skill on the part of the rider, and it was a foregone conclusion that all participants rode only the finest and most well-trained horses.

The competition was still a few months away, but the event was one that called for extensive training. Classes for the semester had ended on Tuesday, and Amanda was heading into exams the following week. It was Wednesday, and Amanda thought it would be wise to go to Muttontown over the weekend to resume training with Paul. She was excelling at the basics, such as always looking in the direction she wanted Pepsi to go next after clearing a fence. Horses could sense their next move based on a rider's intention, which could be conveyed by something as subtle as a quick glance. It was part of the close bond between horse and rider. She also managed to keep her heels down to maintain balance, and she never rushed a jump, which could potentially send a rider catapulting over the horse's head. It was important to let the horse's power execute the jump, not speed. Lately, however, Amanda had developed a small hitch in her riding stance. Her shoulders were leaning slightly forward, but it was imperative to keep them back in order to keep her center of gravity. During a jump, a rider's body left the saddle briefly except for feet in the stirrups. To maintain equilibrium and land safely, riding posture had to be perfect. Amanda and Paul had been working on correcting the problem, and she wanted to get in extra practice time. With the semester's "dead days" now upon her—time between the end of classes and the beginning of exams that allowed students extra time for exam prep—Amanda thought it was the perfect time to work with Paul and Pepsi.

She'd called her father the previous night, but he hadn't answered. She then remembered that he was at a meeting supporting Joseph Papp's proposal for a theater in Central Park that would offer free performances of Shakespeare. He was clearly as passionate about this project as he was the previous year, when he formed a committee to save Claremont Riding Academy. The stables, condemned by the city and marked for demolition, were to be replaced by a residential building. The day the Parks Commission announced a two-year reprieve, Mark sent Amanda flowers, saying he couldn't have achieved the win without her for inspiration.

As an only child, Amanda was extremely close to Mark and her mother, and although there was tension and frequent arguments between her parents, she was devastated when they separated. Fortunately, Mark and Amanda's shared passion for riding and horses kept their bond strong. After two years, Amanda had not only adjusted to Mark being out of the family home, she preferred her undivided time with him in the city as well as their private conversations on the bridle path. She didn't mind that Pepsi was in Muttontown or that she had to ride a Claremont horse in Manhattan. Amanda loved her precious "dad time."

Amanda phoned the office of Senger Display and was lucky enough to catch her dad between meetings. She explained that she wanted extra training time with Paul and asked if her father would call the airline and purchase a plane ticket from Ithaca

Tompkins Regional Airport to LaGuardia for Friday afternoon and a return ticket for Monday morning.

"Sure, sweetie," Mark said. "Do you have time for dinner with me Friday night or do you want to go right to Judd's."

"I want to see you first," Amanda said. "I'll head to Judd's early Saturday morning. I'll take a taxi into Manhattan, but you can arrange a car back to LaGuardia early on Monday. My first exam is at three Monday afternoon."

"Okay, sounds good. I look forward to seeing you, sweetheart. Ready for exams?"

"I'm almost there. See you Friday. Bye, Dad."

Amanda hung up and reviewed notes for her first two exams. She felt prepared but, like her father, she was organized and left nothing to chance, especially when it came to her schoolwork. Later, she packed a suitcase even though the trip was still two days away. She couldn't wait to see Pepsi again and work on her jumping.

Mark hung up the phone and smiled. Amanda was conscientious about school and riding, and lately she talked of little else but her training sessions with Paul and the approaching Hampton Classic. He was fortunate to have such a mature, intelligent daughter, although she was a child when it came to her parents, still hoping they would get back together. The broken marriage was a heartache Mark wished he could have spared her, but she finally seemed to be adjusting to the new family dynamics. Now that she was in college, she was busy planning her future as an equestrian and a veterinarian. On balance, he thought he'd been a pretty good father. Amanda was turning out to be a mature young woman with poise and promise.

He was about to rise from his desk when he remember his plans with Dana. How could he have forgotten? Dana was coming over Friday evening after work. Should he ask her to come over on Saturday instead? His hand reached for the telephone, but he pulled it back. Dana was becoming an important part of his life and he believed Amanda was old enough to accept the relationship, even if it didn't happen overnight. Not one to hesitate, he decided that it was time for Amanda and Dana to meet.

Chapter Twenty-Six

*J*ack arrived home in time for dinner Wednesday night but remained quiet as usual except for the small talk that he made with Patti in the evening. He was in excruciating emotional pain, but after what Andrew had told him on the phone, he decided it would be better if he went home instead of staying late at the office, trying to process Andrew's ultimatum. He felt considerable guilt over what he'd been putting Patti through, and if having dinner with her could provide some small measure of comfort, then it was the least he could do. Inside, however, he was a mass of conflicting emotions, and by bedtime he was ready to collapse after watching a couple of hours of television. He hadn't the slightest idea what he'd seen since his mind was only on Andrew. After putting on his pajamas, he'd gone into the bathroom and taken a Valium.

On Thursday morning, he got up at his normal time, put on a business suit, and had a quick breakfast of coffee and toast. Patti was all smiles, perhaps happy that she'd had the company of her husband for an entire evening at home, quiet though he was, for the first time in several weeks. Her brief display of normalcy tugged at his heart. How was he going to tell his wife that he wanted out of the marriage? He knew that she loved him, and the thought of hurting her was almost inconceivable. But he had discovered over the past several months that he'd been living a lie for most of his life. The idea that he was attracted to men was something that he'd pushed to the back of his mind since he was a teenager. He'd been a good student and had worked hard for Hartlen Oil before being put in charge of Hartlen Response by his father. His college roommate introduced him to Patti, and it seemed natural that he should follow in the footsteps of his dad, settling down and one day having children of his own. Besides, it was expected of him.

Patti was an attractive woman with whom he shared a great deal in common, such as golf, hiking, and reading. The couple got engaged after only a year of dating and married a year later. She worked for a short time at Hartlen Oil as an account executive before beginning her career in philanthropy with the Houston Endowment. Always beneath the surface, however, Jack remained attracted to the same sex, although it wasn't until he met Andrew on a business trip to New York City that he found himself drawn into a close friendship with the display director from B. Altman. The friendship had quickly progressed to a romantic relationship, and it was then that he realized how much he'd repressed his feelings for so many years.

He folded the morning paper, kissed Patti on the cheek, and left for Davis, Konen and Wright. It was time to sign the consortium agreement and get Brett off his back once and for all. In the taxi, he almost instructed the driver to change direction and take him to Hartlen Response, reasoning that if his affair with Andrew was over, then Brett could no longer blackmail him. But in his grief over Andrew's terse words the day before, he'd overlooked the fact that Brett had stumbled upon his slush fund and the investigation by the IRS and the FBI. He could hardly believe how much trouble he had created for himself, but the grim reality was that Brett not only knew too much about his personal life and misuse of company funds, but it was Brett who was going to be able to halt the federal investigation.

He therefore let the taxi proceed to the financial district in lower Manhattan.

• • •

Brett was present in Conference Room Three at Davis, Konen and Wright, as was Richard Patterson, the managing partner and a competitive sailor who had created the consortium in his zeal to keep the oceans clean. Other partners were present as well, knowing how important the agreement was to Richard and the firm. Jack put on his best smile before entering the room lest Brett see that anything was bothering him. If Jack showed the least amount of discomfort, the always-astute Brett might well dig deeper into Jack's personal life, which would certainly compound his almost unmanageable stress. He shook hands and sat at the table as Richard, for the sake of formality, explained the content of every page of the agreement. After Jack affixed his signature multiple times to the lengthy document, two junior partners signed the final page as witnesses and a third notarized the agreement, after which the conference room erupted in applause.

"I only wish Ralph could be here," Richard said, extending his hand to Jack. "It's a great day for Hartlen Oil, too."

"You and Hartlen Oil are making a good strategic move," Brett said, also extending his hand, "not to mention a very lucrative one. Hartlen Oil and Hartlen Response will be seen as environmentally friendly companies, and leasing your response equipment to the other signatories will net you a fortune. Welcome aboard."

Jack hadn't noticed until the flash bulbs went off, but a reporter and photographer from the *New York Times* were present. Such a bold environmental move on the part of big business was unprecedented and newsworthy. He smiled more broadly as he shook hands with Richard and Brett. Perhaps when Patti read about the signing she would realize that he had never stopped conducting business as CEO of Hartlen Response, ameliorating some of her suspicion. He was ready to leave when Richard signaled for the conference room doors to be opened and a cake was wheeled in as champagne corks started popping. Jack's heart sank when he realized that he would have to retain his professional demeanor a little while longer.

"A bit early in the morning for a celebration, but this event is too important," Richard asserted.

For the next hour, Jack shook more hands and spoke with the partners about response technology, but he felt dizzy and began perspiring as the minutes wore on. He managed to wipe his forehead with a handkerchief just before Brett made his way back to have a final word.

"Now that wasn't so bad, was it?" Brett asked.

"I'd rather have waited for the patents, but it's a done deal," Jack said.

"That it is. As I said once before—" Brett paused, frowning. "Are you okay, Jack? You look tired."

"I'm fine. Now if you'll excuse me, I need to get back to the office. Is anything further required here?"

"Nothing at all. Have a good day, Jack."

Jack turned to leave and headed for the hallway, relieved that the signing was over.

"Jack?" Brett said.

"Yes."

"Give my regards to Patti."

Jack turned and left.

• • •

Out on the street, Jack felt as if he were suffocating. He was sweating profusely now, and his breath came in quick, short gasps. He hailed a taxi and gave the driver the address of Hartlen Response. The ride took unusually long because of several traffic jams, and Jack felt as if he might pass out.

Jack's mind was filled with voices: Andrew's, Patti's, Brett's, his father's. But his own mind returned again and again to one single thought: *Why are you doing this to us, Andrew? Why can't you give me time?*

An hour later, Jack seated himself at his desk after getting a copy of the Yellow Pages from his secretary. His right hand shaking, he impatiently thumbed through the large book, looking under Physicians/Psychiatrists. He couldn't deal with his situation any longer without professional help. He knew only one name, a psychiatrist used by his senior vice president, who had gone into grief counseling after his wife had died of a sudden heart attack two months earlier at the age of forty-four. Using his private line, he dialed the number and made an appointment with the receptionist of Dr. Walter Stein.

He then settled back and loosened his tie. Taking several deep breaths, he picked up his telephone and told his secretary to cancel all meetings for the rest of the day. Jack Hartlen felt that he'd lost control of his company, his wife, and his very sanity. The worst part was that he was sure he'd lost Andrew Ricci for good.

*C*hapter *T*wenty-*S*even

*D*ana took off her light spring coat when she arrived at Mark's apartment on Friday afternoon. Anxious about meeting his daughter, she left work early to make sure she wouldn't be late. She would only have one chance to make a first impression.

"I thought Amanda was going to be here," Dana said, stepping into the living room.

"She will be soon," Mark said, kissing Dana on the lips. "Her plane from Ithaca was delayed, and LaGuardia is jammed up with Friday evening traffic."

Dana took a deep breath. "I'm really nervous," she confessed. "I thought I'd meet Amanda for the first time at Claremont, where my presence wouldn't be so … well, conspicuous. I'd be just another rider, and she'd see us as friends and would have time to warm up to me a bit."

Mark took Dana in his arms and gave her a reassuring hug.

"No need to be nervous," he said, "you'll do fine. Just be yourself. What's not to like?"

"What did she say when you told her I was joining you for dinner?"

Mark couldn't help but laugh. "She said 'That's nice.'"

"That doesn't sound very enthusiastic," Dana said.

"No, but that's Amanda being an aloof teenager."

"What if she doesn't like me?"

"And what if she does? Either way, be patient and give it time. And try not to over-think the situation."

"Okay," Dana said. "I'll trust my instincts and—"

The doorbell sounded before Dana could finish her sentence.

Mark admitted Amanda, who dropped her brown leather travel bag in the hall and hugged her father while kissing him on the cheek.

"I called Paul yesterday," Amanda said excitedly. "He said we can start tomorrow morning at nine o'clock. I'll have to be picked up at six. I was thinking that—"

Amanda stopped short, noticing Dana standing in the background.

Mark turned and extended his arm, inviting Dana to join them.

"Sweetheart, I'd like you to meet Dana McGarry. Dana, my daughter, Amanda."

"I'm so happy to meet you," Dana said as she walked towards them and held out her hand. "I was sorry to hear about your delayed flight."

"Nice to meet you," Amanda said, taking Dana's hand and looking back at her father. "It's okay. We're used to it, right, Dad? No on-time flights at LaGuardia."

"Only one more to go and you'll be home for the summer."

"Speaking of summer," Amanda said, "Mom made me promise I'd talk to you about staying here when I'm not in Muttontown. She's going to Italy for a couple of weeks before the Classic, and she wants you to be around."

"Sure, but we can talk about that later. Why don't you put your bag in your room and settle in. I'll have dinner ready in half an hour."

"What?" Amanda said with a pained expression on her face. "You've got to be kidding me. Tell me you didn't cook."

"I didn't cook," Mark said with a laugh, looking at Dana. "That wouldn't be the best way to impress our guest."

"Dad attempted to make pancakes one morning when we were in the middle of a blizzard, and we used them as hockey pucks," Amanda said.

"You'll be happy to know," Mark continued, "that Sal sent over a salad and your favorite baked ziti when I told him we couldn't make the eight o'clock reservation. They were packed for the rest of the night."

"Good," Amanda said. "I'm starved."

Amanda looked at Dana as she grabbed her luggage and disappeared down the hallway.

Dana sat on the couch in the living room, elbows resting on her knees, her head cradled in the palms of her upraised hands.

"Penny for your thoughts?" Mark said.

"Amanda was fine. *I'm* the one feeling awkward. Dating someone's father is a role that I never envisioned. I want to get it right, but I'm not quite sure what to do. It's one thing to get along over dinner, but do you think Amanda is ready for you to have someone in your life?"

Mark sat beside Dana and took her right hand in his. "Honey, we have to take one day at a time. You're brand new in her world right now, and it's normal that she be tentative and a little jealous. I'm her father, and she's always wanted me all for herself. Plus she's an only child, so the bond she has with me and her mother is very strong. She may need time to understand you're not going to interfere with my relationship with her. She's also still a moody teen, so don't be upset if she appears unfriendly at times."

"I'll be sensitive to her feelings, Mark. As a daughter who adores her father, I can relate. I know it can't be easy."

"Here's my advice. Stop worrying about what she's think-ing. Just be yourself. There's such a thing as trying too hard."

Dana cocked her head towards Mark. "So true. I'll try to be a little more relaxed."

"That's really all you can do. I've got to check on dinner, so just sit back and let the evening unfold."

Dana, Mark, and Amanda sat down to dinner in the dining area by the casement windows, the city lights sparkling in the distance beyond the park.

"What courses are you studying at Cornell?" Dana asked. "Your dad says you're in the veterinary medicine program."

" Biology, zoology, and animal physiology. I'm minoring in French."

"What a lovely diversion. Are you fluent?"

"Not quite, but I held my own when we were in France last summer, right Dad?"

"You did better than that. I thought I was traveling with a native."

"Maybe we can go to Quercy for a few days after the Clas-sic," Amanda said, focusing all her attention on her father. "You said you wanted to go there."

"I *would* like to go there," Mark said tuning to Dana. "It's the land of truffles and *foie gras*. Historic inns along the Dordo-gne River. Beautiful countryside for riding and dining."

Interrupting, Amanda said, "Mom wants—"

"And speaking of riding," Mark continued, "Dana is start-ing lessons tomorrow with Larry."

Amanda rested her fork on her plate and stared at her father. The look on her face was that of disbelief. "Claremont?"

"Where else?" her father said with a laugh. "I don't think she's ready for show-jumping lessons with Paul, but I think she'll quickly pick up the basics. You know, Dana's also a very good tennis player. I think you're well-matched."

Amanda smiled thinly and said nothing in response. Her tone became subdued for the rest of the meal, and she asked to be excused before dessert.

"That didn't go well at all," Dana said as she helped clear the table. "Her entire demeanor changed when you brought up Claremont. Listen, I think I should go home early and let the two of you talk."

Mark nodded. "It's probably for the best. I have an idea what's bothering her, but I want to make one thing perfectly clear. I'll do everything I can to respect her feelings, but she's nineteen and can't expect me to live like a hermit or a monk. I'm not putting you on the back burner, and I'm not going to let Amanda control our relationship, Dana. She'll come around when she gets to know you better."

Mark kissed Dana, rode down in the elevator with her, and saw her safely into a cab.

Mark knocked gently on Amanda's door. "May I come in?"

When there was no answer, he opened the door a crack. "Hello? Amanda?"

"I'm studying, Dad," said Amanda, who was seated at her desk in the corner.

Mark opened the door wider, entered, and pulled up a chair next to the desk. "Can we talk?"

"I'd rather not."

Mark paused before speaking. "Look, I know what's on your mind, but I'd like you to tell me so that we can talk this over. Just for a few minutes. What do you say?"

Tears formed at the corners of Amanda's eyes. "Are you going to invite Dana to come with us to Quercy? That was going to be our riding vacation."

"It still is, and I won't ask her if you don't want me to. Besides, that's still a few months away."

"Okay, but why does she have to take riding lessons? Why can't she stick to tennis?"

"Amanda," Mark said slowly, "the riding lessons were my idea. When people date, they naturally share things that interest them. Besides, riding wouldn't be nearly so important to me if it weren't for the time you and I have spent on the trails together, and that won't change."

Amanda turned to face Mark squarely. "But that's just the point, Dad. I feel it already has. It's not going to be just the two of us anymore."

"I was thinking that Dana could come with us once in a while, but not every time. I'll always make sure that we still have our private time together."

Amanda remained quiet as she digested her father's words. "Okay, but it's still going to be hard to get used to. It's ... well, it's the principle of the thing."

"What you're saying is that the very idea of Dana's riding automatically puts her into our own special world. Like I'm giving away part of something that belongs only to us."

"Yeah, something like that."

Mark sighed and chose his words carefully. He understood exactly what Amanda was feeling. "Sweetheart, all I can say is that Dana will never take your place in my life. It's just not possible. But riding is a part of my life and always has been, even before you were born, right?"

"Right."

"So it's naturally something I want to share with Dana because it's who I am. Does that make sense?"

"Yes, but you could have chosen something else to share with her. Why not climb a mountain with her or something?"

Mark laughed, drew closer, and put his arm around Amanda. "Not too many mountains here in Manhattan except the man-made brick and mortar kind. Horseback riding is a bit more accessible."

Amanda wanted to laugh at her father's humor, but she suppressed the urge.

"Listen, sweetheart, I know this will take time to get used to, but there's no deadline and no rules other than being congenial when she's around."

"Okay." Amanda sniffled. "Dad?"

"Yes?"

"I still don't like her. I mean, I'm sure she's a nice person, but I can't make myself warm up to somebody on command."

"Will you give her a chance? For me? Once you get to know her, I'm sure that—"

"You're sure that I'll really like her. She's never going to replace Mom, but I might one day get to be friends with her. Is that the rest of the speech?"

"Pretty much. But you haven't answered my question."

"I will."

"Thanks, sweetheart," Mark said, kissing Amanda on the forehead. "It means a lot to me."

Mark rose and left the room, closing the door behind him. The evening hadn't gone as smoothly as he'd hoped, but he thought that he made progress in the last few minutes. Only time would tell.

Chapter Twenty-Eight

Dana had no desire to begin her riding lessons on Saturday morning, a beautiful warm day in April. Amanda had grown pale at the mention of Claremont, and Dana was smart enough to recognize territoriality when she saw it. And jealousy. She felt foolish for going to Miller's and accepting the riding outfits from Mark, for how could she not have seen this coming? Mark had often talked about his time on the trails with Amanda, as well as her show jumping. *Of course* she wanted Dana excluded from that part of her life. Any child in her situation would feel the very same way. Dana called Mark at eight in the morning, telling him how she felt and that she wanted to return the clothing purchased from Miller's.

"Let's not be too hasty!" Mark stated. "I had a good talk with Amanda after you left last night. She said she understood why I wanted to share riding with you and that she would try to give it a chance."

"It?"

"You and me. It's not easy for her, but she loves me enough to know that I deserve some happiness, too. There's no reason to change our plans."

Dana remained hesitant. "I don't know, Mark. It doesn't feel right. Maybe in time."

Mark was clearly exasperated. "There's never going to be a right time, Dana. We can wait six months to re-introduce you to Amanda, but she would still feel the same way then. She has to get past the idea that I'll never share things with anyone but her. Am I supposed to wait until she's in her twenties or married before I date or enjoy myself? I'm not willing to put my life on hold, especially now that you're a part of that life. And the same goes for your riding lessons. We can put them off, but you're going to feel the same way *whenever* we decide to go to Claremont, whether it's today or next year."

Dana was silent.

"Let me put it another way," Mark continued. "Last December, you decided to divorce Brett. It was painful, but it needed to be done and there was never going to be an opportune time to do it. We have to live our lives without giving power over them to anyone else."

"I can't argue with that logic," Dana admitted. "I surrendered my plans to Brett for too many years."

"I gave Amanda all the reassurances she needs to know that my relationship with her won't be affected by the simple fact that I'm dating, and that's all I can do for the moment. Besides, it's not fair to Amanda to conduct our relationship behind her back. We're not doing her any favors by avoiding these issues."

"What do you mean? I'm not following."

"She's nineteen. She's still got a lot of maturing to do, but life is filled with obstacles, and she has to learn to deal with them."

"And she's okay with my taking lessons?"

"Yes, so put on those breeches and get over here. You have a nine-thirty lesson."

"Okay. I'm convinced."

"Good. See you soon."

• • •

Claremont Stables was located at 175 West 89ᵗʰ Street on the Upper West Side. A former livery stable converted to a riding academy, it was a multi-story barn with several floors connected by ramps. An indoor riding ring gave the academy a unique and homey feel despite being located in Manhattan.

"I pictured something larger," Dana said as she looked at a few riders and their trainers in the crowded ring.

"It's all the space you need to learn the basics," Mark said. "The rest of the building stables one hundred and thirty-nine horses. About half are boarded by owners, and the others are rented for the bridle paths just a block and half away. Here's Larry now. He worked with Amanda when she was just starting."

Larry Cuthbert was one of Claremont's fifteen trainers. He was a tall man in his fifties and walked with a slow easy gait that spoke of someone quite comfortable around horses. He wore jeans, boots, and a blue work shirt, although he spoke with a New York accent.

"Hi, Mark. Good to see you. This must be Dana. Pleased to meet you, Ms. McGarry."

"So what have you picked out for Dana?" Mark asked.

"Follow me," Larry said, leading them to stalls on the second floor. "This is a Tennessee Walker, a chestnut mare named Macy. Pretty gentle and the ideal choice for a beginner. She can rack, foxtrot, and canter, but all you want to do at first, Dana, is follow me while I walk her around the ring downstairs. Let her get to know you. I saddled her just before you arrived."

The three of them took Macy to the ring, Dana walking next to Larry as he led Macy around the circuit a dozen times.

"She's used to your being near her now, Dana, so it's your turn," Larry said. "Take the lead rope, but don't hold it too close to the halter underneath her chin. Loop it around your hand but don't ever wrap it tightly in case a horse decides to get ahead of you. With a gentle horse like Macy, give it some slack. Now stand even with her head, click your tongue, and start walking. I'll be right beside you every step of the way."

Dana led Macy around the ring several times, Macy stopping and shaking her head only once.

"Nothing to worry about," Larry said. "It's not a tug of war, so just stop and wait. When she's steady again, click your tongue and resume walking. You're doing great."

"I'm proud of you, honey," Mark said from the side of the ring.

Dana blushed. "I don't feel like I'm doing anything."

"Sure you are," Larry said, "but it's time for you to mount."

He showed Dana how to climb into the saddle as he held Macy's reins. "The first thing you need to learn is the correct posture. You want to be able to imagine a straight line from your ear through your shoulder and hips and all the way down to your heel. That'll help you keep balanced. I'm going to lead you around the ring a few times, but don't lean left or right. Just stay in alignment. Above all, breathe easy and stay relaxed. Horses can sense the slightest bit of tension in a rider. That's what I want you to take away from today's lesson. The correct sitting position and staying calm."

"You look terrific," Mark commented. "Aren't you glad you came? You look like a natural."

Dana smiled. "I feel pretty comfortable. And I don't feel so intimidated anymore."

"Then the lesson has been a success," Larry declared. He stopped the horse occasionally to adjust Dana's feet in the stirrups. "Don't dig them in all the way. You're walking, not jumping," he said with a smile. He continued to instruct Dana whenever her body came out of alignment, but Macy, Dana, and Larry circled the ring, with Larry moving farther away with each circuit until the lesson was over.

"It gets easier," Larry said as he helped Dana dismount. "I can tell you like animals, and so can Macy. You did really well, Dana. I look forward to our next lesson. We can take her out on a trail, and I'll ride alongside."

"Let's go into the park," Mark said as Larry brought Macy back to her stall. "We'll walk the short bridle path that goes around the reservoir. It's such a beautiful day."

"I'd love to," Dana replied. "We have the entire weekend to ourselves. Let's make the most of it."

They strolled along the bridle path in Central Park, a place for horseback riding, jogging, and enjoying nature. The trees and shrubs were just starting to display varied shades of green as Mark and Dana walked, hand in hand, beneath the path's lush canopy.

"I wish everything were this tranquil," Dana said reflectively. "Or as easy as learning to get on a horse."

"Wishing it were easier to get to know Amanda?" Mark said, looking at the dirt path ahead as two joggers coming from the direction of the reservoir passed them.

Dana smiled and looked sideways at Mark. "Yes, and getting the boutique up and running."

Mark squeezed Dana's hand tighter. "Getting to know the child of someone you're dating always takes time. The boutique is a different story, however. Helen remains an obstacle, but that's no reason why we can't follow our plan." He returned Dana's gaze as he spoke. "I've had to fight for almost everything in my life. The right to take riding lessons, permission to go to the Wharton School and not a medical college, and, later, the way I wanted to run the company. My dad is a difficult guy, always challenging my vision, but we can't live in little bubbles, like the Finzi-Continis. I suppose that's why I create challenges for myself whenever things seem to be sailing along smoothly. It gives me a competitive edge and reminds me that there will always be something to push against what I'm trying to achieve."

They passed several tourists taking pictures. A photographer with half a dozen cameras slung over his shoulder was looking in the distance through a tripod-mounted zoom lens. He smiled at the couple and tipped his cap. Dana smiled back before walking on.

"You didn't have to fight for *me*," she said.

"Yes, it just feels ... right, doesn't it?"

Twenty paces further, Mark stopped and encircled Dana with his arms, drawing her close as he kissed her passionately on the lips.

"For now, it's a perfect bubble, and I'm happy to live in it all weekend," Dana said.

"Then that's just what we'll do. No talk about boutiques, Bauer & Sons , France, or the Hampton Classic. You've had your first riding lesson, met Amanda, and the gears are in motion with Irwin. I think we've both earned a little quiet time."

Dana leaned her body against Mark and put her arm around his waist as they continued to walk. An occasional rider slowly trotted by, and they passed an older man in a brown tweed jacket, obviously a birdwatcher, who was looking up into the trees with binoculars and writing his observations in a spiral notebook.

"Where shall we have dinner tonight?" Dana asked. "Sal's trattoria?"

"I know just the place," Mark said.

"Where?"

"My apartment. We'll drop by your place after lunch. You can change clothes, pack a bag, and pick up Wills. Tonight, everything we need will be at my apartment."

"Everything?"

"Yep. You and me."

"I think you're spoiling me, Mr. Senger."

"Gladly. And you have to start taking care of Dana, too. Stay focused on what you need and what makes you happy."

"That's what Father Macaulay's been telling me."

"The priest in London?"

"Yes. He's a wise man. And kind."

"You'll have to tell me more about him sometime. Anyway, why don't we go over to Sal's for a quick lunch, get our chores done, and be back to my place by four. We'll have a long, leisurely evening. And we'll sleep in tomorrow. Read the *Times* and—"

"And you can make some hockey puck pancakes."

"Amanda was exaggerating. They weren't that bad. They could have been oven mitts, but not hockey pucks. I'll put breakfast into your capable hands. How about a smoked salmon frittata? We'll buy what we need at Zabar's after we pick up Wills."

They kissed again and continued on. Dana leaned her head against Mark's shoulder and closed her eyes to block out the rest of the world. For the moment, there was no B. Altman, in-store boutique, or private label. She had the present moment, which was more than enough to make her happy.

Chapter Twenty-Nine

*D*ana arrived at work early Monday morning since she would be leaving the store at noon to dart home and be ready for Irwin's driver to pick her up and bring her to his factory in Brooklyn. She was meeting with Irwin and his head tailor to present a selection of sportswear from her wardrobe that would inspire the British clothing line. After a romantic weekend with Mark, she felt as energized as when she'd walked the streets of London or shopped the departments at Jaeger. Even her shaky start with Amanda no longer weighed on her mind since Mark was convinced that Amanda would learn to accept his relationship with Dana given time, which was enough to put her mind at ease.

Helen asked her to bring the latest projections on the Nantucket line to her office at ten. This seemed odd to Dana, who had given Helen projections for the line the week before. A little before ten, therefore, Dana gathered up the appropriate file and brought it to the divisional manager, wondering what was really on her mind. Helen glanced at the numbers for all of thirty seconds before dropping them on the side of her desk.

"Have a seat, Dana," Helen said, giving her full attention to Dana instead of occasionally glancing up from the work on her desk.

Dana sat, knowing that she'd been right. Something else was on Helen's mind, not the Nantucket numbers.

Helen smiled and leaned forward, hands clasped. "You're very good at your job, Dana. You continue to bring B. Altman many innovative ideas."

"Thank you, Helen," Dana replied, wondering where the conversation was going.

"As we saw with the teen makeup section, when the location became available in the cosmetic department, we were able to implement your idea. We all agree that it's been a huge success, but timing is everything."

At moments like this, Dana was ready to run from Helen and B. Altman to the position of fashion director at the House of Cirone. Maybe it was Mark's influence, but she was becoming more confident and, as such, less tolerant for these patronizing conversations. She wanted to remind Helen that she'd fought Dana every step of the way and that the only reason the store had a teen cosmetic department was because Dana saw the opportunity to create a location for it. It hadn't magically appeared, as Helen implied. It was Bob Campbell, not Helen, who'd given Dana the green light.

Remaining politically correct, however, Dana agreed with everything Helen said.

"Good," Helen said. "You're a valuable member of our team, and after all the years you've been with the store, we'd hate to ever lose you. So please heed my advice."

Dana was suddenly concerned. Had Helen somehow gotten wind of Johnny's offer to work for the House of Cirone? Had Andrew let a random comment slip by accident, one that had traveled back to Helen's office? It didn't seem likely, but something was on Helen's mind, and Dana didn't have to wait long to find out what it was.

"I'll be perfectly honest," Helen said, "and I'm speaking to you as a friend, not your boss. I've noticed that you spend an awful lot of time looking at the build-out for your Nantucket boutique. When I arrived this morning, I thought that I saw you measuring one of the walls."

"You can't blame a girl for dreaming," Dana said innocently. She hated keeping her plans with Irwin a secret from Helen, but she had no choice. Dana had made the pitch, and Helen had unequivocally refused to consider it.

"Dreaming is fine," Helen said, her expression still pleasant, "as long as you're not entertaining any ideas of resurrecting the boutique. You've gone around me before, but it's not going to happen again. It would mean your job."

Dana was more confused than ever. "You've already made that very clear, Helen."

"I just wanted to make sure that you still understand my position. Like I said, you're a valuable asset to the store, and I'd hate to lose that asset. You know, Dana, I admire your ambition, but there is a chain of command around here, and I suggest you stay in line."

"Of course, Helen."

"By the way, have you seen Andrew? He's not here and hasn't called in."

"He said the other day that he thought he was coming down with something."

"Well, he could at least have the presence of mind to give us a call," Helen said tersely.

Dana left the office, unsure about what had just transpired. When she returned to her office, her assistant handed her three messages, all from Mark, and said, "He says it's urgent."

Dana called Mark's office, and she was put through immediately.

"What's up?" Dana asked him. "First Helen starts acting peculiar, and now you're frantically calling me. It's turning out to be a strange day."

"You talked with Helen this morning?"

"Yes."

"So you already know then. Damn. I was hoping to get in touch first so *I* could break the news."

"News? What news? Somebody please tell me what's going on here. Helen just reiterated that there's not going to be a British boutique, but I already know her position, so that can't be what you're talking about."

"It's not. Helen called me early this morning and told me that she's giving the selling space to Jones New York. She ordered me to dismantle the boutique. Jones is giving B. Altman an exclusive collection, and Helen wants to test the line in that prime selling space since it's right off the escalator."

"This could change everything!" Dana declared. "When does Helen want this in place?"

"As soon as possible from what I can tell."

"It explains my unusual talk with Helen just now," Dana said. "I think she suspects that I haven't given up on my original plan, so she wants to push this through. Mark, this is terrible! If Helen succeeds, then it doesn't matter how good my custom-designed separates line is. There won't be any place to sell it, at least not as I had envisioned. It's the boutique that completes the idea."

"I know, I know," Mark said, "but let's not hit the panic button. I've already called Irwin and told him that time is of the essence. I assume you're still bringing him samples today?"

"Yes, but—"

"No buts. Let's stay focused and get the samples to Irwin. I don't have anyone to dismantle the boutique tomorrow. My crew is in the middle of a major build-out at the Met. We still have a window of opportunity, so let's stay the course."

"Okay, but life sure was easier inside the bubble for the past two days."

"And we'll get there again, but we always knew this was something we'd have to fight for, right?"

"Very true."

"Then let's fight. And don't let on that you know what Helen is up to. Play it close to the vest."

"I'm already there," Dana said. "Helen gave me fair warning, but it's going to be business as usual."

"Perfect," Mark said. "We'll see this through. Don't worry."

Dana hung up and returned to work. On the way to the selling floor, she passed Helen twice and smiled quickly, knowing that Helen was scrutinizing every aspect of her body language. The situation was frustrating, but Dana reminded herself that Helen wasn't an evil genius trying to thwart her career. She was a good woman, but one who was extremely controlling and had her own way of doing things. By noon Dana was exhausted from thinking about her morning conversation with Helen and her subsequent conversation with Mark. She was glad to get back to the carriage house to walk Wills, collect her suitcase of samples, and be whisked away to Brooklyn for a creative session with Irwin. It wouldn't be long before she was lost in a sea of beautiful fabrics on the way to charting a new course for B. Altman.

Women's manufacturers were tucked away on the side streets off Seventh Avenue, but many menswear manufacturers, whose showrooms were on Sixth Avenue, had factories in Brooklyn. Knowing that this location was off Dana's beaten path, Irwin met her at the front door, insisting that she allow him to give her a tour of the entire facility. His pride in his operation was obvious as demonstrated by his warm welcome and eagerness to show her the factory layout. Dana followed him after handing the suitcase of clothes to one of Irwin's assistants.

Bauer & Sons Clothiers was housed in a four-story brick building with loft spaces on every floor crowded with racks of clothing, cutting tables, steam pressers, bolts of fabric, and seamstresses and tailors at their stations. Men and women with tape measures around their necks scurried from one room to another as sewing machines hummed beneath wide lamps hanging from the ceiling. Irwin introduced Dana to his department heads, ending with the head tailor, Steve Palazzo, who'd already hung Dana's samples on a rolling rack.

"Steve has been with me for twenty-eight years," Irwin said. "We met in Milan, and he joined me a month later. You couldn't be in better hands, Dana."

"So nice to meet you, Steve," Dana said with a twinkle in her eyes, no longer showing the stress of the morning. I think I'll be easy to work with. I know exactly what I want."

"Famous last words," Irwin said laughing. "Now where do you want to start? Fabrics or patterns?"

"Fabrics," Dana said.

"Come this way," Steve said as Dana and Irwin followed him into a section across the floor that was shelved with wall-to-wall bolts of fabrics sectioned by color, pattern, and weave.

Dana made her selections in twenty minutes, limiting the coordinated separates line to muted taupe, beige, and cream wool accented with brown tweed, lovat glen plaid, and oatmeal pinwale corduroy. Dana's proposed department would also carry basics in gray flannel and camel hair. A double-face loden was chosen for a duffle coat.

"You *do* know what you want," Irwin said as they walked to the cutting room where the samples were waiting.

"I want to keep the line simple for the launch. The neutral colors will be attractive when displayed with coordinating cashmere sweaters and Jersey shawls. However, I can't get into those showrooms to place orders until Bob approves the concept."

"Mark called this morning and told me that we're under the gun a bit. Is that right?"

"Unfortunately it is. The space we discussed at dinner is being allocated to Jones New York."

"I can tell you're worried," Irwin said, "but I've been under the gun myself more than a few times. Sometimes my customers want their orders yesterday, and I'm accustomed to the pressure. You have a clear vision of what we have to do, so I don't anticipate any down time."

Dana nodded, feeling at least partially relieved.

The next two hours were spent designing the line, with Dana requesting changes to the fit and finishes of the samples.

After Irwin called for the car to bring Dana back to Manhattan, they shared their excitement for the new venture and the business opportunity it represented for both of them.

"I really want this to happen, Irwin. I'm going to prove to my boss that I'm not a dreamer and that my vision is based on solid reasoning and good marketing sense."

"Nothing wrong with dreaming. It's an important first step, but most people don't follow through and do what it takes to turn a dream into a reality."

"I know I'm in good hands with you and Mark," Dana said.

Irwin leaned close to Dana. "Let's make it happen."

"I have no doubt it will!" Dana said.

• • •

Back at Sniffen Court, Dana felt confident once again as a result of her meeting with Irwin. It had served as the perfect counterbalance to Helen's decision to give space to Jones New York—and intimidate Dana in the process. Filled with new hope, she had dinner and was about to go upstairs to read when the phone rang. It was Johnny, who had called as usual in order to take Dana's emotional temperature and fish for an answer regarding his job offer. Dana, however, didn't give him any of the reassurances he was looking for. Instead, she described what she'd been doing for the past few days.

"You're taking riding lessons?" he asked.

"Yes, at Claremont. I did really well. I wasn't at all nervous."

"Who arranged the lessons? Mark?"

"Yes. Mark's been riding since he was a child, and his daughter's a show jumper."

"Have you met his daughter?"

"Yes."

"How old is she?"

"Alright, Johnny. Stop. This has become an interrogation."

"Sorry," Johnny said. "I can't deny it. I'm a bit curious about Mark. I would never have expected that—"

"That *what*?"

"I don't know. He just doesn't seem like your type."

"You're smothering me."

"It looks like Mark is the one being overly protective what with his encouraging you to work with his friend. Sounds a little too cozy. "

"He's trying to help me achieve what I want, and what I want is for B. Altman to carry a private line of British-inspired clothing."

"It sounds like a long shot to me," Johnny said.

"And you sound like a mother hen to me."

Johnny was frustrated with Dana's stubbornness, but he let the comment pass. "Speaking of mothers, your mom has been calling me, asking if you've joined the company yet. She's worried about you, and I'm running out of things to tell her."

"Why doesn't she ask me directly?" Dana asked, getting annoyed. "Am I a hot topic of conversation for you two?"

Johnny was silent for several seconds. "I'll be honest, Dana. We're concerned that you're in over your head. You've only been separated for a few months, and you're jeopardizing your job and rushing into this relationship with Mark."

"Johnny?"

"Yes?"

"You know I love you, but I'm not going to talk about this anymore tonight. I promise I'll be in touch, but I had a long day."

"Okay, Dana. We love you, too. We just want the best for you."

"I'm the best judge of that. Goodnight."

Dana was going to follow Irwin's advice and continue her relationship with Mark. Her mother would be calling any day now, and she was resigned to having her very forceful mother challenge her in a much stronger way than Johnny had. She wished that Father Macaulay was stationed in a parish somewhere in Manhattan. He could listen without offering judgment.

Chapter Thirty

$\mathcal{B}$rett and Janice were going over case files from San Francisco on Tuesday morning when Brett's secretary announced that Wade Forrester was waiting in the outer office.

"Show him in," Brett said, glancing at Janice. "This ought to be quite enlightening," he told his partner, with whom he'd shared all he learned from Johnny.

"Good morning, Mr. McGarry," Forrester said stoically, eyeing Janice cautiously.

"It's okay, Wade. I want her present for your briefing."

"Very well," Forrester said, sitting in a chair, opening his briefcase, and producing several files. "I learned a great deal about Mr. Senger and his activities with Mrs. McGarry."

Brett leaned forward in his desk chair, Janice standing casually in the corner behind him. She folded her arms, leaned against the wall, and fixed her gaze on the private investigator. The news from Johnny had been more than she could have hoped for. Perhaps now she could definitively protect her romantic and financial interests at the expense of Little Miss Priss.

"I think you're familiar with the overview," Forrester began. "Senger is forty-two and president of Senger Display. He lives alone in a very expensive co-op on the Upper West Side and is occasionally visited by his daughter Amanda, who attends

Cornell in the veterinary medicine program. His net worth is several million dollars, although at present that's merely an approximation. I should have details in another week. He's well educated and has a penchant for the finer things in life—food, the arts, travel, and the like. One of my men is running down the paperwork at City Hall to find out the details and timing of his divorce. The records are accessible to the public, but in a city of this size, there's a waiting list to get them unless you grease a few palms. We're working on it. But there's a wealth of information we were able to garner through simple tailing and observation."

Janice moved forward and stood at Brett's side. She took a deep breath in anticipation of what Forrester had found out. Hopefully, it would reveal Dana's feet of clay.

"Let's have it," Brett said.

"Mrs. McGarry is in a serious relationship with Mr. Senger and has been spending the night at his apartment frequently, according to direct surveillance. He recently treated your wife to an expensive riding wardrobe purchased from Miller's. The clothing is estimated to have cost two thousand dollars."

"Riding outfit?" Janice said.

"Yes, ma'am. Senger is paying for lessons for Mrs. McGarry at Claremont Riding Academy. He's given the stables $500 towards the lessons."

"Interesting," Brett said. "Any lavish gifts?"

"None that we've detected. We have pictures of her in her riding clothes, and a consultant of mine was able to trace them to Miller's. I dispatched someone to the store, where he asked a few innocent questions, the answers to which indicated that Senger and your wife indeed visited Miller's recently."

"Tell us more about these lessons," Janice said, glancing down at Brett.

"They went to Claremont on Saturday, where Mrs. Mc-Garry had her first lesson. After that, they went for a walk on one of the bridle paths in Central Park. This is where it gets interesting—and perhaps a bit painful," Forrester said, producing photographs from one of his folders.

"Don't hold back anything," Brett instructed. "It's why I hired you. I already have a pretty good idea where you're going with this."

Forrester nodded and proceeded to give his report in a straightforward manner. He handed Brett the pictures, which showed Mark and Dana walking closely together, embracing, and kissing at several stops along the path.

"It was fairly easy to get these shots since so many photographers are in the park and on the trails almost every day. My men didn't arouse the slightest bit of suspicion."

"Were you able to hear what they were talking about?" Brett asked.

"Absolutely. My main photographer had a great deal of equipment, but mixed in with his cameras were highly sensitive microphones and recording equipment. I also had an extra man—a retired New York City police detective who does freelance work—posing as a naturalist taking notes on birds. Between the two sources, I have a transcript of most of their conversation."

Forrester handed Brett a copy of the document before resuming.

"As you can see," Forrester continued, "they talked about a show jumping contest called the Hampton Classic, which is an upcoming event for Amanda. There's also mention of France, although there's no context for the comment. I would theorize that someone is making travel plans. As you'll see, there's also talk about a boutique and a company called Bauer & Sons Clothiers, which manufactures menswear in Brooklyn. Mrs. McGarry visited Bauer's factory late yesterday evening, carrying a suitcase she took from her apartment overlooking Sniffen Court."

Janice shot Brett a puzzled look.

"Probably samples for Bauer to copy," Brett surmised. "Based on Johnny's information, this is part of her idea to sell a private line of clothes at B. Altman."

"Irwin Bauer is a longtime friend of Senger," Forrester said. "He's also wealthy and his business, while suffering a downturn recently, has generally been quite lucrative. Based on conversation we overheard when Senger and your wife went for a walk on Sunday afternoon, Senger seems to be the guiding hand in implementing Mrs. McGarry's business ideas."

"It all makes sense," Brett said. "I listened to fashion talk for ten years. If Dana wants a private label for Altman, the store would need a manufacturer. From what Johnny Cirone tells me, Dana's boss isn't cooperating, so she and Mark are obviously doing this on their own."

"And she's got the House of Cirone to fall back on if the deal falls through," Janice said.

Brett nodded.

"Do Dana and Senger have any plans to marry?" Janice asked.

"Not as far as I can tell. As the transcript reveals, however, they're quite taken with each other, and the talk is explicitly romantic. And oh, there's one more thing. Dana and Mark share the same divorce attorney, a man named Alan Rudnick. He's a high-priced attorney known for making spouses bleed green." Forrester returned the files to his briefcase. "That's all I have for now."

"I found out that last detail firsthand," Brett said, rolling his eyes. "Excellent work as usual, Wade. Get back to me when you have those public records and more on Senger's assets."

"Shall I keep following them?"

"Yes," Janice said.

Forrester glanced at Brett, who was smiling.

"Yes, Wade. Get me whatever you can and spare no expense."

"Yes, sir."

Forrester left, and Janice moved to the front of the desk, sat and crossed her legs.

"This is absolutely incredible!" Janice exclaimed. "What in the hell does Dana need your generous settlement for? She's going to make a bundle of cash on her own regardless of where she ends up working, plus she's got a wealthy older man on the hook. Are you going to let her get away with this? What she's doing is outrageous. In fact ... "

"Go ahead," Brett said. "You can't say anything that would make me angrier."

"How do we know Dana wasn't involved with Senger last year?"

Brett shook his head. "She was talking about starting a family and buying a home in the country."

"What difference does *that* make? Was she understanding about your desire to make partner?"

"Yes, but she was growing impatient towards the end of the year. I was feeling a lot of pressure from her about my hours here at the firm. She was quite irritable by December over ridiculous stuff, like the choice of a Christmas tree."

"My point exactly. Plenty of people begin flirting or start relationships when they're discontent, but if their spouses suddenly walk the straight and narrow, they abandon their extracurricular activities and begin nesting. Maybe she was testing the waters with this guy."

Brett was clearly agitated. "You know, she ended the marriage so quickly, calling an attorney before I even returned from San Francisco. That's not Dana's style at all."

"And Rudnick is Senger's attorney too. Come on, Brett. Two and two make four. Dana is the type to at least hear you out, think about matters, and probably even go to marriage counseling. Her personality isn't even close to shooting from the hip. She gets a call from her brother, however, and suddenly she has an instant appointment with a shark who handles family law. I'm sorry, but this whole thing stinks. It's five months later and she's getting handouts from this rich old man, staying at his apartment, and positioning herself for megabucks and more European travel—maybe even a partnership with the House of Cirone as she steps up to fashion director. Sounds premeditated, if you ask me."

Brett looked at Janice, unsure of what to say.

"Sounds like Dana may not have been the demure, patient wife you thought you were married to. And you're going to give her alimony and half of your joint assets? For God's sake, fight back!"

Brett stood and sighed. "That's exactly what I'm going to do. I agreed to terms, but in New York State, the initial agreement doesn't roll over into a divorce decree until a couple is separated for a full year. Trust me, I'm going to call my attorney today. Dana is childless and, as we've learned, very employable. I'm going to request that the court evaluate her earning potential."

Janice stood, approached Brett, and put her arms around him. "Aren't you glad I came back to New York? You're doing the right thing."

Brett and Janice kissed tenderly.

"I don't hate Dana," Brett said, "but I'm not going to be played for a fool."

"That's the Brett I love," Janice said, winking. "Keep your edge and don't give away the store."

Janice left the office, delighted at what she'd heard from Wade Forrester. And she was glad that she'd made the decision to keep a closer eye on Brett. After all, somebody had to keep the poor baby on course.

Chapter Thirty-One

*A*ndrew Ricci was at his desk on Tuesday morning. He was well dressed as always and looked alert and upbeat. As far as his coworkers were concerned, he'd been sick. He exhibited no sign that he'd been drinking heavily for the past two nights.

"Hey," Dana said, poking her head into Andrew's office. "Feeling better?"

Andrew looked up and grinned. "I'm over my bug, kiddo. Doing fine. What about you?"

"I took some clothing to Irwin on Monday, and I can't wait to see what he does with the samples. He had amazing fabrics."

"Even though Jones New York is getting the space where your boutique was going?"

"You know about that?"

"I was sick, not dead! Of course I know. And my bet's on you. No fool's errand to Brooklyn for Dana McGarry. Hey, are you and Mark still going full steam ahead?"

"And why wouldn't we be!"

"Oh, you've got it worse than I thought, Dana. Not that it's a bad thing, of course. You look happier than I've seen you in a long time. If you're happy, then I'm all for what you're doing— with Mark, the boutique, whatever."

Dana raised her hands in the air as she spoke. "Yes! Why can't everyone else be happy for me? Johnny's driving me crazy."

"What about Virginia? She's not one to remain silent."

"She's coming over for dinner tomorrow night, which means she and Johnny have been discussing my future again. Mom said my father is busy, which is another way of saying she wants to speak to me alone. She knows Dad allows me to live life the way I want."

"Give me a report," Andrew said, pointing his finger at Dana as he stood. "Every word. Gotta run to the kids' floor. They're installing the carousel. Later!"

Andrew's smile dissolved into a vacant stare for the few moments he rode down in the elevator. He was still tired and had been recovering from a hangover the day before. His sense of responsibility had propelled him to work that morning even though he was severely depressed, unable to think of anyone or anything but Jack. Were he and Patti patching things up? Was Jack at Hartlen Response, carrying on business as usual? Andrew didn't know, for he'd had no contact at all with Jack. He was trying his best to focus on work, but he was merely going through the motions.

At lunch, he left the store and walked aimlessly along the streets, not concentrating on where he was going. He didn't know if he'd walked ten blocks or thirty, but he eventually found himself back at the Fifth Avenue entrance. Taking a deep breath, he stepped inside reluctantly to tackle an afternoon of schematics and meetings.

"Good afternoon, Helen!" he said cheerily as he walked across the main floor, once again reclaiming the face of Andrew Ricci that everyone was familiar with.

"Would you stop by my office later?" she asked. "I want to go over a few design plans. And welcome back!"

Andrew winked. "I'll be there within the hour," he said as he resumed walking briskly to the elevators.

The day dragged on, and Andrew thought that he couldn't possibly muster one more smile. He glanced at his watch several times each hour until, at last, he finished his work for the day. It was five twenty-two.

Andrew grabbed his coat and rode the subway to Greenwich Village, where he headed straight for a gay bar called Out of Bounds. It was a silly name, he thought, but it fit perfectly with the iconoclastic nature of the Village, with an extra pun on the fact that his lifestyle wasn't sanctioned by mainstream culture. He entered the dim upscale establishment and sat at the end of the mahogany bar, staring past hundreds of liquor bottles into the long mirror on the wall opposite his seat. A morose face stared back at him—his own. He ordered a gin and tonic and sat silently, looking at his features, which, after a long day of work, looked tired and drawn.

An hour passed, and he was on his third gin and tonic when a stranger sat beside him. The man, in his thirties and dressed in a blue three-piece pinstripe business suit, ordered scotch neat.

"It's been a long day," the tall, wiry stranger said after five minutes.

Andrew turned his head, surprised by the unprompted conversation.

The stranger lowered his head and grinned. "Sorry. That was a pretty lame introduction. I'm Chad Collins," he said, extending his hand.

Andrew was taken aback by the man's use of his surname. Even in trendier bars, last names were not used at an initial meeting.

"Andrew Ricci. Nice to meet you."

"I haven't seen you here before. I stop in most evenings after work. I'm an investment banker with Dobbs and Haskell." Collins had short blond hair and blue eyes.

"Just passing by and thought I'd stop in," Andrew said. "I work at B. Altman. Display director."

"Interesting! I shop there frequently. But it's off the beaten path for the Out of Bounds bar. Are you sure you were just passing by?"

Andrew nodded at the mild challenge. "Guilty as charged. Wanted to get away from work and my apartment."

"Sorry again. Is my babbling bothering you?" asked Collins. "I'll find a table if you want to be alone."

Andrew paused before speaking as Collins started to slide off the seat. "No. By all means stay. No use staring at that mirror all night."

"All night, eh? From the little you've told me, you just lost a partner. Well, I did, too. Walked out on me after two years. Getting through the day is pretty hard. At least here I don't have to pretend that everything in my life is fine."

Andrew raised his glass. "I know the feeling too well. When did your partner leave you?"

"Six months ago. A shrink told me that my grieving process should be over, but that hasn't proven to be the case. What do they know, huh? What about you?"

"Jack—that's his name—and I split three days ago. We weren't living together because ... well, just because."

"Because he has a wife."

"How did you know?"

"Just a guess. I've known people who've dealt with the same situation. For what it's worth, that kind of triangle never has a happy ending, at least not that I've observed. The pull of family is pretty strong. Did he have kids?"

"No, just a wife and a large Texas oil family that owns two major companies."

"Ouch. Tough odds to beat. My story is more straightforward. Ron left me for a photographer here in the Village, but here's the worst part. The other guy used to be a ski instructor in Aspen before coming to New York. Tall fella with Nordic good looks. Rugged, handsome—the whole nine yards. Does it get any more stereotypical?"

The two men chuckled at the remark, and Andrew realized that he hadn't laughed for days, at least not with sincerity.

"If you're still hurting after six months," Andrew said, "it looks like I have a long way to go. Right now it doesn't feel as if I'll ever get past this."

"We'll both turn the corner one day," Collins asserted. "I've been dumped before. It gets better eventually, but right now? If you didn't feel lousy, you wouldn't be human."

"Jack says he wants time to straighten his life out and explain things to his wife."

"I'm sure he's sincere, but it's always a long shot. Say, you want to grab a table where we can relax a bit more?"

"Sure. Why not?"

They talked for two hours—Andrew speaking of how he'd helped Jack deal with his conflicted sexual identity—before deciding to get dinner and continue their conversation. Afterwards, Andrew went home with Collins and stayed the night. He called Collins after work the next day but got no answer. Leaving the store, he returned to Out of Bounds, but Collins wasn't there. He once again sat alone at the bar, drinking gin and tonic. He contemplated calling Dobbs and Haskell the next day before realizing that it was a futile gesture. The man didn't want to be found.

After a few more drinks, Andrew laughed out loud and thought of how foolish he'd been the night before. Why was he hoping to meet Collins again? He had no feelings for the man. It was Jack he loved. Others approached him, offering to buy him a drink, but he declined.

"This is what comes of desperation," he muttered under his breath as he gave the bartender a tip. He left at ten o'clock and went home, where he drank until midnight.

Chapter Thirty-Two

Patti had just arrived home on Tuesday evening when Jack came through the door ten minutes later, placing his briefcase on the floor as he glanced at the day's mail. It could have been a scene from *Ozzie and Harriet*.

"Jack? Is everything all right?"

Jack smiled. "Why wouldn't it be?"

"Well, because you haven't been home early in ... I mean, you're so busy at work and . . Never mind. Can I get you anything. A drink?"

"Nothing for me, thanks. I'm going to sit and read the paper."

Jack kissed Patti and walked into the den where he removed his suit coat and settled on the couch where he leafed through the *Times*. He checked the headlines before turning to the financial section.

"Where shall we go for dinner?" Patti asked. Normally a decisive woman, she spoke and moved hesitantly, puzzled by Jack's shift in routine.

"Oh, I don't know. Why don't we just eat in?"

"Uh, sure. I'll get dinner started now."

Patti opened drawers in the kitchen and removed food from the pantry and freezer, but she couldn't shake Jack's sudden normalcy from her mind. Was Jack now having mood swings? She decided that she would insist that he make an appointment with his doctor for a check-up. Meanwhile, she started dinner and an hour later found Jack watching the evening news in the den as if it was what he did every evening.

"Dinner's ready," she said.

Jack clicked off the TV with the remote and walked into the dining room. Not once had he complained about being tired.

Their talk over dinner was slightly more animated than usual, with Jack speaking of what had happened at Hartlen Response that day and also about his parents in Houston.

"Dad called this morning and said that he'd like us to fly down in June for the annual family reunion. How does that sound?"

"Sounds great," Patti said. "I really miss our family and friends. Does this mean you're less pressured at work?"

Jack smiled. "I thought you'd be pleased. And yes, things have eased up at the office." Patti listened while Jack continued to talk, but there had been something different about his smile, something that was at odds with his personality. It hadn't been forced, but neither had it fit in with the energy and flow of his usual conversation. By the end of the meal, Patti didn't know whether to be more or less concerned about her husband's behavior.

The evening ended after Jack had watched more television and gone to bed. Patti straightened up, and as she picked up Jack's coat from the couch in the den, she felt a pill bottle in the side pocket. She removed it and saw that a prescription for Valium had been written for Jack that day by a Dr. Walter Stein. She quickly got the telephone book from a desk drawer in Jack's study and looked up Dr. Stein. He was a psychiatrist in midtown Manhattan.

Eyes narrowed, Patti looked at the bottle again before sitting slowly on the couch, her mind racing. Things were falling into place. Patti thought it likely that Jack had arrived home early after a session with the psychiatrist. He had apparently filled the prescription on the way home, and the tranquilizer was obviously responsible for her husband's pleasant but sedate demeanor. But why hadn't Jack told her he was consulting a doctor?

It was a foolish question. Why hadn't Jack told her *anything* about what had driven him to see a psychiatrist? This was final validation, as if she needed it, that Jack was dealing with serious issues. She would talk to him the following morning and pledge her unwavering support for whatever had propelled him to seek professional help. It might be a long road, but Patti had new hope that their lives would finally return to normal.

No, that was the last thing she would do. If Jack had wanted her to know that he was seeing a doctor, he would have told her. The important thing was that he was getting help. She would wait for Jack to come to her, and hopefully she would know in the foreseeable future what lay behind the great mystery of her husband's altered behavior over the past several months. Waiting would test the limits of her patience since she wanted so badly to help Jack get better. She still feared that he was seeing another woman.

Chapter Thirty-Three

*A*lways punctual, Virginia arrived at Sniffen Court at seven o'clock. As Dana scurried around the kitchen preparing baked salmon and orzo, mother and daughter talked about the store, the news, and how Phil was re-landscaping the Martignetti home in Hewlett Harbor now that spring had arrived. Over dinner, Virginia told Dana that Matthew had selected a thesis topic for his major in marine biology at the University of Hawaii: cetacean migratory patterns. The two women also discussed how well Uncle John was doing now that he lived in Manhattan, having finally moved from his family home in Long Island after the death of his wife two years earlier.

"So what have you been up to?" Virginia asked Dana casually. "Dad and I haven't heard from you much lately."

"Keeping busy at work. Going out with friends."

"When you say keeping busy at work, I assume you mean trying to get your own clothes line while putting off Uncle John's offer."

Dana prepared herself for a direct line of questioning. True to character, Virginia hadn't taken long to get to her point.

"A line of clothing for B. Altman, not myself. Why do you and Johnny have to continually scrutinize everything I do? You can't even get the facts straight. This is why you came tonight, isn't it—to discuss my life in light of everything Johnny's been telling you?"

Virginia brushed off the remark. "And when you say you're going out with friends, you mean Mark Senger, who's behind all of this."

"Behind all of *what*?"

"The horseback riding and the boutique. Most of all, avoiding a job that would be perfect for you."

"You mean a job that would be perfect for *you*, but let's take one thing at a time. There's nothing wrong with horseback riding. Millions of people around the world ride, even children. Would you rather I ride a motorcycle?"

"Horseback riding isn't safe! That's what's wrong with it! You used to be afraid of dogs, and now you're on top of a thousand pound animal? It doesn't make sense, Dana. I've been reading about this sport, and did you know that it's even more dangerous when you take it up later in life?"

"I just turned thirty, not sixty. I don't know what you've been reading, Mom, but that's ridiculous."

"No it isn't. When you begin as a child, you're more confident and gain experience over the years, which helps avoid accidents as an adult. Even *Reader's Digest* agrees. Falling from a horse can cause serious brain injury, Dana. Why can't you two just ride bicycles in the park?"

"People fall off bikes, too. And Claremont Riding Academy has excellent riding instructors. My instructor taught Mark's daughter, who happens to be a champion show jumper. She boards her horse in Muttontown."

"Really?" Virginia mumbled, shaking her head. "She boards her horse in Muttontown?"

"Yes. You remember Muttontown, We visited—"

"I do, but I don't know too many young girls who have their own horse. She must be spoiled. How many children does Mark have?"

"Just Amanda. She's a freshman at Cornell, and she's a very good student. She's studying to be a veterinarian."

"Oh, this keeps getting better. An only child with her own horse."

"Mother, I'm not going to listen to this any longer. You haven't even met Mark, and you're saying unkind things about his daughter. In addition, you're not respecting my feelings or my judgment."

"Dana, I always respect your feelings," Virgina said, "but, yes, I'm questioning your judgment. I think you've gotten too serious much too quickly with this man."

Dana leaned back in her chair and crossed her arms defensively. "This *man* is someone I've known for almost four years. We've often worked together at the store, and Mark and Andrew are always in the middle of one project or another. He's president of his family's company Senger Display, and B. Altman has been an account for more than ten years. He grew up on the Upper West Side. He's forty-two and he's divorced. We've only been dating about a month and I'm still getting to know him, but what I know so far, I like."

"A month? And he's already taken over your life and decision-making?"

Fuming, Dana said nothing.

"I'm sorry," Virginia said, sipping from a glass of water. "I'm not giving you a chance to talk, so tell me more about him."

"He's smart, witty, and we share a love of film and literature. And it's important to me that he's interested in my career. Is that so bad?"

"That's it? You're head over heels for this man because he's interested in your career? I think you've been managing your career just fine on your own. Frankly, I think if Mark were really helpful, he'd be encouraging you to take advantage of the opportunity to work with Uncle John. How many young women get a chance like that?"

"I want to make it on my own, Mother. Mark understands that. Frankly, he understands me better than anyone else."

"Time will tell. In the meantime, there's more to life than work. How long has he been divorced?" Virginia asked. "Is he like you—just ending a relationship?"

Dana shrugged. "I don't really know, Mom. It's never come up."

"What do you mean you don't know? That's not a trivial detail, Dana. How could you *not* know? What do you two talk about, for heaven's sake?"

Dana wanted to end the conversation, but this was her mother, not Johnny, and she was sitting in Dana's kitchen. Dana steeled herself for more of her mother's interrogation.

"When Amanda is not in school, she lives with her mother and comes to visit Mark on weekends sometimes. In all the years I've worked with him, I've never heard him talk about his ex, so I imagine that they divorced a long time ago. I'm sure it'll come up in conversation one day. I didn't want to give him the third degree, and he showed me the same consideration. And what difference does it make? Neither of us is married now. Anyway, I trust him. It's not like he was a blind date."

"I know the past year has been difficult," Virginia admitted, "but he's older. With a daughter in college, do you think he's going to want to start a new family at his age? If you married him at some point in the next two years, will he want a newborn in his mid-forties while his daughter graduates from college? You're not thinking clearly. Don't you want a family?"

"Like I said, we just started going out, and when you meet him, you'll understand. He's the type of man who'll never grow old. Anyway, was I supposed to ask him about having children on the second date?"

"No, but you can put two and two together."

"I'm getting aggravated, Mother. Right now, our focus is on the birth of B. Altman's British Shop of private label merchandise."

"But according to Johnny, it's a long shot. You have no idea if B. Altman will accept this … this boutique thing you're pursuing. And it's inconsiderate to keep Uncle John waiting."

"Mark and I think this *thing*, as you put it, will be successful. Besides, Uncle John says I can consider his offer for as long as I want."

"Well, don't take advantage of him because he's like family. They have a business to run. Did you know that they'll be carrying a younger line of eveningwear? Johnny wanted you to attend a meeting to get your opinion of Francis' new sketches, but he couldn't reach you in time."

Dana was ready to explode when she realized how much Johnny was sharing with Virginia, but she calmly said that she would take that into consideration. The last thing she wanted to do was hurt Uncle John or Johnny.

"Everything you say confirms my suspicions more and more, Dana. It's Mark and the boutique that's preventing you from making smart choices."

Dana rose from the table and began clearing dishes, with help from her mother.

"I don't deny that what I'm doing is a risk, but it's a risk I'm willing to take. I didn't ask Brett for a divorce just to jump into another marriage. I now have the time I need to focus on my career, and even though I may not need him, I'm glad to have Mark on my side. He gives me a lot of confidence, and I'm becoming more assertive. We really are a good match, Mom. You'll see."

Virginia was still concerned, but she said, "Parents never stop worrying about their children—you'll find that out on your own some day—and I felt that I had to get all of this off my chest. Can you understand that?"

Dana finished putting the last utensil on the drain board, turned to her mother, and put her arms around her. "Yes, I do. I love you, Mom. All I'm asking is that you and Johnny back away a bit and give me some breathing room. I won't keep Uncle John waiting for an answer forever, but I've got to see how this private label idea plays out. As for Mark ... " Dana raised her eyebrows and looked her mother in the eyes. "You're going to have to trust that I know what I'm doing."

The two women hugged again and Virginia gathered up her things as Dana got Wills ready for his evening walk. They left Sniffen Court, and Virginia quickly found a taxi to take her to Penn Station. "Stay in touch, Dana. And as Uncle John might say, pray. God will steer you in the right direction."

Dana smiled. "I know, Mom. Don't worry. I still go to church. Does Dad know what time your train gets in?"

"Of course. Give him a call and tell him I'm on my way."

When Dana returned, she straightened up and looked at the secretary in her living room. She hoped another letter from Father Macaulay would arrive soon. She'd told her mother the truth. She was indeed anchored by her faith, but she felt more than a little comfort knowing that she had such a wise advisor who kept her in his thoughts and prayers.

She also believed, however, that God helped those who helped themselves. She would stay the course and continue down the paths she'd chosen in the past weeks. It went beyond just taking care of herself, as Father Macaulay had suggested. It was a question of being true to herself and following through on the goals she set.

That would never change.

Chapter Thirty-Four

The telephone was ringing when Dana arrived home on Wednesday evening. If it were her mother or Johnny calling to lecture her again or ask probing questions about her relationship with Mark, she would tell them she was busy and would call back another time. She wasn't going to deal with their intrusions indefinitely. She was relieved, however, to hear Mark's voice on the other end of the line.

"Honey, how would you like to come with me to Muttontown this weekend?" Mark asked. "We can stay at Judd's—he has a wonderful old stone house that you'd love—and the trails are beautiful."

"But I've only had one lesson," Dana replied. "I don't think I'd be the best riding companion."

"Let me be the judge of that, and besides, you need the practice. The next gait to master is the trot, and I can show you that. Frank's great, but wouldn't you rather take lessons from me?"

Dana laughed. "Well, if you put it that way, how can I refuse?"

"You can't. Just being around Judd and his stables will give you a leg up—pardon the pun—with your riding. And we get to have a relaxing weekend in some pretty gorgeous country. Very romantic, I might add."

Dana thought back to the previous weekend and hesitated. "Wait a second. Didn't you tell me that Amanda was going to start spending more time at Judd's beginning this weekend after exams are over?"

"That's right. Amanda will definitely be there. She's usually at Judd's whenever she has time off from school, but even more so when the competition is looming."

"I'm not sure," Dana said. "I know you told me that she's willing to give our relationship a chance, but isn't this pushing things a bit? We only just met last week. Maybe she needs more time before seeing me again. Besides, Muttontown is obviously a special place for you two, just like Claremont."

"It is, but I want it to be a special place for you and me as well. Trust me on this. Judd has a big home and lots of acreage, so there's plenty of room for all of us. I don't see any reason why Amanda should object. We'll certainly see her, but she'll be working on her jumping with Paul most of the time. We'll probably have a couple of meals together, but otherwise she'll be absorbed with Pepsi and her riding. And remember, she has to get used to the idea of our being together. This is the perfect opportunity since we can all be in the same location without having to force her into any social interaction with us."

Dana didn't have to think for long. "I guess that makes good sense. It eases her into accepting our relationship in a more casual way. Okay, I'm in. I'll go."

"Excellent. Pack casually, but be sure to bring your breeches and boots. I'll arrange to have a car take us out there and bring us back late Sunday night. I hate driving in traffic and the Long Island Expressway is bumper-to-bumper from now till Labor Day. By the way, Irwin says that he'll have your samples ready sometime next week."

"Have I told you how wonderful you are?" Dana asked.

"Yes, but I'm not counting."

"Good. You're wonderful."

"Thanks. You too."

Excited by the thought of the coming weekend, Dana hung up and was about to prepare dinner when the phone rang again.

"Johnny, you really have to ease up!" Dana said to herself as she reached for the wall phone in the kitchen.

"Dana, it's Alan Rudnick. I was about to leave for the day when I got a call from Tom Silver, Brett's attorney."

"Is anything wrong?" Dana asked.

"Probably not, but Silver wants me to meet with him and Brett. I think you should be there as well."

"What do they want? I thought everything was agreed upon and signed."

"It was, but they can ask to modify the agreement at any time until the decree is issued by the court after a year of separation."

"Modify? Is that what Brett wants? To change the agreement?"

"That's my guess. Silver won't give me any details, but he says that he and Brett want to revisit, as he put it, some of the language. Translation? They want to modify the original separation document."

Dana sighed heavily. "I really hate the idea of seeing Brett right now, let alone listening to some complaint from his lawyer. This is coming out of the blue, Alan. Why would Brett suddenly ask to change things given that Matthew caught him red-handed with Janice?"

"It happens all the time," Rudnick explained. "Time has passed, Brett's probably not worried any longer about scandal now that his partnership with Davis, Konen and Wright is secure, and he thinks—just guessing here—that he might have been too generous with you. But what the specific catalyst might have been is anybody's guess at this point."

"Okay, but I'm really going to be busy in the next week or so. It's not a good time."

"Not a problem. I'll hold them off until you can find a day to come into my office. And try not to worry about the matter, Dana. We're still holding a strong hand, and I'm not inclined to advise you to change anything based on what we know. For now, we're simply agreeing to listen to what's on Brett's mind."

"Thanks, Alan. I'll be in touch when I know more about my schedule."

"Always a pleasure, Dana. Goodnight."

Dana hung up and wondered how Brett could have the audacity to cause her more grief after what he'd done. After a few moments of reflection, however, she was no longer puzzled. Brett was a shrewd man regardless of his personal behavior. He was also under the spell of the very crude and opportunistic Janice Conlon. The latter pretty much said it all.

Dana put the matter out of her mind and went upstairs to read. When the time came, she was prepared to be as tough with Brett as she needed to be. She'd come a long way since sitting in the Sacred Heart Chapel bordering Mount Street Gardens. Her conscience was clear.

Chapter Thirty-Five

*D*ana returned home at lunchtime on Thursday to give medicine to Wills since his stomach had been upset for the past two days. The vet had prescribed antibiotics and canine antacid tablets to relieve his symptoms. While she was there, she ate a light lunch and received the early afternoon mail delivery. There it was! Another letter from Father Macaulay. Dana glanced at the clock and saw that she had time to spare, so she opened the latest news from London and sat on her couch, eager to see what her unofficial spiritual advisor had to say.

Dear Dana,

Your last letter was the most upbeat one you've sent. You're going to design clothes for the store, you've taken up riding, and you feel that life is currently very good. I'm so happy to hear of these positive developments! Most of all, I'm glad that you don't feel guilty about being happy. A majority of people go through life carrying around guilt, feeling that they never quite measure up to the expectations of others or, more importantly, themselves. In your case, however, it sounds like you're making sound decisions, ones that you're not second guessing. If all of my parishioners were like you, I suspect I'd be out of a job and could take up golf or spend more time singing. Yes, I've found a new pub that allows me to sing my heart out, and

*the people there are so much fun to be with. When I take off my
collar, I'm just one of the mates, a regular bloke as my friend Niles
puts it when we have a pint.*

*Unfortunately, I broke a finger the other day while working
out at the gym. I jammed it while having a go at the hanging
punching bag. I was taking out my frustrations since a parishioner
recently told me that I sounded a little too happy and optimistic
in my sermons. The woman, who is about sixty years old, said
that Catholic priests should behave with more decorum. She also
said that if I continued to preach as I do, she would report me to
my bishop. She's not really a bad soul but has a reputation as a
troublemaker, so I'm not concerned. She is a distraction, however,
and it's a fact of life, I suppose, that no matter how wonderfully
things seem to be going, there's always something or someone that
attempts to detract us from the course we have set for ourselves. I
even doubted myself briefly, wondering if I were being a little too
glib in some of my sermons. I'm afraid the English mindset tends
to gravitate towards a very reserved, almost gloomy, perspective of
life sometimes.*

*I do hope to hear about your riding as you progress. I did some
riding myself when I was younger, but alas, the time just isn't there
anymore. I hope you continue to thrive, and as always, I look forward to your next letter.*

All my best,
Father Charles Macaulay

Dana thought it uncanny that Father Macaulay's experi-
ences matched hers so well, at least in spirit. He was doing
well, but just as in her own life, he had his detractors, as well
as occasional doubts. How wonderfully human he was. She decided to take a few extra minutes before returning to the store
in order to write a reply. So many of his sentiments resonated
with her. She sat at her secretary, got out her stationery, and

didn't have to think twice about what she would write. Her thoughts flowed effortlessly to the paper.

Dear Father Macaulay,

I am so happy whenever I see one of your letters in the mail! I'm delighted you found a new pub. A pub for you and trails and horses for me.

I'm sorry to hear about your thumb, but what you said about the annoying parishioner certainly resonated with me. I'm still happy and working on my career, but Johnny and my mother continue to call me almost every day under the pretense of checking up on me, and each time they try to make decisions for me and determine my future. It's as if they've sealed me in a box with their delivery instructions written on the outside. I wish they'd step back, but I'm beginning to realize that they probably won't until I'm farther along in my decision-making. As of now, I simply can't live up to their expectations, as you so well put it.

My mother, whom I love dearly, can be especially infuriating at times. She has always been a proactive, outspoken woman, and I admire her for that, but she needs to stop attempting to micromanage my life. She recently gave me a rather stern lecture, vehemently protesting my horseback riding on the grounds that it's dangerous. She then proceeded to tell me why my idea of a private label for B. Altman wasn't worth pursuing, advocating instead that I immediately join the House of Cirone without giving my own ideas a chance to succeed. I'm thirty years old and still have to answer to my family! Father, if I weren't in love with New York so much, I would be seriously tempted to move away for a few years. I could be very happy in London, for that matter, where I could still work in fashion while enjoying the arts and the rich culture of England. I do love the rhythms of New York, however, and will stay where my heart flourishes most.

Another thing that my mother is now confronting me with, since my divorce will be final at the end of the year, is finding another husband, settling down, and having children. She acts as if it's a simple matter of replacing one man with another, which is surprising since she is a very modern woman in her own way. But just because Brett is no longer in my life doesn't mean that I have to run out and find an upwardly mobile man, which is what my mother and some of my friends have urged me to do. I have plenty of things to keep me busy and fulfilled, as we have previously discussed.

All this having been said, I must confess that my mother's mention of children did strike a nerve in me. Before we separated, Brett and I had finally started to discuss the possibility of having a family. As career-driven as I may be, I do want children some day, and I suppose my mother knows that. But first things first. I need to recover from Brett's infidelity and establish myself, whether it's with B. Altman or the House of Cirone. Only then will I start to consider the idea of family and children. I'm sure that, as a parish priest, you encounter people rushing from one relationship to another. I hope and pray that my wanting to take things slowly is the right course.

My friend Mark is taking me to his friends' horse farm on Long Island this weekend, where I will hopefully learn to trot, now that I have been taught the basics of how to sit on a horse and stay calm while it's walking. I'm very excited and will tell you about it in my next letter.

Please tell me more about your new pub, and I hope your finger will mend quickly.

Sincerely,
Dana

Dana folded the letter, put it into an envelope, and sealed it. She would mail it on her way back to work. As she walked along the streets, she could think of little else except the coming weekend at Judd's and the samples that Irwin would complete the following week. Slowly but surely, she was finding her way.

Chapter Thirty-Six

"I have good news, Amanda," Mark said over the phone. "I'll be joining you at Judd's this weekend. You're still going, I presume."

"Of course! That's terrific, Dad. I'm almost finished with exams and will be able to concentrate fully on my riding. Maybe on Monday we can ride to the Chelsea Inn. I think the terrace is open for lunch."

"I wish I could, honey, but Dana and I have to be back at work on Monday morning."

"Dana? Did you say Dana?"

"Yes, I did. I'd like to introduce her to Judd and Margaret. His wife will welcome someone to talk with. I'm sure she's tired of hearing Judd and me talk about the markets." There was an ominous silence on the line.

"Amanda?"

"Did you think of asking me first?"

"Asking *what*?"

"Come on, Dad! Ask me whether or not it would be all right to bring Dana to Muttontown."

"I don't need your permission, Amanda. I thought we'd discussed this. If you're going to give my relationship a chance, then it means you're going to try to get to know who Dana is.

It goes without saying that I can't live two different lives, one with you and one with Dana. That should be obvious, especially after our talk Friday night."

"It feels like you're pushing her on me, Dad. It's too much too fast. How am I supposed to focus on my riding while making an effort to get to know your girlfriend? You're asking a lot."

"For the record," Mark said, "Dana was reluctant to accept my invitation when I asked her to go this weekend. She doesn't want to come between us, and that alone speaks volumes for who she is. I reminded her, though, that you'd be busy with Paul most of the time. I just want her to see what a great place Judd has and maybe do some riding with her. Is it too much to ask that you both be on the same grounds together, especially if you don't have to spend any significant time with her?"

"You could have waited!" Amanda shot back. "I'm not ready to deal with her!"

"Her name is Dana," Mark said, "and I'm not asking you to deal with anything. I'm expecting you to behave like an adult and be pleasant when you're together. Just like you are if you meet a friend or business associate of mine when we're running around the city."

"Those are two-minute interruptions, not a weekend. I don't want her to spend that much time with us. At least not yet. Besides, I don't want her watching me practice. I'll be nervous. That means you'll have to entertain her while I'm in the arena with Paul, and you won't see how I'm doing. Then we'll have nothing to talk about over dinner. Don't you see what's happening? Things are changing already, just like I said they would."

"And I can *still* be there with you. Margaret will be happy to spend time with Dana while I'm watching your practices." Mark paused, trying to be patient. "We're talking in circles,

Amanda. I think you're being stubborn. I'm disappointed that you're breaking your promise to try to get to know someone I care about."

"If you wish to date, that's fine, but if you want to be with your girlfriend this weekend, I think you should stay in the city. I don't want Dana at Judd's."

"Will you at least consider the idea of her joining me?"

"What I want is for you to consider *my* request."

Frustrated, Mark took a deep breath. "I will, honey. That's only fair."

Several moments passed before Amanda said, "Thanks. Love you, Dad."

"And I love you. That's never going to change."

Mark could tell that his daughter was holding back tears. "Finish your exams, and I'll see you over the weekend."

"Okay, Dad. Bye."

Mark was out of his office for most of the afternoon. When he returned, he sat quietly for a few moments, thinking of his earlier conversation with Amanda, knowing that he had a decision to make.

He could indeed understand his daughter's feelings about someone new in his life, but Amanda was nineteen, which was old enough to handle his having a relationship, even a serious one. Even more importantly, Amanda needed to realize once and for all that he and her mother were never going to get back together. That being the case, she couldn't expect him to forego all female companionship for the rest of his life, nor was it feasible for him to live a double life, always keeping any woman he was seeing in the shadows. With Dana, the necessity to be open was all the more pressing since he loved her company. She understood him so well, but it was more than that—and more than the fact that they shared the same tastes in so many things. At a deep level, their thoughts were aligned in a way that was rare in any relationship. And they both possessed an energy and zest for life, a willingness to take chances and explore. Life had taught him not to pass up opportunities, and keeping Dana in the background wasn't an option, just as he'd explained it to Amanda. Sooner or later, his daughter would see how happy Dana made him, and he felt certain that, in the long run, Amanda wouldn't begrudge him that happiness. It might be tough on her in the short term, but he was confident that she would come around once she had time to sit down and talk with Dana. Meanwhile, she was capable of tolerating Dana's presence on Judd's large estate for a mere forty-eight hours. It wasn't as if the three of them were going on vacation together.

Mark decided that there was no need to change his plans to bring Dana to Muttontown. He was her father, and his wishes had to be respected. Amanda admired her father's determination and leadership, and this was an instance when she would have to see these qualities demonstrated in his personal life.

He sat at his desk and laughed. So much angst over a weekend at Judd's! It was a tempest in a teapot. As he'd told Dana, Amanda would be busy. Hell, she would be so absorbed in her jumping that Dana's presence would be the last thing she would be thinking of. No, going to Judd's with Dana was the perfect decision. Everything was going to work out.

Mark finished his day's work without giving the matter another thought.

Chapter Thirty-Seven

Patti and Andrew had lunch on Thursday at Charleston Garden. Andrew didn't want to sit with Patti so as to avoid thinking about Jack, but she spotted him as she put her tray down on a table near the colonnade, so he sat in an adjoining chair with his usual charming smile. Besides, trying to avoid thinking about Jack had proved impossible except when he was drinking after work. Alcohol and casual conversation with strangers were the only things that alleviated his pain, however briefly.

Andrew asked Patti about her work with the Altman Foundation in order to steer conversation away from Jack. She related how she was preparing her quarterly report for a board meeting the following week.

"You seem in unusually good spirits," Andrew noted. "The job with the Foundation obviously suits you."

Patti shrugged and smiled. "I do enjoy my job, although the budget crunch every quarter is daunting," she said. "But, most of all, I love it here. And Jack seems to be so much more relaxed in the last couple of days. He's been swamped at work for the last few months, but I think Hartlen Response has turned the corner in its New York operations. Jack says he's solved problems with his suppliers and that we'll have more time together from here on. He looks tired, but he seems content for the first time since we moved to the city. He even suggested that we take a vacation in July."

Andrew had been looking down at his plate as Patti spoke enthusiastically of her domestic situation, but he looked up abruptly after her last comment.

"Really? A vacation?"

"Yes! I told him I'd like to go someplace tropical. It's been a cold winter, and even though I'm getting used to the weather here, I think it would be romantic to rent a bungalow somewhere in the Caribbean."

Andrew put down his fork and took a sip of water at the word "romantic." His right hand experienced a mild tremor, and he took out his handkerchief and wiped his forehead.

"Are you okay?" Patti asked.

Andrew regained his composure and smiled. "Fine. You might have heard that I was sick a few days ago. It's been hard to shake, but my doctor says I'm good to go. I'm glad to hear Jack's doing so well, too."

"Running a family business is never easy, but opening the office here in New York put so much pressure on him, not to mention Hartlen Response becoming part of a consortium to handle oil spills more quickly and efficiently. He now has to coordinate with several other companies, but in the long run, Hartlen Response will have far greater exposure and might even be on the world stage one day. Jack says we'll be doing a lot of traveling in the coming years."

"That's terrific, Patti. You both deserve success after so much hard work. And speaking of work, I have to meet with Helen and then visit the main floor. It's been great catching up." Andrew stood hastily and picked up his tray.

"Have a good afternoon," Patti said. "I'll tell Jack you said hi."

Andrew nodded and left. His entire body was shaking by the time he arrived at his office.

Andrew tried to work, but his mind was too distracted. Had his relationship with Jack been a sham? How could Jack resume his life so quickly, especially after pleading with him for time to explain his situation with Patti? And yet after only a few days, a more relaxed Jack Hartlen was talking with his wife about taking a romantic vacation. Had Andrew merely been an experiment, something Jack had indulged in as a counterbalance to the pressures of relocating from Texas? It was a distinct possibility. Some straight men did indeed try an alternate sexual lifestyle for a brief time before reverting back to their long-standing orientation. But Jack had been so forthcoming when pouring out his heart during the many hours the two men had sat and talked in Andrew's apartment.

Something didn't add up. A piece of the puzzle was missing, but Andrew wasn't inclined to call Jack to find out what it was. Andrew had declared that he would have nothing to do with Jack unless he extricated himself from his marriage, and gauging from what Patti had told him over lunch, Jack was acting once again like a model husband.

For the rest of the day, Andrew went through the motions, performing his job adequately but with little enthusiasm. He left promptly at five and arrived at the Out of Bounds less than an hour later.

"Hey there," Chad Collins said, swiveling in his seat at the bar. "Make yourself comfortable and have a drink."

Andrew sat without saying anything for a full minute. "I haven't seen you since the other night. I thought you stopped in every evening."

"I usually do, but I've been of town on business for the past two days. Hey, are you trying to say that you missed my company, wit, and charm? If so—" Collins opened his arms wide. "Here I am!"

"Yeah," Andrew said. "Something like that."

"Then why don't we pick up where we left off?"

"Sure. Why not."

Andrew ordered a gin and tonic. Two hours later, the men once again returned to Collins' apartment.

Chapter Thirty-Eight

Dana and Mark arrived at Judd's at eight o'clock on Friday night, Wills having been boarded in Manhattan. Judd's farm sat on ten acres near the trails of the Muttontown Preserve and was home to six stables, with his stone house situated on the western end of the property. After settling into their second-floor guest suite, they went downstairs and had drinks with Judd and Margaret before eating a light supper, speaking mostly of Judd's latest acquisitions, which included a Belgian Warmblood, an Irish Sport Horse, and a Friesian. Later, when Margaret gave Dana a tour of the house, Mark and Judd discussed trading and the plan to have Irwin manufacture a line for B. Altman. Dana and Mark went to their room by eleven, however, since they planned on getting up at six and hitting the trails by seven-thirty the following day.

After breakfast on Saturday morning, Dana rode an American Quarter Horse, Mark an Oldenburg. The horses walked along trails cutting through upland forests in which grew oak, red cedar, birch, black walnut, sumac, and cottonwood. It was a warm, sunny day that stood in stark contrast to the shadows cast over the streets of Manhattan.

"You were right," Dana remarked when they stopped on a trail cutting across an old estate road. "Early morning is the most beautiful time to be on the trails. I love the way the morning dew sparkles on the leaves, and the air is so fresh and sweet. Did Judd or Margaret grow up in the area?"

"No, they found the house and property when they visited one summer. Before Christmas they packed up, left Manhattan, and never looked back. I think a couple of weekends a month is all we would need to relax and unwind. This is countrified living at its best. The land has everything—nature swamps, glacial ponds, and abundant wildlife."

"I saw a box turtle about half a mile back," Dana said.

"They have red foxes here as well, although it's rare to catch a glimpse of one since they're both stealthy and quick. But just look around," Mark said lifting himself off his saddle a few inches and craning his neck. "I couldn't begin to count the number of bird species."

"I love it," Dana said. "It's everything you promised it would be."

"And I love your being here by my side. You're doing pretty well on that horse, by the way."

"I'm not doing anything but sitting. The horse seems to be doing all the work."

"But you're sitting properly and getting used to being in the saddle, and that's what counts. You're relaxed. And we're both going to stay that way for the entire weekend, I may add. Amanda will arrive sometime this morning, and other than dinner tonight, I doubt we'll even see her, although I promised to watch one of her practice sessions with Paul today or tomorrow."

"I was wrong to be so worried," Dana said. "She's your daughter, and I need to trust your instincts more. Margaret said that she'd take me to a farmers market this afternoon, so don't worry about spending time with Amanda. I'll be fine."

"I'm just glad that you trusted my instincts when I asked you out. I wasn't sure you'd say yes."

"You mean you weren't sure I'd say yes so quickly," Dana laughed. "You were probably prepared to work a little harder."

"I was prepared to do whatever was necessary," Mark said.

"Obviously I felt the same way or I wouldn't be sitting on this horse," Dana said. "We do share a determination to get what we want."

Mark smiled as the horses moved forward again. "I think we both know each other pretty well, but you know the best part of it?"

"What?"

"We're just getting started."

The pair rode on, listening to the sounds of the rustling leaves and the birds. Dana adored the pastoral setting and the slow, easy gait of the horse. She shook her head and smiled as she recalled her mother's dire warning on the dangers of horse-back riding. Jaywalking in Manhattan posed a greater threat. As for the dangers of dating a forty-two year old man, that, too, seemed ludicrous. There was no way she would ever again be interested in a man her own age, one who was going through the growing pains of establishing a career. Once was enough. It was now time to focus on her career, and Mark was lovingly and enthusiastically supporting her. Right now, she longed for nothing more.

Amanda arrived at eleven o'clock. Judd greeted her person-ally, helping her unload her bags from the car.

"Welcome to your home for the summer!" Judd said, pick-ing up her suitcase and leather tote bag. "Let's get you settled in so you and Paul can get started right after lunch. Your father's out riding, but I expect him back before too long."

Judd and Amanda proceeded into the house, where Judd paused momentarily to hand Amanda a brown package. "This came for you a couple of days ago. I think your Dad's been at it again."

Amanda took the box and saw that the return address indicated that it was from Miller's.

"No, I think they're the khaki breeches that I had to back-order," Amanda said as they moved to the staircase. "Thanks, Judd."

Arriving at her room, Judd made sure that Amanda was comfortable and said, "I'll tell Paul that you've arrived and notify the kitchen that you'll be joining us for lunch."

"Thanks," Amanda said, suddenly curious to open the box that felt a bit heavy for two pairs of breeches. Perhaps it was a surprise gift from her father.

She eagerly tore off the brown parcel paper and opened the box to find a brown tweed hacking jacket, which she quickly tried on. The sleeves were a little long, and a tailor would have to nip in the waist, but it was perfect and she loved it. She decided to change into her riding clothes and wear the jacket to lunch. As she gathered up the tissue paper, she noticed another small gift-wrapped package. Smiling, she carefully untied the burlap ribbon and removed the hunter-green paper. Lifting the top of the crème-colored box, she gasped with excitement when she saw a green enamel dragonfly ascot pin.

"It's beautiful!" she said aloud to an empty room. "I love you, Dad."

She then spied a card in a small gift envelope and opened it. Her excitement faded immediately, blood draining from her face, as she read the message on the card.

For Dana, the prettiest equestrian on the trails and in my heart. Love, Mark

Amanda was crestfallen. It was a foregone conclusion that Miller's thought the package was for her when they saw it was being sent by Mark, who sent all her riding clothes to Judd's. She recalled how her dad had told her that he'd outfitted Dana the previous week. But the words stung her each time she forced her eyes to look down at the card. *Prettiest. Equestrian. Heart. Love.* Was her father in love with this woman? And how could he dare call her an equestrian?

Amanda burst into tears, throwing the pin and the card to the floor before she curled into a ball on the bed and sobbed for several minutes. She felt alone, betrayed, even unloved despite her father's reassurances over the past week. She recalled his words from their last conversation. *I'm expecting you to act like an adult.* Did that include having to look at her father's endearing message to his girlfriend? Was that part of being an adult?

More than ever, Amanda didn't want Dana in her father's life—or hers, not even in the most casual way. Amanda succumbed to a fresh wave of tears. *For Dana, the prettiest equestrian on the trails and in my heart. Love, Mark.* In an instant, all of Amanda's fond memories of time spent riding with her dad were erased. When it came to the trails, she was no longer the prettiest girl in her father's eyes. The black ink said so, written in his own hand. She would give him the pin and the jacket, obviously another gift for his girlfriend, when he returned to the house, but she wasn't sure what she would do after that.

Someone tapped lightly on the door.

"Yes?" Amanda said.

"Your father's back," Judd announced. "Why don't you come downstairs, and we can all have lunch together."

"Okay," Amanda said weakly. "On my way."

Amanda took a deep breath and summoned up every ounce of strength to lift herself off the bed. She took off the jacket and picked up the pin, her hand grasping it tightly until it pressed into the flesh of her palm. She then walked down the stairs, but she wasn't prepared for what she saw in the hallway leading into the dining room.

"Hi, Amanda," Dana said. "I can see why you and your dad are so fond of Muttontown."

"He's apparently a lot more fond of you than me or Muttontown," Amanda said as she handed Mark the jacket, ascot pin, and note. "Here, these are for your girlfriend."

"What are you talking about?" Mark asked.

He looked closely at the pin and read the note. "Honey, I'm sorry," Mark said after a few seconds. "Yes. These were gifts for Dana."

"Well, now you can give them to the prettiest equestrian on the trails yourself," Amanda fired back, breathing heavily.

Dana stepped back, not knowing what to say.

"Oh come on, Amanda," Mark said. "They're just presents!"

Amanda turned around, took three deep breaths, and then faced her father again. "What is *she* doing here anyway? I told you I didn't want her to come with you."

Stung by the remark, Dana put her hand to her mouth as she looked at Mark. "I think I'd better go upstairs and let you two talk."

"No, Dana," Mark said. "Stay right where you are. I told Amanda you were coming with me, and she's not acting like an adult right now."

"What you told me," Amanda said, "was that you would think about my request to either come alone or stay in the city with your girlfriend. You said it was only fair to consider my feelings."

"And I did consider them," Mark said, his voice calm but determined. "But I also explained that I have to lead my life the way I see fit. In the end, I decided that Dana wouldn't intrude on your stay here. You're blowing this way out of proportion."

Amanda was now in tears. "This is my first weekend home for the summer, and I have to concentrate on my jumping. Your stubbornness has ruined everything. You could have brought Dana another time, preferably when I wasn't here."

"But I want you to get to know her. I've made that clear."

"But it's not what *I* want. How many times do I have to tell you that?"

Looking down in frustration, Mark ran his right hand through his hair. He wanted to get matters under control, but he didn't want to give Amanda the upper hand. She was acting childishly.

"There's nothing to stop you from practicing with Paul right now," he said. "You don't have to have lunch with us. Or dinner for that matter. If you want me to watch your practice with Paul, I'll do it. Margaret has plans with Dana this afternoon."

"You didn't even bother to call back and warn me that you'd decided to bring her," Amanda continued, not hearing a word Mark said. "It's the least you could have done. Maybe I'll go riding. Or maybe I'll go upstairs, get my bags, and leave!"

Amanda stormed out of the hallway, the sound of her feet heavy on the stairs beyond.

"I'm sorry, Dana," Mark said, handing Dana the pin and note. "I think Amanda is being unreasonable and rude."

The look on Dana's face was pensive as she read the words that had troubled Amanda so greatly. "Mark, I have to be honest with you. If I were in Amanda's shoes and had received this note, I would be upset, too. It must be terribly hard for her to process such a sentiment. I think Amanda may be right. Maybe I shouldn't have come. You're expecting her to deal with your relationship with me in a logical manner, but emotions aren't always logical. To her, it doesn't matter that Judd has a large estate and that she doesn't have to interact with me if she doesn't want to. The fact is that I *am* here. With you. And that's not what she wants right now. She wants your undivided attention—to know that you're here for her, and her alone. I'm a distraction from her jumping and your usual routine with her."

"But that's my point, Dana. The routine can't go on forever. There's never going to be a good time to change it. I know my daughter, and she can be headstrong. Unfortunately, receiving your gift made matters worse. Frankly, I think that's what's caused her to have such a strong reaction to your being here. But whether it's this weekend or six months from now, my being in a relationship is going to bother her." He paused. "Or am I totally missing the boat here?"

"I think it's a possibility," Dana said. "Look, I'm not trying to judge you. I understand your reasoning, but I'm thinking about how the situation might look to Amanda. Maybe I should go back to the city to show her that we're sensitive to her feelings. Let's give her more time to adjust."

"Why don't we have lunch before making that decision. We need to give Amanda time to settle down. Let's not push the panic button just yet. I still think she's capable of understanding what I've been telling her."

Dana sighed. "I suppose there's nothing else to do for the moment, and I think we all need a break. And Mark? Thank you for the pin. It's beautiful. And so is the note."

"I mean it," Mark said as he kissed Dana.

Amanda reappeared, walking quickly through the hallway in her riding outfit minus her jacket. She said nothing as she passed Mark and Dana.

"At least she's not leaving," Mark said philosophically. "I take that as a good sign. She can work out her frustrations while practicing with Pepsi."

Margaret appeared in the doorway of the dining room. "Hey, everyone! I hope you had a good morning. It's time for lunch. Will Amanda be joining us?"

"No," Mark said. "She's eager to start practice."

"I understand," Margaret said. "It's a beautiful day, so we're lunching on the patio."

Judd walked in the front door and stood by his wife, putting his arm around her shoulder. "That daughter of yours is racing to meet Paul at this very moment. I'd bet money that she's going to wow the judges at the Classic."

"I wouldn't bet against her," Mark said as all four went into the dining room. "She's a force to be reckoned with."

Dana gave Mark a sideways look as she considered the irony of his last remark.

Paul was an easygoing man in his early fifties, a man with a slender but muscular build and a shock of short blond hair. He squinted in the early afternoon sun as Amanda appeared at the barn where Pepsi was stabled.

"Pepsi is saddled and ready," Paul said. "Judd called and said you were on your way."

Amanda gave Paul a perfunctory smile and "hi" before entering the barn. A few minutes later she led Pepsi from the barn by the reins. Paul climbed onto his own horse, and the pair rode to a one-acre field fifty yards away. They were accompanied by a man named Wally, who would help out by picking up any bars that might be dislodged from the fences during practice. The field, surrounded by trees, contained eight fences of varying height, some angled towards the others to force a jumper to change directions after clearing a fence.

"Remember to keep your shoulders back so we can get rid of that hitch," Paul said. "Have you been visualizing the jumps like I told you?"

Amanda nodded. "All week."

"Okay then," Paul said, riding to the edge of the field. "Ride around for a bit. When you're ready, take Pepsi through the paces. Nice and easy. We'll worry about speed when you feel loose."

Amanda made several circuits of the field, not worrying about jumping since neither she nor her horse had warmed up. After fifteen minutes, Amanda jumped a low three-bar fence several times and then jumped three higher fences in succession.

"Nice," Paul said, riding back into the practice area, "but your right shoulder was a little out of alignment on the last jump. You also rushed the second fence."

"What about overall form?" Amanda said.

"It's okay, but slow down a bit. We're just beginning, but you look tense. Just relax so you and Pepsi can get into the proper rhythm."

"Got it," Amanda said as she rode around the field again and then made a single jump.

Next, she moved to a different part of the course, jumping two fences before angling towards a different gate to her right.

"Whoa there!" Paul called, riding forward again. "You came up way too high out of the saddle on that last fence. You're not concentrating."

"I know, I know," Amanda said. "Let me try again."

Amanda returned to making circuits of the field, trying to steady her mind, but she kept returning to the altercation with her father, to Dana's presence, to the ascot pin. She couldn't bear the thought of losing her father, but her heart was aching as though she already had.

Pepsi maintained a steady gait as Amanda kept circling the pasture—two times, three times, four times. Paul was about to ride out and ask if Amanda was all right since she wasn't going for the fences.

Realizing her father wasn't on the field with Paul, she started to cry.

I can't do this without him. I hate her.

Amanda cleared the three gates and started handling the full course. She had one more fence to clear before she would ride over to Paul and ask for feedback. The gate was ten yards ahead. The image of Dana appeared in her mind just as Pepsi started the jump, and Amanda's body was grossly out of position. She was leaning forwards and her feet had slipped back in the stirrups.

Pepsi cleared the fence, but Amanda came out of the saddle, tumbling forward and to the right. Her body did a complete flip, landing on the right side of her back and right shoulder. Paul rode out in a flash to check on her, hopping off his horse before it came to a full stop.

"Amanda! Are you okay? That was a nasty spill."

Amanda made no response.

Paul knelt next to his student and saw that Amanda's head was turned sharply to the left despite her body being tilted to the right. Her right leg was flat on the ground, but her left leg was raised, bent at the knee. Paul knew immediately that something was terribly wrong.

"Don't move!" he ordered. "Stay perfectly still."

He turned to Wally, who had ridden closer from his position on the far side of the field. "Ride back to the house and tell Mark and Judd to get out here right away. And tell them to call an ambulance."

"Is it that bad?" Wally asked.

"Just do it!" Paul said.

Amanda turned her head slowly to look up at Paul. "What happened?"

"You took one nasty fall, young lady."

Amanda tried to sit up, forcing her left hand against the grass, but she could only lift herself a few inches.

"Like I said, Amanda, don't try to move. Help is on the way."

"I have a tingling in my left leg. Pins and needles."

"What about your right leg?"

"I can't feel it."

"Can you wiggle the fingers of either hand?" Paul asked.

"Yeah. A little."

"Good. You just lie quiet for now. Your dad and Judd will be here in two shakes of a lamb's tail, but we'll need to get you checked over by a doctor."

"I don't have time for doctors," Amanda said weakly. "I've got to practice. The … competition. It's … close. Got to … "

"Shhh," said Paul. "Save your energy."

Amanda closed her eyes, her breathing shallow.

This is bad, Paul thought. Really bad.

When Wally rushed into the house, Mark and Judd had already gone into the den to talk, and Margaret and Dana were exiting the back door for the farmers market.

"Mr. Baumann!" Wally cried out. "Mr. Senger! Quick! There's been an accident."

Mark, Judd, Margaret, and Dana all hastened to the main foyer, where Wally stood, out of breath as he tried to speak.

"What's wrong?" Judd asked.

"It's Amanda," Wally replied, gulping for air. "She got thrown."

"Is it serious?" Mark asked, looking rapidly at Dana and then at Wally.

"I don't know, sir. Paul told me to come and get you as soon as possible. And to call an ambulance."

"Ambulance?" Judd said. "Margaret, call for the medics while we ride out to the practice field. Come on, Mark."

Judd, Mark, and Dana quickly piled into Judd's Jeep and rode to the field, where Paul was still kneeling by Amanda's motionless body. Mark jumped from the front passenger seat and ran towards his daughter.

"Amanda, honey," he said. "It's Dad." His hand reached out to lift her head, but Paul grabbed his arm by the wrist as he shook his head. The two men's eyes locked, and Mark knew that this had been no ordinary fall.

"Can you hear me, honey?" Mark asked, his face creased in worry.

"She's lapsing in and out of consciousness," Paul explained. "I suggest we just wait and make sure she doesn't move a muscle. Her breathing was a little shallow at first, but it's steady now. That's a good sign."

Dana stood five feet behind Mark and Paul. "Is she going to be all right?" she asked.

Mark looked up but said nothing, indicating the seriousness of the situation.

"Is there anything I can do?" Dana asked.

"Dana, go to the gate at the edge of the field. Stand by the end of the dirt road where we just drove in. Make sure the ambulance knows where we are. Judd, you get Wally to take Pepsi back to the stable and then drive over to meet Dana."

"Right," Dana said as she ran to the path and stood, waiting nervously.

It was ten minutes before the wail of a siren could be heard approaching in the distance. Minutes after that, the ambulance rumbled to within five yards of Amanda's limp body, two men in white uniforms jumping out and running over to Paul and

Mark. The first man began taking Amanda's vital signs, feeling her pulse and examining the pupils of her eyes. The second listened to Paul explain what had happened.

"We're almost certainly dealing with spinal trauma," the second medic said. "We need to get her to the nearest hospital fast. We'll get a stretcher and use our immobilization protocols."

"Wait," Mark said, standing. "I'm her father, Mark Senger. My daughter is Amanda. I want her taken to New York Hospital."

"That's going to require an airlift and additional time. It's your call, but there could be internal bleeding."

"Call for a helicopter," Mark said. "There's ample room for landing in the field. I'm not familiar with the hospitals on Long Island, and I don't want my daughter being transferred from one facility to another. That might waste valuable time. New York Hospital will have whatever she needs."

"Yes, sir, but we'll need to prepare your daughter so that we can load her directly onto the chopper as soon as it arrives."

"Do what you have to," Mark said, returning his attention to Amanda.

The medics hurried back to their ambulance and called in the request for an air evacuation. They then hurried back with a wooden body board rather than a conventional stretcher, gently lifted Amanda onto its smooth surface, and immobilized her head with a cervical neck collar. They checked her blood pressure every five minutes after strapping her to the board.

"Shouldn't you be doing more?" Mark asked.

"Her color's good," the second medic said. "No need for oxygen. And no fluids since we don't know what internal injuries might have been sustained."

The helicopter arrived thirty minutes later, its rotors causing the branches of nearby trees to sway wildly. The copilot jumped from the cockpit and took the preliminary report from the medics, who then picked up the body board and, under the direction of the copilot, loaded Amanda onto the chopper.

"Room for two family members," the copilot said sternly, holding up two fingers of his right hand as rotor noise filled the field.

Mark motioned to Dana, and they climbed onto the helicopter before turning to Judd to ask him to call Amanda's mother. "Try not to alarm her, but let her know we'll be in the emergency room at New York Hospital within the hour." He then joined Dana on the jump seats behind Amanda.

The copilot hopped aboard and, facing forward, twirled his index finger in the air, signaling the pilot to lift off.

"Where's the airlift medic?" Mark asked.

"I'm a medic," the copilot replied as he sat next to Amanda. "I'm going to listen to her heart and then take her temperature and blood pressure. I also need to check for any visible bruises. Last, I'm going to put EKG leads on her chest so that the hospital can monitor her heartbeat as soon as we hit the ER."

"Daddy?" Amanda said, her voice barely audible.

"Yeah, sweetie. I'm here."

"Am I going to be all right?"

"Of course, you are," Mark said, putting his hand on her left shoulder. "We'll fix you up good as new."

Dana glanced out of the side window, the figures of Judd, Margaret, Paul, and the medics growing smaller and smaller as the helicopter gained altitude. She was already feeling remorse, wondering if her presence had upset Amanda to the point of distraction as she'd tried to take Pepsi over the fences.

She said nothing, but felt certain that she should have trusted her initial instinct. She shouldn't have come to Muttontown.

Chapter Thirty-Nine

The air evacuation chopper carrying Amanda landed at the East 34th Street Public Heliport, where she was transferred to an ambulance and rushed to New York Hospital since it lacked a helipad of its own. Mark and Dana followed the stretcher through the large glass doors of the ER as two nurses and a doctor followed Amanda down the hall while taking the report of the medic. Within minutes, Amanda was wheeled into a cubicle and its curtain pulled for privacy.

"I'm Dr. Rosenbaum," a figure in green scrubs told Mark. "You need to wait outside while we do a preliminary assessment."

"But I'm her father," Mark protested. "My daughter Amanda was thrown from a horse and—"

"I'm aware of the circumstances," Dr. Rosenbaum said with quiet reassurance. "I'll be out in a few minutes when I know more, but you're going to have to let us do our jobs."

"Shouldn't you get a consult from a—"

"Mark, let's wait out here in the hall," Dana said. "The important thing is that Amanda is now in the ER. She's going to be well cared-for. You have to trust the doctors."

"You're right," Mark said, stepping back and leaning against the wall on the opposite side of the corridor. "I should have been in the field watching her. This is my fault."

"You don't know that, nor is it time for self-recrimination. She stormed out of Judd's and you decided to let her cool off. Let's wait to see what the doctor says, okay?"

"That's what's bothering me. I shouldn't have let her ride when she was so upset."

One of several nurses passing through the corridor approached Mark. "Mr. Senger, please follow me," she said. "We're going to need some information at the desk."

"What? Oh, of course."

Mark and Dana walked down the hallway, where Mark filled out insurance forms and a questionnaire listing Amanda's weight, height, age, and medical history.

"Thank you," said the nurse. "Please have a seat in the waiting room to the right. You can get some coffee, and someone will get you as soon as the doctor is ready to speak to the family."

Dana put her arm through Mark's and guided him toward the waiting room when the door to the ER swung open and Susan and Irwin, accompanied by an attractive brunette in her late thirties, rushed in.

"Mark, where is she?" the woman asked.

"She was admitted a few minutes ago," Mark replied. "The doctor's with her now."

"Is she conscious? How serious is it?" The woman spoke urgently as she dabbed away tears with a tissue.

"She was conscious, but I don't know much more." Mark answered. "It's too soon to tell. The medic at Judd's said that he thought there was probably spinal trauma."

"Oh my God!" the woman cried. "That means Amanda could be paralyzed?"

"She has some movement in one of her legs," Mark explained, "but it's a serious injury."

"How did it happen? Wasn't Paul there?"

"Yes, but I don't know anything more than that she was thrown during a jump."

"Marsha," said Irwin as he walked up from behind. "Try to keep calm. Amanda's in good hands. We'll know more very soon. Let's all go into the waiting room and sit down."

Irwin pulled Mark aside as the women continued into the waiting room.

Dana waited for Susan and the brunette to be seated before asking if she could bring them something to drink. For the first time, the brunette looked closely at the woman in riding clothes standing before her and then across the room at Mark in his breeches, a puzzled look on her face.

"Marsha," Susan quickly said, "This is Dana McGarry, a friend of Mark's. Dana, Amanda's mother, Marsha Senger."

"I'm so sorry," Dana said as she looked at the pain on Marsha's face. "I wish—"

"How much do you know," Marsha interrupted. "Were you and Mark there when it happened?"

Mark and Irwin were now standing behind Dana, and Mark replied, "I told you, Marsha, that Amanda was with Paul, and that's all I know. We didn't see it happen."

As Marsha continued to glare at Dana, Mark added, "You're aware that Amanda practices with Paul frequently, and I'm usually not there."

"Only when you have better things to do, and obviously that was the case today," Marsha said.

"Marsha, we're all upset," Mark replied. "You don't have to direct your anger towards Dana."

"Excuse me, Dana," Marsha sarcastically replied. "I should be more sensitive to your feelings."

"Oh no. I understand," Dana said, suddenly feeling that it might be best for her to leave.

Mark, tired and short-tempered, fired back, "All right, Marsha, that's enough."

"Dana and I are developing a line of women's clothing for B. Altman," Irwin said, trying to switch the focus from Mark and Dana's dating. "It's a new opportunity for Bauer & Sons."

"Really?" Marsha said, turning to Susan, "Why haven't you mentioned this? What else are you all keeping from me?"

Dana, looking down, turned to Mark and said, "May I speak with you for a minute? I think I should leave."

As they started to step aside, a nurse approached them.

"The doctor would like to meet with you now, Mr. Senger. Come this way, please."

Mark and Marsha followed the nurse, with Dana, Irwin, and Susan walking closely behind them.

Dr. Rosenbaum, a stethoscope draped around his neck, stepped from the cubicle and directed them into a private office. Marsha stood by Mark on one side of the desk with Susan, Irwin, and Dana on the other side.

"We've completed our initial work-up, and the good news is that Amanda is stable and not in immediate danger."

"Thank goodness," Mark said, letting out a long sigh.

"We need to get her to X-ray now," he said. "I've given her something for the pain in her shoulder and chest, so she won't be very coherent for a while. She's conscious, however."

"Her chest?" Marsha said. "What does that mean?"

"I suspect that she has some bruised ribs," Rosenbaum said, "but her EKG is normal, and there's no sign of internal bleeding in her thoracic cavity."

"What about her legs, doctor?" Mark asked.

"She has feeling in them, although there's more in the left than the right."

"What does that indicate?" Marsha asked.

"I'm afraid it means that Amanda's still not out of the woods. We'll know more after the X-rays. Do you have a family physician for Amanda?"

"Yes," Mark said. "Dr. Russell Nadelman at Greenwich Hosptial."

Rosenbaum nodded. "I'll have someone call his office. We'll also need a consult with a neurosurgeon when the film comes back since there does indeed appear to be some degree of spinal trauma."

"Will she need surgery?" Marsha asked, her face ashen.

"It's a possibility, but let's not get ahead of ourselves. We'll also need some skull X-rays to rule out concussion and brain trauma, and I've ordered one of her right shoulder as well."

"But is she ever going to walk?" Marsha asked, bursting into tears as she clung to Mark and put her head against his shoulder.

"I can't answer that either way," Rosenbaum said candidly. "There could be crushed vertebrae, pinched nerves, and a host of other injuries, but it's really too early to tell. It would be mere speculation. Only a neurosurgeon will be able to give us a definitive diagnosis. I'm sorry, but I would like to speak privately now with Mr. and Mrs. Senger."

"Thank you, doctor," Marsha said, looking directly at Dana. "My husband and I would appreciate some privacy."

Dana, shocked and in disbelief, locked eyes with Mark. His troubled, pained expression, confirmed that what she'd just heard was true.

Dana was emotionally numb as she walked with Irwin and Susan back to the waiting room, barely hearing Irwin's explanation of Mark's situation.

"They've been living apart for two years now," Irwin said when he saw that Dana's face was pale and her lip was trembling.

"And it's not the first time they've separated. It's complicated, but Mark has every intention of getting a divorce. I'm sure he'll tell you everything as soon as things settle down."

Dana, feeling sicker by the minute, remained silent until Irwin finished speaking.

"Irwin, let me know when the samples are ready for my approval," Dana said.

"Susan, I'm sorry we had to see each other under these circumstance. Take care."

"She's one tough cookie," Susan said as she watched Dana turn and walk out of the ER waiting room.

"For God's sake, Susan," Irwin said. "She's in shock. Give her a break."

Using every bit of strength she could muster, Dana remained composed until she found herself on the cardiology floor. Tears streaming, she asked the head nurse if Dr. Phoebe Cirone was on duty. Concerned about Dana's condition, the nurse put Dana in a private room and explained that Dr. Cirone was off for the weekend but that she would call her in an emergency.

"I'm Phoebe's childhood friend," Dana explained. "I know how to reach her. May I have an outside line?"

"Dr. Cirone here," was the steady voice that Dana needed to hear in order to unleash her emotions resulting from the traumatic events of the day and the heartbreaking news that Mark was married.

"I need to see you, Phoebe," Dana said in between sobs.

"Where are you?" Phoebe asked. "I'm coming."

"I'm two blocks away at New York Hospital. I need some air, so I'll walk over."

"I'm coming down to meet you," Phoebe said.

Blinded by tears, Dana made her way through the pedestrians on First Avenue until Phoebe took her arm and guided her up to her apartment. Dana never uttered a word. A few hours earlier, she and Mark had been riding through the bucolic countryside of Muttontown, believing Mark when he said that their beautiful relationship was just getting started. Now, with that dream abruptly ended, Mark remained at New York Hospital to comfort his injured daughter.

And his angry wife.

Chapter Forty

Dana sat in a daze on Phoebe's sofa as her friend handed her a cup of tea.

"I've never seen you look so frightened, Dana. Tell me, what happened?"

Fighting back tears, Dana slowly related the events at Muttontown, beginning with her leisurely ride with Mark along the trails that morning and ending with her abrupt, chilly meeting with Marsha in the emergency room.

"I'm having trouble processing everything," Dana said. "One minute I'm upset over Amanda's accident, the next minute I'm angry with Mark because he wasn't forthcoming with me. Most of all, I'm overwhelmed with guilt."

"Guilt?" Phoebe said.

"I didn't want to go to Judd's, but Mark was sure it was the right thing to do. Deep down I knew better. My instinct told me Amanda wasn't ready."

"I don't understand."

"Amanda has been very distant with me from the first time I met her. And you should have witnessed the disdain on her face and in her voice when she saw me right before the accident. Literally just minutes before it happened! She and Mark apparently had a conversation during which she was adamant that I not go to Muttontown. To make matters worse, not only did I show up, but so did a gift from an equestrian shop. The gift was accompanied by a romantic note from Mark. It was inadvertently sent to Amanda at Judd's, where she receives all of her riding clothes. She was apparently livid when she saw the note, but my presence sent her over the edge. Believe me when I say she held nothing back."

Phoebe said nothing for a minute, reflecting on what Dana had told her. "No question, the gift and note were an unfortunate mishap, but you and Mark aren't mind readers, and even Mark couldn't have predicted his daughter's reaction."

"I think Mark and I were both blinded by how much we wanted to be together," Dana said as she lowered her head. "That seems so selfish now. All I know is that if I hadn't gone to Muttontown, Amanda wouldn't be in a hospital, possibly paralyzed."

"You must stop thinking about what might have been," Phoebe said, moving from her chair to sit next to her distraught friend. "It will torment you, Dana. Assuming Mark should have honored Amanda's request, the fact is he didn't. I suspect he was hoping that the weekend would be an opportunity for you and Amanda to get to know each other better."

Dana nodded. "That was his desire from the beginning."

"Then he made the decision for the right reason."

"And what about his decision not to tell me that he's still married," Dana said, turning to look at Phoebe. "Was that, too, for the right reason?"

"Soon enough, Dana, Mark will explain. For now, try not to speculate."

"Irwin tried to comfort me," Dana continued as her body trembled, "but what he said was more confusing than enlightening. Something about Mark's situation being complicated—how many times have people heard that one?—and that he's been living apart from his wife for two years and wants a divorce. Years? A week is a lifetime for Mark. He makes decisions in a New York minute. It doesn't make sense."

"I learned in my psychiatric rotation that people's lives, especially their relationships and marriages, are both complex and unique."

"Well, Mom looks at life simply and, in this case, she was right. She told me last week that I should have known how long ago Mark got a divorce. For him to say nothing was to leave me with the impression that he's divorced. What else was I to assume?"

"I would have thought the same thing," Phoebe said, "but again, you don't know the entire story yet, certainly not from Mark's perspective."

"You're right, but ..." Dana broke down in tears. "I feel like Mark and I stepped in a minefield and that our lives will never be the same. Worst of all, Amanda may be the one to pay the heaviest price and never walk again and—"

"You don't know that," Phoebe interrupted. "I'm not a neurosurgeon, but the outcome of a spinal injury can be very hard to predict."

"Okay, but she has serious injuries nonetheless, and her condition is a result of Mark and me being together. That's a fact, Phoebe."

"The fact is that there are many variables to consider. Things are too up in the air right now to make assumptions. I'll call the hospital in a little while and get an update on Amanda's condition. In the meantime, you need to rest, Dana. Doctor's orders."

"But—"

"I'm not taking no for an answer," Phoebe said patiently. "Get some rest."

As Dana rose from the sofa, the doorman called to announce that Johnny was on his way up.

"It's Johnny," Phoebe said. "We were going to dinner."

"Oh, great," Dana said. "He has to be told, of course, but I don't think I can listen to him berating Mark when he hears the gory details. I'm going to take that nap now. I'll see you when you return. Johnny should be calm by then." Dana walked down the hall to Phoebe's bedroom.

Walking past Dana's riding boots at the door, Johnny teased Phoebe as he gave her a kiss. "Don't tell me you're taking up riding, too?"

"Let's go," Phoebe said as she quickly put on her sweater.

Noticing the tea cups on the table as well as Dana's hacking jacket on the sofa, Johnny pointed to the closed bedroom door and said, "Dana's here, isn't she? What happened? Was she in an accident?"

"She's fine, but she's resting. I'll tell you everything over dinner."

The telephone rang as Phoebe and Johnny were heading for the door.

"She's sleeping, Mark," Phoebe said after taking the call. "How's Amanda?"

"What happened?" Johnny said, looking confused.

Putting her hand up, Phoebe signaled for him to remain silent.

Phoebe listened carefully for several minutes as Johnny paced the room, looking concerned.

"Yes … yes … okay," Phoebe said. "Thanks for the news. We'll be praying for Amanda." She hung up and turned to Johnny, apprising him of the riding accident.

"What's Amanda's condition?" Johnny asked.

She's suffered a thoracolumbar fracture of two of her vertebrae. The breaks are between the ribcage and pelvis. She's scheduled for surgery tomorrow morning."

"But what about—" Johnny began.

"Not here," Phoebe whispered. "I don't want to wake Dana. Let's go."

"I was on the line, Phoebe," Dana said, sobbing as she appeared in the hallway. "I heard everything. Amanda may never walk again. Dear God, it's all my fault."

Johnny immediately went to Dana to comfort her.

"Dana, there's no way you can take responsibility for Amanda's accident," Johnny said. "That's crazy."

"No, you don't understand," Dana said. "I shouldn't have been there and—"

"Dana, you can't go through the story again," Phoebe said. "I'll explain everything to Johnny later. In the meantime, you need to have faith that Amanda will be okay. You heard what Mark said, and I can confirm it. Amanda's surgeon is world-renowned. She's in excellent hands."

"Mark sounded so upset, Phoebe," Dana said. "I'm sure Marsha is adding to his misery, reminding him that he was with me when Amanda had the accident."

"Who's Marsha?" Johnny asked.

"His wife!" Dana said as she buried her head in Johnny's shoulder, deeply regretting her words.

"What did you say?" Johnny asked, looking with disbelief at Phoebe. "Senger's married?"

Phoebe nodded.

"I'm going to wring his neck," Johnny said.

"Johnny, you're not helping Dana or the situation," Phoebe said. "On the contrary, you're making matters worse."

"I knew there was something that wasn't quite right about Mark from the beginning," Johnny continued, his voice rising in pitch.

"That's ridiculous," Dana said, moving away from Johnny. "There was no way you could have surmised that he was married."

"True, but I felt that *something* wasn't adding up." He shook his head. "How could anyone be that deceptive, especially to you? He's worse than I imagined."

"Irwin told me that Mark has every intention of getting a divorce," Dana said, feeling the need to defend Mark.

"And I have every intention of getting married," Johnny said. "But here's the difference. One day, I will. Can you tell me that Mark will follow through as well?"

"It's not like Dana didn't know the man," Phoebe retorted.

"Actually, it is," Johnny said as he folded his arms. "She worked with the guy for years, and during that entire time everyone assumed he was divorced. I've made my opinion clear from the outset that Dana's been too trusting of Mark. They've only been going out a short time, and she gave him her heart without knowing his background, which he knowingly withheld. Mark has been blatantly dishonest with her. It's all black and white."

"Nothing is black and white," Phoebe chimed in. "As I told Dana, Mark deserves the right to explain."

Johnny was clearly frustrated and couldn't hold his tongue. Turning to Dana, he said, "Okay, fine. Let him explain, but he concealed the truth once, regardless of his reasoning, so I say make a clean break after you speak with him and then come work with us, trustworthy friends who love you."

"I'm not walking away from my plans to open The British Shop, no matter what happens to my relationship with Mark," Dana said adamantly.

"But how can you trust anything he tells you from this point on, Dana? What isn't he telling you about this deal with Bauer & Sons ?"

"You're letting your imagination run away with you," Dana replied. "I trust Irwin implicitly."

"Just like you trusted Mark? It's your life and your career that are on the line. Your mother would agree with me if she were here." Johnny's voice continued to grow in pitch as he spoke.

"That's enough, Johnny," Phoebe said. "I want you to stop all this——"

"It's okay," Dana said with resignation. "Johnny's entitled to his opinion. Please understand, I just want to go home now."

"I think it's best if you stay overnight," Phoebe suggested. "You definitely shouldn't be alone right now."

"I agree," Johnny said. "And I'm sorry, Dana. I know this has been a hard day for you, and I guess I haven't made it any easier. Please stay with Phoebe tonight."

"I promise I'll call you both in the morning," Dana said, "but I need to be alone right now."

After several more protests from her friends, Dana convinced Johnny to hail a cab on First Avenue while she put her riding clothes back on. Thirty minutes later, Dana, Phoebe, and Johnny had Wills in the taxi and were on their way to Sniffen Court.

Once inside, Dana sat on the edge of her bed and cried harder than she had all day. When her sobs had run their course, she got undressed, put on pajamas, and knelt by her bedside, praying for Amanda. In the morning, she would go to early mass and then jog in the park. She would wait until the surgery was over and Amanda was out of immediate danger to deal with her relationship with Mark. And on Monday morning, she would be back at work as usual.

Dana got into bed, trying to remember lines from a poem that she loved, one that was appropriate for the way she felt, but her mind was too tired to retrieve them. They would come, she thought, some other time. She was asleep by eight o'clock.

Chapter Forty-One

*J*ack had only had three sessions with his psychiatrist thus far, but he was already feeling guilt and remorse about his recent neglect of Patti. The psychiatrist, of course, only asked leading questions to elicit his patient's true feelings so as to help him make his own decisions: *Why do you think that Andrew distanced himself from you? Do you love your wife? Do you think it likely that you might one day leave Patti for Andrew? If so, how much time would you need to break the news to her? Have you contacted Andrew since he broke up with you? Do you still have a slush fund with Hartlen Response?*

Jack had been shocked at his own answers. As he told Dr. Stein, he could not envision himself actually revealing to Patti that he was gay and wanted a divorce even though he and Andrew had talked of such a hypothetical conversation on many occasions. He'd been determined to seek a divorce and move in with Andrew, but now that Andrew no longer believed in his sincerity, his resolve had dissipated like so much smoke. And the plain truth was that he loved his wife and had no idea how long it would take him to work up the nerve to break such news to her face-to-face. Andrew had no doubt sensed all of Jack's inner conflict, and it was not long afterwards that Andrew had broken off their relationship. And had he, Jack, really created a slush fund with the intent of building a nest egg should his family not accept his new lifestyle? He'd broken the law and, but for Brett McGarry, he might have faced federal criminal charges. At his doctor's suggestion, he would continue therapy for a full year, and probably longer, but he would make no attempt to reach out to Andrew with the intent for a reconciliation. He would throw himself upon Patti's mercy and hope she would forgive him for the pain he'd caused her.

Jack sat alone in his office on Saturday afternoon, the entire suite to himself. He looked out over the city, a city that had seemed alien to him ten months earlier when he and his father had come to New York City with the intention of opening an office in the north to take better advantage of their response technology that would revolutionize the oil industry. The city had seemed cold and impersonal. There was no grass, no room to breathe. There was no opportunity to walk out into a field and look at blue sky in every direction.

But he'd met Andrew in those early days, and everything had changed, including his perspective on New York. Andrew had helped Jack acclimate himself to the city and appreciate its richness, even its faster pace. But that's not why he'd fallen in love with Andrew. His feelings for the man had been genuine, and suddenly his life in Texas, including his marriage, had seemed irrelevant and outdated. He placed his hand on the telephone on his desk but pulled it back abruptly.

He was accustomed to the city now, and he could survive without Andrew. Patti awaited him at their apartment, and where would he have been back in Texas without her confidence in him? He would still have become CEO of Hartlen Response—it was his family legacy—but it had been Patti, a woman of strength and determination, who had always been at his side, helping him to realize his full potential as a CEO in his own right, not just a son standing in his father's shadow. And despite the distance he'd imposed on them for so many months, she was still there. She still believed in him, and he doubted if other women in her position would have demonstrated the same faith and loyalty in a man seemingly adrift. The first few steps of therapy had been excruciatingly painful, but slivers of light had already penetrated his mind. His answers to Doctor Stein's questions had been honest. There would be no desperation call to Andrew from the safety of his office. His mind was made up.

He got up slowly from his desk and walked through the empty offices of Hartlen Response. It was time to go home in more ways than one.

"Back so soon?" Patti asked as Jack entered the den. "I thought you were going to catch up on some work today."

"And I did," Jack said with a smile. "Very minor stuff that's been bugging me. But I'm going to relax for the rest of today."

"That's good," Patti said, running her hand along Jack's shoulders. "You deserve some rest."

Jack grabbed Patti's hand and gently turned her to face him. "I suppose I do, but you deserve more, too."

"I do?"

Jack took both of Patti's hands in his. "I know I've been distant during the past months. Downright neglectful, in fact. I'm sorry, Patti. I haven't been a very good husband, but all that's going to change." Jack paused, realizing that he sounded like a soap opera character spouting clichés. "I mean it."

Suppressing tears, Patti looked deeply into Jack's eyes and saw that he was speaking from the heart. "What's important is that we're here now, together," she said, circling her husband's waist with her arms while laying her head against his shoulder.

They stood in their embrace for several minutes without saying a word. It was Jack who at last broke the silence.

"You see, Patti," he said, "the truth is that—"

Patti quickly covered Jack's lips with her hand.

"No, Jack. I don't need to know the particulars. I've been waiting for you to open up to me, and you've done that today. I know you've been consulting a psychiatrist because I found your bottle of Valium."

"You mean that—"

"Wait, Jack. Let me finish. I know the move to New York has been tougher on you than it has been on me, and I'm also aware that you've had a lot of challenges at work with your suppliers, the consortium agreement, and other matters. What you say to your doctor is private. It's enough to know that you're seeking help and still want to be with me."

"I do very much," Jack said, kissing Patti on the cheek. He was no longer physically attracted to her in the way he once had been, but maybe that would change in time as well. "You've been so patient with me. I wish there were something I could do to make up for these past months."

Patti stepped back and patted Jack's chest lightly with both of her hands. "Just stay in therapy and we'll get through this," she said, wiping a single tear from her cheek. "That's enough for me."

They sat together on the couch, holding hands for the next hour while reminiscing on the good times they'd had in Texas.

"We'll have to get back there more often," Jack said. "Maybe buy a second home and spend a few months there every year. Meanwhile, I promised you a vacation."

"That sounds great," Patti said, her body leaning against Jack's. "Why don't we plan it tonight? It'll be fun."

Later, Patti went into the kitchen to prepare dinner. Her patience had paid off. Her husband had finally confided in her that he needed help. She still suspected that he'd had an affair—isn't that what he was on the verge of confessing?—but she didn't want to know either way. Their road ahead would be difficult enough without the added burden of an affair hanging over their heads for the rest of their lives. While Patti was shrewd and observant, she was also wise. In the end, she simply wanted her husband back. What was paramount was that they move forward.

Still in the den, Jack remained on the couch, reflecting on the day. He was certain that he'd done the right thing. But what if Andrew should call? What if he had a sudden change of heart? Jack let out a sigh. That was an unlikely scenario, and even if he did, Jack had made his decision. His history and love for Patti went too far back, too deep. Thinking of Andrew was still painful, but his sense of peace outweighed his discomfort.

He was home.

Chapter Forty-Two

$\mathcal{A}$ndrew lay in Chad Collins' queen size bed on Sunday morning while Chad went to get the *New York Times* and croissants. Andrew got up, put on a blue velour robe, and began making coffee. He inhaled the aroma from the pot and thought it a stark contrast to sitting at the Out of Bounds and drinking endless cocktails.

"Here we go," announced Chad when he returned to the apartment. "This is really all anyone needs on a Sunday morning in New York City—besides the right company, that is." He moved towards Andrew and gave him a warm hug.

The two sat at the butcher block kitchen counter as they ate.

"I should have seen it coming," Andrew said as he sipped from a coffee mug.

"Seen what coming?" Chad asked.

"Jack's getting cold feet. Not being able to commit to our relationship."

"Don't beat yourself up about it. Do you remember that I told you during our first meeting in the Village that I knew people who'd been in your shoes?"

"Yes."

"Well, I actually know only one person, and that someone is me."

Andrew sat back in his chair, his eyebrows raised in surprise.

"Why didn't you just tell me straight out? I thought you got dumped by some guy named Ron. The ski instructor."

"Because it would have sounded like a lame pickup line. Yeah, there was a guy named Ron—that was real enough—but before him I went out with an older man named Arthur. We met at work. Arthur had been married for ten years but had no children. I asked him why one day, and he suddenly broke into tears and told me that he didn't really love his wife, that the marriage always been a sham and a pretense to please his family."

"How long were you two together?"

"Two years, believe it or not. He even separated from his wife—her name was Doris—but on the two-year anniversary of our meeting, he said he'd made an awful mistake. Doris never took him back, but one day he up and resigned from the company, and I never saw nor heard from him again. Someone told me later that he moved to LA."

"I'm sorry. Did you love him?"

Chad nodded. "I did, but that's ancient history now. I'm here with you. I guess what I'm saying is that this kind of thing happens, and it's possible to recover from it." He reached across the table and covered Andrew's hand with his.

"I guess we're kindred spirits," Andrew said. "I'm glad you were there when I wandered into the Out of Bounds."

"You looked pretty lost, but hey—sometimes people are just in the right place at the right time. Call it kismet."

The couple raised their coffee mugs.

"To kismet," Andrew said.

"Say, want to take in a matinee this afternoon? I'll look in the movie section."

"Sure," Andrew said. "That's what I do most Sundays."

Andrew had thought of Jack many times since giving him an ultimatum, and he'd been tempted to pick up the phone on more than one occasion and call his private number at Hartlen Response and tell him that he was sorry, that he'd been too harsh and judgmental. Each time, however, he'd changed his mind. Something deep inside told him that he was right, that Jack was enmeshed with his family and would never leave the nest, least of all Patti. Living in the shadows since last December had been too much of a strain, and he couldn't handle it any longer. In his estimation, Jack wasn't going to ask for a divorce, but even if Andrew was correct on that count, he might have ended up living in the shadows for another year, maybe longer, and the cloak and dagger would have been intolerable.

It had been serendipitous that he'd met Chad Collins, someone who knew exactly how he felt, having lived through a similar drama himself. Was Chad a rebound relationship? Technically yes, but Andrew thought it had potential, and he had to start somewhere, had to start living again and not stay holed up in his apartment. He would miss Jack, always retaining a soft spot for him in his heart, but for now, he was starting to come to terms that the relationship was over. It happened all the time, as Chad had stated so philosophically.

Today, he would go to a movie with Chad Collins.

Chapter Forty-Three

For Dana, work at B. Altman on Monday was like any other day. She went about her business, and Andrew seemed in unusually high spirits. Even Helen smiled at her several times when they passed each other in the fifth floor hallway. Dana's thoughts, however, were never far from Mark and Amanda, and she prayed silently every hour for Amanda's recovery and for guidance on her relationship with Mark. She hoped for a phone call, however brief, that would update her on Amanda's progress. Couldn't Mark take five minutes to call, knowing how concerned she was? If he couldn't, perhaps something bad had happened. Perhaps Amanda was in the ICU—or worse. Maybe she hadn't pulled through. As the day wore on, Dana grew more worried and told Andrew of Saturday's events at Muttontown and New York Hospital.

"Slow down," Andrew said, sitting in Dana's office. "Spinal surgery is delicate and can take several hours. The operation may have lasted all day yesterday, and Amanda may not even be out of the recovery room. Mark is probably worried sick, and I suspect he may also be preoccupied with the doctors. I doubt that he wants to disappear for even a second. Give it time."

Dana sighed. "I suppose you're right. It's just hard not to think about Amanda."

"I know," Andrew said, "but as the old saying goes, this too shall pass."

"You seem awfully optimistic today," Dana observed.

"I've had my ups and downs in the past weeks, but I'm trying to take my own advice and do the best I can from moment to moment."

"Good for you," Dana said. "And thanks."

At home, Dana took Wills for his evening walk. When she returned, the telephone was ringing, and she unhooked Wills from the leash and dashed for the telephone.

"It's Irwin, Dana. I wanted you to know that Amanda's surgery went well, although it lasted until ten last night. She was taken from recovery to ICU late this morning and might be there a day or two. Thankfully, she's in stable condition. The surgeon performed something called spinal fusion by inserting titanium rods into the affected vertebrae."

"What's the long-term outlook?" Dana asked.

"That's hard to say. The disks are going to need time to heal, and the doctors naturally aren't going to commit to any hard and fast prediction. The waiting is going to be hard on all of us."

"How is Mark?"

"He hasn't left the hospital since Saturday except to get a change of clothes and shower at his apartment early Sunday morning before the surgery, which was scheduled for noon. Otherwise, he's been by Amanda's bedside the entire time. He sleeps in the chair in her room and eats in the cafeteria."

"I wish so much that I could be there to help him."

"I know, but Marsha's right beside him, and I think you know what that means. But here's some good news. He's going back to his apartment tomorrow afternoon if Amanda remains stable, and he hopes that you'll meet him there for dinner. He's going to check in at work on Wednesday morning, and then be back at the hospital in the afternoon. He'll probably take some time off but work half days if the need arises. Amanda is going to be in the hospital for at least two weeks, maybe longer. She'll have to remain immobile for a long time until her disks start to heal. However this plays out, the surgeon admitted that she has a lot of rehab ahead of her."

"Thank you so much for calling, Irwin. I've been thinking about Amanda all day. Tell Mark I'll be over at six thirty."

"He'll be happy to hear. And by the way, I'm going to drop the clothing samples off at your apartment on Wednesday evening if you're going to be home. I know you're under the gun, so I made them a priority."

"No, I'll come to Brooklyn," Dana insisted. "You've done too much already. Please don't inconvenience yourself anymore."

"Hey, I'm your partner, and it's no trouble. I know you have a lot on your mind, and I'll be in the city anyway. It's what friends are for, Dana. I'll see you Wednesday night."

Dana felt somewhat relieved after she hung up. Knowing that Amanda was out of immediate danger was of some comfort, although the weeks of waiting to see what kind of recovery she'd make would be agonizing.

Before going upstairs, she glanced at the mail, hoping to see a letter from Father Macaulay. She realized, however, that any response he might have sent wouldn't have had time to reach her yet.

She went to bed early, not wanting to dwell on what Mark would say at dinner the following evening. Everything was up in the air, but as Father Macaulay had told her from their very first meeting, she had to take care of herself.

• • •

Dana was at her desk on Tuesday morning when Alan Rudnick called.

"Good morning, Dana," the attorney said. "I was wondering if you could come in tomorrow morning and meet with Brett and his attorney, Tom Silver."

"Can you hold him off a bit longer?" Dana asked. "I don't think I could get all my work done even if there were three of me."

"I'm afraid not. I put Silver off once, but he's adamant that we meet as soon as possible. As we discussed, they almost certainly want to amend the initial agreement Brett signed in January before the final divorce decree goes into effect, and I'd like to know the chapter and verse of what they're going to propose. The sooner we know what they're up to, the sooner I can frame a response that's to our advantage."

"All right," Dana said, flustered. "If there's no way around it, I'll be there."

"Thanks," Rudnick said. "The meeting's at ten o'clock tomorrow morning."

Dana sat at her desk, dreading seeing Brett again. Of all the people in the world she didn't want to deal with right now, it was her husband. Amanda, Mark, The British Shop, Helen—she had so many things on her mind, not to mention her routine duties as buyer. There just weren't enough hours in the day. And now Brett was going to renege on their agreement? She wished she were in a quiet room at the Lansdowne Club in London.

• • •

Unlike Monday, Tuesday was not a day like any other for Dana. She was not only preoccupied with what Mark was going to say about his marriage to Marsha, but now the meeting with

Brett loomed over her head. She was distracted while meeting with other buyers, and during a meeting with Helen, she became so lost in thought that she had to ask Helen to repeat herself.

"Are you all right, Dana?" Helen asked. "You don't look well."

"I'm fine. Just juggling a lot of balls right now."

"Well, get your head back in the game," Helen said. "We're all juggling a dozen things at once. It's what we do every day."

Dana smiled at the curt remark and left, returning to her office while attempting to concentrate.

When the clock on her desk mercifully read five o'clock, Dana gathered up her things quickly, went home to walk Wills, then grabbed a taxi and headed for the Upper West Side. There was no need to bring Wills. She would be coming home tonight. For the past two days and nights her thoughts and prayers were for Amanda's recovery, suppressing the shock and hurt on learning of Mark's marriage. Now it was time for them to face another trauma, and, hopefully, they, too, would recover. She had no idea how she would feel after hearing Mark's explanation but in her heart she still trusted him.

Mark greeted Dana with a hug as soon as he opened the door.

"Amanda?" Dana asked.

"Out of ICU and on a ward, but she's on a lot of pain medication. At least she made it through the surgery without complications."

"I'm so glad, Mark," Dana said, fighting back tears. I feel so bad, so responsible. I should never have—"

"Stop right there," Mark said. "I know where you're going, and you're not to blame."

"But—"

"We've got other things to discuss now, so let's sit down and talk about Marsha. Would you like a glass of wine?"

Dana shook her head. "No, thanks."

"Okay then," Mark began when they were seated on his couch. "What I'm about to tell you, I should have mentioned weeks ago, but I didn't, and all I can do is ask for your forgiveness. I was caught up in feeling so good about our relationship. I'd like to think that I would have said something shortly, but the truth unfortunately came out at a very unfortunate time."

"It was quite a shock, Mark," Dana said quietly. "But I realized that you needed a chance to tell me your side of the story. I'm here to listen."

Mark took Dana's hand and inhaled, as if ready to go deeper into his personal history.

"Marsha and I shared similar backgrounds and our families encouraged the relationship. We were caught up in everyone's euphoria and, before we knew it, we were engaged. Unfortunately, after the marriage, we learned that we didn't have much in common. When Amanda came along, we put aside our differences like so many young parents do. Our focus was totally on our baby daughter. As Amanda grew older, however, I was absorbed in my career, and problems in the marriage surfaced again as Amanda became more independent and didn't need us hovering over her every minute. As time wore on, I didn't want to subject her to our arguments, so I moved out in 1971 and rented a small apartment here on the Upper West Side, although we hadn't filed for a legal separation. Amanda was devastated, and I was worried sick about her every minute of every day. She had a lot of problems with the visitation schedule Marsha and I worked out, so we decided to make another go of it after Amanda's Sweet Sixteen party, when so many family and friends gathered to celebrate the occasion. It was a reminder of how important family is in the lives of children.

I moved back in, and for six months or so, things went back to normal. It was a relief to see Amanda return to her normal routine, but nothing had changed between Marsha and me. We couldn't agree on anything. She resented my long hours at work, and I also think she was jealous of how close Amanda and I were. My time alone with Amanda on the trails was something that especially irritated Marsha, plus she didn't like my friends and I didn't like hers. We rarely went out together, and our lives were as miserable as they'd always been."

"It sounds like you did everything humanly possible for the good of Amanda," Dana noted.

"We tried, but Amanda definitely picked up on the tension—keep in mind that she was much older by then—and so I decided once again to move out, this time in 1973. Marsha and I filed for a legal separation, although working out terms would prove difficult, if not impossible. I nevertheless knew that the marriage was over and bought into this co-op."

"How did Amanda take the second separation?" Dana asked.

"Not well. Even though she saw the strain in our marriage, she, like any kid, wanted her parents to stay together. As she once said, why can't the two of you just get along? Sometimes divorce can be harder on older kids than younger ones. As a psychologist friend of mine explained it, older children begin to wonder if what they saw while growing up was real or just a pretense. Anyway, the visitations started again, and Amanda threw herself into her riding more than ever as a way to cope. She became even more serious about competitive jumping, I think, as a way to please me or perhaps to prove her self-worth, since kids of divorce tend to blame themselves."

"I think I understand Amanda a lot better now," Dana remarked. "No wonder she's been upset."

Mark nodded. "She's also been affected by the inability of Marsha and me to bring any closure to our relationship. In fact, I've been thinking since the accident that maybe Amanda half expected us to reconcile for a second time. It wasn't going to happen, though, and Marsha kept throwing up roadblocks that prevented my getting a final divorce decree."

Dana squeezed Mark's hand as he spoke, realizing for the first time how much pressure he'd been under for the past several years. He was always the sunny, charming, consummate professional when she ran into him at B. Altman, but she now understood the great stress he'd been under, stress that he'd concealed almost too well.

"With the help of our lawyers, Marsha and I reached an agreement by September of 1974," Mark continued. "I agreed to maintain our home in Greenwich until Amanda was twenty-two, at which time Marsha would sell the house, with both of us receiving equal shares of the profit. Marsha balked, however, and decided she wanted to live in the house for as long as she wanted, with me covering all the costs. The agreement was too open-ended, and I couldn't agree to it." Mark paused, sighed, and went forward with his account. "And then there was the financial settlement. I agreed to give her a very generous sum in the agreement, but she changed her mind and decided that she wanted alimony as well so that she could better budget her month-to-month income. Alan, therefore, insisted that the settlement amount would have to be reduced to offset the alimony payments, but Marsha and her attorney to this day cannot agree as to how much the settlement should be scaled down. In fact, there have been some meetings in which she didn't want the settlement reduced a dime."

"Her position doesn't sound the least bit reasonable," Dana observed.

Mark rolled his eyes. "It's not reasonable at all. She wants the right to live in the house in Greenwich forever at my expense, as well as alimony and a small fortune in the form of a very large settlement. I've never been opposed to giving her fair and generous terms, but over a lifetime, Marsha could end up gaining millions of dollars by doing absolutely nothing, which leaves me totally unable to budget my own life. I get together with Marsha and her attorney every few months to try to find some common ground, but she won't budge. She feels entitled to my wealth, but my lawyer and I are in agreement. Marsha wants a divorce decree that essentially has no limits on how much she can collect over the years, and I'm not going to give it to her."

"I can relate," Dana said. "My attorney and I have to meet Brett tomorrow. It seems that he wants to change the terms of our own separation agreement, although I'm not asking for any kind of open-ended agreement like the one Marsha wants."

"Sorry you have to go through that kind of annoyance too," Mark said. "Why can't people just move on with their lives?"

Dana closed her eyes and took a deep breath. "I'd like to move on with ours," she said. "Now that you've given me the details, I can see how you're handcuffed by Marsha's excessive demands."

Dana had never seen the always-confident Mark look vulnerable before. Telling his story had obviously drained him emotionally.

"Are you sure?" he asked. "I don't know how long it might take to get an acceptable legal agreement from Marsha, especially now that she and I have to deal with Amanda's recuperation."

"I'm not a fair-weather friend," Dana said, leaning closer to Mark and kissing him on the cheek. "I'm here for you. It's obvious that you've done everything you can to finalize the divorce, and it's not your fault that Marsha won't cooperate. It's just a matter of time before you'll come to an agreement. I'm sure of that."

Mark put his arm around Dana's shoulder and pulled her tightly against his body.

"I know the doctors can't commit to an exact prognosis yet," Dana said, "but I'm sure that Amanda will be home soon and be able to walk. I think we all know that she won't be competing in the Hampton Classic this year, but in time I'm sure she will ride again. The one thing I'm certain of is that she has her father's indomitable spirit. She's going to pull through, Mark, and there's no reason we can't be together."

"You're pretty amazing," he said, "which is something I don't tell you enough."

"You make me very happy, Mark," Dana said, optimistic for the first time in four days. "and that's more important than anything you could possibly say."

Mark kissed Dana and the smile that she loved and hadn't seen since Saturday morning finally returned. "We won't know for a couple of days when Amanda will be released, Mark said. "Thankfully, she's out of danger and there's no paralysis, even though her movements are quite restricted, but I agree with you. She's going to conquer this given her willpower and determination. And, Dana, thank you for your determination to stay with me after all I told you and considering the few challenges that I have ahead."

"I think I'm ready for that glass of wine," Dana said as she smiled and gave Mark a kiss.

An hour later, Mark and Dana sat at the dining room table eating pasta from Sal's while discussing The British Shop and Irwin's delivery of the samples Wednesday evening.

"He's been such a comfort," Dana said.

"He's a great guy and one of the best friends I have. It's why I felt the two of you would make such good business partners. Are you ready to take B. Altman by storm?"

"As ready as I'll ever be," Dana replied.

Mark grinned. "I have every confidence that you'll make it happen, with or without Helen's approval. People like her forget that they got to where they are today because they, too, were young once and wouldn't take no for an answer."

"I've had that same thought myself," Dana said, "and when I make my mark, I'm not going to shut the door on younger women trying to establish themselves."

"Hold on a minute," Mark said, laughing. "Don't age yourself prematurely. You're going to make your mark long before you qualify to speak about younger women."

They toasted to Dana's success, cleared the table, and sat in the living room briefly before Dana rose to leave.

"Call me at the office tomorrow if you get a chance," Dana said. "My meeting with Rudnick is in the morning, but try me in the afternoon."

"I will," Mark whispered in her ear as they embraced. "Let's go downstairs and get you a cab."

Back at Sniffen Court, Dana got into her pajamas after taking Wills for a final evening walk, but she couldn't fall asleep. Her mind was racing after hearing all the details about Mark and Marsha's tumultuous marriage. She was relieved that Amanda had made it through surgery safely and that she and Mark still had a future together. She felt so grateful that her prayers had been answered that she went downstairs and wrote a long letter to Father Macaulay, chronicling everything that had happened during the past week. She held back nothing, including everything about her relationship with Mark, Amanda's accident, Mark's legal problems with Marsha, the progress she'd made towards making The British Shop a reality, and her renewed confidence that everything was going to work out.

It took thirty minutes to complete the letter, but afterwards she felt as if a burden had been lifted from her shoulders. The day had come to a satisfactory conclusion, and confiding in Father Macaulay had been the perfect way to give one final release to her emotions before bed. If she'd called her mother, she would have been up half the night answering questions and listening to new warnings and I-told-you-so's, and she didn't want to burden Phoebe, who had so little free time.

She went upstairs and fell asleep, confident in the future, which included her meeting the following morning with Brett.

Chapter Forty-Four

Alan Rudnick escorted Dana into his conference room shortly after ten o'clock on Wednesday morning. Tom Silver and Brett were already present and rose as Dana entered. Silver and Dana shook hands politely while Brett stood to the side and smiled as if all parties were assembled to conduct a real estate transaction. Dana looked at him and nodded, but she said nothing.

At forty-eight, Tom Silver was prematurely gray, and his short hair was parted neatly on the side. Examining his gray goatee and gray pinstripe suit, Dana thought that he was a portrait in gray, a middle-aged man who seemed older than his years.

After they took their seats on opposite sides of the conference table—Rudnick facing Brett, and Dana facing Silver—Silver pushed copies of the separation agreement across the polished mahogany table so that everyone could consult the same document.

"My client and I feel that we need to revisit the initial agreement that Mr. and Mrs. McGarry signed in January, doing so with an eye to modifying some of the clauses," Silver stated.

"For what purpose?" Rudnick asked. "I've reviewed the agreement, and I believe that the existing terms are entirely fair.

Mr. McGarry is now a partner with Davis, Konen and Wright, and his salary and future earning potential are considerable. And I don't have to remind you of the circumstances leading to my client's filing for separation. Mr. and Mrs. McGarry talked last December of possibly starting a family and buying a weekend home in the country, but Mr. McGarry's actions prompted my client to abruptly change the course of her life and rapidly adjust the expectations for her future. We can all agree that starting a new life isn't easy. That alone justifies what she's asking for."

"I'm not here to discuss my client's alleged actions," Silver said as he leaned back and smiled affably. "Just the terms of the agreement. No other suit was brought against Mr. McGarry, so let's stick to matters of the settlement so that everyone can move forward. Frankly, we're not interested in rehashing any personal history which, at this point, is irrelevant."

Dana bristled at the word "alleged" but kept her gaze fixed on Silver.

"It may not be relevant to you," Rudnick shot back, "but it is to us. Just so we're clear on that. It's not too late for me to file an additional suit, as you must certainly know."

Silver ignored the remark. "You mentioned earning potential," he continued, "and that's exactly why we're here today, only not to talk of my client's financial opportunities. It's Mrs. McGarry's earning potential that we're here to discuss. She's currently employed at B. Altman as a buyer for the Junior Division. Is that correct?"

Rudnick glanced at Dana, who said, "Yes, I'm a buyer."

"Exactly," Silver said, "which represents a promotion. What was omitted from the original discussion was Mrs. McGarry's future career track and—" Silver paused to lean over and confer with Brett in a whisper "—and any other assets she may have."

"What kind of assets are you talking about?" Rudnick asked, looking puzzled.

Silver spread his arms wide as he responded. "Oh, come on, Alan. Don't be coy. *Any* kind of assets whatever. Everything's on the table when it comes to settling the community."

It was now Dana and Rudnick who quickly and quietly conferred.

"We have no assets to report," Rudnick asserted. "My client lives in a modest carriage house that she's subletting from a friend. You're more than aware, Tom, that all assets for this couple have always been held jointly, so the holdings are known to all parties. As I said, we have nothing new to add."

Silver looked at Dana as he spoke. "Is it true that Mrs. Mc-Garry plans on developing and launching a clothing line for B. Altman? I'll remind you, Alan, that Mr. and Mrs. McGarry still have mutual friends——Johnny Cirone, for example, whose family owns the House of Cirone, a very successful manufacturing company."

Dana and Rudnick conferred for a second time.

"There is currently no new line of clothing at B. Altman developed by my client," Rudnick said. "There's a Nantucket line that falls under her assigned duties, but nothing beyond her present job description."

"That's not what I asked, Alan," Silver countered. "Are you telling me that no line of clothing for B. Altman is currently in the development stage under Mrs. McGarry's direction?"

Dana began to speak, but Rudnick interrupted as he put his hand on her forearm. "The department store has not authorized Mrs. McGarry to develop any new line, but let me emphasize that it would be totally unethical to divulge any marketing plans on the part of B. Altman should they ever request Mrs. McGarry to do so. That information is totally confidential."

Silver's jaw jutted out as he fluttered the palm of his right hand from side to side as if to say "maybe." "Okay, Alan, I'll concede the latter point, but my client is totally within his rights to determine his wife's future earning potential before committing to generous monthly alimony payments. I regard it as axiomatic that Mrs. McGarry's salary has already increased as buyer since she was promoted from"—Silver glanced at the legal pad before him—"promoted from special events coordinator, and her salary will almost certainly increase, perhaps significantly, over the years. There are even speculations from a mutual friend that your client may one day work alongside the owner of the House of Cirone, earning an equity position that will provide her with substantial wealth."

Rudnick didn't hesitate for a second. "We're not here to deal in rumors or speculation, Tom. My client has indeed had a slight increase in salary, but nothing that would warrant any kind of modification to their initial separation agreement."

"Very well," Silver said, looking at Brett, "but I'm still going to insist that you provide an assessment of earning potential for Mrs. McGarry according to the existing guidelines and income formulas currently used for family law in New York State. It's standard. In addition, Mr. McGarry is not prepared to pay the entire settlement on December 31st. He's obligated to pay into his partnership with the firm, and without the partnership, Mrs. McGarry would not be receiving a fraction of this generous settlement to begin with. He will pay one-fifth at the end of December, with equal payments resuming annually for four years, beginning in 1977."

"In all my years of practice, I've never heard of such an arrangement," Rudnick said. "If your client can't afford the settlement he willingly agreed to in December, he's in a good enough position to secure a loan to satisfy his obligations. Mrs. McGarry isn't going to put her life on hold for four years."

"On hold?" Silver said, looking at Dana. "These terms don't prevent Mrs. McGarry from going on with her life in the least. And if she chooses not to remarry during this time, she'll have peace of mind knowing that Mr. McGarry will be providing her a secure future."

"This settlement is hardly a guarantee for a secure future," Rudnick said. "Why didn't you ask for these changes sooner?"

"Because we're asking now," Silver said, his polite demeanor fading as he leaned forward with clasped hands. "Negotiation remains open until a divorce decree is issued. My formal request will arrive in your afternoon mail."

"Do we have anything else to discuss?" Rudnick asked with no inflection in his voice.

Silver grinned as he stood. "Nothing else for now. Mrs. McGarry, it's been a pleasure to meet you."

Dana made no reply. She and Rudnick stood as Brett looked at his wife with a Cheshire cat grin before leaving the room with his attorney.

"What was that all about?" Dana asked.

"They've been doing some homework," Rudnick said. "Tell me what's going on at work and about Johnny and the House of Cirone."

Dana related her plans for The British Shop but explained that it lacked formal approval since she hadn't yet presented the samples to Bob Campbell and that the idea had even been rejected by her immediate boss. "As for Johnny," Dana said, "he probably still plays squash with Brett, who helped him out of a legal jam last year. And he has indeed made me an offer to join his family business."

"Let me get this straight," Rudnick said. "I assume you're going to jump ship with B. Altman in favor of the House of Cirone if The British Shop doesn't get approval."

"Exactly."

"Let me ask one more question. Are you seeing anyone? Anyone wealthy?"

"Well," Dana said, looking down and feeling a bit embarrassed, "I am. Actually, someone you know very well. The man who referred me to you. Mark Senger."

"That's very nice to hear, Dana," Rudnick said with a smile. "Pardon me for asking, but has he given you expensive presents?"

"Just riding clothes and an ascot pin."

"Riding clothes?" Rudnick asked

"Yes. Mark's been an equestrian since his childhood, and he wanted me to join him on the bridle paths. I've started lessons at Claremont."

"They've obviously had you followed by a private investigator. Easy to do in Central Park, and that explains the meeting we just had, as well as Silver's veiled sarcasm. Brett and Silver are perfectly aware of what your present assets are, but they obviously know a bit about Mark. If you were ever to marry him, your financial profile might change appreciably. Add to that an ownership position with the House of Cirone and you might end up being worth more than Brett."

"So what do we do?" Dana asked.

"For now? Nothing. They're on a fishing expedition, and in the process, they're trying to intimidate us. Mark is currently just a boyfriend—they can't ask for modification based on that—and your career options are just that for the moment—options. I'll give them a formal answer about your earning potential that will simply outline your present job and salary. Nothing more. That's all that's required to comply with Silver's request, despite his bluster. If anything in your life changes significantly, however, let me know as soon as possible, but I don't think any career advancement on your part would be so rapid as to sway a judge to amend your original agreement.

Meanwhile, we'll see if Silver makes any further requests beyond an extension on the payment schedule."

"What might he ask for?" Dana said.

"Hard to say. Perhaps a smaller amount of either the settlement sum or the alimony. Maybe both. The finances of divorce can be very fluid, but we shouldn't panic or change our position until we have more information."

"I understand," Dana said.

"And one more thing," Rudnick said. "Be careful what you say and where you say it. You might still be under surveillance, and private investigators can be anywhere. And they don't always fit stereotypes. I've even heard of investigators posing as blind men with tin cups on street corners. It only takes a cheap pair of sunglasses. They also use some pretty sophisticated equipment and can record you from great distances. Go about your business, but just be mindful that you're probably being watched."

"It's enough to make somebody paranoid," Dana said.

"It is, but it will be over soon. Believe me, Brett wants to get this settled as much as you do. He's well aware that you have those damaging photos of him and his mistress. He also knows that, if pushed too hard, you might use them. He obviously has some regrets about his quick agreement to your settlement proposal and may think your new relationship with Mark has softened your heart. He no doubt figures it's worth a try."

"Janice Conlon," Dana uttered.

"Who?"

"The mistress. She's a scheming woman who, I'm guessing, might be egging him on so there's more money for her if they stay together."

"It wouldn't be the first time something like that has happened," Rudnick said, "but it sounds like you've moved on with your life, so leave Brett to me. And don't have any contact with him in case he tries to manipulate or intimidate you. I'll be in touch if I hear anything."

Rudnick stood and ushered Dana from the conference room.

As Dana returned to B. Altman, she couldn't help but study people lining the street or standing on the main buying floor. She'd been followed for the past two weeks—maybe longer— and she now had to be extra careful in conversation. *And to think that I broke down in tears over Brett while I was at the Sacred Heart Chapel in London*, Dana thought. *That won't ever happen again, and unless Alan Rudnick tells me otherwise, Brett's going to pay me everything I asked for. And he can take that back to his blond bombshell.*

Dana resumed her work, excited that Irwin would be at her apartment later.

Chapter Forty-Five

*I*rwin arrived at Dana's shortly before seven o'clock on Wednesday evening accompanied by his driver and head tailor, Steve, who helped him carry several large suitcases of merchandise for Dana to inspect.

"I brought Steve along in case you wanted to make a few last minute changes," Irwin said. "He can make the adjustments tomorrow, and you'll have them back on Friday."

"Good idea," Dana said as Steve unpacked the samples, hanging them on a portable rack he quickly assembled in the living room.

Dana could barely contain her excitement as she saw the luxury sportswear line appear, one tailored garment at a time: a camel hair blazer with matching pants and skirt, full-cut trousers in gray flannel and Irish tweed, the lovat glen plaid kilt, and a loden duffle coat.

"Close your eyes, Dana," Irwin teased as he unpacked the four-button navy twill blazer.

"No peaking." Holding up the blazer, he said, "Now let's slip it on. There you go. Okay, what do you see?"

"Irwin, I love them!" Dana said in disbelief as she admired the pheasants on the navy enamel buttons. I was only joking when I showed you the photograph. Where did you get them?"

"I have my connections. In fact, look at *all* the buttons. They're antique leather and the finest horn. We aim to impress and want you to succeed. We want that account!"

"The British Shop ~ B. Altman," Dana said aloud as she read the silk label. "We're going to do it, Irwin."

"Do you really think so? You really think you can sell the whole new concept?"

"More than ever," Dana answered. "Bob Campbell is holding a meeting for buyers tomorrow morning. Rumor has it that he's going to announce some big initiative for the coming months. With any luck, I'll see an opportunity to pitch The British Shop based on what he says."

"So tomorrow's the big day? Are you sure you have everything you need?"

"I won't need the samples for a day or two," Dana said. "So if I think of anything, I'll call. Tomorrow I make the sales pitch."

"Who can say no to you, Dana?" Irwin asked. "Your enthusiasm is seductive."

"I hope you're right."

"No doubt about it. My money's on you." Irwin turned to leave with Steve, but turned and added, "Literally!"

Dana and Irwin burst out laughing, and she gave him a warm hug before seeing him out.

Dana poured herself a sherry and looked at the clothing samples for over an hour while preparing her presentation to Bob. Steve and Irwin had gone the extra mile on every front: the silk linings, the top stitching, the label, and the buttons—all the details to set apart merchandise worthy of its own boutique. She didn't think Bob would be able to resist either her concept or the marketing potential for the store. It would be a win-win situation, followed by a full-page spread in *Vogue*. Dana was sure that, too, would happen. Dream big or don't dream at all.

It was Grace Mirabella's personal style, and the editor-in-chief of *Vogue* was redefining the magazine to reflect the new American working woman, whose preference was classic separates. The timing of The British Shop would be perfect.

Dana was also happy that she and Mark were back on track now that Amanda was out of danger. His explanation for not having secured a divorce made perfect sense. He was clearly trying, but Marsha's demands were unreasonable. Frankly, she had too much time on her hands and used it to think of ways to aggravate Mark. What a waste of a life, as though the extra money she was demanding would make her happy. Why would she want to live in a big house by herself? Amanda was either in college or at Judd's. No, she didn't need the home and was only using it as a means to get more money and attention from Mark. Dana knew with certainty that Mark, with his dogged determination, as well as Alan Rudnick on his side, would eventually free himself from this miserable situation. In the meantime, she would not allow Marsha to drive a wedge between them.

There had been many bumps in the road over the past month, but Dana had learned the previous year that problems existed to be solved, not to discourage or deter, and that was Mark's philosophy as well. It was one of dozens of things that made them perfectly suited for one another.

The storm clouds were moving away, and for Dana Mc-Garry, it was still a very good life.

Dana joined the other buyers in the Charleston Garden restaurant for an eight o'clock meeting Thursday morning. Bob entered carrying several folders and flashed a big grin to the room as he said, "Good morning, everyone! I've got a lot to talk about, so let's get started."

Bob opened the top folder as he stood at a podium at the head of the room, paused, and began speaking.

"As most of you already know, it's a tough economic climate out there, and it's getting tougher by the day. Inflation remains high and sales are … well, I don't have to tell you. They're soft." He pursed his lips, narrowed his eyes, and continued. "I'm therefore going to ask buyers to find a single line in their departments that can be made price-sensitive for a holiday promotion. We can offer our customers good value with a higher markup."

Men and women around the room nodded their heads, understanding the wisdom of the proposal and its sound economic sense. Bob elaborated on his idea, taking questions from various buyers about items in their respective departments. Everyone, however, seemed in total agreement as to the merits of the executive vice-president's strategy.

"Excellent," Bob said as he gathered up his papers and folders at the end of the meeting. "Everybody get your favorite manufacturers to sharpen their pencils so we can be ready well before the season goes into high gear. I'll be meeting with division heads in a month for an update." He quickly exited the room and was out the door, moving on to his next meeting.

In a flash, Dana knew where her opening lay to pitch The British Shop if she could only get a few moments alone with Bob. She dashed to the front of the restaurant, flew through the door while others stood and spoke of the meeting, and caught up with him as he hurried down the hall.

"Great meeting, Bob," Dana said, glancing over her shoulder to make sure Helen wasn't in view. "Can I have a few minutes alone? I have an idea that will take your directive to another level."

"I'm intrigued," he said with a smile, "but it'll have to wait until this evening. I have one meeting after another scheduled today, and I'm already late for my next one. Can you keep a lid on that enthusiasm of yours for a few hours?"

"Absolutely," Dana said. "What time should I stop by your office?"

"Five thirty."

"I'll be there," Dana said as she turned and headed back to her office.

Andrew popped in for a quick hello and saw her standing behind her desk, hands on her hips.

"You look like you're about to explode with energy," Andrew commented. "I heard about Bob's pricing strategy, and I'm guessing that today is the day you're going to drop the bomb and pitch the boutique. What's your angle?"

"A good one," Dana responded. "It seems to me that the price-sensitive approach is—"

"Andrew, do you have a minute?" one of his assistants asked as she craned her neck around the doorframe of Dana's office.

"Duty calls," Andrew said, shrugging. "Good luck."

Dana could hardly concentrate on anything except her meeting with Bob. It seemed that the hours were dragging by, the hands of the clock hardly seeming to move as she glanced at it every few minutes. She passed Helen in the hall at eleven o'clock, prompting the head of the junior department to stop and ask, "Are you working on price-sensitive merchandise for Bob?"

"Harder than you can imagine," Dana replied.

"Good. I suspect you'll want to select the Nantucket line, which is the most logical choice," Helen said, resuming her quick stride without waiting for a response.

Bob Campbell's secretary unexpectedly called Dana at noon to notify her that her boss would like to see her now. He had thirty minutes before he had to leave for the day.

Dana took a deep breath and walked quickly to Bob's office. Everything she and Mark had planned came down to a single meeting with Bob Campbell. It might be all or nothing.

"You have that look I've come to recognize," Bob said from behind his desk. "I take it that there's some kind of project percolating in your very fertile mind. Have a seat and tell me about it."

Dana sat opposite the executive vice-president, and although she'd been preparing what she would say all day long, she abandoned all the phrases she'd rehearsed in her mind and spoke from her heart.

"Bob," she began, "what if I brought you not one line, but a whole department of merchandise that would guarantee a higher profit margin, one that would also provide a marketing opportunity that promoted B. Altman?"

"I'm listening," Bob said, sitting back in his chair, hands behind his head.

"First, the concept. A free-standing women's boutique of coordinated separates. Bob, you know it's time we had a boutique. Second, the name. The British Shop by B. Altman. Just picture the silk label."

"But—"

"Wait a second," Dana interrupted, not wanting to delay her pitch. "I've saved the best for last. All the merchandise would be made exclusively for B. Altman! Camel hair and navy blazers, gray flannel and tweed trousers, long wool jersey culotte skirts—even selective outerwear. And all the separates will have dyed-to-match knitwear within steps of each other. Think of the multiple sales! And the merchandise will be designed just for us, cutting out the middleman, thus affording a higher markup and lower prices."

Bob sat forward, the smile on his face mixed with a look of incredulity. "It would be great, but I still want to see your magic wand. An exclusive B. Altman line? Wow. You've caught me off guard here, Dana. Have you sat in on a board of directors meeting that I missed? You're talking about something that would take an enormous amount of work, not to mention money." He glanced at his watch, knowing he had to leave in twenty minutes.

"Actually, Bob, virtually everything is already in place. For the first season, we won't have to buy the piece goods, just pay for manufacturing."

"You've completely lost me."

Dana smiled. "I know it sounds too good to be true, but I have it all worked out. Mark Senger introduced me to a friend of his, Irwin Bauer."

"I've heard the name," Bob said. "Bauer & Sons Clothiers."

"The very same. I brought my favorite Jaeger sportswear to Irwin and asked him to produce samples using his menswear fabrics," Dana said, beaming. "What we have to show you is the beginning of a polished American line with British style, which is exactly what today's career-minded businesswoman wants, not to mention that the look is on the editorial pages of *Vogue* every month. Irwin is ready to expand his business and would love to be a vendor for B. Altman. Believe me—he'll sharpen his pencil."

Bob nodded thoughtfully. "And you're convinced the boutique is the way to go?"

"Yes, the clothing needs its own setting to make a statement. We won't overstock items but rather be selective with the merchandise and the number of pieces made. Customers will return often to see what's new. The concept is perfect for the boutique model, which should be original, unique, and have a concentrated look. Plus the boutique already partially exists."

"I thought Helen was getting rid of it?"

"True. Mark was ordered to halt the build-out, but he's had his hands full because of his daughter's riding accident."

"Yes, I've heard. Terrible news."

"It would take no time to add wood-paneled walls and display cases, wool plaid upholstered chairs, and mahogany tables for sweaters, like Brooks Brothers does. The sales staff would be asked to wear the merchandise—tweed skirts and cashmere sweaters. We can serve Fortnum & Mason tea and sell silk tartan shirts at Christmas with black velvet skirts. There's no end to the merchandising potential, and you can open a menswear boutique just like it on the second floor."

"I can see where you're going, Dana." Bob said. "I've been talking all morning, but you've left me speechless. There's bound to be a downside."

"Just one," Dana said. "Helen, who has sworn that no boutique will ever grace the interior of B. Altman. Otherwise, we have the merchandise, the manufacturer, the floor space, and the concept. The question is whether or not you'll let me run with it."

Bob was silent for almost a full minute. "Dana," he said at last, "the idea is nothing short of brilliant. I'd have to see the samples, of course. How soon can you arrange that?"

"The samples are on a rolling rack in my coach house. I'll get a cover from one of the departments, and Andrew and I can walk it over." Dana paused, looking Bob directly in the eye. "I've worked really hard on this, and I'm convinced it would be a winner. We have a target audience that wants classic but luxurious sportswear at less than designer prices. And we finally can become competitive with others, like Bloomies, who are embracing the boutique concept. The feather in our cap is that we get a private label in the process from a manufacturer who is enthusiastic to work with us."

Bob leaned back and ran his hand through his hair. "Hell of an idea, Dana. It's hard not to say yes. This could be a grand slam home run if the numbers add up."

"They will, but what about Helen?"

"It's going to be a tough sell—no denying it. I don't want to steamroll her or anybody else for that matter, but I like what I'm hearing, and at the end of the day, Helen has to go along with what's best for the store. It's a small investment in the larger scheme of things, and it has a huge upside. Bring in the samples."

"Thank you, Bob. They'll be here when you arrive in the morning."

Dana returned to her office and sat in silence. She took a deep breath, clenched her fist, and whispered, "Yes!" Her over-whelming instinct was to call Mark and tell him that she was on her way to finally getting The British Shop approved, but she didn't want to disturb him at the hospital, and she knew he would be with Amanda. She had no doubt that he'd be proud of her.

She'd come a long way from the afternoon she'd shopped at Jaeger and had her epiphany about the possibilities of a British boutique of color-coordinated separates. It was finally going to happen. She could see it as clear as day.

Chapter Forty-Six

*A*fter a late lunch, Dana and Andrew rolled the rack of samples to the store, leaving them in the conference room next to Bob's office. Dana then went about her usual duties, trying to keep her mind off The British Shop, which proved impossible. At three thirty, Mark called as she sat at her desk, reviewing her open-to-buy for the Nantucket line.

"I've got great news," he said. "Amanda is on less pain medication, and she has more movement in her toes and ankles. The doctors are encouraged and say that she might be able to return home in three to four weeks. Moving her before then might jeopardize the spinal tissue that needs to close around the fusion points, but the neurosurgeon feels certain that she's turned a corner."

"That's wonderful!" Dana exclaimed. "I'm so happy to hear such an optimistic outlook from the doctors themselves."

"It's the best news I've heard in the past week. Marsha took yesterday off from hospital duty, and I'm going to do the same tomorrow. We're no good to Amanda if we're both run down."

"I've got some pretty amazing news myself," Dana said.

"The boutique?"

"Yes!" Dana related the details of her meeting with Bob Campbell and how The British Shop represented such a great alternative to Bob's line-specific measures to boost sales in other departments. He's going to see the samples tomorrow morning and was very enthusiastic about the whole idea."

"Great news, Dana. Listen, I know it's last minute, but are you free for dinner tonight? I miss you and want us to get back on track."

"I would love to see you tonight," Dana said. "But why don't you come here for dinner. I think it would be more relaxing. You could use a change of scenery."

"You've got that right. It's a date. I'll see you at seven thirty. Can't wait."

"Me, too."

She slipped into her new cream and white Diane wrap dress and sling-backs, lit candles and the fire, and placed flowers on the small round dining table in the book corner of the living room. It was going to be a perfect evening—indeed, almost a reunion with her lover.

Mark was buzzed in a few minutes late, wearing a sports coat and dress trousers, looking totally refreshed as opposed to the tired, drawn figure Dana had seen at the hospital on Saturday. He entered the carriage house, and Dana immediately threw her arms around him. He pulled her close and kissed her on the lips, a long and sensuous kiss.

"Why does it seem like an eternity since we've done that?" Mark asked.

"Because it has been," Dana said, kissing him again.

They hugged for several minutes, Mark's hands caressing Dana's neck and shoulders.

Mark poured a scotch for himself and sherry for Dana. Sitting in front of the fire, Dana expressed her appreciation for

Irwin and Steve's efforts and how proud she was to present the line to Bob.

"Judging from Bob's eagerness to see the samples," Mark said, "The British Shop looks like a done deal."

Dana served dinner, and their conversation seemed as normal and relaxed as the night they'd had dinner and discussed *The Garden of the Finzi-Continis*. Mark spoke of his new project at the Met, which had been on hold while he spent night and day at the hospital. He also urged Dana to resume her lessons at Claremont. When they were finished eating, Mark reached across the small table and touched Dana's arm, noting how the skin of her face glowed in the soft candlelight.

" Let's enjoy our wine by the fire," Mark said as he stood up, taking Dana's hand.

Dana sat on the sofa, nestled against Mark's body, her head resting on his shoulder.

"I finally see daylight, Mark," Dana said, raising her head to look at him. "We've been in such a scary, dark place for the past few days."

"Another reminder of why we have to live each day to the fullest," Mark said, giving Dana a kiss.

"I think we can do that now, knowing that Amanda is going home to recuperate."

"And that she'll be able to walk," Mark added. "God, what a relief. She can't wait to see Rex, and Marsha is busy planning for her arrival. She's redecorating the guest room on the first floor to accommodate Amanda's bedroom furniture. It'll be easier for us and Amanda's friends if we don't have to run up and down the stairs to see her throughout the day. I was planning on using that room, but Marsha was right. Amanda shouldn't be cloistered on the second floor. She needs to interact with us as much as possible. In fact, the doctors are more concerned about depression than her spinal injury."

He took a sip of his wine and squeezed Dana's shoulder gently.

Dana was quiet for a few minutes, trying to process all she'd just heard.

"Honey, what's the matter?" Mark asked. "Did you remember something you didn't do at work? You look worried."

"I feel awkward asking, Mark," Dana said as she sat up, reaching for her wine. "How often do you plan to be in Connecticut?"

Mark clasped his hands, resting his elbows on his knees

"We've all been so worried about Amanda's walking again," Mark began while staring at the rug, "that we didn't think about how the recuperation was going to affect her mental state."

"Do the doctors have an idea how long the recuperation period will be?" Dana asked.

Turning to Dana, Mark explained his daughter's recovery process. "Despite the surgical correction of her spine, bed rest will be crucial for a full recovery. If Amanda resumes activities too quickly, even something as simple as walking, the reconstruction might fail. Unfortunately, there are limited treatment options after a relapse. The doctors are now predicting twelve months of bed rest, although they'll conduct a six-month follow-up evaluation."

"And the doctors believe that you can help Amanda's spirits by returning to Connecticut?" Dana said, feeling she was heading into that dark tunnel.

"Honey, listen," Mark said, putting his hand on her cheek. "Please look at me. It's not going to be forever. It's just that she's really depressed. She knows she can't compete in the Classic this summer, but what's really going to upset her is finding out that she'll miss her entire sophomore year. We know in the greater scheme of life that this won't matter, but for a nineteen year old, it seems like an eternity, further delaying her dream of starting veterinary school."

"I understand," Dana said, fighting back tears.

"Of course, I'm keeping my apartment, which you know I love. I have to be in town for board meetings, and, well ... for us."

Needing to move away from Mark, Dana got up and walked to the mantle. Looking into the fire, her back to Mark, she asked, "What do you mean by 'us'? I don't know where I'll fit into your life as you've described the months you'll be living in your Connecticut home with Amanda and Marsha."

"My feelings haven't changed, Dana, and I believe you feel the same. If anything, this situation will bring us closer."

"Mark," Dana said as she fought harder not to cry, "I want to believe that I can handle this new arrangement. I desperately want to go on, business as usual. But I know myself too well. I can't. There are too many people in our relationship, and 'us' will become just a nice diversion from Marsha. Our times together would be fun and loving, but that's not all that life is. I know that, over time, I wouldn't like myself for seeing you under these conditions."

Seeming desperate, Mark approached Dana and put his hands on her shoulders, his face inches from hers. "What if I agree to Marsha's settlement proposal and get a divorce. I'll give her everything she wants and rent a nearby house while Amanda recovers."

Dana couldn't hold back the tears any longer, and Mark turned her around to hold her.

"Mark, as much as we care for each other, I can't let you make that decision to appease me. I don't want the burden of knowing I was responsible for your giving in to Marsha's demands, which you've already explained are unacceptable."

"Damn it, that's my decision to make."

"It's too messy."

"Dana, life is messy. It isn't the perfect world you want it to be, but we can get through this."

"Then let's trust Fate and believe that when you're divorced and ready for a new phase of your life, we'll find a way back to each other. I know that I'll regret what I'm saying the moment you leave, but I also know that I can't tolerate our relationship as you envision it. It's better that we part feeling as we do rather than in anger. I want to believe that it may not be forever."

Mark wrapped his arms around Dana, and they held each other for several minutes without speaking.

"You're right," he said at last, his voice low and filled with resignation. "About everything. I can't expect you to put your life on hold, but I also can't bear the thought of losing you."

"You can't risk losing Amanda," Dana said quietly.

"I know."

Mark kissed Dana softly on the lips. "I, uh, think I should be going now," he said, his voice breaking.

Mark backed away, his hand holding Dana's until their fingertips slid from each other. He lowered his eyes before turning and walking to the door, looking defeated.

Wills, who had been sleeping on the library landing, came down when he heard the door close. Without thinking, Dana attached his leash, and they went into the dark, warm night for a long walk, ending on the steps of the Morgan Library, where she sat and cried. Looking for comfort, she found it in Father Macaulay's message to take care of herself. Her heart would heal in its own time. She decided that she would not take her tears back to the coach house, which only last December represented a new life, a good life, and she wasn't ready to give up on that dream. She knew in her heart that she'd made the right decision, as painful as it was. Because of their deep feelings, she believed that if they were truly destined to be together, they would find each other again.

Entering the coach house, Dana quickly put out the fire, turned off the lights, and left the dishes for the morning. The sooner the day was over, the better. Looking around the living room and recalling her last moments with Mark, she felt disoriented, believing for a split second that their conversation had been just a bad dream. To imagine that he was out of her life was surreal. Despondent, she walked upstairs, stopping in front of the bookcase to find a poem in the collection she'd recently bought in London, and then proceeded to her bedroom.

It was now that she recalled the lines of poetry that her mind had searched for a few days earlier. They were from a poem called "The April Snow-Storm—1858" by Charles Sangster.

Frail type of life thou art:
At first, pure as the snow
We come—abide—depart;
What more, th' Immortals know ...

Spread gently, virgin shower,
Your winding sheet of snow;
My heart has lost its power,
But mock not at its woe.

Fall not so cold and bleak,
Treat not her corse with scorn;
Gently. My heart is weak;
She, too, was April born.

Fall gently, virgin shower;
The heart once strong and brave
Hath lost its wonted power;
'Tis buried in her grave.

Dana's heart had indeed lost its power. The promise of a life with Mark, born in the spring days in Manhattan—in April—had run its course too briefly. People could be strong and courageous, but each day was a gift that was gone too quickly. *We come—abide—depart.* Frailty sometimes ruled even the most promising lives and relationships.

Dana was at peace. She knew that God would see her through the painful days ahead. She would get up the following morning and, as always, do what she had to do at work. But tonight? Her heart was broken and weak. Tonight, she wouldn't pretend to be brave. There was April snow in her heart.

Chapter Forty-Seven

*D*ana arrived at work the following morning, but her life still seemed surreal. The day before, she'd been in her office, speaking excitedly to Mark over the phone about a celebratory dinner and a romantic evening. Today, she was merely going through the motions. She was accomplishing what needed to be done—paperwork, meetings, calls to manufacturers—but she performed everything with a noticeable lack of enthusiasm. By eleven o'clock, she realized that she hadn't thought of the boutique a single time all morning. It was Helen who abruptly grabbed her attention at ten minutes after eleven.

"Dana!" Helen said, appearing in the doorway of Dana's office. This in itself was unprecedented. If Helen wished to speak to employees, they were always summoned to her office. Dana knew what kind of verbal assault was coming and steeled her mind for Helen's stern words.

"I just spoke with Bob after discovering a rack of separates in his conference room," Helen said. "He told me that you'd brought in samples for—what's the lovely name you've chosen—The British Shop, I believe."

"Bob asked me to bring them in," Dana explained.

"And he made this request based on what? Is he a seer, a prophet? How did he know that any samples existed in the first place? Let's be candid, Dana. Bob told me that you've enlisted the aid of a *menswear* manufacturer in Brooklyn to produce an exclusive line of clothes for B. Altman."

"It cost the store nothing," Dana retorted, "and I did it all on my own time."

"That's not the point, and you damn well know it."

Dana had witnessed Helen's anger before, whether directed at herself or at others, but this morning she was filled with outright wrath. Her words were venomous.

"I told you that there would be no B. Altman line and no boutique, which I ordered to be dismantled. We had that discussion more than once, and I was unequivocal. You've deliberately defied my directives, Dana. Who do you think you are? Dawn's replacement? Do you think you have carte blanche to do whatever you please even when your superiors have expressly forbidden you to explore your wild concepts?"

"Bob doesn't think they're so wild," Dana said, holding her ground. "He believes that my idea could be a game-changer for the store. There would no longer be a need to tap into every department to choose a price-sensitive line to tout for the holidays. I'm talking profit and sales, not wild concepts."

Helen folded her arms, tapped her right foot impatiently, and exhaled as she looked down at the floor, unable to comprehend the aggressive challenge Dana was making to her authority.

"You didn't tell me about this, Dana!"

"I did, Helen. Many times, in fact. But you weren't interested. When Bob gave us a directive for holiday selling, I simply followed his orders. Just doing my job."

Helen's eyes narrowed as she breathed even harder. "I told you, there is a pecking order around here and you're expected to stay in line like the other buyers in this division. It's *my* job to take recommendations to Bob, not yours. It's protocol,

Dana. I don't come here every day to simply fill a vacant chair. And going to a manufacturer, a menswear manufacturer no less, to have clothing made for a women's department is ... well, it's unthinkable."

"Irwin Bauer is a friend of mine and he was overstocked with beautiful woolen fabrics. Did you feel them? You can't find more luscious gray flannel or camel hair in any of the women's lines throughout the store. He made samples based on my own British wardrobe. I don't think that's anybody's business but mine."

"We're talking in circles, Dana. Have Irwin Bauer make all the samples you want! Knock yourself out. Just don't bring them to Bob and then pitch your boutique when I've already passed on the idea."

Dana sighed. She hadn't eaten breakfast that morning—her appetite had faded after her decision to stop seeing Mark—and her head was now pounding.

"I understand your position, Helen. I'm sorry. I didn't think it would hurt if Bob looked at my samples. The matter is out of my hands now."

"No, Dana. It's a moot issue. The space is no longer available, and I reiterated that to Bob a few minutes ago. This British boutique of yours isn't going to happen, so you'd better get used to the idea." Helen paused. "You're still an accessories buyer, Dana, not the fashion director. I suggest you act like one or I'll recommend this very week that you be replaced with someone who can bring team spirit to our family here at B. Altman. I'm not interested in having a maverick constantly second-guessing all of my decisions. I climbed the ranks to get where I am, and in the process I did what I was told. In fact, I suggest that you consider whether or not you're suited to work here at B. Altman any longer. If you wish to make executive decisions, then you should apply to stores with openings in upper-level management."

Helen turned on her heels and left without waiting for a response.

Dana briefly thought of Johnny and the House of Cirone—-independence, creativity, and travel. This was the one day that she had no stomach for store politics and drama. If Bob wasn't going to overrule Helen and go with what he knew to be right, then it was time to move on.

Maybe, but Dana summoned her strength and recalled her conversation with Bob Campbell the day before. The British Shop wasn't dead yet. She wasn't going to give Helen the satisfaction of submitting her resignation until she'd heard back from Bob personally. She'd come too far to let Helen's dressing-down stop her from doing everything in her power to turn her dream into a reality.

Chapter Forty-Eight

Dana sat across the table from Andrew at the Charleston Garden restaurant, Andrew having persuaded Dana to accompany him when he'd seen how despondent she looked after stopping by her office at one o'clock.

"Is everything all right with Amanda?" Andrew asked, looking concerned. "She hasn't taken a turn for the worse, has she?"

"No, thank goodness," Dana answered.

"Something's wrong," Andrew said, "and I'm guessing that either you and Mark are having trouble or else the boutique isn't panning out."

"The boutique is on life support," Dana said, her head lowered as she stared lethargically at a cup of tea. "Helen blew a fuse when she saw the rack of separates in Bob's conference room. She suggested I consider resigning from B. Altman."

"Resign? Wow. That's tough even by Helen's standards. And Mark?"

Dana looked up at Andrew, wiping moisture from the corner of her left eye. "I've called it off. He has to move in with his wife at their Connecticut home when Amanda is discharged from the hospital. His time would be so—"

"Whoa there," Andrew said. "Back up the train. Did you say his *wife*?"

"He's legally separated, but his wife Marsha wants him to give her a small fortune before she'll sign any divorce decree. His hands have been tied for a while now. I told him last night that I thought it best if we went our own way. I wouldn't have had the strength to end it if he were living in New York, but now that he and Marsha are under the same roof, I can no longer deny the fact that he's still a married man. If I'd agreed to keep the relationship going, which is what Mark wanted, I'd only see him a few days here and there around board meetings and business dinners. Andrew, I'm going to miss him terribly, but I won't date a married man or be at the mercy of Marsha and Amanda's whims and moods. I hope the future brings us back together, but for now, I have to move on."

"That's a lot to assimilate in less than twenty-four hours. No wonder you look glum."

Dana shrugged. "I'll be okay. I'm still waiting to hear from Bob, but Helen reiterated that the space where the boutique was being built is no longer available."

"There's always Johnny. I assume that his offer to work for the House of Cirone is still on the table."

"I thought of that briefly this morning after Helen took me down a few notches, but I think Mark was right about making such a move. Just look at how persistent Johnny's been to get an answer from me, not to mention his insistence that I dump Mark. I don't think I could work by his side with pressure constantly coming from a self-styled big brother, as well-meaning as he is. As for Uncle John, I want him as a trusted family friend, not my boss. Working at the House of Cirone would probably jeopardize my relationship with his family, so I've decided that it's just not the right thing to do."

"Do you want some company tonight?" Andrew asked. "We could go out to dinner or a movie."

"No, but thanks. I need some peace and quiet to sort things out in my mind. I'm going to stay home and try to rest."

"Makes sense," Andrew said. "But I've got an idea. When was the last time you went to The Frick?"

"Early last year. Why?"

"They have a special exhibition right now—Goya's Last Works. Miniatures painted on ivory. You visited a miniature collection while in London, didn't you?"

"I did. I even brought home a book on eighteenth and nineteenth century portrait miniatures."

"Then why not check out the exhibit this afternoon? Leave work early and spend some time doing something you enjoy rather than dragging through the day. You'll still get home in time to walk Wills and be alone with your thoughts."

"Maybe. Sounds tempting."

Andrew looked at Dana after finishing his coffee. "Hey, kiddo, you'll get through this. Correction—*we'll* get through this. I had a pretty bad breakup recently, but I'm still standing, as they say. There's life on the other side. I'm always here for you."

"You are, Andrew. You're a great friend."

"Ditto," he said with an encouraging smile.

Dana squeezed Andrew's hand and got up to leave. Sitting at the adjoining table was a man in his seventies wearing a brown suit. He was doing the *New York Times* daily crossword puzzle, and Dana noted that he, like most other crossword puzzle addicts, had endless scribbles in the margins of the paper. He looked up and smiled, and Dana returned the gesture.

"I think that old geezer was listening to every word we said," Andrew stated as they left the restaurant.

"He needs to get a life," Dana said. "My woes must have bored him silly."

They both laughed and returned to their offices.

• • •

Dana left work at two thirty, deciding to take Andrew's advice and go to The Frick. As anxious as she was to speak with Bob, Helen seemed to be frequenting the fifth floor hallway for the last two hours, as if she were looking for an excuse to fire Dana were she to see her talking with the executive vice-president.

The Frick was an art collection on Fifth Avenue between 70th and 71st Streets. It was housed in a mansion once owned by industrialist Henry Clay Frick, the mansion having been converted to a public museum in 1931. It had the reputation for being one of the finest small museums in the United States, housing well-known paintings by European masters. It also contained porcelain, sculpture, and eighteenth-century French furniture. Some of its most famous paintings were by Johannes Vermeer and Jean-Honoré Fragonard.

Dana took a cab to the Upper East Side and found herself quickly immersed in the Goya exhibition after entering the mansion. In his first year in Bordeaux, 1824, Goya had experimented in the medium of painting miniatures on ivory. She walked several times through the two rooms where the exhibit was being held, stopping frequently to examine and reexamine the miniatures. On Dana's final pass through the exhibit, she noticed a woman across the room who looked familiar even though she was facing the wall. Dana studied the back of the woman more closely, noting a slender frame and hair rolled into a bun behind her head. And there was something about the slope of her shoulders and the way her sweater fell to the top of her tweed skirt. Yes, it was none other than Abby Kempf, whom Dana had met at a lecture at the Wallace Collection in London.

"Abby?" Dana said, crossing the room.

The petite figure whirled around. "Dana!" Abby said. "How have you been? Why am I not surprised to see you here? Isn't this exhibition exceptional?"

"It's incredible," Dana said, trying to keep her voice low.

"You know," Abby said, "Goya's miniatures bear almost no resemblance to Italian miniatures, or any others, for that matter. Not one to imitate anybody, him. Did you know that he blackened the ivory plaques and then put a single drop of water on the surfaces to slightly dissipate the black backgrounds, producing lighter areas where he would trace marvelous images with a tiny sharp instrument. It's how he was able to achieve such a diversity of shadows and highlights. I could look at these all day. In fact, I literally have."

"No, I didn't know any of that, but it's fascinating."

Dana noted that Abby's speech was far more animated than her conversation at the Wallace Collection or during their subsequent lunch. Her eyes sparkled, and her enthusiasm for the artwork shone through every word she spoke.

The two women moved to the foyer of the museum so they could speak more openly.

"I thought you weren't going to be intown until the fall," Dana commented.

"Yes, I'll be traveling to France and Italy this summer to look at various works of art for an upcoming series of lectures," Abby said, "but I have a few weeks before I'm due in Florence, so I thought I'd enjoy a little springtime in Manhattan and visit my family in Bernardsville. I just can't stay still when I've got so many ideas going through my head."

"That's right! You mentioned your art lectures when we had lunch in London."

"I just put the finishing touches on a lecture and slide show on miniatures that I'm delivering right here at The Frick since they're staging the current Goya exhibit. I'm going to be comparing Goya's techniques with those of other artists, such as the ones we saw in London. Isn't it amazing that there can be so many variations in technique when dealing with small pictures on porcelain or ivory? I'll never cease to be amazed by the diversity of the art form."

"I agree," Dana said. "Abby, my apologies for this urgent last minute request, but are you available to deliver your lecture on contrasting techniques at the Colony Club this coming Saturday? We have a luncheon scheduled, but the guest speaker had to cancel. She was going to talk on the rise of expressionism, but I know that your lecture and slide show would capture everyone's attention, especially due to The Frick's exhibit. Members have an opportunity to attend a private showing next Thursday evening, so the timing of your lecture would be perfect. "

"You don't have to ask twice," Abby replied. "I'd be delighted. The more people I can get interested in miniatures, the happier I am. I'm quite sure that we didn't run into each other by accident today, Dana. This fits perfectly into my schedule and makes my little trip to New York even more worthwhile. Here's my number," Abby said, handing Dana the phone number of her New York apartment. "Call me with the details and I'll be there! If I'm not home, just leave a message on my answering machine."

"Thank you so much, Abby. Would you like to have some coffee now?"

"I'd love to, but I'm pressed for time," Abby said, glancing at her watch. "I have an appointment to keep in Midtown." She leaned forward and kissed Dana on the cheek. "It was wonderful to see you again. Until Saturday!"

Abby turned quickly and walked out of the museum.

Dana felt better than she had all day, not that she was exuberant by any means, but Andrew's suggestion had been a good one. She'd enjoyed meeting Abby again, and the luncheon at the Colony Club would be a pleasant diversion.

Still, Abby seemed like a different person than the Abby Kempf she'd met in London, where she was quiet and subdued. And a kiss on the cheek? Ah well, Dana thought—she didn't know Abby that well, and perhaps environment was everything. Maybe Abby displayed more decorum when in a proper, staid English environment as opposed to the noisy, bustling borough of Manhattan.

Chapter Forty-Nine

When Dana arrived home from The Frick, she was happy to finally see a letter postmarked London, England. Father Macaulay had responded, and as usual she couldn't wait to see what he had to say, especially in reference to her last letter, in which she'd told him all about Amanda's accident and her relationship with Mark. What he'd written, however, stunned and saddened her.

Dear Dana,

Please forgive the lateness of my response. I'm afraid I was hit with some tragic and unexpected news. My mother passed away shortly before I received your last letter. She was eighty-seven and died in her sleep. The doctors say she had a heart attack. My father died when I was in my thirties, and since then my mother and I have seen each other for tea once a week. The last time I saw her, she looked like her cheerful old self, and I was always convinced that she'd live to be a hundred. She was usually a gentle person, very intelligent, but had a bit of a feisty streak in her sometimes, which is why I think she lived so long. I'm not grief-stricken, mind you, since my mother had a rich and happy life, and I was blessed to have her for many years. Her death was sudden, however, and life is now so very different. I have felt numb ever since we buried her. Life goes on as it must, but it just isn't the same, of course.

Because of my faith, I know I will see her again one day, but for now I have no relish for singing songs in a pub or working out with the punching bag. It takes time, I suppose, to understand the losses in our lives, and for now I will simply go about my duties as parish priest and be content with that. The joy will return later.

The past several days have been a reminder of how short life really is and that we must make use of every single moment, which is a precious gift, whether we mourn or laugh. There is so much to accomplish in life, and we must somehow find a way past our setbacks.

I am so sorry to hear of poor Amanda's accident. I do keep her in my prayers and hope that she will one day ride again. As for your relationship with Mark, your mind and heart seem to be in conflict. Pray for guidance and then trust your instincts. I have no doubt that you will know what to do.

Please let me know how things are working out. It sounds like both of us have been given certain trials lately, and I'm certain that we will both come through them. I will also pray for the success of your boutique.

God bless you,
Father Charles Macaulay

Dana could relate to everything Father Macaulay had written. They were indeed going through difficult times, and she was touched by his vulnerability and humanity. He'd been wounded by great sorrow but didn't expect any kind of pious, superhuman reaction from himself. As he'd said, loss was an inevitable part of life, and one had to marshal on. Dana had trusted her instincts with Mark, knowing that Amanda's welfare was more important than trying to grasp at a relationship that would not have allowed either of them to grow or move forward in a healthy manner.

Dana was particularly touched by Macaulay's statement that one had to perform his or her duties until a spirit of joy returned to one's life. Macaulay's letter validated that she was on the right course. And wasn't that the theme of all of his letters, that we must retain a balance in life? There was great joy and great sadness at times, but in between these extremes, there was so much to accomplish. She was much younger than Macaulay, but she would always remember his advice: not to take any day for granted. Tomorrow, she was determined to see where Bob Campbell stood on The British Shop. She'd done everything she could. It was now out of her hands. She had to trust that her efforts would pay off.

Chapter Fifty

*B*rett was putting on his suit coat, ready to leave his office for the day, when his secretary informed him that Tom Silver was calling.

"Put him through," Brett said anxiously, taking his seat behind the desk. He hoped that Dana would no longer be able to hide her true financial circumstances and professional aspirations.

"Brett, I don't have good news," Silver began. "In fact, I think the entire renegotiation of your settlement is going to be a nonstarter."

"What? Dana hasn't been forthcoming with us, Tom. I'm not going to cut her a huge check when she's poised to be so wealthy. It's outrageous. Am I supposed to give her more than half our assets simply because I'm a partner?"

"Just hear me out," Silver said. "First, Rudnick has sent me a formal response to our request. It details Dana's current financial situation and doesn't list anything in the way of astronomical future earning potential. In fact, it only lists her position as buyer at B. Altman."

"She's hiding something, Tom. I know Johnny Cirone, and he's always been straight with me. I have no reason to doubt that Dana's star is on the rise in more ways than one."

"That's my second point," Silver continued. "As per your request, Dana has remained under surveillance. One of your investigator's assistants, a man in his seventies, sat next to Dana and her friend Andrew at Charleston Garden early this afternoon and heard every word of their conversation while he pretended to work the *Times* crossword puzzle."

"And? He must have gotten everything we needed!"

"Quite to the contrary, sad to say. Dana's boutique idea with the store seems to have crashed and burned. She's also decided against taking the position with the House of Cirone for personal reasons. As for Mark Senger, the guy is married. She broke it off with him two days ago. The bottom line is that Dana, except for becoming a buyer at B. Altman, is no different than when you two separated in terms of financial standing and her career, nor is there anything on the horizon that says she's about to live a life of fame and fortune. In short, we've got nothing."

There was a pause on the line while Brett tried to think of any remaining options.

"Then I want to at least change the payment schedule," he said at last. "Just as you specified in the meeting."

"Rudnick is having none of that. He knows you can afford to pay the settlement, and if you push Dana on the matter, my hunch is that he's going to file suit for your dalliance with Janice. That's old news, of course, but it's not going to sit well with your partners, and at the very least, it's going to cost you a lot of money and would drag on for months. Nothing but a headache. You're going to end up losing money, not gaining it."

Brett sighed and spoke in a weary, defeated tone. "Yeah, well … thanks, Tom. Can't win 'em all. At least we tried."

"Sorry, Brett. Just move on, and give my best to Janice. Try to be happy and put the past behind you."

"I guess I have no choice. Bye, Tom."

Brett hung up and sat in his chair, a scowl on his face. He exhaled and rested his head against the back of his chair, looking at the ceiling. The private investigators, the plan to keep more of his money—it had all been a massive waste of time. Dana had caught him red-handed with Janice, but he thought he'd have the last word by renegotiating the divorce settlement. He didn't hate Dana or wish her any harm or discomfort, but neither did he believe that she deserved so large a settlement, which he'd agreed to in a knee-jerk reaction given his fear of being exposed within the ranks of the firm after committing adultery. But there was nothing to do now but follow Tom Silver's advice: move on with his life.

The door to his office opened, startling him from his musings. It was Janice.

"I've been waiting for you in my office for fifteen minutes," she said. "I thought we were going out to dinner to celebrate our victory over Dana."

"As it turns out," Brett said dispiritedly, "our plans to celebrate were premature."

"Now what?" Janice asked, closing the door and sitting across from Brett.

"Tom Silver just called. None of Dana's career plans can be validated. I'd look foolish taking her to court."

"Then we'll just have to work harder to validate them," Janice said harshly. "We can't let Dana get away with—"

"She's not getting away with anything," Brett interrupted. "She was overheard today saying that the boutique fell through and that she's taking a pass on the House of Cirone."

"What?" Janice asked, fire in her eyes. "What about everything Johnny told you? Was that all just a pack of lies? Are you going to just give up?"

"Not lies, but things didn't work out the way Dana anticipated."

"But what about this Senger character that she's involved with. His money could choke a pig?"

"You do have a way with words, Janice. Senger's out of the picture. He and Dana broke up. Tom advises that we move on with our lives. There's not going to be any amending of the separation agreement."

"That *we* move on? *We?*"

"Yes. There's nothing else to do." He shrugged. "Let's go grab dinner."

"You really screwed this up, Brett," Janice said with indignation. "Why don't you go have a cozy romantic dinner with *yourself?* I'm going to pack and catch the red-eye to San Francisco."

"I didn't screw up anything," Brett said defensively. "My information from Johnny was solid, but Dana's prospects didn't firm up."

Janice rose to leave. "You should have vetted his information better before setting up a meeting with Rudnick. And your investigators leave a lot to be desired. Dana's playing you like a fiddle."

"Wait a minute, Janice!" Brett called. "I don't need your attitude tonight. I have no control over Dana's life. I left her for *you*, if you recall." There was an edge of sarcasm in his voice.

"You left her? If I recall, she threw you out! Little Miss Priss seems to call all the shots. Go ahead and let her bleed you dry."

"For God's sake, Janice, I'm far from broke. Let's just drop it. I'll fly back with you tonight."

"Take your time. I'm going by myself."

"What are you saying?"

Janice left the office without responding.

Brett sat alone. Janice was a loose cannon. Would she be waiting for him when he arrived in San Francisco? Had she just terminated their relationship? He didn't know. He decided to go to a nearby bar and have a drink with colleagues from the firm. Janice had made him feel like a fool.

Chapter Fifty-One

Dana went into work on Saturday and searched for Bob on the fifth floor, but he wasn't in his office, although she knew that he had weekend meetings scheduled. His secretary said that he would return later that morning.

Dana walked down the hall in frustration. She'd been waiting for two days to get a definitive answer from Bob, and he still hadn't weighed in on the samples she'd brought to the conference room. Had he seen them and decided that they weren't right for an exclusive B. Altman line? Worse yet, had Helen succeeded in talking him out of the idea, convincing him that the boutique concept didn't have all the perks touted by Dana? She decided that she wasn't going to leave the store that day until she saw Bob face-to-face and knew whether or not The British Shop was going to be embraced by the store.

Dana decided to get some work done in her office before checking on the Nantucket display as well as other lines that were traditionally hot summer items. Two hours later, she was on the selling floor when she spied Andrew talking with a salesman from Jones New York near the escalator—and the boutique build-out. Andrew had some schematics in his hand, and judging from their sweeping hand gestures, the two men were obviously discussing what kind of display would be appropriate for the Jones New York line when the boutique was finally dismantled. The salesman had a Madras jacket draped over his arm, and Dana's curiosity was piqued both by the good-looking fabric and what appeared to be plans to finally utilize the boutique space for something other than The British Shop. She approached them, prompting Andrew to interrupt the articulation of how the schematics would be implemented.

"Pleased to meet you," the salesman said. "I'm Jeff Stravitz. Jones New York."

"Dana McGarry. I'm the teen accessories buyer. Pleased to meet you."

Dana extended her hand and smiled politely, but her heart was sinking as she stood next to the boutique where she'd dreamt that her British-inspired separates were to have been displayed. In her mind, she saw the build-out and every little detail, down to the tartan-green shopping bags with The British Shop logo. She couldn't believe it was slipping away right before her eyes.

As the salesman resumed talking about the space he envisioned where the boutique now stood, Andrew shrugged his shoulders slightly as he silently mouthed the word "Helen," indicating to Dana that the matter was out of his hands—he was just doing what he'd been told.

"Is that the new non-bleeding Madras plaid from India?" Dana asked, referring to the jacket Stravitz was holding. "Do you mind if I have a closer look?"

Caught off guard, the salesman smiled. "It is! We're making it the centerpiece of our new Regatta division."

"What else is in the collection?" Dana asked as she inspected the trendsetting fabric.

"In addition to the jacket, we'll have matching Madras Bermuda shorts, skirts, and pants. We're introducing our own prep blazer, cotton-striped shirtdresses, and floral-print wrap skirts."

"Look at their logo," Andrew said, holding up a piece of distressed wood with the Regatta name in nautical letters.

"What a great match for my accessories in the Nantucket boutique," Dana said while glancing furtively at Andrew.

"You have a Nantucket boutique?" Stravitz asked. "For accessories?"

"No Nantucket boutique on the horizon I'm afraid," Dana laughed, "but I know your Regatta division will be a hit. The preppy look is really hot with juniors."

"I'm going to contact Bass and see if they want a section in our department to sell penny and tassle Weejuns," Jeff said.

"Great idea, Jeff," Andrew said.

"I have a better one," Dana said with a sly smile.

"Really? For the Regatta line?" Jeff said. "Tell me quickly. The suspense is killing me."

"Follow me," Dana said as Andrew shook his head, not sure what Dana had in mind.

Dana led Andrew and Jeff into The Shop for Pappagallo, which was packed with Saturday shoppers trying on brightly colored flats and buying ribbon stripe belts and Bermuda bags.

"Where did you find that jacket?" one young woman asked when she spotted the Madras jacket Jeff was holding.

"Do you like it?" Jeff asked. "Here. Let's try it on."

The jacket caught the attention of two other shoppers, and they also wanted to know where to find more Madras pieces.

"Can I buy it?" the young girl said as she turned to her mother for approval.

Jeff explained that the new line would be available in the next few weeks and that he would send her and the others in the group a personal invitation to the Regatta fashion show.

While Andrew took the girls' mailing addresses, Dana turned to Jeff and said, "Need I say more? The Pappagallo Shop is where you should be. Your customer is already here and waiting for you!"

"You're absolutely right!" Jeff said. "I know Ben Goldberg at the US Shoe Corporation. I'm sure I can sell him on the idea to sell our line in The Pappagallo Shop. It's a win-win for both of us."

"You know, Jeff," Dana said, "US Shoe is leasing the space, so I'm sure he would be happy to expand and have you share the cost."

"Really, Dana?" Jeff said. "Good information. Andrew, I'm late for a meeting back at the showroom. Tell Helen I don't want the space by the escalator. Let's quickly work up a new design incorporating Pappagallo, and I'll present it to Goldberg at US Shoe next week. Dana, I owe you a nice lunch. The three of us will celebrate when this gets put together."

"We'd love that," Dana said, looking at Andrew.

"I think you've made a wise decision," Andrew said. "I have no doubt that we can put the space by the escalator to good use for another line." He winked and smiled at Dana as he spoke.

"It's been a pleasure to meet you," Dana told Stravitz. "I look forward to our lunch. Now if you'll excuse me, I have a million things to do. Good luck with the Regatta line! I love it!"

Dana whirled about and returned to the fifth floor, adrenaline pumping through her veins, new enthusiasm propelling her to the office of Bob Campbell, who was walking briskly down the hallway straight towards her.

"I was planning on finding you today," Bob said with a telling grin. "Come on in and we'll talk. Sorry I've been so busy for the past two days."

Dana followed Bob into his office, where they sat on opposite sides of his desk.

"Have you looked at the separates?" Dana asked eagerly. "What do you think?"

"The samples are stunning," he said. "Irwin and his team are obviously very talented."

"Can you see where I'm going with this, Bob?" Dana asked, her hands folded on his desk. "Aren't the fabrics luscious? Now, add four-ply cashmere sweaters, wool jersey shawls, and dyed-to-match merino wool knits and we're making a statement. All items within irresistible reach of each other!"

Bob nodded slowly. "Uh ... yes, I can."

Dana couldn't understand the reticence of the executive vice president. Why was he drawing out the conversation? Dana wanted a simple yes or no, but Bob seemed so tentative in his answers.

"And the boutique?" she asked.

"Helen gave me an earful the other day, telling me that she wanted to see the boutique chopped into kindling. I told you ahead of time that she was going to be a tough sell, didn't I?"

"Yes, but you also said that she has to get on board with what's best for the store. Bob, we can't give up on Ira and Dawn's vision to bring B. Altman into mainstream retailing. This is not such a big risk, for goodness sake! Why are you hesitating?"

"Well, you already know that the boutique space has been promised to Jones New York. How do we get around that?"

"That problem has been solved," Dana said proudly. "I was just with Jeff Stravitz, the head sales rep with Jones, and he told Andrew to inform Helen that he doesn't want that space. We toured Pappagallo, and the young women there were wild about the Madras plaid jacket he was carrying. The new non-bleeding Madras is the focus of their new preppy line, and the Pappagallo customer is made for it. He knows a top executive at US Shoe, and he's pitching him on expanding the

Pappagallo shop to incorporate their new line. Plus he'll share the cost of the leased space."

"I wonder who might have put that particular bug in Stravitz's ear," Bob remarked.

"I just led him to the Pappagallo Shop and the customers took over from there," Dana said innocently. "The kids were all over the jacket, pleading to know when his entire line would be available."

"I see," Bob said thoughtfully as he looked up, weighing the decision he needed to make. Then he leaned forward and burst out laughing.

Dana was confused. "What's the matter?"

"You're the new buyer of The British Shop," he declared. "And you've got your boutique, which I'll instruct Mark to complete. I wanted you to take the lead in solving this problem, just as you did last year with the teen makeup counter and the B. Altman Teen Contest. And you did just that. There's really no objection Helen can make anymore, although she'll grumble a bit as always. Over the long haul, we'll give her some input, but this will be your baby, Dana. In time, Helen will brag about how she brought you along and challenged you so that you could make the whole project a success."

Dana was speechless, her mouth hanging open.

"You can breathe now," Bob said. "And congratulations. I've never been more impressed with your initiative and vision for the store. The concept, the fabrics, bringing Irwin on board, the coordinated separates—what you did was amazing, and it's going to send ripples through the other departments. This is just the beginning of private label merchandise at B. Altman."

Dana let out the air she'd been holding in her lungs. "Thank you, Bob. I'm so grateful. I don't have the words to tell you how much I appreciate your confidence in me."

"No words are needed, Dana. Your work speaks for itself."

Dana returned to her office and called Irwin.

"Hello, partner," Dana said.

"Dana, do you mean you did it?" Irwin said in disbelief.

"Yes!" Dana said. "Bob loved the samples, and the deal is done. I'll tell you all about it over lunch. Are you free on Monday? We have lots to discuss."

"I'm all yours. Monday it is. How about twelve thirty at Giambelli's?"

"Perfect."

"Does Mark know?" Irwin asked.

"No," Dana said, having decided that she would write him a note instead of calling. "Would you mind telling him for me? I know he'll be very happy for both of us."

"Are you sure, Dana?" Irwin asked.

"I am."

Dana then called her mother and father and gave them the good news.

"You've got to come over for dinner tomorrow so we can celebrate," Virginia said. She paused for several seconds. "And bring Mark if you like."

Dana related recent events about Mark and Amanda in broad strokes, telling her that she'd be delighted to see them for dinner. She knew that her mother had endless questions about her breakup with Mark, but Virginia withheld them all.

Filled with energy, Dana decided that she needed a long jog in the park. She ran five miles and felt delightfully tired when she returned home at three o'clock. Upon awaking from a nap, she decided to go to church and offer a brief prayer of thanksgiving for the success of the boutique.

As Father Macaulay might have said, she had once again found her balance.

Chapter Fifty-Two

Sunday was a gorgeous display of May in Hewlett Harbor on Macy Channel. Dana arrived to find that Johnny, Phoebe, and Uncle John had also been invited to her celebratory dinner.

Dana walked into the Martignetti den and froze. "I just told Mom yesterday about The British Shop," Dana said, looking at the beaming faces staring at her in the den, the French doors open to the patio. "How could all of you possibly make it here on such short notice?"

"The hospital lets me out for some fresh air occasionally," Phoebe said with a laugh.

"Dad and I wouldn't have missed this for anything," Johnny added. "It's your greatest professional accomplishment to date."

Phil passed a tray of champagne flutes upon Dana's entrance and handed one to her.

"To my daughter!" Phil said, giving Dana a kiss and raising his glass in the air as everyone joined him in the toast.

"To Dana!" said Phoebe.

"Dana," said Uncle John, "your good fortune is my loss, but I wouldn't have wanted you to work for the House of Cirone in the first place if you didn't have the kind of initiative it took to get a line of clothing for B. Altman, not to mention a specialized boutique. The store is lucky to have you. But I must warn you—the more success you have, the more I'm going to court you to change horses one day and come work with Johnny and me. There will always be a place at the House of Cirone for someone with your talent and determination. But for now, I hope that The British Shop is—" He paused to find the right words. "A smashing success, as the English say! And I have no doubt that it will be, with you as its buyer."

Dana advanced and hugged Uncle John. "I wanted to tell you my decision in person, not over the phone last night," Dana said, "so I'm glad that you were able to make it today."

"And you managed to get the entire idea approved despite Helen's unreasonable objections," Johnny noted.

"Helen clearly underestimated Dana's determination," Virginia said. "It seems we all did."

"I couldn't give up without doing everything possible to open B. Altman's first boutique," Dana said. "I knew Bob would come around when he saw it from my point of view."

"Now who does Dana sound like?" Phil asked with a smile as he looked around the room.

"Her mother," Virginia said, putting her arm around Dana and giving her kiss, "and if everyone will excuse me, I'm going to see how dinner is coming along. Phoebe made Lena's Sunday gravy, so we're in for a special treat."

"It's a beautiful day," Johnny told Dana. "Would you like to walk out on the dock?"

"Sure," Dana said as the pair walked past the French doors.

"I guess I've been more than a little overbearing," Johnny said contritely. "You're right. I've been a mother hen, and while I didn't think that the boutique would fly, I was equally worried that one day it might, since that would mean losing you. I was really looking forward to your working with us. The House of Cirone is sometimes a bit too stuffy for me. You would have been the perfect catalyst to stir things up and bring a little energy to the business. But I'm happy things worked out. Forgive me?"

"Of course, Johnny. After all is said and done, it's nice knowing that you and Mom were so worried about me, although if you tell her I said that, I'll kill you. As for the House of Cirone, why don't *you* give it the energy it needs? Build a new team. It's not like you're an outsider. Uncle John would be open to your new ideas to grow the company."

Johnny shrugged. "I've asked myself that same question a thousand times. I can handle the business end of things pretty well, but when it comes to design and predicting trends, I wouldn't know where to begin or who to hire."

"It doesn't sound like you're very happy at work," Dana said.

"I enjoy running the business most of the time. As Dad likes to remind me, it's in my blood, but there are days when I think I need to go out on my own."

"And do what?"

"That's the problem. I'm just not sure. All in good time, though. Today is about you."

The two longtime friends stared at the afternoon sun's golden reflection on the waters of Macy Channel for several minutes without speaking.

"I'm sorry to hear about Mark," Johnny said at last. "You're putting on a brave face."

"Thanks, but something tells me you're relieved that it didn't work out."

Johnny sighed. "To be honest, I never did see you and him together, but I've been on the outside looking in. What's important is that you must still be hurting, and that doesn't make me happy regardless of what I think of Mark."

"You know, Johnny," Dana said, "that's why I love you. You can be honest and sympathetic at the same time. Really. I appreciate your candor. If you'd had a chance to get to know Mark, I think you'd have felt differently about him, but that's a moot point now. And yes, I'm still hurting. After all, Mark and I were together up until a few days ago. It's going to take some time for my heart to heal, even with all the frenzy of working with Irwin while the boutique is set up to house the collection. I suppose people are right in saying that I'm feisty like my mother when I have to be, but nobody is immune from the pain of loss. I fall apart like anybody else sometimes."

"But you always put yourself back together," Johnny said, "and you don't need all the king's horses and all the king's men to do it."

"Just between you and me, I have a friend in London who gives me some spiritual Band Aids from time to time."

"You've lost me."

"Just a priest I met when I was in Europe at the beginning of April. We've kept in touch, and he's given me some advice that's helped keep me together lately."

Johnny nodded. "I think we all need somebody like that." He turned and looked into Dana's eyes. "You called it off with Mark because of Marsha, didn't you?"

Dana swallowed hard. "Yes, I did. Once he moved home, regardless of the reason, which was indeed to help Amanda, I couldn't deny that he was still a married man. Adjusting to this single life is difficult enough, but there are some boundaries I'm not crossing."

Johnny faced forward again. "You know," he said, "I think people get what they deserve in life."

"What are you getting at?" Dana asked puzzled.

"In spite of the heartache you knew would come, you made for a principled decision, and you did the right thing for you, Mark, and Amanda. You deserve the very best, and one day you'll get just that: the best."

Dana showed the hint of a smile. "I hope so, but I'm not interested in meeting anyone right now. Mark will be a hard act to follow. I'm just going to enjoy work and take care of myself."

"Nothing wrong with that," Johnny said.

"If I get really stressed, of course, I might start singing Cole Porter songs in an English pub."

"Huh?"

Dana waved off the reference and took a sip of her wine.

"Advice from the priest?" Johnny said.

"In a manner of speaking."

The dinner was delicious as always and seemed to go on forever. The Martignettis and Cirones were in good spirits, and Dana realized just how much enjoyment, not to mention comfort, she derived from family get-togethers.

When it was time to leave, Phil hugged his daughter and gave her a kiss on the cheek.

"You haven't had much to say in the past several weeks," Dana commented.

"Because I trust your judgment," he said.

"That seems to be the theme of the afternoon," Dana said, "but there are times when not everybody believes in me."

"But I always have," Phil said with a wink. "And always will."

And Dana knew what her father said was right. She did indeed get drive from her mother, but her father's lifelong trust in his daughter's decisions had given her something equally important: confidence. It was because of Phil Martignetti that Dana always found the kind of inner balance—and moral compass—that Father Macaulay wrote of frequently.

She had two great parents.

Back at Sniffen Court, Dana took Wills for a late-evening walk and then looked at her book on portrait miniatures. She could hardly wait until the following Saturday, when Abby would deliver her lecture on Goya's miniatures. She picked up the phone and called the number that Abby had given her, but she reached Abby's answering machine. She left the time that Abby should arrive at the Colony Club so that she could set up her slides and then hung up.

Later that evening, Dana was about to go to bed when she reread Father Macaulay's last letter. She was struck by one line in particular: Once we have let things go and put them in God's hands, our job is to move forward ...

That's exactly what Dana was doing: making healthy choices and getting on with her life. If there was another way to live wisely, she didn't know what it might be.

Chapter Fifty-Three

*U*nder a tight deadline for holiday selling in The British Shop, Dana worked with Irwin for much of the next week planning production for the new line of clothing. As before, Dana, Irwin, and Steve put their own mark on existing designs and new patterns, and Dana had never felt more energized in her whole career since she was helping to launch, not just new merchandise, but an exclusive label for B. Altman. At the store, she passed Helen several times each day, but the junior buyer uttered not a single word to Dana. She suspected that Helen's chilly demeanor would change over the weeks and months ahead, but if not, Dana had more than proved herself to the store's management.

Dana called Abby's number several more times during the week to make sure that she'd received her initial message, but Dana always got the answering machine. Dana had also wanted to ask Abby to lunch just to chat and to see if she needed any help for the coming weekend. Perhaps Abby was busy preparing for her trip to Florence, but why hadn't she bothered to return Dana's call? It was likely, Dana thought, that Abby was spending time with her family in Bernardsville. Whatever the case, the lecture promised to be a fascinating look at a period of Goya's career that not everyone was acquainted with. Dana was sure that Abby's passion for miniatures would resonate with the members.

• • •

Dana arrived at the Colony Club on Park Avenue early in order to help Abby set up. In the last message she'd left on the answering machine, Dana had asked Abby to be at the club by eleven o'clock so that she could not only make any last minute preparations but also meet some of its members. Abby, however, was nowhere to be seen. The lecture was scheduled for after the luncheon, which was to be held at one o'clock, and Dana reasoned that Abby was merely running late or caught in traffic. Still, Dana was nervous since the seat of honor for the guest lecturer—someone whom Dana had recommended—remained empty as the luncheon began.

"I hope nothing's happened to Abby," Dana remarked to those seated at her table.

"When was the last time you spoke with her?" asked Grace Stanford, a member seated next to Dana.

"Over a week ago," Dana said. "We met at the Goya exhibit at The Frick. I had just heard that Carla Bertolli couldn't speak today, and when I learned that Abby had prepared a lecture on Goya miniatures for The Frick, I asked her if she would mind helping us out at the last minute."

"I was looking forward to seeing Abby today, too," Grace whispered to Dana. "I went to Sarah Lawrence with her, and we were together for a year in Florence. The better I knew her, however, the more aloof she became. She was unpredictable and extremely undependable."

"That's clearly the case today," Dana said with a sigh. "I'm so disappointed and embarrassed. She had such an impressive resume, so I naturally didn't anticipate that something like this would ever happen. We first met at a lecture in London and had a lovely lunch afterward. I do know what you mean, however. She suddenly became aloof and distant as we were saying goodbye, but I'm still concerned, Grace. I'll let you know if I hear from her. "

Dana went to the podium in the corner of the room, apologized for Abby's absence, and said that she looked forward to seeing the ladies at the private Goya showing the following Thursday.

Dana went home and called Abby's number yet again. She didn't anticipate anyone answering, but it was the most logical thing to do.

"Abby," Dana said after the answering machine beeped, "this is Dana. I'm very worried since you didn't show up at the Colony Club and haven't returned any of my calls this week."

Grace had said that Abby was unpredictable. Dana began to wonder if Abby was ever going to return her calls.

The mystery was solved the following Wednesday. Dana had just returned to her desk after lunch when she received a call from Joseph Cunningham, the manager of the Colony Club, informing her that a letter had been hand delivered for her and that he would keep it in his office.

"Is there a return address?" Dana asked.

"I'm afraid not, Mrs. McGarry," the manager replied. "Just your name on the envelope."

"Thank you, Mr. Cunningham," Dana said. "I'll pick it up before five today."

Dana had an appointment at Pringle of Scotland on Seventh Avenue at three o'clock and decided that she would go to the club immediately afterwards as the suspense was more than she could tolerate. Did the letter have something to do with Abby's failure to deliver the lecture?

Mr. Cunningham was speaking with the doorman at the entrance to the Colony Club when Dana arrived, and together they went to his office on the fifth floor. He handed her the white linen envelope, and Dana, after thanking him, went to the drawing room on the second floor. Relieved to find it empty, she poured a cup of tea and sat in one of the wing chairs, staring at her name in distinct script before finally opening the letter.

Neatly inscribed, the letter read:

Dear Ms. McGarry,

I would like to introduce myself. My name is Peter Sitwell, the husband of Abby Kempf.

Sadly, Abby died in an automobile accident ten days ago while visiting her family in Bernardsville. I was at our home in London when I learned the devastating news and went straightaway to Bernardsville for the funeral. I returned to our New York apartment yesterday, which is when I retrieved your messages.

On behalf of Abby, I apologize for your embarrassment on the day of the lecture. I am sure that you went from being distraught with concern to feeling confused and perhaps even angry. Rightly so, but now you understand.

I don't know of your connection to Abby other than your shared fondness for portrait miniatures, and under the circumstances, I would like to give you Abby's collection. The three fine pieces were wedding gifts from my mother. I know that Abby would want you to have them.

I am returning to London this afternoon, and I'm not sure when I will again be in New York. However, the miniatures are in England, either at my mother's home in Wiltshire or somewhere safe in London. Forgive me if I'm in a bit of fog about all this, but people will help me sort it out when I'm back home. In the meantime, please consider accepting the miniatures as a fond remembrance of Abby. You may write me of your decision or telephone at 9a Hays Mews, London, W1J 5PY, telephone 020-7298-3321

Yours sincerely,
Peter Sitwell

Dana read the letter twice more, each time finding it harder to hide her tears. Not wanting to cry in the drawing room, she put the letter back in the envelope and left the club. It was five o'clock, and she was oblivious to the crowded sidewalks, with pedestrians pushing one another and rushing to make trains and buses. In a daze, she slowly made her way down Park Avenue to her neighborhood church at Park and Thirty-seventh Street, where she stopped in to light a candle and pray for Abby and her husband. More than anything at that moment, she needed to get home and write to Father Macaulay.

Dana sat at her secretary and began a letter to Father Macaulay, expressing her sympathy on the loss of his mother and that he would remain in her thoughts and prayers. She then shared everything about her decision to terminate her relationship with Mark, as well as the details related to the approval of the boutique by Bob. She ended the letter with a long description of Abby Kempf's tragic death and the totally unexpected letter from Peter Sitwell and his offer of Abby's miniatures. *Father,* she wrote, *I can tell that Mr. Sitwell is sincere in his wish for me to have the miniatures, and I will accept them. I don't know when that will be as Mr. Sitwell doesn't know when he will return to New York, but that doesn't matter. I will write him a letter to express my sympathy and to accept his kind offer. I must tell you, however, that I feel that you and I have a connection to Mr.*

Sitwell aside from the fact that we are each suffering a loss. He's a neighbor of yours at 9a Hays Mews, a home on my path to Farm Street Church. I don't think he's one of your parishioners, but you would probably recognize him from the neighborhood. I hope that, in time, the three of us will meet. By then, we all may be ready to enjoy a Cole Porter tune.

Dana placed the letter in an envelope and sealed it. For the rest of the evening, she tried to read, but she couldn't stop thinking about Abby's sudden death, the first of someone so close to Dana's age. It was impossible in this melancholy mood not to remember her last evening with Mark and his words emphasizing that they had to learn to live each day to the fullest. In the brief encounters she had with Abby, Dana realized that Abby did just that. Although married, she clearly had the freedom to travel around the world as an independent woman, pursuing her love of art and the joy of lecturing. And yet, while Dana wanted to believe that Abby had lived a happy life, her erratic behavior and mood swings were indications of something more troubling. Perhaps she would indeed meet with Mr. Sitwell at some point in the future and learn more about Abby, putting her mind at ease. Until then, she would have to be content to continue living with the mystery of Abby Kempf.

Chapter Fifty-Four

Dana received a letter from Father Macaulay the following week. She hadn't expected a reply yet since the priest was surely grieving for his deceased mother, but she found a letter in her afternoon mail the following Thursday when she returned home from work.

Dear Dana,

Thank you for your last letter and your condolences. While it is still strange, indeed almost beyond belief, to realize that my mother is no longer with me, life goes on. I sometimes find myself stopping in the course of a day, reflecting on her death but feeling that it must have been a bad dream. Only a few weeks ago I could call her on the phone and chat about the weather. I then recall my vocation and remember that we are all on a journey that extends far beyond the life we live here on earth.

I am sorry that your relationship with Mark ended so abruptly, but I believe that you have chosen the correct path. If you were not true to yourself and your core beliefs, you would not have been happy for long. As difficult as it was, you parted with feelings and respect for one another, and if your paths cross again, that's a nice place to begin. There is, of course, your very exciting news about the boutique. You have what we English call an indomitable spirit. You worked very hard to make the shop at B. Altman a reality, and

I'm sure it will keep you quite busy, which is the best thing perhaps in the face of loss.

I am not familiar with Mr. Sitwell, but you are quite correct. His flat is a stone's throw from Farm Street Church and I'm sure we've passed each other many times in Mount Street Gardens and Berkeley Square. I will keep alert should I hear or see the name anywhere since the area is not so big that people can go unnoticed for very long. But Abby's death is a tragedy, another loss at a time when loss has been too much a part of your life.

I will leave you for now with two brief lines from one of the psalms, lines that I find comforting in the wake of my mother's passing. They say that "With the evening there comes weeping, but with the dawn there is rejoicing." I believe that is very true, for regardless of the harsh realities that life sometimes forces us to endure, there is always another chance, another day, another opportunity to find happiness. I am convinced that no mystery or loss can deprive us of that joy. In fact, it is sometimes through our very losses that we discover a new path to our destiny.

Be well!

Sincerely,
Father Charles Macaulay

Dana folded the letter and put it with the others she'd received from Father Macaulay over the weeks. They were treasures that she would always keep, and she had no doubt that she would return to them when necessary and read them in order to absorb their simple wisdom.

With the lengthening days of summer, Dana went for what was becoming her daily jog in Central Park. She was enjoying the workout when she suddenly crossed the bridle path where she and Mark had walked after her lesson at Claremont. She was unexpectedly overwhelmed with sadness and cut short her jog to return home. Her heart was still healing, and for the first time in several days, she experienced a renewed sense of loss that caused her to briefly shed tears for a relationship that had been so promising despite its brevity. Yes, in the evening, there were still tears to be shed, as Father Macaulay had sagely pointed out.

She woke the next morning to the ringing of the telephone. It was seven o'clock, and Dana usually didn't get such early calls.

"You've got to get here right away!" Andrew said excitedly.

"What's going on?" Dana asked, not fully awake.

"Mark's team has just finished putting the name on the boutique. *Your* boutique! They were here during the night to finish the installation before the store opens. I thought you should be here when we start setting up the display cases. It's a winner, kiddo!"

"Thank you, Andrew!" Dana said. "I'm on my way."

Dana quickly showered and dressed, walked Wills, and left for B. Altman without having breakfast. Thirty minutes later, she was striding across the main selling floor, headed for the boutique.

"Dana!" called Helen. "Do you have a moment?"

"Gee, Helen, can it wait until I get upstairs? I was told that—"

"It will only take a minute," Helen said, taking Dana by the arm, pulling her to the side, and handing her a book of tartan silk swatches. "I found these in the market yesterday— my favorites are marked—and I thought they'd make gorgeous holiday shirts for The British Shop. I included the name of a vendor you might want to call." Helen patted Dana on the shoulder and turned away quickly. "Keep the swatches," she said. "I'm late for a meeting."

Dana laughed as she tucked the book under her arm and rode up the escalator. There it was, just as Andrew had described it. Above the entrance to the boutique, which had been constructed with brown, rustic, wooden shingles on its exterior, was the name that Dana had carried with her for so long: The British Shop. The letters, written in gold, were stylized and looked exactly like signs she'd seen on Regent Street shops in London.

Irwin was making great progress finishing the line, and soon the boutique would be open for business. Even Helen had abandoned her curmudgeonly personality, just as Bob had predicted.

It didn't take Dana long to instruct Andrew's display team on the placement of fixtures and display cases—she'd been documenting every detail for months. As Dana had learned the previous year with the teen cosmetic counter, and now with The British Shop, there was no easy path, no shortcut to achieving success. If you believed in yourself, however, you'd find a way to make it happen. What had been an artistic vision two months earlier had become a solid, three-dimensional reality. Nothing was impossible.

Dana went up to her office, a smile still on her face. She had a million things to do and she didn't know where to start. And that, of course, was exactly how Dana liked it.

Although Lynn Steward's debut novel, *A Very Good Life* Vol. 1 in the Dana McGarry series, takes place in 1970s New York City, the emotional story transcends any period. Dana McGarry is an "it" girl, living a privileged lifestyle of a well-heeled junior executive at B. Altman, a high end department store. With a storybook husband and a fairytale life, change comes swiftly and unexpectedly. Cracks begin to appear in the perfect facade. Challenged at work by unethical demands, and the growing awareness that her relationship with her distant husband is strained, Dana must deal with the unwanted changes in her life. Can she find her place in the new world where women can have a voice, or will she allow herself to be manipulated into doing things that go against her growing self-confidence?

A Very Good Life chronicles the perils and rewards of Dana's journey, alongside some of the most legendary women of the twentieth century. From parties at Café des Artistes to the annual Rockefeller Center Christmas tree lighting ceremony, from meetings with business icons like Estée Lauder to cocktail receptions with celebrity guests like legendary *Vogue* editor

Diana Vreeland. Steward's intimate knowledge of the period creates the perfect backdrop for this relatable story about a woman's quest for self-identity.

A Very Good Life ranked #1 on Amazon's list of 100 Top Free eBooks in Literary and Fiction

Available on Amazon.com for Kindle and all devices that support the Kindle App

ABOUT THE AUTHOR

Lynn Steward is a successful business woman who spent many years in New York City's fashion industry in marketing and merchandising, including the development of the first women's department at a famous men's clothing store. Through extensive research, and an intimate knowledge of the period, Steward created the characters and stories for a series of five authentic and heartwarming novels about New York in the seventies. *April Snow* is the second volume in the Dana McGarry Series. *A Very Good Life,* Steward's debut novel, was published in March 2014.

Visit Lynn's Website ~ **LynnSteward.com**
Join Lynn on Facebook ~ **Facebook.com/LynnStewardnyc**
Follow Lynn on Pinterest ~ **Pinterest.com/LynnStewardny**

www.ingramcontent.com/pod-product-compliance
Lightning Source LLC
Chambersburg PA
CBHW030547180626
46816CB00005B/1432